WORKS

OF

WILLIAM MAKEPEACE THACKERAY

THE

VIRGINIANS

VOL. III

EDITED BY

WALTER JERROLD

ILLUSTRATED BY

CHARLES E. BROCK

LONDON

J. M. DENT & CO.

NEW YORK

FRED DE FAU & COMPANY

CONTENTS

iii

LIST OF ILLUSTRATIONS

The Virginians

Mr. Johnson had been asleep for some time.

CHAPTER LXIII

MELPOMENE

GEORGE WARRINGTON by no means allowed his legal
studies to obstruct his comfort and pleasures, or
interfere with his precious health. Madam Esmond
had pointed out to him in her letters that, though he
wore a student's gown, and sat down with a crowd of
nameless people to hall commons, he had himself a
name, and a very ancient one, to support, and could
take rank with the first persons at home or in his
own country; and desired that he would study as a

gentleman, not a mere professional drudge. With
this injunction the young man complied obediently
enough : so that he may be said not to have belonged
to the rank and file of the law, but may be considered
to have been a volunteer in her service, like some
young gentlemen of whom we have just heard.
Though not so exacting as she since has become—
though she allowed her disciples much more leisure,
much more pleasure, much more punch, much more
frequenting of coffee-houses and holiday-making,
than she admits now-a-days, when she scarce gives
her votaries time for amusement, recreation, instruction, sleep, or dinner—the law a hundred years ago
was still a jealous mistress, and demanded a pretty
exclusive attention.   Murray, we are told, might
have been an Ovid, but he preferred to be Lord Chief
Justice, and to wear ermine instead of bays.   Perhaps
Mr. Warrington might have risen to a peerage and
the woolsack, had he studied very long and assiduously,
—had he been a dexterous courtier, and a favourite of
attorneys : had he been other than he was, in a word.
He behaved to Themis with a very decent respect
and attention ; but he loved letters more than law
always ; and the black letter of Chaucer was infinitely
more agreeable to him than the Gothic pages of Hale
and Coke.
    Letters were loved indeed in those quaint times,
and authors were actually authorities.   Gentlemen
appealed to Virgil or Lucan in the courts or the
House of Commons.   What said Statius, Juvenal—
let alone Tully or Tacitus—on such and such a
point ?   Their reign is over now, the good old
Heathens : the worship of Jupiter and Juno is not
more out of mode than the cultivation of Pagan
poetry or ethics.   The age of economists and calcu-
lators has succeeded, and Tooke's Pantheon is deserted

and ridiculous. Now and then, perhaps, a Stanley kills a kid, a Gladstone hangs up a wreath, a Lytton burns incense, in honour of the Olympians. But what do they care at Lambeth, Birmingham, the Tower Hamlets, for the ancient rites, divinities, worship? Who the plague are the Muses, and what is the use of all that Greek and Latin rubbish? What is Helicon, and who cares? Who was Thalia, pray, and what is the length of her i? Is Melpomene's name in three syllables or four?

Now, it has been said how Mr. George in his youth, and in the long leisure which he enjoyed at home, and during his imprisonment in the French fort on the banks of Monongahela, had whiled away his idleness by paying court to Melpomene; and the result of their union was a tragedy, which has been omitted in Bell's 'Theatre,' though I dare say it is no worse than some of the pieces printed there. Most young men pay their respects to the Tragic Muse first, as they fall in love with women who are a great deal older than themselves. Let the candid reader own, if ever he had a literary turn, that his ambition was of the very highest, and that however in his riper age he might come down in his pretensions, and think that to translate an ode of Horace, or to turn a song of Waller or Prior into decent alcaics or sapphics, was about the utmost of his capability, tragedy and epic only did his green unknowing youth engage, and no prize but the highest was fit for him.

George Warrington, then, on coming to London, attended the theatrical performances at both houses, frequented the theatrical coffee-houses, and heard the opinions of the critics, and might be seen at the 'Bedford' between the plays, or supping at the 'Cecil' along with the wits and actors when the performances were over. Here he gradually became acquainted with the players and such of the writers and poets as were known to the public. The tough old Macklin, the frolicsome Foote, the vivacious Hippisley, the sprightly Mr. Garrick himself, might occasionally be seen at these houses of entertainment ; and our gentleman, by his wit and modesty, as well, perhaps, as for the high character for wealth which he possessed, came to be very much liked in the coffee-house circles, and found that the actors would drink a bowl of punch with him, and the critics sup at his expense with great affability. To be on terms of intimacy with an author or an actor has been an object of delight to many a young man ; actually to hob and nob with Bodadil or Henry the Fifth or Alexander the Great, to accept a pinch out of Aristarchus's own box, to put Juliet into her coach, or hand Monimia to her chair, are privileges which would delight most young men of a poetic turn ; and no wonder George Warrington loved the theatre. Then he had the satisfaction of thinking that his mother only half approved of plays and play-houses, and of feasting on fruit forbidden at home. He gave more than one elegant entertainment to the players, and it was even said that one or two distinguished geniuses had condescended to borrow money of him.

And as he polished and added new beauties to his masterpiece, we may be sure that he took advice of certain friends of his, and that they gave him applause and counsel. Mr. Spencer, his new acquaintance of the Temple, gave a breakfast at his chambers in Fig Tree Court, when Mr. Warrington read part of his play, and the gentlemen present pronounced that it had uncommon merit. Even the learned Mr. Johnson, who was invited, was good enough to say that the piece showed talent. It warred against the unities, to be sure; but these had been violated by other authors, and Mr. Warrington might sacrifice them as well as another. There was in Mr. W.'s tragedy a something which reminded him both of 'Coriolanus' and 'Othello.' 'And two very good things too, sir!' the author pleaded. 'Well, well, there was no doubt on that point; and 'tis certain your catastrophe is terrible, just, and being in part true, is not the less awful,' remarks Mr. Spencer.

Now the plot of Mr. Warrington's tragedy was quite full indeed of battle and murder. A favourite book of his grandfather had been the life of old George Frundsberg of Mindelheim, a colonel of foot-folk in the Imperial service at Pavia fight, and during the wars of the Constable Bourbon: and one of Frundsberg's military companions was a certain Carpzow, or Carpezan, whom our friend selected as his tragedy hero.

His first act, as it at present stands in Sir George Warrington's manuscript, is supposed to take place before a convent on the Rhine, which the Lutherans, under Carpezan, are besieging. A godless gang these Lutherans are. They have pulled the beards of Roman friars, and torn the veils of hundreds of religious women. A score of these are trembling within the walls of the convent yonder, of which the garrison, unless the expected succours arrive before mid-day, has promised to surrender. Meanwhile there is armistice, and the sentries within look on with hungry eyes, as the soldiers and camp people gamble on the grass before the gate. Twelve o'clock, ding, ding, dong! it sounds upon the convent bell. No succours have arrived. Open gates, warder! and give admission to the famous Protestant hero, the terror of Turks on the Danube, and Papists in the Lombard plains—Colonel *Carpezan!* See, here he comes, clad in complete steel, his hammer of battle over his shoulder, with which he has battered so many infidel sconces, his flags displayed, his trumpets blowing. ' No rudeness, my men,' says Carpezan, ' the wine is yours, and the convent larder and cellar are good ; the church plate shall be melted : any of the garrison who choose to take service with Gaspar Carpezan are welcome, and shall have good pay. No insult to the religious ladies ! I have promised them a safe-conduct, and he who lays a finger on them, hangs ! Mind that, Provost Marshal !' The Provost Marshal, a huge fellow in a red doublet, nods his head.

'We shall see more of that Provost Marshal, or executioner,' Mr. Spencer explains to his guests.

'A very agreeable acquaintance, I am sure,—shall be delighted to meet the gentleman again !' says Mr. Johnson, wagging his head over his tea. ' This scene of the mercenaries, the camp-followers, and their wild sports, is novel and stirring, Mr. Warrington, and I make you my compliments on it. The Colonel has gone into the convent, I think ? Now let us hear what he is going to do there.'

The Abbess, and one or two of her oldest ladies, make their appearance before the conqueror. Conqueror as he is, they beard him in their sacred halls. They have heard of his violent behaviour in conventual establishments before. That hammer, which he always carries in action, has smashed many sacred images in religious houses. Pounds and pounds of convent plate is he known to have melted, the sacrilegious plunderer ! No wonder the Abbess-Princess of Saint Mary's, a lady of violent prejudices, free language, and noble birth, has a dislike to the low-born heretic who lords it in her convent, and tells Carpezan a bit of her mind, as the phrase is. This

scene, in which the lady gets somewhat better of the
Colonel, was liked not a little by Mr. Warrington's
audience at the Temple. Terrible as he might be in
war, Carpezan was shaken at first by the Abbess's
brisk opening charge of words; and, conqueror as he
was, seemed at first to be conquered by his actual
prisoner. But such an old soldier was not to be beaten
ultimately by any woman. 'Pray, madam,' says he,
'how many ladies are there in your convent, for whom
my people shall provide conveyance?' The Abbess,
with a look of much trouble and anger, says that,
'besides herself, the noble Sisters of Saint Mary's
House are twenty—twenty-three.' She was going to
say twenty-four, and now says twenty-three! 'Ha!
why this hesitation?' asks Captain Ulric, one of
Carpezan's gayest officers.

The dark chief pulls a letter from his pocket. 'I
require from you, madam,' he says sternly to the Lady
Abbess, 'the body of the noble Lady Sybilla of Hoya.
Her brother was my favourite captain, slain by my
side, in the Milanese. By his death, she becomes
heiress of his lands. 'Tis said a greedy uncle brought
her hither; and fast immured the lady against her
will. The damsel shall herself pronounce her fate—
to stay a cloistered sister of Saint Mary's, or to return
to home and liberty, as Lady Sybil, Baroness of——'
Ha! The Abbess was greatly disturbed by this question. She says, haughtily : 'There is no Lady Sybil in
this house : of which every inmate is under your protection, and sworn to go free. The Sister Agnes was a
nun professed, and what was her land and wealth revert
to this Order.'

'Give me straightway the body of the Lady Sybil of
Hoya!' roars Carpezan in great wrath. 'If not, I
make a signal to my reiters, and give you and your
convent up to war.'

'Faith, if I lead the storm and have my right, 'tis not my Lady Abbess that I'll choose,' says Captain Ulric, 'but rather some plump, smiling, red-lipped maid like—like——' Here, as he, the sly fellow, is looking under the veils of the two attendant nuns, the stern Abbess cries, 'Silence, fellow, with thy ribald talk! The lady, warrior, whom you ask of me is passed away from sin, temptation, vanity, and three days since our Sister Agnes—*died*.'

At this announcement Carpezan is immensely agitated. The Abbess calls upon the Chaplain to confirm her statement. Ghastly and pale, the old man has to own that three days since the wretched Sister Agnes was buried.

This is too much! In the pocket of his coat of mail Carpezan has a letter from Sister Agnes herself, in which she announces that she is going to be buried indeed, but in an *oubliette* of the convent, where she may either be kept on water and bread, or die starved outright. He seizes the unflinching Abbess by the arm, whilst Captain Ulric lays hold of the Chaplain by the throat. The Colonel blows a blast upon his horn; in rush his furious lanzknechts from without. Crash, bang! They knock the convent walls about. And in the midst of flames, screams and slaughter, who is presently brought in by Carpezan himself, and fainting on his shoulder, but Sybilla herself? A little sister nun (that gay one with the red lips) had pointed out to the Colonel and Ulric the way to Sister Agnes's dungeon, and, indeed, had been the means of making her situation known to the Lutheran chief.

'The convent is suppressed with a vengeance,' says Mr. Warrington. 'We end our first act with the burning of the place, the roars of triumph of the soldiery, and the outcries of the nuns. They had best go change their dresses immediately, for they will

have to be Court ladies in the next act—as you will
see.' Here the gentlemen talked the matter over.
If the piece were to be done at 'Drury Lane,' Mrs.
Pritchard would hardly like to be Lady Abbess, as she
doth but appear in the first act. Miss Pritchard might
make a pretty Sybilla, and Miss Gates the attendant
nun. Mr. Garrick was scarce tall enough for Carpezan
—though, when he is excited, nobody ever thinks of
him but as big as a grenadier. Mr. Johnson owns
Woodward will be a good Ulric, as he plays the
Mercutio parts very gaily ; and so, by one and t'other,
the audience fancies the play already on the boards,
and casts the characters.

In act the second, Carpezan has married Sybilla.
He has enriched himself in the wars, has been ennobled
by the Emperor, and lives at his castle on the Danube
in state and splendour.

But, truth to say, though married, rich, and ennobled, the Lord Carpezan was not happy. It may
be that in his wild life, as condottiere on both sides,
he had committed crimes which agitated his mind
with remorse. It may be that his rough soldier-
manners consorted ill with his imperious high-born
bride. She led him such a life—I am narrating as it
were the Warrington manuscript, which is too long
to print in entire—taunting him with his low birth,
his vulgar companions, whom the old soldier loved to
see about him, and so forth—that there were times
when he rather wished that he had never rescued this
lovely, quarrelsome, wayward vixen from the *oubliette*
out of which he fished her. After the bustle of the
first act this is a quiet one, and passed chiefly in
quarrelling between the Baron and Baroness Carpezan,
until horns blow, and it is announced that the young
King of Bohemia and Hungary is coming hunting
that way.

Act III. is passed at Prague, whither His Majesty
has invited Lord Carpezan and his wife, with noble
offers of preferment to the Baron. From Baron he
shall be promoted to be Count ; from Colonel he shall
be General-in-Chief. His wife is the most brilliant
and fascinating of all the ladies of the Court—and as
for Carpzoff—

'Oh, stay—I have it—I know your story, sir, now,'
says Mr. Johnson. ''Tis in "Meteranus," in the
"Theatrum Universum." I read it in Oxford as a
boy—Carpezanus or Carpzoff——'

'That is the fourth act,' says Mr. Warrington.
In the fourth act the young King's attentions towards
Sybilla grow more and more marked ; but her husband,
battling against his jealousy, long refuses to yield to
it, until his wife's criminality is put beyond a doubt—
and here he read the act, which closes with the terrible
tragedy which actually happened. Being convinced
of his wife's guilt, Carpezan caused the executioner
who followed his regiment to slay her in her own
palace. And the curtain of the act falls just after the
dreadful deed is done, in a side-chamber illuminated
by the moon shining through a great oriel window,
under which the King comes with his lute, and plays
the song which was to be the signal between him and
his guilty victim.

This song (writ in the ancient style, and repeated in
the piece, being sung in the third act previously at a
great festival given by the King and Queen) was pronounced by Mr. Johnson to be a happy imitation of
Mr. Waller's manner, and its gay repetition at the
moment of guilt, murder, and horror, very much
deepened the tragic gloom of the scene.

'But whatever came afterwards?' he asked. 'I
remember in the "Theatrum," Carpezan is said to
have been taken into favour again by Count Mansfield,

and doubtless to have murdered other folks on the re-
formed side.'

Here our poet has departed from historic truth.
In the fifth act of 'Carpezan' King Louis of
Hungary and Bohemia (sufficiently terror-stricken, no
doubt, by the sanguinary termination of his intrigue)
has received word that the Emperor Solyman is invading his Hungarian dominions. Enter two noblemen who relate how, in the council which the King
held upon the news, the injured Carpezan rushed in-
furiated into the Royal presence, broke his sword, and
flung it at the King's feet—along with a glove which
he dared him to wear, and which he swore he would
one day claim. After that wild challenge the rebel
fled from Prague, and had not since been heard of;
but it was reported that he had joined the Turkish
invader, assumed the turban, and was now in the
camp of the Sultan, whose white tents glance across
the river yonder, and against whom the King was now
on his march. Then the King comes to his tent with
his generals, prepares his order of battle, and dismisses
them to their posts, keeping by his side an aged and
faithful knight, his master of the horse, to whom he
expresses his repentance for his past crimes, his esteem
for his good and injured Queen, and his determination
to meet the day's battle like a man.

'What is this field called?'

'Mohacz, my liege!' says the old warrior, adding
the remark that 'Ere set of sun, Mohacz will see a
battle bravely won.'

Trumpets and alarms now sound; they are the
cymbals and barbaric music of the janissaries; we are
in the Turkish camp, and yonder, surrounded by
turbaned chiefs, walks the Sultan Solyman's friend,
the conquerer of Rhodes, the redoubted Grand
Vizier.

Who is that warrior in an Eastern habit, but with
a glove in his cap? 'Tis Carpezan. Even Solyman
knew his courage and ferocity as a soldier. He knows
the ordnance of the Hungarian host; in what arms
King Louis is weakest: how his cavalry, of which the
shock is tremendous, should be received, and inveigled
into yonder morass, where certain death may await
them—he prays for a command in the front, and as
near as possible to the place where the traitor King
Louis will engage. ''Tis well,' says the grim Vizier,
'our invincible Emperor surveys the battle from yonder
tower. At the end of the day, he will know how to
reward your valour.' The signal-guns fire — the
trumpets blow—the Turkish captains retire, vowing
death to the infidel, and eternal fidelity to the
Sultan.

And now the battle begins in earnest, and with
those various incidents which the lover of the theatre
knoweth. Christian knights and Turkish warriors
clash and skirmish over the stage. Continued alarms
are sounded. Troops on both sides advance and
retreat. Carpezan, with his glove in his cap, and his
dreadful hammer smashing all before him, rages about
the field, calling for King Louis. The renegade is
about to slay a warrior who faces him, but recognising
young Ulric, his ex-captain, he drops the uplifted
hammer, and bids him fly and think of Carpezan.
He is softened at seeing his young friend, and thinking
of former times when they fought and conquered
together in the cause of Protestantism. Ulric bids
him to return, but of course that is now out of the
question. They fight, Ulric *will* have it, and down
he goes under the hammer. The renegade melts in
sight of his wounded comrade, when who appears but
King Louis, his plumes torn, his sword hacked, his
shield dented with a thousand blows which he has

received and delivered during the day's battle. Ha! who is this? The guilty monarch would turn away (perhaps Macbeth may have done so before), but Carpezan is on him. All his softness is gone. He rages like a fury. 'An equal fight!' he roars. 'A traitor against a traitor! Stand, King Louis! False King, false knight, false friend—by this glove in my helmet, I challenge you!' And he tears the guilty token out of his cap, and flings it at the King.

Of course they set to, and the monarch falls under the terrible arm of the man whom he has injured. He dies uttering a few incoherent words of repentance, and Carpezan, leaning upon his murderous mace, utters a heartbroken soliloquy over the royal corpse. The Turkish warriors have gathered meanwhile: the dreadful day is their own. Yonder stands the dark Vizier, surrounded by his janissaries, whose bows and swords are tired of drinking death. He surveys the renegade standing over the corpse of the King.

'Christian renegade!' he says, 'Allah has given us a great victory. The arms of the Sublime Emperor are everywhere triumphant. The Christian King is slain by you.'

'Peace to his soul! He died like a good knight,' gasps Ulric, himself dying on the field.

'In this day's battle,' the grim Vizier continues, 'no man hath comported himself more bravely than you. You are made Bassa of Transylvania! Advance, bowmen—Fire!'

An arrow quivers in the breast of Carpezan.

'Bassa of Transylvania you were a traitor to your King, who lies murdered by your hand!' continues grim Vizier. 'You contributed more than any soldier to this day's great victory. 'Tis thus my sublime Emperor meetly rewards you. Sound trumpets! We march for Vienna to-night!'

And the curtain drops as Carpezan, crawling towards his dying comrade, kisses his hand, and gasps—

'Forgive me, Ulric!'

When Mr. Warrington has finished reading his tragedy, he turns round to Mr. Johnson, modestly, and asks—

'What say you, sir? Is there any chance for me?'

But the opinion of this most eminent critic is scarce to be given, for Mr. Johnson had been asleep for some time, and frankly owned that he had lost the latter part of the play.

The little auditory begins to hum and stir as the noise of the speaker ceased. George may have been very nervous when he first commenced to read; but everybody allows that he read the last two acts uncommonly well, and makes him a compliment upon his matter and manner. Perhaps everybody is in good humour because the piece has come to an end. Mr. Spencer's servant hands about refreshing drinks. The Templars speak out their various opinions whilst they sip the negus. They are a choice band of critics, familiar with the pit of the theatre, and they treat Mr. Warrington's play with the gravity which such a subject demands.

Mr. Fountain suggests that the Vizier should not say 'Fire!' when he bids the archers kill Carpezan, —as you certainly don't *fire* with a bow and arrows. A note is taken of the objection.

Mr. Figtree, who is of a sentimental turn, regrets that Ulric could not be saved, and married to the comic heroine.

'Nay, sir, there was an utter annihilation of the Hungarian army at Mohacz,' says Mr. Johnson, 'and

Ulric must take his knock on the head with the rest. He could only be saved by flight, and you wouldn't have a hero run away ! Pronounce sentence of death against Captain Ulric, but kill him with honours of war.'

Messrs. Essex and Tanfield wonder to one another who is this queer-looking *put* whom Spencer has invited, and who contradicts everybody ; and they suggest a boat up the river and a little fresh air after the fatigues of the tragedy.

The general opinion is decidedly favourable to Mr. Warrington's performance ; and Mr. Johnson's opinion, on which he sets a special value, is the most favourable of all. Perhaps Mr. Johnson is not sorry to compliment a young gentleman of fashion and figure like Mr. W. 'Up to the death of the heroine,' he says, 'I am frankly with you, sir. And I may speak, as a playwright who have killed my own heroine, and had my share of the *plausus in theatro.* To hear your own lines nobly delivered to an applauding house, is indeed a noble excitement. I like to see a young man of good name and lineage who condescends to think that the Tragic Muse is not below his advances. It was to a sordid roof that I invited her, and I asked her to rescue me from poverty and squalor. Happy you, sir, who can meet her upon equal terms, and can afford to marry her without a portion.'

'I doubt whether the greatest genius is not debased who has to make a bargain with Poetry,' remarks Mr. Spencer.

'Nay, sir,' Mr. Johnson answered, 'I doubt if many a great genius would work at all without bribes and necessities ; and so a man had better marry a poor Muse for good and all, for better or worse, than dally with a rich one. I make you my compliment of your

play, Mr. Warrington, and if you want an introduction to the stage, shall be very happy if I can induce my friend Mr. Garrick to present you.'

'Mr. Garrick shall be his sponsor,' cried the florid
Mr. Figtree. 'Melpomene shall be his godmother,
and he shall have the witches' cauldron in "Macbeth"
for a christening font.'

'Sir, I neither said font nor godmother,' remarks
the man of letters. 'I would have no play contrary
to morals or religion : nor, as I conceive, is Mr.
Warrington's piece otherwise than friendly to them.
Vice is chastised, as it should be, even in kings,
though perhaps we judge of their temptations too
lightly. Revenge is punished—as not to be lightly
exercised by our limited notion of justice. It may
have been Carpezan's wife who perverted the King,
and not the King who led the woman astray. At any
rate, Louis is rightly humiliated for his crime, and
the Renegade most justly executed for his. I wish
you a good afternoon, gentlemen.' And with these
remarks, the great author took his leave of the
company.

Towards the close of the reading, General Lambert
had made his appearance at Mr. Spencer's chambers,
and had listened to the latter part of the tragedy.
The performance over, he and George took their way
to the latter's lodgings in the first place, and subsequently to the General's own house, where the
young author was expected, in order to recount the
reception which his play had met from his Temple
critics.

At Mr. Warrington's apartments in Southampton
Row, they found a letter awaiting George, which the
latter placed in his pocket unread, so that he might
proceed immediately with his companion to Soho.
We may be sure the ladies there were eager to know

about the Carpezan's fate in the morning's small rehearsal. Hetty said George was so shy, that perhaps it would be better for all parties if some other person had read the play. Theo, on the contrary, cried out—

'Read it, indeed! Who can read a poem better than the author who feels it in his heart? And George had his whole heart in the piece!'

Mr. Lambert very likely thought that somebody else's whole heart was in the piece, too, but did not utter this opinion to Miss Theo.

'I think Harry would look very well in your figure of a Prince,' says the General. 'That scene where he takes leave of his wife before departing for the wars reminds me of your brother's manner not a little.'

'Oh, papa! surely Mr. Warrington himself would act the Prince's part best!' cries Miss Theo.

'And be deservedly slain in battle at the end?' asks the father of the house.

'I did not say that; only that Mr. George would make a very good Prince, papa!' cries Miss Theo.

'In which case he would find a suitable Princess, I have no doubt. What news of your brother Harry?'

George, who has been thinking about theatrical triumphs; about *monumentum ære perennius*; about lilacs; about love whispered and tenderly accepted, remembers that he has a letter from Harry in his pocket, and gaily produces it.

'Let us hear what Mr. Truant says for himself, Aunt Lambert!' cries George, breaking the seal.

Why is he so disturbed, as he reads the contents of his letter? Why do the women look at him with alarmed eyes? And why, above all, is Hetty so pale?

'Here is the letter,' says George, and begins to read it :—

'RYDE : *June* 1, 1758.

'I DID not tell my dearest George what I hoped and intended, when I left home on Wednesday. 'Twas to see Mr. Webb at Portsmouth or the Isle of Wight, wherever his Reg^t was, and if need was to *go down on my knees* to him to take me as volunteer with him on the Expedition. I took boat from Portsmouth, where I learned that he was with *our regiment* incampt at the village of Ryde. Was received by him most kindly, and my petition granted out of hand. That is why I say our regiment. We are eight gentlemen volunteers with Mr. Webb, all men of birth, and *good fortunes* except poor me, who don't deserve one. We are to mess with the officers ; we take the right of the collumn, *and have always the right to be in front*, and in an hour we embark on board His Majesty's Ship the " Rochester " of 60 guns, while our Commodore's, Mr Howe's, is the " Essex," 70. His squadron is about 20 ships, and I should think 100 transports at least. Though 'tis a secret expedition, we make no doubt France is our destination—where I hope to see my friend the Monsieurs once more, and win my colours *à la poinct de mon épée,* as we used to say in Canada. Perhaps my service as interpreter may be useful ; I speaking the language not so well *as someone I know*, but better than most here.

'I scarce venture to write to our mother to tell her of this step. Will you, who have a *coxing tongue will wheadle any one*, write to her as soon as you have finisht the famous *tradgedy?* Will you give my affectionate respects to dear General Lambert and ladies ; and if any accident should happen, I know you will take care of poor Gumbo as belonging to my dearest best George's most affectionate brother, HENRY E. WARRINGTON.

'P.S.—Love to all at home when you write, including Dempster, Mountain, and Fanny M. and all the people, and duty to my honored mother, wishing I had pleased her better. And if I said anything unkind to dear Miss Hester Lambert, I know she will forgive me, and pray God bless all.   H. E. W.

'To G. Esmond Warrington, Esq.,
    'At Mr. Scrace's house in Southampton Row,
        opposite Bedford House Gardens, London.'

He has not read the last words with a very steady voice. Mr. Lambert sits silent, though not a little moved. Theo and her mother look at one another; but Hetty remains with a cold face and a stricken heart. She thinks, 'He is gone to danger, perhaps to death, and it was I sent him!'

CHAPTER LXIV

IN WHICH HARRY LIVES TO FIGHT ANOTHER DAY

The trusty Gumbo could not console himself for the departure of his beloved master: at least, to judge from his tears and howls on first hearing the news of Mr. Harry's enlistment, you would have thought the negro's heart must break at the separation. No wonder he went for sympathy to the maidservants at Mr. Lambert's lodgings. Wherever that dusky youth was, he sought comfort in the society of females. Their fair and tender bosoms knew how to feel pity for the poor African, and the darkness of Gumbo's complexion was no more repulsive to them than Othello's to Desdemona. I believe Europe has never been so squeamish in regard to Africa, as a certain other respected quarter. Nay, some Africans —witness the Chevalier de St. Georges, for instance —have been notorious favourites with the fair sex.

So, in his humbler walk, was Mr. Gumbo. The Lambert servants wept freely in his company : the maids kindly considered him not only Mr. Harry's man, but their brother. Hetty could not help laughing when she found Gumbo roaring because his master had gone a volunteer, as he called it, and had not taken him. He was ready to save Master Harry's life any day, and would have done it, and had himself cut in twenty tousand hundred pieces for Master Harry, that he would ! Meanwhile, Nature must be supported, and he condescended to fortify her by large supplies of beer and cold meat in the kitchen. That he was greedy, idle, and told lies, is certain ; but yet Hetty gave him half-a-crown, and was especially kind to him. Her tongue, that was wont to wag so pertly, was so gentle now, that you might fancy it had never made a joke. She moved about the house mum and meek. She was humble to mamma ; thankful to John and Betty when they waited at dinner ; patient to Polly when the latter pulled her hair in combing it ; long-suffering when Charley from school trod on her toes, or deranged her workbox ; silent in papa's company,— oh, such a transmogrified little Hetty ! If papa had ordered her to roast the leg of mutton, or walk to church arm-in-arm with Gumbo, she would have made a curtsey, and said, ' Yes, if you please, dear papa !' Leg of mutton ! What sort of meal were some poor volunteers having, with the cannon-balls flying about their heads ? Church ? When it comes to the prayer in time of war, oh how her knees smite together as she kneels, and hides her head in the pew ! She holds down her head when the parson reads out, ' Thou shalt do no murder,' from the communion-rail, and fancies he must be looking at her. How she thinks of all travellers by land or by water !

How she sickens as she runs to the paper to read if
there is news of the Expedition ! How she watches
papa when he comes home from his Ordnance Office,
and looks in his face to see if there is good news or
bad ! Is he well ? Is he made a General yet ? Is he
wounded and made a prisoner ? ah me ! or, perhaps,
are both his legs taken off by one shot, like that
pensioner they saw in Chelsea Garden t'other day ?
She would go on wooden legs all her life, if his can
but bring him safe home ; at least, she ought never
to get up off her knees until he is returned. 'Haven't
you heard of people, Theo,' says she, 'whose hair has
grown grey in a single night? I shouldn't wonder
if mine did—shouldn't wonder in the least.' And she
looks in the glass to ascertain that phenomenon.

'Hetty dear, you used not to be so nervous when
papa was away in Minorca,' remarks Theo.

'Ah, Theo ! one may very well see that George is
not with the army, but safe at home,' rejoins Hetty ;
whereat the elder sister blushes and looks very pensive.
Au fait, if Mr. George had been in the army, that, you
see, would have been another pair of boots. Meanwhile, we don't intend to harrow anybody's kind feelings any longer, but may as well state that Harry is,
for the present, as safe as any officer of the Life Guards
at Regent's Park Barracks.

The first expedition in which our gallant volunteer
was engaged may be called successful, but certainly
was not glorious. The British Lion, or any other lion,
cannot always have a worthy enemy to combat, or a
battle royal to deliver. Suppose he goes forth in quest
of a tiger, who won't come, and lays his paws on a
goose and gobbles him up ? Lions, we know, must
live like any other animals. But suppose, advancing
into the forest in search of the tiger aforesaid, and
bellowing his challenge of war, he espies not one but

six tigers coming towards him? This manifestly is
not his game at all. He puts his tail between his Royal
legs, and retreats into his own snug den as quickly as
he may. Were he to attempt to go and fight isix
tigers, you might write that Lion down an Ass.

Now Harry Warrington's first feat of war was in
this wise. He and about 13,000 other fighting men
embarked in various ships and transports on the 1st of
June, from the Isle of Wight, and at daybreak on the
5th the fleet stood in to the Bay of Cancale in Brittany.
For a while he and the gentlemen volunteers had the
pleasure of examining the French coast from their
ships, whilst the Commander-in-Chief and the Commodore reconnoitred the bay in a cutter. Cattle were
seen and some dragoons, who trotted off into the
distance; and a little fort with a couple of guns had
the audacity to fire at his Grace of Marlborough and
the Commodore in the cutter. By two o'clock the
whole British fleet was at anchor, and signal was made
for all the grenadier companies of eleven regiments, to
embark on board flat-bottomed boats and assemble
round the Commodore's ship, the 'Essex.' Meanwhile,
Mr. Howe, hoisting his broad pennant on board the
'Success' frigate, went in as near as possible to shore,
followed by the other frigates to protect the landing
of the troops; and, now, with Lord George Sackville
and General Drury in command, the gentlemen volunteers, the grenadier companies, and three battalions of
Guards pulled to shore.

The gentlemen volunteers could not do any heroic
deed upon this occasion, because the French, who
should have stayed to fight them, ran away, and the
frigates having silenced the fire of the little fort which
had disturbed the reconnaissance of the Commander-
in-Chief, the army presently assaulted it, taking the
whole garrison prisoner, and shooting him in the leg.

Indeed he was but one old gentleman, who gallantly had fired his two guns, and who told his conquerors, 'If every Frenchman had acted like me, you would not have landed at Cancale at all.'

The advanced detachment of invaders took possession of the village of Cancale, where they lay upon their arms all night : and our volunteer was joked by his comrades about his eagerness to go out upon the war-path, and bring in two or three scalps of Frenchmen. None such, however, fell under his tomahawk ; the only person slain on the whole day being a French gentleman, who was riding with his servant, and was surprised by volunteer Lord Downe, marching in the front with a company of Kingsley's. My Lord Downe offered the gentleman quarter, which he foolishly refused, whereupon he, his servant, and the two horses, were straightway shot.

Next day the whole force was landed, and advanced from Cancale to St. Malo. All the villages were emptied through which the troops passed, and the roads were so narrow in many places that the men had to march single file, and might have been shot down from behind the tall leafy hedges had there been any enemy to disturb them.

At nightfall the army arrived before St. Malo, and were saluted by a fire of artillery from that town, which did little damage in the darkness. Under cover of this, the British set fire to the ships, wooden buildings, pitch and tar magazines in the harbour, and made a prodigious conflagration that lasted the whole night.

This feat was achieved without any attempt on the part of the French to molest the British force ; but, as it was confidently asserted that there was a considerable French force in the town of St. Malo, though they wouldn't come out, his Grace the Duke of Marlborough and my Lord George Sackville determined not to dis-

turb the garrison, marched back to Cancale again, and
—and so got on board their ships.

If this were not a veracious history, don't you see
that it would have been easy to send our Virginian on
a more glorious campaign ? Exactly four weeks after
his departure from England, Mr. Warrington found
himself at Portsmouth again, and addressed a letter to
his brother George, with which the latter ran off to
Dean Street so soon as ever he received it.

'Glorious news, ladies !' cries he, finding the Lambert family all at breakfast. 'Our champion has come
back. He has undergone all sorts of dangers, but has
survived them all. He has seen dragons—upon my
word, he says so.'

'Dragons ! What do you mean, Mr. Warrington ?'

'But not killed any—he says so, as you shall hear.
He writes :—

'DEAREST BROTHER,—I think you will be glad to hear
that I am returned, without any commission as yet ; without any wounds or glory ; but at any rate, *alive and harty*.
On board our ship, we were almost as crowded as poor Mr.
Holwell and his friends in their Black Hole at Calcutta.
We had rough weather, and some of the gentlemen volunteers, who prefer smooth water, grumbled not a little. My
gentlemen's stomachs are dainty ; and after Braund's
cookery and White's kickshaws, they don't like plain
sailor's *rum and bisket*. But I, who have been at sea before,
took my rations and can of flip very contentedly : being
determined to put a good face on everything before our fine
English *macaronis*, and show that a Virginia gentleman is as
good as the best of 'em. I wish, for the honour of old
Virginia, that I had more to brag about. But all I can say
in truth is, that we have been to France and come back
again. Why, I don't think even *your tragick pen* could make
anything of such a campaign as ours has been. We landed
on the 6 at Cancalle Bay, we saw a few dragons on a hill——'

'There! Did I not tell you there were dragons?'
asks George, laughing.

'Mercy! What can he mean by dragons?' cries
Hetty.

'Immense, long-tailed monsters, with steel scales on
their backs, who vomit fire, and gobble up a virgin
a-day. Haven't you read about them in "The Seven
Champions"?' says papa. 'Seeing St. George's flag,
I suppose, they slunk off.'

'I have read of 'em,' says the little boy from Chartreux, solemnly. 'They like to eat women. One
was going to eat Andromeda, you know, papa: and
Jason killed another, who was guarding the apple-tree.'

'—A few dragons on a hill,' George resumes, 'who rode
away from us without engaging. We slept under canvass.
We marched to St. Malo, and burned ever so many privateers there. And we went on board shipp again, without
ever crossing swords with an enemy or meeting any except
a few poor devils whom the troops plundered. Better luck
next time! This hasn't been very much nor *particular
glorious;* but I have liked it for my part. I have *smelt
powder,* besides a deal of rosn and pitch we burned. I've
seen the enemy; have sleppt under canvass, and been dreadful crowdid and sick at sea. I like it. My best compliments to dear Aunt Lambert, and tell Miss Hetty I wasn't
very much fritened when I saw the French horse. ·

'Your most affectionate brother,
'H. E. WARRINGTON.'

We hope Miss Hetty's qualms of conscience were
allayed by Harry's announcement that his expedition
was over, and that he had so far taken no hurt. Far
otherwise. Mr. Lambert, in the course of his official
duties, had occasion to visit the troops at Portsmouth
and the Isle of Wight, and George Warrington bore
him company. They found Harry vastly improved

in spirits and health from the excitement produced by
the little campaign, quite eager and pleased to learn
his new military duties, active, cheerful, and healthy,
and altogether a different person from the listless
moping lad who had dawdled in London coffee-houses
and Mrs. Lambert's drawing-room. The troops were
under canvas ; the weather was glorious, and George
found his brother a ready pupil in a fine brisk open-
air school of war. Not a little amused, the elder
brother, arm-in-arm with the young volunteer, paced
the streets of the warlike city, recalled his own brief
military experiences of two years back, and saw here
a much greater army than that ill-fated one of which
he had shared the disasters. The expedition, such as
we have seen it, was certainly not glorious, and yet
the troops and the nation were in high spirits with it.
We were said to have humiliated the proud Gaul.
We should have vanquished as well as humbled him
had he dared to appear. What valour, after all, is
like British valour ? I dare say some such expressions
have been heard in later times. Not that I would
hint that our people brag much more than any
other, or more now than formerly. Have not these
eyes beheld the battle-grounds of Leipzig, Jena,
Dresden, Waterloo, Blenheim, Bunker's Hill, New
Orleans ? What heroic nation has not fought, has
not conquered, has not run away, has not bragged in
its turn ? Well, the British nation was much excited
by the glorious victory of St. Malo. Captured
treasures were sent home and exhibited in London.
The people were so excited, that more laurels and
more victories were demanded, and the enthusiastic
army went forth to seek some.

With this new expedition went a volunteer so
distinguished, that we must give him precedence of
all other amateur soldiers or sailors. This was our

sailor prince, H.R.H. Prince Edward, who was conveyed on board the 'Essex' in the ship's twelve-oared
barge, the standard of England flying in the bow of
the boat, the Admiral with his flag and boat following
the Prince's, and all the captains following in
seniority.

Away sails the fleet, Harry, in high health and
spirits, waving his hat to his friends as they cheer from
the shore. He must and will have his commission
before long. There can be no difficulty about that,
George thinks. There is plenty of money in his
little store to buy his brother's ensigncy ; but if he
can win it without purchase by gallantry and good
conduct, that were best. The colonel of the regiment
reports highly of his recruit ; men and officers like him.
It is easy to see that he is a young fellow of good
promise and spirit.

Hip, hip, huzzay ! What famous news is this
which arrives ten days after the expedition has sailed ?
On the 7th and 8th of August His Majesty's troops
have affected a landing in the Bay des Marais, two
leagues westward of Cherbourg, in the face of a large
body of the enemy. Awed by the appearance of
British valour, that large body of the enemy has
disappeared. Cherbourg has surrendered at discretion ;
and the English colours are hoisted on the three outlying forts. Seven-and-twenty ships have been burned
in the harbours, and a prodigious number of fine brass
cannon taken. As for your common iron guns, we
have destroyed 'em, likewise the basin (about which
the Mounseers bragged so), and the two piers at the
entrance to the harbour.

There is no end of jubilation in London ; just as
Mr. Howe's guns arrive from Cherbourg, come Mr.
Wolfe's colours captured at Louisbourg. The
colours are taken from Kensington to St. Paul's,

escorted by fourscore Life Guards and fourscore Horse Grenadiers with officers in proportion, their standards, kettle-drums, and trumpets. At St. Paul's they are received by the Dean and Chapter at the West Gate, and at that minute—bang, bong, bung— the Tower and Park guns salute them ! Next day is the turn of the Cherbourg cannon and mortars. These are the guns *we* took. Look at them with their carving and flaunting emblems—their lilies, and crowns, and mottoes ! Here they are, the Téméraire, the Malfaisant, the Vainqueur (the Vainqueur, indeed ! a pretty *vainqueer* of Britons !), and ever so many more. How the people shout as the pieces are trailed through the streets in procession ! As for Hetty and Mrs. Lambert, I believe they are of opinion that Harry took every one of the guns himself, dragging them out of the batteries, and destroying the artillery- men. He has immensely risen in the general estima- tion in the last few days. Madame de Bernstein has asked about him. Lady Maria has begged her dear Cousin George to see her, and, if possible, give her news of his brother. George, who was quite the head of the family a couple of months since, finds himself deposed, and of scarce any account, in Miss Hetty's eyes at least. Your wit, and your learning, and your tragedies, may be all very well ; but what are these in comparison to victories and brass cannon ? George takes his deposition very meekly. They are fifteen thousand Britons. Why should they not march and take Paris itself ? Nothing more probable, think some of the ladies. They embrace, they congratulate each other ; they are in a high state of excitement. For once, they long that Sir Miles and Lady Warrington were in town, so that they might pay her Ladyship a visit, and ask, ' What do you say to your nephew, now, pray ? Has he not taken twenty-one finest brass cannon ; flung a hundred and twenty iron guns into the water, seized twenty-seven ships in the harbour, and destroyed the basin and the two piers at the entrance ? ' As the whole town rejoices and illuminates, so these worthy folks display brilliant red hangings in their cheeks, and light up candles of joy in their eyes, in honour of their champion and conqueror.

But now, I grieve to say, comes a cloudy day after the fair weather. The appetite of our commanders, growing by what it fed on, led them to think they had not feasted enough on the plunder of St. Malo ; and thither, after staying a brief time at Portsmouth, and the Wight, the conquerors of Cherbourg returned. They were landed in the bay of St. Lunar, at the distance of a few miles from the place, and marched towards it intending to destroy it this time. Meanwhile the harbour of St. Lunar was found insecure, and the fleet moved up to St. Cas, keeping up its communication with the invading army.

Now the British Lion found that the town of St. Malo—which he had proposed to swallow at a single mouthful—was guarded by an army of French, which the Governor of Brittany had brought to the succour of his good town, and the meditated *coup de main* being thus impossible, our leaders marched for their ships again, which lay duly awaiting our warriors in the Bay of St. Cas.

Hide, blushing glory, hide St. Cas's day ! As our troops were marching down to their ships they became aware of an army following them, which the French governor of the province had sent from Brest. Two-thirds of the troops, and all the artillery, were already embarked, when the Frenchmen came down upon the remainder. Four companies of the First Regiment of Guards and the Grenadier companies of the army, faced about on the beach to await the enemy, whilst the remaining troops were carried off in the boats. As the French descended from the heights round the bay, these Guards and Grenadiers marched out to attack them, leaving an excellent position which they had occupied—a great dyke raised on the shore, and behind which they might have resisted to advantage. And now, eleven hundred men were engaged with six—nay, ten times their number; and, after a while, broke and made for the boats with a *sauve qui peut!* Seven hundred out of the eleven were killed, drowned, or taken prisoners—the General himself was killed — and ah! where were the volunteers?

A man of peace myself, and little intelligent of the practice or the details of war, I own I think less of the engaged troops than of the people they leave behind. Jack the Guardsman and La Tulipe of the Royal Bretagne are face to face, and striving to knock each other's brains out. Bon! It is their nature to—like the bears and lions—and we will not say Heaven, but some power or other has made them so to do. But the girl of Tower Hill, who hung on Jack's neck before he departed; and the lass at Quimper, who gave the Frenchman his *brûle-gueule* and tobacco-box before he departed on the *noir trajet?* What have you done, poor little tender hearts, that you should grieve so? My business is not with the army, but with the people left behind. What a fine state Miss Hetty Lambert must be in, when she hears of the disaster to the troops and the slaughter of the Grenadier companies! What grief and doubt are in George Warrington's breast; what commiseration in Martin Lambert's, as he looks into his little girl's face and reads her piteous story there? Howe, the brave Commodore, rowing in his barge under the enemy's fire, has rescued with his boats scores and scores of our flying people. More are drowned; hundreds are prisoners, or shot on the beach. Among these where is our Virginian?

CHAPTER LXV

SOLDIER'S RETURN

GREAT Powers! will the vainglory of men, especially of Frenchmen, never cease? Will it be believed, that after the action of St. Cas—a mere affair of cutting off a rearguard, as you are aware—they were so unfeeling as to fire away I don't know how much powder at the Invalides at Paris, and brag and bluster over our misfortune? Is there any magnanimity in hallooing and huzzaying because five or six hundred brave fellows have been caught by ten thousand on a sea-shore, and that fate has overtaken them which is said to befall the hindmost? I had a mind to design an authentic picture of the rejoicings at London upon our glorious success at St. Malo. I fancied the polished guns dragged in procession by our gallant tars; the stout Horse Grenadiers prancing by; the mob waving hats, roaring cheers, picking pockets, and our friends in a balcony in Fleet Street looking on and blessing this scene of British triumph. But now that the French Invalides have been so vulgar as to imitate the Tower, and set up their St. Cas against our St. Malo, I scorn to allude to the stale subject. I say Nolo, not Malo: content, for my part, if Harry has returned from one expedition and t'other with a whole skin. And have I ever said he was so much as bruised? Have I not, for fear of exciting my fair young reader, said that he was as well as ever he had been in his life? The sea air had browned his cheek, and the ball whistling by his side-curl had spared it. The ocean had wet his gaiters and other garments, without swallowing up his body. He had, it is true, shown the lapels of his coat to the enemy; but for as short a time as possible, withdrawing out of their sight as quick as might be. And what, pray, are lapels but reverses? Coats have them, as well as men; and our duty is to wear them with courage and good-humour.

'I can tell you,' said Harry, 'we all had to run for it; and when our line broke, it was he who could get to the boats who was most lucky. The French horse and foot pursued us down to the sea, and were mingled among us, cutting our men down, and bayoneting them on the ground. Poor Armytage was shot in advance of me, and fell: and I took him up and staggered through the surf to a boat. It was lucky that the sailors in our boat weren't afraid; for the shot were whistling about their ears, breaking the blades of their oars, and riddling their flag with shot; but the officer in command was as cool as if he had been drinking a bowl of punch at Portsmouth, which we had one on landing, I can promise you. Poor Sir John was less lucky than me. He never lived to reach the ship, and the service has lost a fine soldier, and Miss Howe a true gentleman to her husband. There must be these casualties, you see; and his brother gets the promotion—the baronetcy.'

'It is of the poor lady I am thinking,' says Miss Hetty (to whom haply our volunteer is telling his story); 'and the King. Why did the King encourage Sir John Armytage to go? A gentleman could not refuse a command from such a quarter. And now the poor gentleman is dead! Oh, what a state His Majesty must be in!'

'I have no doubt His Majesty will be in a deep state of grief,' says papa, wagging his head.

'Now you are laughing! Do you mean, sir, that when a gentleman dies in his service, almost at his feet, the King of England won't feel for him?' Hetty asks. 'If I thought that, I vow I would be for the Pretender!'

'The sauce-box would make a pretty little head for Temple Bar,' says the General, who could see Miss Hetty's meaning behind her words, and was aware in what a tumult of remorse, of consternation, of gratitude that the danger was over, the little heart was beating. 'No,' says he, 'my dear. Were kings to weep for every soldier, what a life you would make for them! I think better of His Majesty than to suppose him so weak; and, if Miss Hester Lambert got her Pretender, I doubt whether she would be any the happier. That family was never famous for too much feeling.'

'But if the King sent Harry—I mean Sir John Armytage—actually to the war in which he lost his life, oughtn't His Majesty to repent very much?' asks the young lady.

'If Harry had fallen, no doubt the Court would have gone into mourning: as it is, gentlemen and ladies were in coloured clothes, yesterday,' remarks the General.

'Why should we not make bonfires for a defeat, and put on sackcloth and ashes after a victory?' asks George. 'I protest I don't want to thank Heaven for helping us to burn the ships at Cherbourg.'

'Yes, you do, George! Not that I have a right to speak, and you ain't ever so much cleverer. But when your country wins you're glad—I know I am. When I run away before Frenchmen I'm ashamed— I can't help it, though I *done* it,' says Harry. 'It

don't seem to me right somehow that Englishmen should have to do it,' he added gravely.
And George smiled; but did not choose to ask his
brother what, on the other hand, was the Frenchman's opinion.

''Tis a bad business,' continued Harry gravely :
' but 'tis lucky 'twas no worse. The story about the
French is, that their Governor, the Duke of Aiguillon,
was rather what you call a *moistened chicken*. Our
whole retreat might have been cut off, only, to be sure,
we ourselves were in a mighty hurry to move. The
French local militia behaved famous, I am happy to
say ; and there was ever so many gentlemen volunteers
with 'em, who showed, as they ought to do, in the
front. They say the Chevalier of Tour d'Auvergne
engaged in spite of the Duke of Aiguillon's orders.
Officers told us, who came off with a list of our
prisoners and wounded to General Bligh and Lord
Howe. He is a Lord now, since the news came of
his brother's death to home, George. He is a brave
fellow, whether lord or commoner.'

' And his sister, who was to have married poor
Sir John Armytage, think what *her* state must
be ! ' sighs Miss Hetty, who has grown of late so
sentimental.

' And his mother,' cries Mrs. Lambert. ' Have you
seen her Ladyship's address in the papers to the electors
of Nottingham ? " Lord Howe being now absent
upon the publick service and Lieutenant-Colonel
Howe with his regiment at Louisbourg, it rests upon
me to beg the favour of your votes and interests that
Lieutenant-Colonel Howe may supply the place of
his late brother as your representative in Parliament."
Isn't this a gallant woman ? '

' A laconic woman,' says George.

' How can sons help being brave who have

been nursed by such a mother as that?' asks the
General.

Our two young men looked at each other.

'If one of us were to fall in defence of his country,
we have a mother in Sparta who would think and
write so too,' says George.

'If Sparta is anywhere Virginia way, I reckon
we have,' remarks Mr. Harry. 'And to think that
we should both of us have met the enemy, and
both of us been whipped by him, brother!' he adds
pensively.

Hetty looks at him, and thinks of him only as he
was the other day, tottering through the water towards
the boats, his comrade bleeding on his shoulder, the
enemy in pursuit, the shot flying round. And it was
she who drove him into the danger! Her words
provoked him. He never rebukes her now he is
returned. Except when asked he scarcely speaks
about his adventures at all. He is very grave and
courteous with Hetty; with the rest of the family
especially frank and tender. But those taunts of hers
wounded him. 'Little hand!' his looks and
demeanour seem to say, 'thou shouldst not have been
lifted against me! It is ill to scorn any one, much
more one who has been so devoted to you and all yours.
I may not be over quick of wit, but in as far as the
heart goes, I am the equal of the best, and the best
of my heart your family has had.'

Harry's wrong, and his magnanimous endurance of
it, served him to regain in Miss Hetty's esteem that
place which he had lost during the previous month's
inglorious idleness. The respect which the fair pay
to the brave she gave him. She was no longer pert
in her answers, or sarcastic in her observations regarding his conduct. In a word, she was a humiliated, an
altered, an improved Miss Hetty.

And all the world seemed to change towards Harry, as he towards the world. He was no longer sulky and indolent ; he no more desponded about himself, or defied his neighbours. The colonel of his regiment reported his behaviour as exemplary, and recommended him for one of the commissions vacated by the casualties during the expedition. Unlucky as its termination was, it at least was fortunate to him. His brother volunteers, when they came back to St. James's Street, reported highly of his behaviour. These volunteers and their actions were the theme of everybody's praise. Had he been a general commanding, and slain in the moment of victory, Sir John Armytage could scarce have had more sympathy than that which the nation showed him. The papers teemed with letters about him, and men of wit and sensibility vied with each other in composing epitaphs in his honour. The fate of his affianced bride was bewailed. She was, as we have said, the sister of the brave Commodore who had just returned from this unfortunate expedition, and succeeded to the title of his elder brother, an officer as gallant as himself, who had just fallen in America.

My Lord Howe was heard to speak in special praise of Mr. Warrington, and so he had a handsome share of the fashion and favour which the town now bestowed on the volunteers. Doubtless there were thousands of men employed who were as good as they : but the English ever love their gentlemen, and love that they should distinguish themselves ; and these volunteers were voted Paladins and heroes by common accord. As our young noblemen will, they accepted their popularity very affably. White's and Almack's illuminated when they returned, and St. James's embraced its young knights. Harry was restored to full favour amongst them. Their hands were held out eagerly to him again. Even his relations congratulated him; and there came a letter from Castlewood, whither Aunt Bernstein had by this time betaken herself, containing praises of his valour, and a pretty little bank-bill, as a token of his affectionate aunt's approbation. This was under my Lord Castlewood's frank, who sent his regards to both his kinsmen, and an offer of the hospitality of his country house, if they were minded to come to him. And besides this there came to him a private letter through the post—not very well spelt, but in a hand-writing which Harry smiled to see again, in which his affectionate cousin, Maria Esmond, told him she always loved to hear his praises (which were in every-body's mouth now), and sympathised in his good or evil fortune; and that, whatever occurred to him, she begged to keep a little place in his heart. Parson Sampson, she wrote, had preached a beautiful sermon about the horrors of war, and the noble actions of men who volunteered to face battle and danger in the service of their country. Indeed, the chaplain wrote himself, presently, a letter full of enthusiasm, in which he saluted Mr. Harry as his friend, his benefactor, his glorious hero. Even Sir Miles Warrington de-spatched a basket of game from Norfolk: and one bird (shot sitting), with love to my cousin, had a string and paper round the leg, and was sent as the first victim of young Miles's fowling-piece.

And presently, with joy beaming in his counten-ance, Mr. Lambert came to visit his young friends at their lodgings in Southampton Row, and announced to them that Mr. Henry Warrington was forthwith to be gazetted as Ensign in the Second Battalion of Kingsley's, the 20th Regiment, which had been engaged in the campaign, and which now at this time was formed into a separate regiment, the 67th.

Its colonel was not with his regiment during its expedition to Brittany. He was away at Cape Breton, and was engaged in capturing those guns at Louisbourg, of which the arrival in England had caused such exultation.

CHAPTER LXVI

IN WHICH WE GO A-COURTING

SOME of my amiable readers no doubt are in the custom of visiting that famous garden in the Regent's Park, in which so many of our finned, feathered, four-footed fellow-creatures are accommodated with board and lodging, in return for which they exhibit themselves for our instruction and amusement : and there, as a man's business and private thoughts follow him everywhere and mix themselves with all life and nature round about him, I found myself, whilst looking at some fish in the aquarium, still actually thinking of our friends the Virginians. One of the most beautiful motion-masters I ever beheld, sweeping through his green bath in harmonious curves, now turning his black glistening back to me, now exhibiting his fair white chest, in every movement active and graceful, turned out to be our old homely friend the flounder, whom we have all gobbled up out of his bath of water souchy at Greenwich, without having the slightest idea that he was a beauty.

As is the race of man, so is the race of flounders. If you can but see the latter in his right element, you may view him agile, healthy, and comely : put him out of his place, and behold his beauty is gone, his motions are disgraceful ; he flaps the unfeeling ground ridiculously with his tail, and will presently gasp his

feeble life out. Take him up tenderly, ere it be too
late, and cast him into his native Thames again——
But stop : I believe there is a certain proverb about
fish out of water, and that other profound naturalists
have remarked on them before me. Now Harry
Warrington had been floundering for ever so long a
time past and out of his proper element. As soon as
he found it, health, strength, spirits, energy, returned
to him, and with the tap of the epaulet on his
shoulder he sprang up an altered being. He delighted in his new profession ; he engaged in all its
details, and mastered them with eager quickness.
Had I the skill of my friend Lorrequer, I would
follow the other Harry into camp, and see him on the
march, at the mess, on the parade-ground ; I would
have many a carouse with him and his companions ;
I would cheerfully live with him under the tents ; I
would knowingly explain all the manœuvres of war,
and all the details of the life military. As it is the
reader must please, out of his experience and imagina-
tion, to fill in the colours of the picture of which I
can give but meagre hints and outlines, and, above
all, fancy Mr. Harry Warrington in his new red
coat and yellow facings, very happy to bear the
King's colours, and pleased to learn and perform
all the duties of his new profession.

As each young man delighted in the excellence of
the other, and cordially recognised his brother's superior
qualities, George, we may be sure, was proud of
Harry's success, and rejoiced in his returning good
fortune. He wrote an affectionate letter to his mother
in Virginia, recounting all the praises which he had
heard of Harry, and which his brother's modesty,
George knew, would never allow him to repeat. He
described how Harry had won his own first step in the
army, and how he, George, would ask his mother

leave to share with her the expense of purchasing a higher rank for him.

Nothing, said George, would give him a greater delight, than to be able to help his brother, and the more so, as, by his sudden return into life as it were, he had deprived Harry of an inheritance which he had legitimately considered as his own. Labouring under that misconception, Harry had indulged in greater expenses than he ever would have thought of incurring as a younger brother : and George thought it was but fair, and, as it were, as a thank-offering for his own deliverance, that he should contribute liberally to any scheme for his brother's advantage.

And now, having concluded his statement respecting Harry's affairs, George took occasion to speak of his own, and addressed his honoured mother on a point which very deeply concerned himself. She was aware that the best friends he and his brother had found in England were the good Mr. and Mrs. Lambert, the latter Madam Esmond's schoolfellow of earlier years. Where their own blood relations had been worldly and unfeeling, these true friends had ever been generous and kind. The General was respected by the whole army, and beloved by all who knew him. No mother's affection could have been more touching than Mrs. Lambert's for both Madam Esmond's children ; and now, wrote Mr. George, he himself had formed an attachment for the elder Miss Lambert, on which he thought the happiness of his life depended, and which he besought his honoured mother to approve. He had made no precise offers to the young lady or her parents ; but he was bound to say that he had made little disguise of his sentiments, and that the young lady, as well as her parents, seemed favourable to him. She had been so admirable and exemplary a daughter to her own mother, that he felt sure she would do her duty by his. In a word, Mr. Warrington described the young lady as a model of perfection, and expressed his firm belief that the happiness or misery of his own future life depended upon possessing or losing her. Why do you not produce this letter? haply asks some sentimental reader, of the present Editor, who has said how he has the whole Warrington correspondence in his hands. Why not? Because 'tis cruel to babble the secrets of a young man's love: to overhear his incoherent vows and wild raptures, and to note, in cold blood, the secrets—it may be, the follies—of his passion. Shall we play eavesdropper at twilight embrasures, count sighs and hand-shakes, bottle hot tears: lay our stethoscope on delicate young breasts, and feel their heart throbs? I protest for one, love is sacred. Wherever I see it (as one sometimes may in this world) shooting suddenly out of two pair of eyes; or glancing sadly even from one pair; or looking down from the mother to the baby in her lap; or from papa at his girl's happiness as she is whirling round the room with the captain; or from John Anderson, as his old wife comes into the room—the *bonne vieille*, the ever peerless among women: wherever we see that signal, I say, let us salute it. It is not only wrong to kiss and tell, but to tell about kisses. Everybody who has been admitted to the mystery,—hush about it. Down with him *qui Deæ sacrum vulgarit arcanæ*. Beware how you dine with him: he will print your private talk; as sure as you sail with him, he will throw you over.

Whilst Harry's love of battle has led him to smell powder—to rush upon *reluctantes dracones*, and to carry wounded comrades out of fire, George has been pursuing an amusement much more peaceful and delightful to him: penning sonnets to his mistress's eyebrow, mayhap; pacing in the darkness under her window, and watching the little lamp which shone upon her in her chamber; finding all sorts of pretexts for sending little notes which don't seem to require little answers, but get them; culling bits out of his favourite poets, and flowers out of Covent Garden for somebody's special adornment and pleasure; walking to St. James's Church, singing very likely out of the same Prayer-book, and never hearing one word of the sermon, so much do other thoughts engross him; being prodigiously affectionate to all Miss Theo's relations—to her little brother and sister at school; to the elder at college; to Miss Hetty with whom he engages in gay passages of wit; and to mamma, who is half in love with him herself, Martin Lambert says; for if fathers are sometimes sulky at the appearance of the destined son-in-law, is it not a fact that mothers become sentimental, and, as it were, love their own loves over again?

Gumbo and Sady are for ever on the trot between Southampton Row and Dean Street. In the summer months, all sorts of junketings and pleasure-parties are devised; and there are countless proposals to go to Ranelagh, to Hampstead, to Vauxhall, to Marylebone Gardens, and what not? George wants the famous tragedy copied out fair for the stage, and who can write such a beautiful Italian hand as Miss Theo? As the sheets pass to and fro they are accompanied by little notes of thanks, of interrogation, of admiration, always. See, here is the packet, marked in Warrington's neat hand, 'T's letters, 1758-9.' Shall we open them and reveal their tender secrets to the public gaze? Those virgin words were whispered for one ear alone. Years after they were written, the husband read, no doubt, with sweet pangs of remembrance, the fond lines addressed to the lover. It were a sacrilege to show the pair to public eyes: only let

kind readers be pleased to take our word that the
young lady's letters are modest and pure, the gentleman's most respectful and tender. In fine, you see,
we have said very little about it ; but, in these few last
months, Mr. George Warrington has made up his
mind that he has found the woman of women. She
mayn't be the most beautiful. Why, there is Cousin
Flora, there is Cœlia, and Ardelia, and a hundred
more, who are ever so much more handsome : but her
sweet face pleases *him* better than any other in the
world. She mayn't be the most clever, but her voice
is the dearest and pleasantest to hear ; and in her
company he is so clever himself; he has such fine
thoughts ; he uses such eloquent words ; he is so
generous, noble, witty, that no wonder he delights in it.
And, in regard to the young lady,—as thank Heaven
I never thought so ill of women as to suppose them to
be just,—we may be sure that there is no amount of
wit, of wisdom, of beauty, of valour, of virtue with
which she does not endow her young hero.

When George's letter reached home, we may fancy
that it created no small excitement in the little circle
round Madam Esmond's fireside. So he was in love,
and wished to marry ! It was but natural, and would
keep him out of harm's way. If he proposed to unite
himself with a well-bred Christian young woman,
Madam saw no harm.

'I knew they would be setting their caps at him,'
says Mountain. 'They fancy that his wealth is as great
as his estate. He does not say whether the young
lady has money. I fear otherwise.'

'People would set their caps at him here, I dare
say,' says Madam Esmond, grimly looking at her
dependant, 'and try and catch Mr. Esmond
Warrington for their own daughters, who are no
richer than Miss Lambert may be.'

'I suppose your ladyship means me!' says Mountain. 'My Fanny is poor, as you say; and 'tis kind of you to remind me of her poverty!'

'I said people would set their caps at him. If the cap fits you, *tant pis!* as my papa used to say.'

'You think, madam, I am scheming to keep George for my daughter? I thank you, on my word! A good opinion you seem to have of us after the years we have lived together!'

'My dear Mountain, I know you much better than to suppose you could ever fancy your daughter would be a suitable match for a gentleman of Mr. Esmond's rank and station,' says Madam, with much dignity.

'Fanny Parker was as good as Molly Benson at school, and Mr. Mountain's daughter is as good as Mr. Lambert's!' Mrs. Mountain cries out.

'Then you *did* think of marrying her to my son? I shall write to Mr. Esmond Warrington, and say how sorry I am that you should be disappointed!' says the mistress of Castlewood. And we, for our parts, may suppose that Mrs. Mountain was disappointed, and had some ambitious views respecting her daughter—else, why should she have been so angry at the notion of Mr. Warrington's marriage?

In reply to her son, Madam Esmond wrote back that she was pleased with the fraternal love George exhibited; that it was indeed but right in some measure to compensate Harry, whose expectations had led him to adopt a more costly mode of life than he would have entered on had he known he was only a younger son. And with respect to purchasing his promotion, she would gladly halve the expense with Harry's elder brother, being thankful to think his own gallantry had won him his first step. This bestowal of George's money, Madam Esmond added, was at least much more satisfactory than some other extravagances to which she would not advert.

The other extravagance to which Madam alluded was the payment of the ransom to the French captain's family, to which tax George's mother never would choose to submit. She had a determined spirit of her own, which her son inherited. *His* persistence she called pride and obstinacy. What she thought of her own pertinacity, her biographer who lives so far from her time does not pretend to say. Only I dare say people a hundred years ago pretty much resembled their grandchildren of the present date, and loved to have their own way, and to make others follow it.

Now, after paying his own ransom, his brother's debts, and half the price for his promotion, George calculated that no inconsiderable portion of his private patrimony would be swallowed up : nevertheless he made the sacrifice with a perfect good heart. His good mother always enjoined him in her letters to remember who his grandfather was, and to support the dignity of his family accordingly. She gave him various commissions to purchase goods in England, and though she as yet had sent him very trifling remittances, she alluded so constantly to the exalted rank of the Esmonds, to her desire that he should do nothing unworthy of that illustrious family ; she advised him so peremptorily and frequently to appear in the first society of the country, to frequent the Court where his ancestors had been accustomed to move, and to appear always in the world in a manner worthy of his name, that George made no doubt his mother's money would be forthcoming when his own ran short, and generously obeyed her injunctions as to his style of life. I find in the Esmond papers of this period, bills for genteel entertainments, tailors' bills for Court suits supplied, and liveries for his honour's negro servants and chairmen, horse-dealers' receipts, and so forth; and am thus led to believe that the elder of our Virginians was also after a while living at a considerable expense.

He was not wild or extravagant like his brother. There was no talk of gambling or race-horses against Mr. George; his table was liberal, his equipages handsome, his purse always full, the estate to which he was heir was known to be immense. I mention these circumstances because they may probably have influenced the conduct both of George and his friends in that very matter concerning which, as I have said, he and his mother had been just corresponding. The young heir of Virginia was travelling for his pleasure and improvement in foreign kingdoms. The queen his mother was in daily correspondence with his Highness, and constantly enjoined him to act as became his lofty station. There could be no doubt from her letters that she desired he should live liberally and magnificently. He was perpetually making purchases at his parent's order. She had not settled as yet; on the contrary, she had wrote out by the last mail for twelve new sets of waggon-harness, and an organ that should play fourteen specified psalm-tunes; which articles George dutifully ordered. She had not paid as yet, and might not to-day or to-morrow, but eventually, of course, she would: and Mr. Warrington never thought of troubling his friends about these calculations, or discussing with them his mother's domestic affairs. They, on their side, took for granted that he was in a state of competence and ease, and, without being mercenary folks, Mr. and Mrs. Lambert were no doubt pleased to see an attachment growing up between their daughter and a young gentleman of such good principles, talents, family, and expectations. There was honesty in all Mr. Esmond Warrington's words and actions, and in his behaviour to the world a certain grandeur and simplicity, which showed him to be a true gentleman. Somewhat cold and haughty in his demeanour to strangers, especially towards the great, he was not in the least supercilious: he was perfectly courteous towards women, and with those people whom he loved, especially kind, amiable, lively, and tender.

No wonder that one young woman we know of got to think him the best man in all the world—alas! not even excepting papa. A great love felt by a man towards a woman makes him better, as regards her, than all other men. We have said that George used to wonder himself when he found how witty, how eloquent, how wise he was, when he talked with the fair young creature whose heart had become all his. . . . I say we will not again listen to their love whispers. Those soft words do not bear being written down. If you please—good sir, or madam, who are sentimentally inclined—lay down the book and think over certain things for yourself. You may be ever so old now; but you remember. It may be all dead and buried; but in a moment, up it springs out of its grave, and looks, and smiles, and whispers as of yore when it clung to your arm, and dropped fresh tears on your heart. It is here, and alive, did I say? O far far away! O lonely hearth and cold ashes! Here is the vase, but the roses are gone; here is the shore, and yonder the ship was moored; but the anchors are up, and it has sailed away for ever.

Et cetera, et cetera, et cetera. This, however, is mere sentimentality; and as regards George and Theo, is neither here nor there. What I mean to say is, that the young lady's family were perfectly satisfied

with the state of affairs between her and Mr. Warrington ; and though he had not as yet asked the decisive
question, everybody else knew what the answer would
be when it came.

Mamma perhaps thought the question was a long
time coming.

'Psha ! my dear !' says the General. 'There is
time enough in all conscience. Theo is not much
more than seventeen ; George, if I mistake not, is
under forty ; and, besides, he must have time to write
to Virginia, and ask mamma.'

'But suppose she refuses ?'

''That will be a bad day for old and young,' says the
General. 'Let us rather say, suppose she consents,
my love ?—I can't fancy anybody in the world
refusing Theo anything she has set her heart on,' adds
the father : 'and I am sure 'tis bent upon this match.'

So they all waited with the utmost anxiety until an
answer from Madam Esmond should arrive ; and
trembled lest the French privateers should take the
packet-ship by which the precious letter was conveyed.

CHAPTER LXVII

IN WHICH A TRAGEDY IS ACTED, AND TWO MORE ARE BEGUN

JAMES WOLFE, Harry's new Colonel, came back from America a few weeks after our Virginian had joined his regiment. Wolfe had previously been Lieutenant-Colonel of Kingsley's, and a second battalion of the regiment had been formed and given to him in reward for his distinguished gallantry and services at Cape Breton. Harry went with quite unfeigned respect and cordiality to pay his duty to his new commander, on whom the eyes of the world began to be turned now,—the common opinion being that he was likely to become a great General. In the late affairs in France, several officers of great previous repute had been tried and found lamentably wanting. The Duke of Marlborough had shown himself no worthy descendant of his great ancestor. About my Lord George Sackville's military genius there were doubts, even before his unhappy behaviour at Minden prevented a great victory. The nation was longing for military glory, and the Minister was anxious to find a General who might gratify the eager desire of the people. Mr. Wolfe's and Mr. Lambert's business keeping them both in London, the friendly intercourse between those officers was renewed, no one being more delighted than Lambert at his younger friend's good fortune.

Harry, when he was away from his duty, was never tired of hearing Mr. Wolfe's details of the military operations of the last year, about which Wolfe talked very freely and openly. Whatever thought was in his mind, he appears to have spoken it out generously. He had that heroic simplicity which distinguished Nelson afterwards : he talked frankly of his actions. Some of the fine gentlemen at St. James's might wonder and sneer at him ; but amongst our little circle of friends we may be sure he found admiring listeners. The young General had the romance of a boy on many matters. He delighted in music and poetry. On the last day of his life he said he would rather have written Gray's ' Elegy ' than have won a battle. We may be sure that with a gentleman of such literary tastes our friend George would become familiar ; and as they were both in love, and both accepted lovers, and both eager for happiness, no doubt they must have had many sentimental conversations together, which would be very interesting to report could we only have accurate accounts of them. In one of his later letters, Warrington writes :—

' I had the honour of knowing the famous General Wolfe, and seeing much of him during his last stay in London. We had a subject of conversation then which was of unfailing interest to both of us, and I could not but admire Mr. Wolfe's simplicity, his frankness, and a sort of glorious bravery which characterised him. He was much in love, and he wanted heaps and heaps of laurels to take to his mistress. "If it be a sin to covet honour," he used to say with Harry the Fifth (he was passionately fond of plays and poetry), " I am the most offending soul alive." Surely on his last day he had a feast which was enough to satisfy the greediest appetite for glory. He hungered after it. He seemed to me not merely like a soldier going resolutely to do his duty, but rather like a knight in quest of dragons and giants. My own country has furnished of late a chief of a very different order, and quite an opposite genius. I scarce know which to admire most, the Briton's chivalrous ardour, or the more than Roman constancy of our great Virginian.'

As Mr. Lambert's official duties detained him in London, his family remained contentedly with him, and I suppose Mr. Warrington was so satisfied with the rural quiet of Southampton Row and the beautiful flowers and trees of Bedford Gardens, that he did not care to quit London for any long period. He made his pilgrimage to Castlewood, and passed a few days there, occupying the chamber of which he had often heard his grandfather talk, and which Colonel Esmond had occupied as a boy : and he was received kindly enough by such members of the family as happened to be at home. But no doubt he loved better to be in London by the side of a young person in whose society he found greater pleasure than any which my Lord Castlewood's circle could afford him, though all the ladies were civil, and Lady Maria especially gracious, and enchanted with the tragedy which George and Parson Sampson read out to the ladies. The chaplain was enthusiastic in its praises, and indeed it was through his interest, and not through Mr. Johnson's after all, that Mr. Warrington's piece ever came on the stage. Mr. Johnson, it is true, pressed the play on his friend Mr. Garrick for 'Drury Lane,' but Garrick had just made an arrangement with the famous Mr. Home for a tragedy from the pen of the author of 'Douglas.' Accordingly, 'Carpezan' was carried to Mr. Rich at 'Covent Garden,' and accepted by that manager.

On the night of the production of the piece, Mr. Warrington gave an elegant entertainment to his friends at the 'Bedford Head' in Covent Garden, whence they adjourned in a body to the theatre ; leaving only one or two with our young author, who remained at the Coffee-house, where friends from time to time came to him with an account of the performance. The part of Carpezan was filled by Barry, Shuter was the old nobleman, Reddish, I need scarcely say, made an excellent Ulric, and the King of Bohemia was by a young actor from Dublin, Mr. Geoghegan, or Hagan, as he was called on the stage, and who looked and performed the part to admiration. Mrs. Woffington looked too old in the first act as the heroine, but her murder in the fourth act, about which great doubts were expressed, went off to the terror and delight of the audience. Miss Wayn sang the ballad which is supposed to be sung by the King's page, just at the moment of the unhappy wife's execution, and all agreed that Barry was very terrible and pathetic as Carpezan, especially in the execution scene. The grace and elegance of the young actor, Hagan, won general applause. The piece was put very elegantly on the stage by Mr. Rich, though there was some doubt whether, in the march of janissaries in the last, the manager was correct in introducing a favourite elephant, which had figured in various pantomimes, and by which one of Mr. Warrington's black servants marched in a Turkish habit. The other sat in the footman's gallery, and uproariously wept and applauded at the proper intervals.

The execution of Sybilla was the turning-point of the piece. Her head off, George's friends breathed freely, and one messenger after another came to him at the Coffee-house, to announce the complete success of the tragedy. Mr. Barry, amidst general applause, announced the play for repetition, and that it was the work of a young gentleman of Virginia, his first attempt in the dramatic style.

We should like to have been in the box where all our
friends were seated during the performance, to have
watched Theo's flutter and anxiety whilst the success
of the play seemed dubious, and have beheld the
blushes and the sparkles in her eyes, when the victory
was assured. Harry, during the little trouble in the
fourth act, was deadly pale—whiter, Mrs. Lambert
said, than Barry, with all his chalk. But if Briareus
could have clapped hands, he could scarcely have made
more noise than Harry at the end of the piece. Mr.
Wolfe and General Lambert huzzayed enthusiastically.
Mrs. Lambert, of course, cried ; and though Hetty
said, 'Why do you cry, mamma ? you don't want any
of them alive again ; you know it serves them all
right :'—the girl was really as much delighted as any
person present, including little Charley from the
Chartreux, who had leave from Dr. Crusius for that
evening, and Miss Lucy, who had been brought from
boarding-school on purpose to be present on the great
occasion. My Lord Castlewood and his sister, Lady
Maria, were present ; and his Lordship went from his
box and complimented Mr. Barry and the other actors
on the stage ; and Parson Sampson was invaluable in
the pit, where he led the applause, having, I believe,
given previous instructions to Gumbo to keep an eye
upon him from the gallery, and do as he did.

Be sure there was a very jolly supper of Mr. Warrington's friends that night—much more jolly than
Mr. Garrick's, for example, who made but a very
poor success with his 'Agis' and its dreary choruses,
and who must have again felt that he had missed a
good chance, in preferring Mr. Home's tragedy to
our young author's. A jolly supper, did we say ?
—many jolly suppers. Mr. Gumbo gave an entertainment to several gentlemen of the shoulder-knot,
who had concurred in supporting his master's master-

piece : Mr. Henry Warrington gave a supper at
the 'Star and Garter,' in Pall Mall, to ten officers
of his new regiment, who had come up for the express
purpose of backing ' Carpezan ; ' and finally, Mr. Warrington received the three principal actors of the tragedy,
our family-party from the side-box, Mr. Johnson and his
ingenious friend, Mr. Reynolds the painter, my Lord
Castlewood and his sister, and one or two more. My
Lady Maria happened to sit next to the young actor
who had performed the part of the King. Mr Warrington somehow had Miss Theo for a neighbour,
and no doubt passed a pleasant evening beside her.
The greatest animation and cordiality prevailed, and
when toasts were called, Lady Maria gaily gave
' The King of Hungary ' for hers. That gentleman,
who had plenty of eloquence and fire, and excellent
manners, on as well as off the stage, protested that
he had already suffered death in the course of the
evening, hoped that he should die a hundred times
more on the same field ; but, dead or living, vowed he
knew whose humble servant he ever should be. Ah,
if he had but a real crown in place of his diadem of
pasteboard and tinsel, with what joy would he lay
it at her Ladyship's feet ! Neither my Lord nor Mr.
Esmond were over well pleased with the gentleman's
exceeding gallantry—a part of which they attributed,
no doubt justly, to the wine and punch, of which
he had been partaking very freely. Theo and her
sister, who were quite new to the world, were a
little frightened by the exceeding energy of Mr.
Hagan's manner—but Lady Maria, much more experienced, took it in perfectly good part. At a late
hour coaches were called, to which the gentlemen
attended the ladies, after whose departure some of
them returned to the supper-room, and the end was
that Carpezan had to be carried away in a chair, and

that the King of Hungary had a severe headache;
and that the Poet, though he remembered making
a great number of speeches, was quite astounded
when half-a-dozen of his guests appeared at his house
the next day, whom he had invited overnight to
come and sup with him once more.

As he put Mrs. Lambert and her daughters into
their coach on the night previous, all the ladies
were flurried, delighted, excited; and you may be
sure our gentleman was with them the next day,
to talk of the play and the audience, and the actors,
and the beauties of the piece, over and over again.
Mrs. Lambert had heard that the ladies of the
theatre were dangerous company for young men.
She hoped George would have a care, and not
frequent the green-room too much.

George smiled, and said he had a preventive against
all green-room temptations, of which he was not in
the least afraid; and as he spoke he looked in Theo's
face, as if in those eyes lay the amulet which was to
preserve him from all danger.

'Why should he be afraid, mamma?' asks the
maiden simply. She had no idea of danger or of
guile.

'No, my darling, I don't think he need be afraid,'
says the mother, kissing her.

'You don't suppose Mr. George would fall in love
with that painted old creature who performed the
chief part?' asks Miss Hetty, with a toss of her
head. 'She must be old enough to be his mother.'

'Pray, do you suppose that at our age nobody can
care for us, or that we have no hearts left?' asks
mamma, very tartly. 'I believe, or I may say, I
hope and trust, your father thinks otherwise. *He*
is, I imagine, perfectly satisfied, miss. *He* does not
sneer at age, whatever little girls out of the school-

room may do. And they had much better be back there, and they had much better remember what the fifth commandment is—that they had, Hetty!'

'I didn't think I was breaking it by saying that an actress was as old as George's mother,' pleaded Hetty.

'George's mother is as old as I am, miss!—at least she was when we were *at school*. And Fanny Parker—Mrs. Mountain who now is—was seven months older, and we were in the French class together; and I have no idea that our age is to be made the subject of remarks and ridicule by our children, and I will thank you to spare it, if you please! Do you consider your mother too old, George?'

'I am glad my mother is of your age, Aunt Lambert,' says George, in the most sentimental manner.

Strange infatuation of passion—singular perversity of reason! At some period before his marriage, it not unfrequently happens that a man actually is fond of his mother-in-law! At this time our good General vowed, and with some reason, that he was jealous. Mrs. Lambert made much more of George than of any other person in the family. She dressed up Theo to the utmost advantage in order to meet him; she was for ever caressing her, and appealing to her when he spoke. It was 'Don't you think he looks well?' —'Don't you think he looks pale, Theo, to-day?'— 'Don't you think he has been sitting up over his books too much at night?' and so forth. If he had a cold, she would have liked to make gruel for him and see his feet in hot water. She sent him recipes of her own for his health. When he was away, she never ceased talking about him to her daughter. I dare say Miss Theo liked the subject well enough. When he came

she was sure to be wanted in some other part of the
house, and would bid Theo take care of him till she
returned. Why, before she returned to the room,
could you hear her talking outside the door to her
youngest innocent children, to her servants in the
upper regions, and so forth? When she re-appeared,
was not Mr. George always standing or sitting at a
considerable distance from Miss Theo—except, to be
sure, on that one day when she had just happened to
drop her scissors, and he had naturally stooped down
to pick them up? Why was she blushing? Were
not youthful cheeks made to blush, and roses to bloom
in the spring? Not that mamma ever noted the
blushes, but began quite an artless conversation about
this or that, as she sat down brimful of happiness to
her work-table.

And at last there came a letter from Virginia in
Madam Esmond's neat well-known hand, and over
which George trembled and blushed before he broke
the seal. It was in answer to the letter which he had
sent home, respecting his brother's commission and
his own attachment to Miss Lambert. Of his intentions respecting Harry, Madam Esmond fully
approved. As for his marriage, she was not against
early marriages. She would take his picture of Miss
Lambert with the allowance that was to be made for
lover's portraits, and hope, for his sake, that the young
lady was all he described her to be. With money, as
Madam Esmond gathered from her son's letter, she
did not appear to be provided at all, which was a pity,
as, though wealthy in land, their family had but little
ready-money. However, by Heaven's blessing, there
was plenty at home for children and children's children,
and the wives of her sons should share all she had.
When she heard more at length from Mr. and Mrs.
Lambert, she would reply for her part more fully.

She did not pretend to say that she had not greater
hopes for her son, as a gentleman of his name and
prospects might pretend to the hand of the first lady
of the land ; but as Heaven had willed that her son's
choice should fall upon her old friend's daughter, she
acquiesced, and would welcome George's wife as her
own child.   This letter was brought by Mr. Van den
Bosch of Albany, who had lately bought a very large
estate in Virginia, and who was bound for England
to put his granddaughter to a boarding-school.   She,
Madam Esmond, was not mercenary, nor was it
because this young lady was heiress of a very great
fortune that she desired her sons to pay Mr. Van d. B.
every attention.   Their properties lay close together,
and could Harry find in the young lady those qualities
of person and mind *suitable for a companion for life*, at
least she would have the satisfaction of seeing both
her children near her in her declining years.   Madam
Esmond concluded by sending her affectionate compliments to Mrs. Lambert, from whom she begged to
hear further, and her blessing to the young lady who
was to be her daughter-in-law.

The letter was not cordial, and the writer evidently
but half-satisfied ; but, such as it was, her consent was
here formally announced.   How eagerly George ran
away to Soho with the long-desired news in his
pocket !   I suppose our worthy friends there must
have read his news in his countenance—else why
should Mrs. Lambert take her daughter's hand and
kiss her with such uncommon warmth, when George
announced that he had received letters from home ?
Then, with a break in his voice, a pallid face, and a
considerable tremor, turning to Mr. Lambert, he said :
'Madam Esmond's letter, sir, is in reply to one of
mine, in which I acquainted her that I had formed an
attachment in England, for which I asked my

mother's approval. She gives her consent, I am grateful to say, and I have to pray my dear friends to be equally kind to me.'

'God bless thee, my dear boy!' says the good General, laying a hand on the young man's head. 'I am glad to have thee for a son, George. There, there, don't go down on your knees, young folks! George may, to be sure, and thank God for giving him the best little wife in all England. Yes, my dear, except when you were ill, you never caused me a heartache —and happy is the man, I say, who wins thee!'

I have no doubt the young people knelt before their parents, as was the fashion in those days; and am perfectly certain that Mrs. Lambert kissed both of them, and likewise bedewed her pocket-handkerchief in the most plentiful manner. Hetty was not present at this sentimental scene, and when she heard of it, spoke with considerable asperity, and a laugh that was by no means pleasant, saying: 'Is this all the news you have to give me? Why, I have known it these months past. Do you think I have no eyes to see, and no ears to hear, indeed?' But in private she was much more gentle. She flung herself on her sister's neck, embracing her passionately, and vowing that never never would Theo find any one to love her like her sister. With Theo she became entirely mild and humble. She could not abstain from her jokes and satire with George, but he was too happy to heed her much, and too generous not to see the cause of her jealousy.

When all parties concerned came to read Madam Esmond's letter, that document, it is true, appeared rather vague. It contained only a promise that she would receive the young people at her house, and no sort of proposal for a settlement. The General shook his head over the letter—he did not think of examin-

ing it until some days after the engagement had been
made between George and his daughter : but now he
read Madam Esmond's words, they gave him but small
encouragement.

'Bah !' says George. 'I shall have three hundred
pounds for my tragedy. I can easily write a play a
year ; and if the worst comes to the worst, we can live
on that.'

'On that and your patrimony,' says Theo's father.

George now had to explain, with some hesitation,
that what with paying bills for his mother, and
Harry's commission and debts, and his own ransom—
George's patrimony proper was well nigh spent.

Mr. Lambert's countenance looked graver still at
this announcement, but he saw his girl's eyes turned
towards him with an alarm so tender, that he took
her in his arms and vowed that, let the worst come to
the worst, his darling should not be balked of her
wish.

About the going back to Virginia, George frankly
owned that he little liked the notion of returning
to be entirely dependent on his mother. He gave
General Lambert an idea of his life at home, and explained how little to his taste that slavery was. No.
Why should he not stay in England, write more
tragedies, study for the bar, get a place, perhaps?
Why, indeed ? He straightway began to form a plan
for another tragedy. He brought portions of his work,
from time to time, to Miss Theo and her sister ; Hetty
yawned over the work, but Theo pronounced it to be
still more beautiful and admirable than the last, which
was perfect.

The engagement of our young friends was made
known to the members of their respective families,
and announced to Sir Miles Warrington, in a ceremonious letter from his nephew. For a while Sir

Miles saw no particular objection to the marriage; though, to be sure, considering his name and prospects, Mr. Warrington might have looked higher. The truth was, that Sir Miles imagined that Madam Esmond had made some considerable settlement on her son, and that his circumstances were more than easy. But when he heard that George was entirely dependent on his mother, and that his own small patrimony was dissipated, as Harry's had been before, Sir Miles's indignation at his nephew's imprudence knew no bounds; he could not find words to express his horror and anger at the want of principle exhibited by both these unhappy young men : he thought it his duty to speak his mind about them, and wrote his opinion to his sister Esmond in Virginia. As for General and Mrs. Lambert, who passed for respectable persons, was it to be borne that such people should inveigle a penniless young man into a marriage with their penniless daughter ? Regarding them, and George's behaviour, Sir Miles fully explained his views to Madam Esmond, gave half a finger to George whenever his nephew called on him in town, and did not even invite him to partake of the famous family small-beer. Towards Harry his uncle somewhat unbent; Harry had done his duty in the campaign, and was mentioned with praise in high quarters. He had sowed his wild oats,—he at least was endeavouring to amend ; but George was a young prodigal, fast careering to ruin, and his name was only mentioned in the family with a groan. Are there any poor fellows nowadays, I wonder, whose polite families fall on them and persecute them ; groan over them and stone them, and hand stones to their neighbours that they may do likewise ? All the patrimony spent ? Gracious heavens ! Sir Miles turned pale when he saw his nephew coming. Lady Warrington prayed for him

as a dangerous reprobate; and, in the meantime,
George was walking the town, quite unconscious that
he was occasioning so much wrath and so much devotion. He took little Miley to the play and brought
him back again. He sent tickets to his aunts and
cousins which they could not refuse, you know; it
would look too marked were they to break altogether.
So they not only took the tickets, but whenever
country constituents came to town they asked for
more, taking care to give the very worst motives to
George's intimacy with the theatre, and to suppose
that he and the actresses were on terms of the most
disgraceful intimacy. An august personage having
been to the theatre, and expressed his approbation of
Mr. Warrington's drama to Sir Miles, when he
attended his R-y-l H-gh-n-ss's levée at Saville House,
Sir Miles, to be sure, modified his opinion regarding
the piece, and spoke henceforth more respectfully of
it. Meanwhile, as we have said, George was passing
his life entirely careless of the opinion of all the uncles,
aunts, and cousins in the world.

Most of the Esmond cousins were at least more
polite and cordial than George's kinsfolk of the
Warrington side. In spite of his behaviour over the
cards, Lord Castlewood, George always maintained,
had a liking for our Virginians, and George was
pleased enough to be in his company. He was a far
abler man than many who succeeded in life. He had
a good name, and somehow only stained it; a considerable wit, and nobody trusted it; and a very shrewd
experience and knowledge of mankind, which made
him mistrust them, and himself most of all, and which
perhaps was the bar to his own advancement. My
Lady Castlewood, a woman of the world, wore always
a bland mask, and received Mr. George with perfect
civility, and welcomed him to lose as many guineas as

he liked at her Ladyship's card-tables. Between Mr.
William and the Virginian brothers there never was
any love lost ; but, as for Lady Maria, though her
love-affair was over, she had no rancour ; she professed
for her cousins a very great regard and affection, a part
of which the young gentlemen very gratefully returned. She was charmed to hear of Harry's valour
in the campaign; she was delighted with George's
success at the theatre ; she was for ever going to the
play, and had all the favourite passages of 'Carpezan'
by heart. One day, as Mr. George and Miss Theo
were taking a sentimental walk in Kensington
Gardens, whom should they light upon but their
cousin Maria in company with a gentlemen in a smart
suit and handsome laced hat, and who should the
gentleman be but His Majesty King Louis of
Hungary, Mr. Hagan ? He saluted the party, and
left them presently. Lady Maria had only just
happened to meet him. Mr. Hagan came sometimes,
he said, for quiet, to study his parts in Kensington
Gardens, and George and the two ladies walked
together to Lord Castlewood's door in Kensington
Square, Lady Maria uttering a thousand compliments to Theo upon her good looks, upon her
virtue, upon her future happiness, upon her papa
and mamma, upon her destined husband, upon her
paduasoy cloak and dear little feet and shoe-
buckles.

Harry happened to come to London that evening,
and slept at his accustomed quarters. When George
appeared at breakfast, the Captain was already in the
room (the custom of that day was to call all army
gentlemen Captains), and looking at the letters on the
breakfast-table.

'Why, George,' he cries, 'there is a letter from
Maria !'

'Little boy bring it from Common Garden last night—Master George asleep,' says Gumbo.

'What can it be about?' asks Harry, as George peruses his letter with a queer expression of face.

'About my play, to be sure,' George answers, tearing up the paper, and still wearing his queer look.

'What, she is not writing love-letters to *you*, is she, Georgy?'

'No, certainly not to me,' replies the other. But he spoke no word more about the letter; and when at dinner in Dean Street, Mrs. Lambert said, 'So you met somebody walking with the King of Hungary yesterday in Kensington Gardens?'

'What little tell-tale told you? A mere casual rencontre—the King goes there to study his parts, and Lady Maria happened to be crossing the garden to visit some of the *other* King's servants at Kensington Palace.' And so there was an end to that matter for the time being.

Other events were at hand fraught with interest to our Virginians. One evening after Christmas, the two gentlemen, with a few more friends, were met round General Lambert's supper-table, and among the company was Harry's new Colonel of the 67th, Major-General Wolfe. The young General was more than ordinarily grave. The conversation all related to the war. Events of great importance were pending. The great Minister now in power was determined to carry on the war on a much more extended scale than had been attempted hitherto: an army was ordered to Germany to help Prince Ferdinand; another great expedition was preparing for America, and here says Mr. Lambert, 'I will give you the health of the Commander—a glorious campaign, and a happy return to him!'

'Why do you not drink the toast, General James?' asked the hostess of her guest.

'He must not drink his own toast,' says General Lambert; 'it is we must do that!'

What, was James appointed?—All the ladies must drink such a toast as that, and they mingled their kind voices with the applause of the rest of the company.

Why did he look so melancholy? the ladies asked of one another when they withdrew. In after days they remembered his pale face.

'Perhaps he has been parting from his sweetheart,' suggests tender-hearted Mrs. Lambert. And at this sentimental notion, no doubt all the ladies looked sad.

The gentlemen, meanwhile, continued their talk about the war and its chances. Mr. Wolfe did not contradict the speakers when they said that the expedition was to be directed against Canada.

'Ah, sir,' says Harry, 'I wish your regiment was going with you, and that I might pay another visit to my old friends at Quebec.'

What, had Harry been there? Yes. He described his visit to the place five years before, and knew the city, and the neighbourhood, well. He lays a number of bits of biscuit on the table before him, and makes a couple of rivulets of punch on each side. 'This fork is the Isle d'Orleans,' says he, 'with the north and south branches of St. Lawrence on each side. Here's the Low Town, with a battery —how many guns was mounted there in our time, brother?—but at long shots from the St. Joseph shore you might play the same game. Here's what they call the little river, the St. Charles, and bridge of boats with a *tête de pont* over to the place of arms. Here's the citadel, and here's convents — ever so many convents—and the cathedral ; and here, outside the lines to the west and south, is what they call the Plains of Abraham—where a certain little affair took place, do you remember, brother ? He and a young officer of the Roussillon regiment *ça-ça'd* at each other for twenty minutes, and George pinked him, and then they *juré'd* each other an *amitié éternelle*. Well it was for George : for his second saved his life on that awful day of Braddock's defeat. He was a fine little fellow, and I give his toast : Je bois à la santé du Chevalier de Florac !'

'What, can you speak French, too, Harry ?' asks Mr. Wolfe. The young man looked at the General with eager eyes.

'Yes,' says he, 'I can speak, but not so well as George.'

'But he remembers the city, and can place the batteries, you see, and knows the ground a thousand times better than I do!' cries the elder brother.

The two elder officers exchanged looks with one another ; Mr. Lambert smiled and nodded, as if in reply to the mute queries of his comrade : on which the other spoke. 'Mr. Harry,' he said, 'if you have had enough of fine folks, and White's and horse-racing——'

'Oh, sir !' says the young man, turning very red.

'And if you have a mind to a sea-voyage at a short notice, come and see me at my lodgings to-morrow.'

What was that sudden uproar of cheers which the ladies heard in their drawing-room ? It was the hurrah which Harry Warrington gave when he leaped up at hearing the General's invitation.

The women saw no more of the gentlemen that

night. General Lambert had to be away upon his business early next morning, before seeing any of his family; nor had he mentioned a word of Harry's outbreak on the previous evening. But when he rejoined his folks at dinner, a look at Miss Hetty's face informed the worthy gentleman that she knew what had passed on the night previous, and what was about to happen to the young Virginian. After dinner Mrs. Lambert sat demurely at her work, Miss Theo took her book of Italian poetry. Neither of the General's customary guests happened to be present that evening.

He took little Hetty's hand in his, and began to talk with her. He did not allude to the subject which he knew was uppermost in her mind, except that by a more than ordinary gentleness and kindness he perhaps caused her to understand that her thoughts were known to him.

'I have breakfasted,' says he, 'with James Wolfe this morning, and our friend Harry was of the party. When he and the other guests were gone, I remained and talked with James about the great expedition on which he is going to sail. Would that his brave father had lived a few months longer to see him come back covered with honours from Louisbourg, and knowing that all England was looking to him to achieve still greater glory! James is dreadfully ill in body—so ill that I am frightened for him—and not a little depressed in mind at having to part from the young lady whom he has loved so long. A little rest, he thinks, might have set his shattered frame up, and to call her his has been the object of his life. But, great as his love is (and he is as romantic as one of you young folks of seventeen), honour and duty are greater, and he leaves home, and wife, and ease, and health, at their bidding. Every man of honour would do the like; every woman

who loves him truly would buckle on his armour for
him.   James goes to take leave of his mother to-night ;
and though she loves him devotedly, and is one of the
tenderest women in the world, I am sure she will
show no sign of weakness at his going away.'

'When does he sail, papa ?' the girl asked.

'He will be on board in five days.'   And Hetty
knew quite well who sailed with him.

CHAPTER LXVIII

IN WHICH HARRY GOES WESTWARD

OUR tender hearts are averse to all ideas and descriptions of parting ; and I shall therefore say nothing of
Harry Warrington's feelings at taking leave of his
brother and friends.   Were not thousands of men in
the same plight ?   Had not Mr. Wolfe his mother to
kiss (his brave father had quitted life during his son's
absence on the glorious Louisbourg campaign), and
his sweetheart to clasp in a farewell embrace ?   Had
not stout Admiral Holmes, before sailing westward,
with his squadron, the 'Somerset,' the 'Terrible,' the
'Northumberland,' the 'Royal William,' the 'Trident,'
the 'Diana,' the 'Sea-horse'—his own flag being
hoisted on board the 'Dublin'—to take leave of Mrs.
and the Misses Holmes ?   Was Admiral Saunders,
who sailed the day after him, exempt from human
feeling ?   Away go William and his crew of jovial
sailors, ploughing through the tumbling waves, and
poor Black-eyed Susan on shore watches the ship as
it dwindles in the sunset !

It dwindles in the west.   The night falls darkling
over the ocean.   They are gone : but their hearts
are at home yet awhile.   In silence, with a heart

inexpressibly soft and tender, how each man thinks of those he has left! What a chorus of pitiful prayer rises up to the Father, at sea and on shore, on that parting night: at home by the vacant bedside, where the wife kneels in tears; round the fire, where the mother and children together pour out their supplications; or on deck, where the seafarer looks up to the stars of heaven, as the ship cleaves through the roaring midnight waters! To-morrow the sun rises upon our common life again, and we commence our daily task of toil and duty.

George accompanies his brother, and stays a while with him at Portsmouth whilst they are waiting for a wind. He shakes Mr. Wolfe's hand, looks at his pale face for the last time, and sees the vessels depart amid the clangour of bells, and the thunder of cannon from the shore. Next day he is back at his home, and at that business which is sure one of the most selfish and absorbing of the world's occupations, to which almost every man who is thirty years old has served, ere this, his apprenticeship. He has a pang of sadness as he looks in at the lodgings to the little room which Harry used to occupy, and sees his half-burned papers still in the grate. In a few minutes he is on his way to Dean Street again, and whispering by the fitful firelight in the ear of the clinging sweetheart. She is very happy—oh, so happy! at his return. She is ashamed of being so. Is it not heartless to be so, when poor Hetty is so melancholy? Poor little Hetty! Indeed, it *is* selfish to be glad when she is in such a sad way. It makes one quite wretched to see her. 'Don't, sir! Well I *ought* to be wretched, and it's very very wicked of me if I'm not,' says Theo; and one can understand her soft-hearted repentance. What she means by 'Don't' who can tell? I have said the room was dark, and the fire burned fitfully—

and 'Don't' is no doubt uttered in one of the dark
fits. Enter servants with supper and lights. The
family arrives ; the conversation becomes general. The
destination of the fleet is known everywhere now.
The force on board is sufficient to beat all the French
in Canada ; and, under such an officer as Wolfe, to
repair the blunders and disasters of previous campaigns.
He looked dreadfully ill, indeed. But he has a great
soul in a feeble body. The Ministers, the country
hope the utmost from him. After supper, according
to custom, Mr. Lambert assembles his modest household, of whom George Warrington may be said quite
to form a part ; and as he prays for all travellers by
land and water, Theo and her sister are kneeling
together. And so, as the ship speeds farther and
farther into the West, the fond thoughts pursue it ;
and the night passes, and the sun rises.

A day or two more, and everybody is at his books
or his usual work. As for George Warrington, that
celebrated dramatist is busy about another composition. When the tragedy of 'Carpezan' had run
some thirty or twoscore nights, other persons of
genius took possession of the theatre.

There may have been persons who wondered how
the town could be so fickle as ever to tire of such a
masterpiece as the tragedy—who could not bear to see
the actors dressed in other habits, reciting other men's
verses ; but George, of a sceptical turn of mind, took
the fate of his tragedy very philosophically, and
pocketed the proceeds with much quiet satisfaction.
From Mr. Dodsley, the bookseller, he had the usual
compliment of a hundred pounds ; from the manager
of the theatre two hundred or more ; and such praises
from the critics and his friends that he set to work to
prepare another piece, with which he hoped to achieve
even greater successes than by his first performance.

Over these studies, and the other charming business which occupies him, months pass away. Happy business! Happiest time of youth and life, when love is first spoken and returned; when the dearest eyes are daily shining welcome, and the fondest lips never tire of whispering their sweet secrets: when the parting look that accompanies 'Good night!' gives delightful warning of to-morrow; when the heart is so overflowing with love and happiness, that it has to spare for all the world; when the day closes with glad prayers, and opens with joyful hopes; when doubt seems cowardice, misfortune impossible, poverty only a sweet trial of constancy! Theo's elders, thankfully remembering their own prime, sit softly by and witness this pretty comedy performed by their young people. And in one of his later letters, dutifully written to his wife during a temporary absence from home, George Warrington records how he had been to look up at the windows of the dear old house in Dean Street, and wondered who was sitting in the chamber where he and Theo had been so happy.

Meanwhile we can learn how the time passes, and our friends are engaged, by some extracts from George's letters to his brother.

'From the old Window opposite Bedford Gardens,
this 20th August, 1759.

'WHY are you gone back to rugged rocks, bleak shores, burning summers, nipping winters, at home, when you might have been cropping ever so many laurels in Germany? Kingsley's are coming back as covered with 'em as Jack-a-Green on May-day. Our six regiments did wonders; and our horse would have done if my Lord George Sackville only had let them. But when Prince Ferdinand said "Charge!" his Lordship could not hear, or could not translate the German word for "Forward;" and so we only beat the French, without utterly annihilating them, as we might, had Lord Granby or Mr. Warrington had the command. My Lord is come back to town, and is shouting for a Court-Martial. He held his head high enough in prosperity: in misfortune he shows such a constancy of arrogance that one almost admires him. He looks as if he rather envied poor Mr. Byng, and the not shooting him were a *manque d'égards* towards him.

'The Duke has had notice to get himself in readiness for departing from this world of grandeurs and victories, and downfalls and disappointments. An attack of palsy has visited His Royal Highness; and *pallida mors* has just peeped in at his door, as it were, and said, "I will call again." Tyrant as he was, this Prince has been noble in disgrace; and no king has ever had a truer servant than ours has found in his son. Why do I like the losing side always, and am I disposed to revolt against the winners? Your famous Mr. P——, your chief's patron and discoverer, I have been to hear in the House of Commons twice or thrice. I revolt against his magniloquence. I wish some little David would topple over that swelling giant. His thoughts and his language are always attitudinising. I like Barry's manner best, though the other is the more awful actor.

'Pocahontas gets on apace. Barry likes his part of Captain Smith; and, though he will have him wear a red coat and blue facings and an epaulet, I have a fancy to dress him exactly like one of the pictures of Queen Elizabeth's gentlemen at Hampton Court; with a ruff and a square beard and square shoes. "And Pocahontas— would you like her to be tattooed?" asks Uncle Lambert. Hagan's part as the warrior who is in love with her, and, seeing her partiality for the Captain, nobly rescues him from death, I trust will prove a hit. A strange fish is this Hagan: his mouth full of stage-plays and rant, but good, honest, and brave, if I don't err. He is angry at having been cast lately for Sir O'Brallaghan, in Mr. Macklin's new farce of "Love A-la-mode." He says that he does not keer to disgreece his tongue with imiteetions of that rascal brogue. As if there was any call for imiteetions, when he has such an admirable twang of his own !

'Shall I tell you ? Shall I hide the circumstance ? Shall I hurt your feelings ? Shall I set you in a rage of jealousy, and cause you to ask for leave to return to Europe ? Know, then, that though Carpezan is long since dead, Cousin Maria is for ever coming to the playhouse. Tom Spencer has spied her out night after night in the gallery, and she comes on the nights when Hagan performs. Quick, Borroughs, Mr. Warrington's boots and portmanteau ! Order a chaise and four for Portsmouth immediately ! The letter which I burned one morning when we were at breakfast (I may let the cat out of the bag, now puss has such a prodigious way to run) was from Cousin M., hinting that she wished me to tell no tales about her : but I can't help just whispering to you that Maria at this moment is busy consoling herself as fast as possible. Shall I spoil sport? Shall I tell her brother ? Is the affair any business of mine ? What have the Esmonds done for you and me but win our money at cards ? Yet I like our noble cousin. It seems to me that he would be good if he could—or rather, he would have been once. He has been set on a wrong way of life, from which 'tis now probably too late to rescue him. O beati agricolæ ! Our Virginia was dull, but let us thank Heaven we were bred there. We were made little slaves, but not slaves to wickedness, gambling, bad male and female company. It was not until my poor Harry left home that he fell among thieves. I mean thieves en grand such as waylaid him and stripped him on English highroads. I consider you none the worse because you were the unlucky one, and had to deliver your purse up. And now you are going to retrieve, and make a good name for yourself ; and kill more "French dragons," and become a great commander. And our mother will talk of her son the Captain, the Colonel, the General, and have his picture painted with all his stars and epaulets, while poor I shall be but a dawdling poetaster, or, if we may hope for the best, a snug-place man, with a little box at Richmond or Kew, and a half-score of little picaninnies, that will come and bob curtseys at the garden-gate when their uncle the General rides up on his great charger, with his aide-de-camp's pockets filled with gingerbread for the nephews and nieces. 'Tis for you to brandish the sword of Mars. As for me I look forward to a quiet life: a quiet little home, a quiet little library full of books, and a little Some-one *dulce ridentem, dulce loquentem,* on t'other side of the fire, as I scribble away at my papers. I am so pleased with this prospect, so utterly contented and happy, that I feel afraid as I think of it, lest it should escape me : and even to my dearest Hal, am shy of speaking of my happi-ness. What is ambition to me, with this certainty ? What do I care for wars, with this beatific peace smiling near ?

'Our mother's friend, Mynheer Van den Bosch, has been away on a tour to discover his family in Holland, and, strange to say, has found one. Miss (who was intended by maternal solicitude to be a wife for your worship) has had six months at Kensington School, and is coming out with a hundred pretty accomplishments, which are to complete her a perfect fine lady. Her grandpapa brought her to make a curtsey in Dean Street, and a mighty elegant curtsey she made. Though she is scarce seventeen, no dowager of sixty can be more at her ease. She conversed with Aunt Lambert on an equal footing ; she treated the girls as chits—to Hetty's wrath and Theo's amusement. She talked politics with the General, and the last routs, dresses, operas, fashions, scandal, with such perfect ease that, but for a blunder or two, you might have fancied Miss Lydia was born in Mayfair. At the Court end of the town she will live, she says ; and has no patience with her grandfather, who has a lodging in Monument Yard. For those who love a brown beauty, a prettier little *mignonne* creature cannot be seen. But my taste, you know, dearest brother, and . . .'

Here follows a page of raptures and quotations of verse, which, out of a regard for the reader, and the

writer's memory, the Editor of the present pages
declines to reprint. Gentlemen and ladies of a certain
age may remember the time when they indulged in
these rapturous follies on their own accounts ; when
the praises of the charmer were for ever warbling from
their lips or trickling from their pens ; when the
flowers of life were in full bloom, and all the birds of
spring were singing. The twigs are now bare,
perhaps, and the leaves have fallen ; but, for all that,
shall we not remember the vernal time ? As for you,
young people, whose May (or April, is it ?) is not
commenced yet, you need not be detained over other
folks' love-rhapsodies ; depend on it, when your spring
season arrives, kindly Nature will warm all your
flowers into bloom, and rouse your glad bosoms to
pour out their full song.

CHAPTER LXIX

A LITTLE INNOCENT

GEORGE WARRINGTON has mentioned in the letter
just quoted, that in spite of my Lord Castlewood's
previous play transactions with Harry, my Lord and
George remained friends, and met on terms of good
kinsmanship. Did George want franks, or an introduction at Court, or a place in the House of Lords to
hear a debate, his cousin was always ready to serve him,
was a pleasant and witty companion, and would do
anything which might promote his relative's interests,
provided his own were not prejudiced.

Now he even went so far as to promise that he
would do his best with the people in power to provide
a place for Mr. George Warrington, who daily
showed a greater disinclination to return to his native

country, and place himself once more under the
maternal servitude. George had not merely a sentimental motive for remaining in England : the pursuits
and society of London pleased him infinitely better
than any which he could have at home. A planter's
life of idleness might have suited him could he have
enjoyed independence with it. But in Virginia he
was only the first, and, as he thought, the worst
treated, of his mother's subjects. He dreaded to think
of returning with his young bride to his home, and of
the life which she would be destined to lead there.
Better freedom and poverty in England, with congenial
society, and a hope perchance of future distinction,
than the wearisome routine of home life, the tedious
subordination, the frequent bickerings, the certain
jealousies and differences of opinion, to which he must
subject his wife so soon as they turned their faces
homeward.

So Lord Castlewood's promise to provide for George
was very eagerly accepted by the Virginian. My
Lord had not provided very well for his own brother
to be sure, and his own position, peer as he was, was
anything but enviable : but we believe what we wish
to believe, and George Warrington chose to put great
stress upon his kinsman's offer of patronage. Unlike
the Warrington family, Lord Castlewood was quite
gracious when he was made acquainted with George's
engagement to Miss Lambert ; came to wait upon her
parents ; praised George to them and the young lady
to George, and made himself so prodigiously agreeable
in their company that these charitable folk forgot his
bad reputation, and thought it must be a very wicked
and scandalous world which maligned him. He said,
indeed, that he was improved in their society, as every
man must be who came into it. Among them he was
witty, lively, good for the time being. He left his

wickedness and worldliness with his cloak in the hall, and only put them on again when he stepped into his chair. What worldling on life's voyage does not know of some such harbour of rest and calm, some haven where he puts in out of the storm? Very likely Lord Castlewood was actually better whilst he stayed with those good people, and for the time being at least, no hypocrite.

And, I daresay, the Lambert elders thought no worse of his Lordship for openly proclaiming his admiration for Miss Theo. It was quite genuine, and he did not profess it was very deep.

'It don't affect my sleep, and I am not going to break my heart because Miss Lambert prefers somebody else,' he remarked. 'Only I wish when I was a young man, madam, I had had the good fortune to meet with somebody so innocent and good as your daughter. I might have been kept out of a deal of harm's way: but innocent and good young women did not fall into mine, or they would have made me better than I am.'

'Sure, my Lord, it is not too late!' says Mrs. Lambert, very softly.

Castlewood started back, misunderstanding her.

'Not too late, madam?' he inquired.

She blushed. 'It is too late to court my dear daughter, my Lord, but not too late to repent. We read, 'tis never too late to do that. If others have been received at the eleventh hour, is there any reason why you should give up hope?'

'Perhaps I know my own heart better than you,' he says, in a plaintive tone. 'I can speak French and German very well, and why? because I was taught both in the nursery. A man who learns them late can never get the practice of them on his tongue. And so 'tis the case with goodness, I can't learn it at my age. I can only see others practise it, and admire them. When I am on—on the side opposite to Lazarus, will Miss Theo give me a drop of water? Don't frown! I know I shall be there, Mrs. Lambert. Some folks are doomed so; and I think some of our family are amongst these. Some people are vacillating, and one hardly knows which way the scale will turn. Whereas some are predestined angels, and fly heavenwards naturally, and do what they will.'

'Oh, my Lord, and why should you not be of the predestined? Whilst there is a day left—whilst there is an hour—there is hope!' says the fond matron.

'I know what is passing in your mind, my dear madam—nay, I read your prayers in your looks; but how can they avail?' Lord Castlewood asked sadly. 'You don't know all, my good lady. You don't know what a life ours is of the world: how early it began; how selfish nature, and then necessity and education have made us. It is Fate holds the reins of the chariot, and we can't escape our doom. I know better: I see better people: I go my own way. My own? No, not mine—Fate's: and it is not altogether without pity for us, since it allows us, from time to time, to see such people as you.' And he took her hand, and looked her full in the face, and bowed with a melancholy grace. Every word he said was true. No greater error than to suppose that weak and bad men are strangers to good feelings, or deficient of sensibility. Only the good feeling does not last— nay, the tears are a kind of debauch of sentiment, as old libertines are said to find that the tears and grief of their victims add a zest to their pleasure. But Mrs. Lambert knew little of what was passing in this man's mind (how should she?), and so prayed for him with the fond persistence of woman. He was much better—yes, much better than he was supposed to be.

He was a most interesting man. There were hopes, why should there not be the most precious hopes for him still ?

It remains to be seen which of the two speakers formed the correct estimate of my Lord's character. Meanwhile, if the gentleman was right, the lady was mollified, and her kind wishes and prayers for this experienced sinner's repentance, if they were of no avail for his amendment, at least could do him no harm. Kind-souled doctors (and what good woman is not of the faculty ?) look after a reprobate as physicians after a perilous case. When the patient is converted to health their interest ceases in him, and they drive to feel pulses and prescribe medicines elsewhere.

But, while the malady was under treatment, our kind lady could not see too much of her sick man. Quite an intimacy sprang up between my Lord Castlewood and the Lamberts. I am not sure that some worldly views might not suit even with good Mrs. Lambert's spiritual plans (for who knows into what pure Eden, though guarded by flaming-sworded angels, worldliness will not creep ?). Her son was about to take orders. My Lord Castlewood feared very much that his present chaplain's, Mr. Sampson's, careless life and heterodox conversation might lead him to give up his chaplaincy : in which case, my Lord hinted, the little modest cure would be vacant, and at the service of some young divine of good principles and good manners, who would be content with a small stipend, and a small but friendly congregation.

Thus an acquaintance was established between the two families, and the ladies of Castlewood, always on their good behaviour, came more than once to make their curtseys in Mrs. Lambert's drawing-room. They were civil to the parents and the young ladies.

My Lady Castlewood's card-assemblies were open to
Mrs. Lambert and her family. There was play,
certainly—all the world played—His Majesty, the
Bishops, every Peer and Peeress in the land. But
nobody need play who did not like ; and surely nobody
need have scruples regarding the practice when such
august and venerable personages were daily found to
abet it. More than once Mrs. Lambert made her
appearance at her Ladyship's routs, and was grateful
for the welcome which she received, and pleased with
the admiration which her daughters excited.

Mention has been made, in a foregoing page and
letter, of an American family of Dutch extraction,
who had come to England very strongly recommended
by Madam Esmond, their Virginian neighbour, to her
sons in Europe. The views expressed in Madam
Esmond's letter were so clear, that that arch match-
maker, Mrs. Lambert, could not but understand them.
As for George, he was engaged already ; as for poor
Hetty's flame, Harry, he was gone on service, for
which circumstance Hetty's mother was not very
sorry perhaps. She laughingly told George that he
ought to obey his mamma's injunctions, break off his
engagement with Theo, and make up to Miss Lydia,
who was ten times—ten times ! a hundred times as
rich as her poor girl, and certainly much handsomer.
'Yes, indeed,' says George, 'that I own : she is
handsomer, and she is richer, and perhaps even
cleverer.' (All which praises Mrs. Lambert but half
liked.) 'But say she is all these ! So is Mr. Johnson
much cleverer than I am : so is whom shall we say ?—
so is Mr. Hagan the actor much taller and handsomer :
so is Sir James Lowther much richer : yet pray,
ma'am, do you suppose I am going to be jealous of
any one of these three, or think my Theo would jilt
me for their sakes ? Why should I not allow that

Miss Lydia is handsomer, then? and richer, and
clever too, and lively, and well-bred, if you insist on it,
and an angel if you will have it so? Theo is not
afraid : art thou, child ?'

'No, George,' says Theo, with such an honest
look of the eyes, as would convince any scepticism, or
shame any jealousy. And if after this pair of speeches,
mamma takes occasion to leave the room for a minute
to fetch her scissors, or her thimble, or a boot-jack and
slippers, or the cross and ball on the top of St. Paul's,
or her pocket-handkerchief which she has forgotten in
the parlour,—if, I say, Mrs. Lambert quits the room
on any errand or pretext, natural or preposterous, I
shall not be in the least surprised if, at her return in a
couple of minutes, she finds George in near proximity
to Theo, who has a heightened colour, and whose hand
George is just dropping—I shall not have the least
idea of what they have been doing. Have you,
madam? Have you any remembrance of what used
to happen when Mr. Grundy came a-courting? Are
you, who, after all, were not in the room with our
young people, going to cry out fie and for shame?
Then fie and for shame upon you, Mrs. Grundy!

Well, Harry being away, and Theo and George
irrevocably engaged, so that there was no possibility
of bringing Madam Esmond's little plans to bear, why
should not Mrs. Lambert have plans of her own ; and
if a rich, handsome, beautiful little wife should fall in
his way, why should not Jack Lambert from Oxford
have her? So thinks mamma, who was always thinking of marrying and giving in marriage, and so she
prattles to General Lambert, who, as usual, calls her a
goose for her pains. At any rate, Mrs. Lambert says
beauty and riches are no objection ; at any rate,
Madam Esmond desired that this family should be
hospitably entertained, and it was not her fault that

Harry was gone away to Canada.   Would the General
wish him to come back ; leave the army and his
reputation, perhaps ; yes, and come to England and
marry this American, and break poor Hetty's heart—
would her father wish that ?   Let us spare further
arguments, and not be so rude as to hint that Mr.
Lambert was in the right in calling a fond wife by
the name of that absurd splay-footed bird annually
sacrificed at the feast of St. Michael.

In those early days, there were vast distinctions of
rank drawn between the Court and City people :
and Mr. Van den Bosch, when he first came to
London, scarcely associated with any but the latter
sort.   He had a lodging near his agent's in the City.
When his pretty girl came from school for a holiday,
he took her an airing to Islington or Highgate, or
an occasional promenade in the Artillery Ground in
Bunhill Fields.   They went to that Baptist meeting-
house in Finsbury Fields, and on the sly to see Mr.
Garrick once or twice, or that funny rogue Mr.
Foote, at the Little Theatre.   To go to a Lord
Mayor's feast was a treat to the gentleman of the
highest order ; and to dance with a young mercer
at Hampstead Assembly gave the utmost delight to
the young lady.   When George first went to wait
upon his mother's friends, he found our old acquaintance, Mr. Draper, of the Temple, sedulous in his
attentions to her ; and the lawyer, who was married,
told Mr. Warrington to look out, as the young lady
had a plum to her fortune.   Mr. Drabshaw, a young
Quaker gentleman, and nephew of Mr. Trail, Madam
Esmond's Bristol agent, was also in constant attendance upon the young lady, and in dreadful alarm and
suspicion when Mr. Warrington first made his appearance.   Wishing to do honour to his mother's
neighbours, Mr. Warrington invited them to an

entertainment at his own apartments: and who should so naturally meet them as his friends from Soho? Not one of them but was forced to own little Miss Lydia's beauty. She had the foot of a fairy: the arms, neck, flashing eyes of a little brown huntress of Diana. She had brought a little plaintive accent from home with her—of which I, *moi qui vous parle*, have heard a hundred gross Cockney imitations, and watched as many absurd disguises, and which I say (in moderation) is charming in the mouth of a charming woman. Who sets up to say No, forsooth? You dear Miss Whittington, with whose *h*'s fate has dealt so unkindly?—you lovely Miss Nicol Jarvie, with your Northern burr? — you beautiful Miss Molony, with your Dame Street warble? All accents are pretty from pretty lips, and who shall set the standard up? Shall it be a rose, or a thistle, or a shamrock, or a star and stripe? As for Miss Lydia's accent, I have no doubt it was not odious even from the first day when she set foot on these polite shores, otherwise Mr. Warrington, as a man of taste, had certainly disapproved of her manner of talking, and her schoolmistress at Kensington had not done her duty by her pupil.

After the six months were over, during which, according to her grandfather's calculation, she was to learn all the accomplishments procurable at the Kensington Academy, Miss Lydia returned nothing loth to her grandfather, and took her place in the world. A narrow world at first it was to her; but she was a resolute little person, and resolved to enlarge her sphere in society: and whither she chose to lead the way, the obedient grandfather followed her. He had been thwarted himself in early life, he said, and little good came of the severity he underwent. He had thwarted his own son, who had turned out but ill. As for little Lyddy, he was determined she should have as pleasant a life as was possible. Did not Mr. George think he was right? 'Twas said in Virginia—he did not know with what reason— that the young gentlemen of Castlewood had been happier if Madam Esmond had allowed them a little of their own way. George could not gainsay this public rumour, or think of inducing the benevolent old gentleman to alter his plans respecting his grand- daughter. As for the Lambert family, how could they do otherwise than welcome the kind old man, the parent so tender and liberal, Madam Esmond's good friend?

When Miss came from school, grandpapa removed from Monument Yard to an elegant house in Blooms- bury ; whither they were followed at first by their City friends. There were merchants from Virginia Walk : there were worthy tradesmen, with whom the worthy old merchant had dealings ; there were their ladies and daughters and sons, who were all highly gracious to Miss Lyddy. It would be a long task to describe how these disappeared one by one— how there were no more junketings at Belsize, or trips to Highgate, or Saturday jaunts to deputy Higgs's villa, Highbury, or country-dances at honest Mr. Lutestring's house at Hackney. Even the Sunday practice was changed ; and, O abomination of abomina- tions ! Mr Van den Bosch left Bethesda Chapel in Bunhill Row, and actually took a pew in Queen Square Church !

Queen Square Church, and Mr. George Warring- ton lived hard by in Southampton Row ! 'Twas easy to see at whom Miss Lyddy was setting her cap, and Mr. Draper, who had been full of her and her grand- father's praises before, now took occasion to warn Mr. George, and gave him very different reports regarding

Mr. Van den Bosch to those which had first been current. Mr. Van d. B., for all he bragged so of his Dutch parentage, came from Albany, and was nobody's son at all. He had made his money by land speculation, or by privateering (which was uncommonly like piracy), and by the Guinea trade. His son had married—if marriage it could be called, which was very doubtful—an assigned servant, and had been cut off by his father, and had taken to bad courses, and had died, luckily for himself, in his own bed.

'Mr. Draper has told you bad tales about me,' said the placid old gentleman to George. 'Very likely we are all sinners, and some evil may be truly said of all of us, with a great deal more that is untrue. Did he tell you that my son was unhappy with me? I told you so too. Did he bring you wicked stories about my family? He liked it so well that he wanted to marry my Lyddy to his brother. Heaven bless her! I have had a many offers for her. And you are the young gentleman I should have chose for her, and I like you none the worse because you prefer somebody else ; though what you can see in your Miss, as compared to my Lyddy, begging your honour's pardon, I am at a loss to understand.'

'There is no accounting for tastes, my good sir,' said Mr. George, with his most superb air.

'No, sir ; 'tis a wonder of nature, and daily happens. When I kept store at Albany, there was one of your tip-top gentry there that might have married my dear daughter that was alive then, and with a pretty piece of money, whereby—for her father and I had quarrelled—Miss Lyddy would have been a pauper, you see ; and in place of my beautiful Bella, my gentleman chooses a little homely creature, no prettier than your Miss, and without a dollar to her fortune. The more fool he, saving your presence, Mr. George.'

'Pray don't save my presence, my good sir,' says George, laughing. 'I suppose the gentleman's word was given to the other lady, and he had seen her first, and hence was indifferent to your charming daughter.'

'I suppose when a young fellow gives his word to perform a cursed piece of folly, he always sticks to it, my dear sir, begging your pardon. But Lord, Lord, what am I speaking of? I am a-speaking of twenty year ago. I was well-to-do then, but I may say Heaven has blessed my store, and I am three times as well off now. Ask my agents how much they will give for Joseph Van den Bosch's bill at six months on New York—or at sight may be—for forty thousand pound? I warrant they will discount the paper.'

'Happy he who has the bill, sir!' says George, with a bow, not a little amused with the candour of the old gentleman.

'Lord, Lord, how mercenary you young men are!' cries the elder simply. 'Always thinking about money nowadays! Happy he who has the girl, I should say—the money ain't the question, my dear sir, when it goes along with such a lovely young thing as that—though I humbly say it, who oughtn't, and who am her fond silly old grandfather. We were talking about you, Lyddy darling—come, give me a kiss, my blessing! We were talking about you, and Mr. George said he wouldn't take you with all the money your poor old grandfather can give you.'

'Nay, sir,' says George.

'Well, you are right to say nay, for I didn't say all, that's the truth. My Blessing will have a deal more than that trifle I spoke of, when it shall please Heaven to remove me out of this world to a better—when poor old Gappy is gone, Lyddy will be a rich little

Lyddy, that she will.   But   she don't wish me
to go yet, does she?'

'Oh,   you   darling   dear   grandpapa!'   says
Lyddy.

'This young gentleman won't have you.' (Lyddy
looks an arch, 'Thank you, sir,' from her brown eyes.)
'But at any rate he is honest, and that is more than
we can say of some folks in this wicked London.
Oh, Lord, Lord, how mercenary they are!   Do
you know that yonder, in Monument Yard, they
were all at my poor little Blessing for her money?
There was Tom Lutestring; there was Mr. Draper,
your precious lawyer; there was actually Mr. Tubbs,
of Bethesda Chapel; and they must all come buzzing
like flies round the honey-pot.   That is why we came
out of the quarter where my brother tradesmen live.'

'To avoid the flies, to be sure!' says Miss Lydia,
tossing up her little head.

'Where my brother tradesmen live,' continues the
old gentleman.   'Else who am I to think of consorting with your grandees and fine folk?   I don't care
for the fashions, Mr. George; I don't care for plays
and poetry, begging your honour's pardon; I never
went to a play in my life, but to please this little
minx.'

'Oh, sir, 'twas lovely! and I cried so, didn't I,
grandpapa?' says the child.

'At what, my dear?'

'At—at Mr. Warrington's play, grandpapa.'

'Did you, my dear?   I dare say; I dare say.   It
was mail day: and my letters had come in: and my
ship the "Lovely Lyddy" had just come into
Falmouth: and Captain Joyce reported how he had
mercifully escaped a French privateer; and my head
was so full of thanks for that escape, which saved me
a deal of money, Mr. George—for the rate at which

ships is underwrote this war-time is so scandalous that
I often prefer to venture than to insure—that I confess I didn't listen much to the play, sir, and only
went to please this little Lyddy.'

'And you *did* please me, dearest Gappy!' cries the
young lady.

'Bless you! then it's all I want. What does a man
want more here below than to please his children, Mr.
George? especially me, who knew what it was to be
unhappy when I was young, and to repent of having
treated this darling's father too hard.'

'Oh, grandpapa!' cries the child, with more
caresses.

'Yes, I *was* too hard with him, dear; and that's
why I spoil my little Lydkin so!'

More kisses ensue between Lyddy and Gappy.
The little creature flings the pretty polished arms
round the old man's neck, presses the dark red lips on
his withered cheek, surrounds the venerable head with
a halo of powder beaten out of his wig by her caresses;
and eyes Mr. George the while, as much as to say,
There, sir! should you not like me to do as much for
you!

We confess;—but do we confess all? George
certainly told the story of his interview with Lyddy
and Gappy, and the old man's news regarding his
granddaughter's wealth; but I don't think he told
everything; else Theo would scarce have been so
much interested, or so entirely amused and good-
humoured with Lyddy when next the two young
ladies met.

They met now pretty frequently, especially after
the old American gentleman took up his residence in
Bloomsbury. Mr. Van den Bosch was in the City for
the most part of the day, attending to his affairs, and
appearing at his place upon 'Change. During his

absence Lyddy had the command of the house, and received her guests there like a lady, or rode abroad in a fine coach, which she ordered her grandpapa to keep for her, and into which he could very seldom be induced to set his foot. Before long Miss Lyddy was as easy in the coach as if she had ridden in one all her life. She ordered the domestics here and there; she drove to the mercer's and the jeweller's, and she called upon her friends with the utmost stateliness, or rode abroad with them to take the air. Theo and Hetty were both greatly diverted with her: but would the elder have been quite as well pleased had she known all Miss Lyddy's doings? Not that Theo was of a jealous disposition—far otherwise; but there are cases when a lady has a right to a little jealousy, as I maintain, whatever my fair readers may say to the contrary.

It was because she knew he was engaged, very likely, that Miss Lyddy permitted herself to speak so frankly in Mr. George's praise. When they were alone—and this blessed chance occurred pretty often at Mr. Van den Bosch's house, for we have said he was constantly absent on one errand or the other—it was wonderful how artlessly the little creature would show her enthusiasm, asking him all sorts of simple questions about himself, his genius, his way of life at home and in London, his projects of marriage, and so forth.

'I am glad you are going to be married,—oh, so glad!' she would say, heaving the most piteous sigh the while; 'for I can talk to you frankly, quite frankly, as a brother, and not be afraid of that odious politeness about which they were always scolding me at boarding-school. I may speak to you frankly; and if I like you, I may say so, mayn't I, Mr. George?'

'Pray, say so,' says George, with a bow and a smile.

'That is a kind of talk which most men delight to hear, especially from such pretty lips as Miss Lydia's.

'What do you know about my lips?' says the girl, with a pout and an innocent look into his face.

'What, indeed?' asks George. 'Perhaps I should like to know a great deal more.'

'They don't tell nothin' but truth, anyhow!' says the girl; 'that's why some people don't like them! If I have anything on my mind, it must come out. I am a country-bred girl, I am—with my heart in my mouth—all honesty and simplicity; not like your English girls, who have learned I don't know what at their boarding-schools, and from the men afterwards.'

'Our girls are monstrous little hypocrites, indeed!' cries George.

'You are thinking of Miss Lamberts? and I might have thought of them; but I declare I did not then. They have been at boarding-school; they have been in the world a great deal—so much the greater pity for them, for be certain they learned no good there. And now I have said so, of course you will go and tell Miss Theo, won't you, sir?'

'That she has learned no good in the world? She has scarce spoken to men at all, except her father, her brother, and me. Which of us would teach her any wrong, think you?'

'Oh, not you! Though I can understand its being very dangerous to be with you!' says the girl, with a sigh.

'Indeed there is no danger, and I don't bite!' says George, laughing.

'I didn't say bite,' says the girl softly. 'There's other things dangerous besides biting, I should think. Aren't you very witty? Yes, and sarcastic, and clever, and always laughing at people? Haven't you

a coaxing tongue? If you was to look at me in that
kind of way, I don't know what would come to me.
Was your brother like you as I was to have married?
Was he as clever and witty as you? I have heard he
was like you: but he hadn't your coaxing tongue.
Heigho! 'Tis well you are engaged, Master George,
that is all. Do you think if you had seen me first,
you would have liked Miss Theo best?'

'They say marriages are made in heaven, my dear,
and let us trust that mine has been arranged there,'
says George.

'I suppose there was no such thing never known,
as a man having two sweethearts?' asks the artless
little maiden. 'Guess it's a pity. Oh me! What
nonsense I'm a-talking; there now! I'm like the
little girl who cried for the moon; and I can't have
it. 'Tis too high for me—too high and splendid and
shining; can't reach up to it nohow. Well, what a
foolish, wayward, little spoilt thing I am now! But
one thing you promise—on your word and your
honour, now, Mr. George?'

'And what is that?'

'That you won't tell Miss Theo, else she'll hate
me.'

'Why should she hate you?'

'Because I hate her and wish she was dead!'
breaks out the young lady. And the eyes that were
looking so gentle and lachrymose but now, flame with
sudden wrath, and her cheeks flush up. 'For shame!'
she adds, after a pause. 'I'm a little fool to speak!
But whatever is in my heart must come out. I am
a girl of the woods, I am. I was bred where the sun
is hotter than in this foggy climate. And I am not
like your cold English girls; who, before they speak,
or think, or feel, must wait for mamma to give leave.
There, there! I may be a little fool for saying what

I have. I know you'll go and tell Miss Lambert. Well, do!'

But, as we have said, George didn't tell Miss Lambert. Even from the beloved person there must be some things kept secret : even to himself, perhaps, he did not quite acknowledge what was the meaning of the little girl's confession ; or, if he acknowledged it, did not act on it ; except in so far as this, perhaps, that my gentleman, in Miss Lydia's presence, was particularly courteous and tender ; and in her absence thought of her very kindly, and always with a certain pleasure. It were hard, indeed, if a man might not repay by a little kindness and gratitude the artless affection of such a warm young heart.

What was that story meanwhile which came round to our friends, of young Mr. Lutestring and young Mr. Drabshaw the Quaker having a boxing-match at a tavern in the City, and all about this young lady? They fell out over their cups, and fought probably. Why did Mr. Draper, who had praised her so at first, tell such stories now against her grandfather? 'I suspect,' says Madame de Bernstein, 'that he wants the girl for some client or relation of his own ; and that he tells these tales in order to frighten all suitors from her. When she and her grandfather came to me, she behaved perfectly well ; and I confess, sir, I thought it was a great pity that you should prefer yonder red - cheeked countrified little chit, without a halfpenny, to this pretty, wild, artless girl, with such a fortune as I hear she has.'

'Oh, she has been with you, has she, aunt?' asks George of his relative.

'Of course she has been with me,' the other replies curtly. 'Unless your brother has been so silly as to fall in love with that other little Lambert girl——'

'Indeed, ma'am, I think I can say he has not,' George remarks.

'Why, then, when he comes back with Mr. Wolfe should he not take a fancy to this little person, as his mamma wishes—only, to do us justice, we Esmonds care very little for what our mammas wish—and marry her, and set up beside you in Virginia? She is to have a great fortune, which you won't touch. Pray, why should it go out of the family?'

George now learned that Mr. Van den Bosch and his granddaughter had been often at Madame de Bernstein's house. Taking his favourite walk with his favourite companion to Kensington Gardens, he saw Mr. Van den Bosch's chariot turning into Kensington Square. The Americans were going to visit Lady Castlewood then? He found, on some little inquiry, that they had been more than once with her Ladyship. It was, perhaps, strange that they should have said nothing of their visits to George; but, being little curious of other people's affairs, and having no intrigues or mysteries of his own, George was quite slow to imagine them in other people. What mattered to him how often Kensington entertained Bloomsbury, or Bloomsbury made its bow at Kensington?

A number of things were happening at both places, of which our Virginian had not the slightest idea. Indeed, do not things happen under our eyes, and we not see them? Are not comedies and tragedies daily performed before us of which we understand neither the fun nor the pathos? Very likely George goes home thinking to himself, 'I have made an impression on the heart of this young creature. She has almost confessed as much. Poor artless little maiden! I wonder what there is in me that she should like me?' Can he be angry with her for this unlucky preference? Was ever a man angry at such a reason? He would not have been so well pleased, perhaps, had he known all ; and that he was only one of the performers in the comedy, not the principal character by any means ; Rosencrantz and Guildenstern in the tragedy, the part of Hamlet by a gentleman unknown. How often are our little vanities shocked in this way, and subjected to wholesome humiliation ! Have you not fancied that Lucinda's eye beamed on you with a special tenderness, and presently become aware that she ogles your neighbour with the very same killing glances ? Have you not exchanged exquisite whispers with Lalage at the dinner-table (sweet murmurs heard through the hum of the guests, and clatter of the banquet !), and then overheard her whispering the very same delicious phrases to old Surdus in the drawing-room ? The sun shines for everybody ; the flowers smell sweet for all noses ; and the nightingale and Lalage warble for all ears— not your long ones only, good brother !

CHAPTER LXX

IN WHICH CUPID PLAYS A CONSIDERABLE PART

WE must now, however, and before we proceed with the history of Miss Lydia and her doings, perform the duty of explaining that sentence in Mr. Warrington's letter to his brother which refers to Lady Maria Esmond, and which, to some simple readers, may be still mysterious. For how, indeed, could well-regulated persons divine such a secret ? How could innocent and respectable young people suppose that a woman of noble birth, of ancient family, of mature experience,—a woman whom we have seen exceedingly in love only a score of months ago,— should so far forget herself as (oh, my very finger-

tips blush as I write the sentence !),—as not only to
fall in love with a person of low origin, and very
many years her junior, but actually to marry him
in the face of the world? That is, not exactly in
the face, but behind the back of the world, so to
speak ; for Parson Sampson privily tied the indissoluble knot for the pair at his chapel in Mayfair.

Now stop before you condemn her utterly. Because
Lady Maria had had, and overcome, a foolish partiality
for her young cousin, was that any reason why she
should never fall in love with anybody else? Are
men to have the sole privilege of change, and are
women to be rebuked for availing themselves, now
and again, of their little chance of consolation? No
invectives can be more rude, gross, and unphilosophical
than, for instance, Hamlet's to his mother about her
second marriage. The truth very likely is, that that
tender parasitic creature wanted a something to cling
to, and, Hamlet senior out of the way, twined herself
round Claudius. Nay, we have known females so
bent on attaching themselves, that they can twine
round two gentlemen at once. Why, forsooth, shall
there not be marriage-tables after funeral baked-
meats? If you said grace for your feast yesterday,
is that any reason why you shall not be hungry to-
day? Your natural fine appetite and relish for this
evening's feast, shows that to-morrow evening at
eight o'clock you will most probably be in want of
your dinner. I, for my part, when Flirtilla or Jiltissa
were partial to me (the kind reader will please to
fancy that I am alluding here to persons of the most
ravishing beauty and lofty rank), always used to bear
in mind that a time would come when they would
be fond of somebody else. We are served *à la Russe,*
and gobbled up a dish at a time, like the folks in
Polyphemus's cave. 'Tis *hodie mihi, cras tibi :* there

are some Anthropophagi who devour dozens of us,—
the old, the young, the tender, the tough, the plump,
the lean, the ugly, the beautiful : there's no escape,
and one after another, as our fate is, we disappear
down their omnivorous maws. Look at Lady Ogre-
sham ! We all remember, last year, how she served
poor Tom Kydd : seized upon him, devoured him,
picked his bones, and flung them away. Now it is
Ned Suckling she has got into her den. He lies
under her great eyes, quivering and fascinated. Look
at the poor little trepid creature, panting and helpless
under the great eyes ! She trails towards him nearer
and nearer : he draws to her, closer and closer.
Presently, there will be one or two feeble squeaks
for pity, and—hobblegobble—he will disappear ! Ah
me ! it is pity, too. I knew, for instance, that Maria
Esmond had lost her heart ever so many times before
Harry Warrington found it ; but I liked to fancy
that he was going to keep it ; that bewailing mis-
chance and times out of joint, she would yet have
preserved her love, and fondled it in decorous celibacy.
If, in some paroxysm of senile folly, I should fall in
love to-morrow, I shall still try and think I have ac-
quired the fee-simple of my charmer's heart ;—not
that I am only a tenant, on a short lease, of an old
battered furnished apartment, where the dingy old
wine-glasses have been clouded by scores of pairs of
lips, and the tumbled old sofas are muddy with the
last lodger's boots. Dear dear nymph ! Being
beloved and beautiful ! Suppose I had a little passing
passion for Glycera (and her complexion really was
as pure as splendent Parian marble) ; suppose you had
a fancy for Telephus, and his low collars and absurd
neck ;—those follies are all over now, aren't they ?
We love each other for good now, don't we ?
Yes, for ever ; and Glycera may go to Bath, and

Telephus take his *cervicem roseam* to Jack Ketch, *n'est-ce pas?*

No. *We* never think of changing, my dear. However winds blow, or time flies, or spoons stir, *our* pottage, which is now so piping hot, will never get cold. Passing fancies we may have allowed ourselves in former days; and really your infatuation for Telephus (don't frown so, my darling creature: and make the wrinkles in your forehead worse)—I say, really it was the talk of the whole town; and as for Glycera, she behaved confoundedly ill to me. Well, well, now that we understand each other it is for ever that our hearts are united, and we can look at Sir Cresswell Cresswell, and snap our fingers at his wig. But this Maria of the last century was a woman of an ill-regulated mind. You, my love, who know the world, know that in the course of this lady's career a great deal must have passed that would not bear the light, or edify in the telling. You know (not, my dear creature, that I mean you have any experience; but you have heard people say —you have heard your mother say) that an old flirt, when she has done playing the fool with one passion, will play the fool with another; that flirting is like drinking; and the brandy being drunk up, you— no, not you—Glycera—the brandy being drunk up, Glycera, who has taken to drinking, will fall upon the gin. So, if Maria Esmond has found a successor for Harry Warrington, and set up a new sultan in the precious empire of her heart, what, after all, could you expect from her? That territory was, like the Low Countries, accustomed to being conquered, and for ever open to invasion.

And Maria's present enslaver was no other than Mr. Geoghegan, or Hagan, the young actor who had performed in George's tragedy. His tones were so

thrilling, his eyes so bright, his mien so noble, he
looked so beautiful in his gilt leather armour and
large buckle periwig, giving utterance to the poet's
glowing verses, that the lady's heart was yielded up
to him, even as Ariadne's to Bacchus when her affair
with Theseus was over. The young Irishman was
not a little touched and elated by the high-born
damsel's partiality for him. He might have preferred
a Lady Maria Hagan more tender in years, but one
more tender in disposition it were difficult to discover.
She clung to him closely, indeed. She retired to his
humble lodgings in Westminster with him, when it
became necessary to disclose their marriage, and
when her furious relatives disowned her.

General Lambert brought the news home from his
office in Whitehall one day, and made merry over it
with his family. In those homely times a joke was
none the worse for being a little broad; and a fine
lady would laugh at a jolly page of Fielding, and
weep over a letter of Clarissa, which would make
your present Ladyship's eyes start out of your head
with horror. He uttered all sorts of waggeries, did
the merry General, upon the subject of this marriage ;
upon George's share in bringing it about ; upon
Harry's jealousy when he should hear of it. He
vowed it was cruel that Cousin Hagan had not
selected George as groomsman ; that the first child
should be called Carpezan or Sybilla, after the tragedy,
and so forth. They would not quite be able to keep
a coach, but they might get a chariot and pasteboard dragons from Mr. Rich's theatre. The baby
might be christened in Macbeth's cauldron : and
Harry and harlequin ought certainly to be godfathers.

'Why shouldn't she marry him if she likes him ?'
asked little Hetty. 'Why should he not love her
because she is a little old ? Mamma is a little old,

and you love her none the worse. When you married
my mamma, sir, I have heard you say you were very
poor; and yet you were very happy, and nobody
laughed at you!' Thus this impudent little person
spoke by reason of her tender age, not being aware of
Lady Maria Esmond's previous follies.

So her family has deserted her? George described
what wrath they were in; how Lady Castlewood had
gone into mourning; how Mr. Will swore he would
have the rascal's ears; how furious Madame de
Bernstein was, the most angry of all. 'It is an insult
to the family,' says haughty little Miss Het; 'and I
fancy how ladies of that rank must be indignant at
their relative's marriage with a person of Mr. Hagan's
condition; but to desert her is a very different
matter.'

'Indeed, my dear child,' cries mamma, 'you are
talking of what you don't understand. After my
Lady Maria's conduct, no respectable person can go
to see her.'

'What conduct, mamma?'

'Never mind,' cries mamma. 'Little girls can't
be expected to know, and ought not to be too curious
to inquire, what Lady Maria's conduct has been!
Suffice it, miss, that I am shocked her Ladyship
should ever have been here; and I say again, no
honest person should associate with her!'

'Then, Aunt Lambert, I must be whipped and
sent to bed,' says George, with mock gravity. 'I
own to you (though I did not confess sooner, seeing
that the affair was not mine) that I have been to see
my cousin the player, and her Ladyship his wife. I
found them in very dirty lodgings in Westminster,
where the wretch has the shabbiness to keep not only
his wife, but his old mother, and a little brother,
whom he puts to school. I found Mr. Hagan, and

came away with a liking, and almost a respect for him, although I own he has made a very improvident marriage. But how improvident some folks are about marriage, aren't they, Theo?'

'Improvident, if they marry such spendthrifts as you,' says the General. 'Master George found his relations, and I'll be bound to say he left his purse behind him.'

'No, not the purse, sir,' says George, smiling very tenderly. 'Theo made that. But I am bound to own it came empty away. Mr. Rich is in great dudgeon. He says he hardly dares have Hagan on his stage, and is afraid of a riot, such as Mr. Garrick had about the foreign dancers. This is to be a fine gentleman's riot. The macaronis are furious, and vow they will pelt Mr. Hagan, and have him cudgelled afterwards. My cousin Will, at Arthur's, has taken his oath he will have the actor's ears. Meanwhile, as the poor man does not play, they have cut off his salary ; and without his salary, this luckless pair of lovers have no means to buy bread and cheese.'

'And you took it to them, sir? It was like you, George!' says Theo, worshipping him with her eyes.

'It was your purse took it, dear Theo!' replies George.

'Mamma, I hope you will go and see them to-morrow!' prays Theo.

'If she doesn't I shall get a divorce, my dear!' cries papa. 'Come and kiss me, you little wench—that is, avec la bonne permission de monsieur mon beau-fils.'

'Monsieur mon beau fiddlestick, papa!' says Miss Lambert, and I have no doubt complies with the paternal orders. And this was the first time George Esmond Warrington, Esquire, was ever called a fiddlestick.

Any man, even in our time, who makes an imprudent marriage, knows how he has to run the gauntlet of the family, and undergo the abuse, the scorn, the wrath, the pity of his relations. If your respectable family cry out because you marry the curate's daughter, one in ten, let us say, of his charming children ; or because you engage yourself to the young barrister whose only present pecuniary resources come from the court which he reports, and who will have to pay his Oxford bills out of your slender little fortune ;—if your friends cry out for making such engagements as these, fancy the feelings of Lady Maria Hagan's friends, and even those of Mr. Hagan's, on the announcement of this marriage.

There is old Mrs. Hagan, in the first instance. Her son has kept her dutifully and in tolerable comfort, ever since he left Trinity College at his father's death, and appeared as Romeo at Crow Street Theatre. His salary has sufficed of late years to keep the brother at school, to help the sister who has gone out as companion, and to provide fire, clothing, tea, dinner, and comfort for the old clergyman's widow. And now, forsooth, a fine lady, with all sorts of extravagant habits, must come and take possession of the humble home, and share the scanty loaf and mutton ! Were Hagan not a high-spirited fellow, and the old mother very much afraid of him, I doubt whether my Lady's life at the Westminster lodgings would be very comfortable. It *was* very selfish perhaps to take a place at that small table, and in poor Hagan's narrow bed. But Love in some passionate and romantic dispositions never regards consequences, or measures accommodation. Who has not experienced that frame of mind ; what thrifty wife has not seen and lamented her husband in that condition ; when, with rather a heightened colour and a deuce-may-care smile on his

face, he comes home and announces that he has asked
twenty people to dinner next Saturday? He doesn't
know whom exactly; and he does know the dining-
room will only hold sixteen. Never mind! Two of
the prettiest girls can sit upon young gentlemen's
knees: others won't come: there's sure to be plenty!
In the intoxication of love people venture upon this
dangerous sort of housekeeping; they don't calculate
the resources of their dining-table, or those inevitable
butchers' and fishmongers' bills which will be brought
to the ghastly housekeeper at the beginning of the
month.

Yes: it was rather selfish of my Lady Maria to seat
herself at Hagan's table and take the cream off the
milk, and the wings of the chickens, and the best half
of everything where there was only enough before;
and no wonder the poor old mamma-in-law was
disposed to grumble. But what was her outcry
compared to the clamour at Kensington among Lady
Maria's noble family? Think of the talk and scandal
all over the town! Think of the titters and whispers
of the ladies in attendance at the Princess's Court,
where Lady Fanny had a place; of the jokes of Mr.
Will's brother officers at the usher's table; of the
waggeries in the daily prints and magazines; of the
comments of outraged prudes; of the laughter of the
clubs and the sneers of the ungodly! At the receipt
of the news Madam Bernstein had fits and ran off to
the solitude of her dear rocks at Tunbridge Wells,
where she did not see above forty people of a night at
cards. My Lord refused to see his sister: and the
Countess, in mourning, as we have said, waited upon
one of her patronesses, a gracious Princess, who was
pleased to condole with her upon the disgrace and
calamity which had befallen her house. For one, two,
three whole days the town was excited and amused by

the scandal; then there came other news—a victory
in Germany : doubtful accounts from America; a
general officer coming home to take his trial; an
exquisite new soprano singer from Italy; and the
public forgot Lady Maria in her garret, eating the
hard-earned meal of the actor's family.

This is an extract from Mr. George Warrington's
letter to his brother, in which he describes other
personal matters, as well as a visit he had paid to the
newly-married pair :—

'My dearest little Theo,' he writes, 'was eager to
accompany her mamma upon this errand of charity; but
I thought Aunt Lambert's visit would be best under the
circumstances, and without the attendance of her little
spinster *aide-de-camp*. Cousin Hagan was out when we
called; we found her Ladyship in a loose undress, and
with her hair in not the neatest papers, playing at cribbage
with a neighbour from the second-floor, while good Mrs.
Hagan sat on the other side of the fire with a glass of
punch, and the "Whole Duty of Man."

'Maria, your Maria once, cried a little when she saw us;
and Aunt Lambert, you may be sure, was ready with her
sympathy. While she bestowed it on Lady Maria, I paid
the best compliments I could invent to the old lady.
When the conversation between Aunt L. and the bride
began to flag, I turned to the latter, and between us we did
our best to make a dreary interview pleasant. Our talk
was about you, about Wolfe, about war; you must be
engaged face to face with the Frenchmen by this time, and
God send my dearest brother safe and victorious out of the
battle ! Be sure we follow your steps anxiously—we fancy
you at Cape Breton. We have plans of Quebec, and
charts of the St. Lawrence. Shall I ever forget your face
of joy that day when you saw me return safe and sound
from the little combat with the little Frenchman ? So
will my Harry, I know, return from his battle. I feel
quite assured of it; elated somehow with the prospect of

your certain success and safety. And I have made all here
share my cheerfulness. We talk of the campaign as over,
and Captain Warrington's promotion as secure. Pray
Heaven all our hopes may be fulfilled one day ere long.

'How strange it is that you who are the mettlesome
fellow (you know you are) should escape quarrels hitherto,
and I, who am a peaceful youth, wishing no harm to anybody, should have battles thrust upon me! What do you
think actually of my having had another affair upon my
wicked hands, and with whom, think you? With no less
a personage than your old enemy, our kinsman Mr. Will.

'What or who set him to quarrel with me, I cannot
think. Spencer (who acted as second for me, for matters
actually have gone this length ; don't be frightened ; it is
all over, and nobody is a scratch the worse) thinks some
one set Will on me : but who, I say? His conduct has
been most singular ; his behaviour quite unbearable. We
have met pretty frequently lately at the house of good Mr.
Van den Bosch, whose pretty granddaughter was consigned
to both of us by our good mother. Oh, dear mother ! did
you know that the little thing was to be such a *causa belli*,
and to cause swords to be drawn, and precious lives to be
menaced ? But so it has been. To show his own spirit,
I suppose, or having some reasonable doubt about mine,
whenever Will and I have met at Mynheer's house—and
he is for ever going there—he has shown such downright
rudeness to me, that I have required more than ordinary
patience to keep my temper. He has contradicted me
once, twice, thrice, in the presence of the family, and out
of sheer spite and rage, as it appeared to me. Is he paying
his addresses to Miss Lydia, and her father's ships, negroes,
and forty thousand pounds ? I should guess so. The old
gentleman is for ever talking about his money, and adores
his granddaughter, and as she is a beautiful little creature,
numbers of folk here are ready to adore her too. Was
Will rascal enough to fancy that I would give up my
Theo for a million of guineas, and negroes, and Venus to
boot ? Could the thought of such baseness enter into the
man's mind ? I don't know that he has accused me of

stealing Van den Bosch's spoons and tankards when we dine there, or of robbing on the highway. But for one reason or the other he has chosen to be jealous of me, and as I have parried his impertinences with little sarcastic speeches (though perfectly civil before company), perhaps I have once or twice made him angry. Our little Miss Lydia has unwittingly added fuel to the fire on more than one occasion, especially yesterday, when there was talk about your worship.

'"Ah!" says the heedless little thing, as we sat over our dessert, "'tis lucky for you, Mr. Esmond, that Captain Harry is not here."

'"Why, miss?" asks he, with one of his usual conversational ornaments. He must have offended some fairy in his youth, who has caused him to drop curses for ever out of his mouth, as she did the girl to spit out toads and serpents. (I know some one from whose gentle lips there only fall pure pearls and diamonds.) "Why?" says Will, with a cannonade of oaths.

'"O fie!" says she, putting up the prettiest little fingers to the prettiest little rosy ears in the world. "O fie, sir! to use such naughty words. 'Tis lucky the Captain is not here, because he might quarrel with you; and Mr. George is so peaceable and quiet, that he won't. Have you heard from the Captain, Mr. George?"

'"From Cape Breton," says I. "He is very well, thank you; that is——" I couldn't finish the sentence, for I was in such a rage, that I scarce could contain myself.

'"From the Captain, as you call him, Miss Lyddy," says Will. "He'll distinguish himself as he did at St. Cas. Ho, ho!"

'"So I apprehend he did, sir," says Harry's brother.

'"Did he?" says our dear cousin; "always thought he ran away; took to his legs; got a ducking, and ran away as if a bailiff was after him."

'"La!" says miss, "did the Captain ever have a bailiff after him?"

'"Didn't he! Ho, ho!" laughs Mr. Will.

'I suppose I must have looked very savage, for Spencer, who was dining with us, trod on my foot, under the table. "Don't laugh so loud, cousin," I said, very gently; "you may wake good old Mr. Van den Bosch." The good old gentleman was asleep in his arm-chair, to which he commonly retires for a nap after dinner.

'"Oh, indeed, cousin," says Will, and he turns and winks at a friend of his, Captain Deuceace, whose own and whose wife's reputation I dare say you heard of when you frequented the clubs, and whom Will has introduced into this simple family as a man of the highest fashion. "Don't be afraid, miss," says Mr. Will, "nor my cousin needn't be."

'"Oh, what a comfort!" cries Miss Lyddy. "Keep quite quiet, gentlemen, and don't quarrel, and come up to me when I send to say the tea is ready." And with this she makes a sweet little curtsey and disappears.

'"Hang it, Jack, pass the bottle, and don't wake the old gentleman!" continues Mr. Will. "Won't you help yourself, cousin?" he continues; being particularly facetious in the tone of that word cousin.

'"I am going to help myself," I said, "but I am not going to drink the glass; and I'll tell you what I am going to do with it, if you will be quite quiet, cousin?" (Desperate kicks from Spencer all this time.)

'"And what the deuce do I care what you are going to do with it?" asks Will, looking rather white.

'"I am going to fling it into your face, cousin," says I, very rapidly performing that feat.

'"By Jove, and no mistake!" cries Mr. Deuceace; and as he and William roared out an oath together, good old Van den Bosch woke up, and, taking the pocket-handkerchief off his face, asked what was the matter.

'I remarked it was only a glass of wine gone the wrong way; and the old man said, "Well, well, there is more where that came from! Let the butler bring you what you please, young gentlemen!" and he sank back in his great chair, and began to sleep again.

'"From the back of Montagu House Gardens there is

a beautiful view of Hampstead at six o'clock in the morning ; and the statue of the King on St. George's Church is reckoned elegant, cousin!'' says I, resuming the conversation.

'"D—— the statue!" begins Will : but I said, "Don't, cousin! or you will wake up the old gentleman. Had we not best go upstairs to Miss Lyddy's tea-table?"

'We arranged a little meeting for the next morning ; and a coroner might have been sitting upon one or other, or both, of our bodies this afternoon ; but—would you believe it?—just as our engagement was about to take place, we were interrupted by three of Sir John Fielding's men, and carried to Bow Street, and ignominiously bound over to keep the peace.

'Who gave the information? Not I, or Spencer, I can vow. Though I own I was pleased when the constables came running to us, bludgeon in hand : for I had no wish to take Will's blood, or sacrifice my own to such a rascal. Now, sir, have you such a battle as this to describe to me —a battle of powder and no shot?—a battle of swords as bloody as any on the stage? I have filled my paper, without finishing the story of Maria and her Hagan. You must have it by the next ship. You see, the quarrel with Will took place yesterday, very soon after I had written the first sentence or two of my letter. I had been dawdling till dinner-time (I looked at the paper last night, when I was grimly making certain little accounts up, and wondered shall I ever finish this letter?), and now the quarrel has been so much more interesting to me than poor Molly's love-adventures, that behold my paper is full to the brim! Wherever my dearest Harry reads it, I know that there will be a heart full of love for his loving brother,   G. E. W.'

CHAPTER LXXI
WHITE FAVOURS

THE little quarrel between George and his cousin caused the former to discontinue his visits to Bloomsbury in a great measure; for Mr. Will was more than ever assiduous in his attentions; and, now that both were bound over to peace, so outrageous in his behaviour, that George found the greatest difficulty in keeping his hands from his cousin. The artless little Lydia had certainly a queer way of receiving her friends. But six weeks before madly jealous of George's preference for another, she now took occasion repeatedly to compliment Theo in her conversation. Miss Theo was such a quiet, gentle creature, Lyddy was sure George was just the husband for her. How fortunate that horrible quarrel had been prevented! The constables had come up just in time; and it was quite ridiculous to hear Mr. Esmond cursing and swearing, and the rage he was in at being disappointed of his duel! 'But the arrival of the constables saved your valuable life, dear Mr. George, and I am sure Miss Theo ought to bless them for ever,' says Lyddy, with a soft smile. 'You won't stop and meet Mr. Esmond at dinner to-day? You don't like being in his company! He can't do you any harm; and I am sure you will do him none.' Kind speeches like these addressed by a little girl to a gentleman, and spoken by a strange inadvertency in company, and when other gentlemen and ladies were present, were not likely to render Mr. Warrington very eager for the society of the young American lady.

George's meeting with Mr. Will was not known for some days in Dean Street, for he did not wish to disturb those kind folks with his quarrel; but when the ladies were made aware of it, you may be sure there was a great flurry and to do. 'You were actually going to take a fellow-creature's life, and you came to see us, and said not a word! Oh, George, it was shocking!' said Theo.

'My dear, he had insulted me and my brother,' pleaded George. 'Could I let him call us both cowards, and sit by and say, Thank you?'

The General sat by and looked very grave.

'You know you think, papa, it is a wicked and un-Christian practice; and have often said you wished gentlemen would have the courage to refuse!'

'To refuse? Yes,' says Mr. Lambert, still very glum.

'It must require a prodigious strength of mind to refuse,' says Jack Lambert, looking as gloomy as his father; 'and I think if any man were to call me a coward, I should be apt to forget my orders.'

'You see brother Jack is with me!' cries George.

'I must not be against you, Mr. Warrington,' says Jack Lambert.

'Mr. Warrington!' cries George, turning very red.

'Would you, a clergyman, have George break the Commandments, and commit murder, John?' asks Theo, aghast.

'I am a soldier's son, sister,' says the young divine drily. 'Besides, Mr. Warrington has committed no murder at all. We must soon be hearing from Canada, father. The great question of the supremacy of the two races must be tried there ere long!' He turned his back on George as he spoke, and the latter eyed him with wonder.

Hetty, looking rather pale at this original remark of
brother Jack, is called out of the room by some artful
pretext of her sister.   George started up and followed
the retreating girls to the door.

'Great powers, gentlemen!' says he, coming back,
'I believe, on my honour, you are giving me the
credit of shirking this affair with Mr. Esmond!' The
clergyman and his father looked at one another.

'A man's nearest and dearest are always the first to
insult him,' says George, flashing out.

'You mean to say, "Not guilty?"   God bless thee,
my boy!' cries the General.   'I told thee so, Jack.'
And he rubbed his hand across his eyes, and blushed,
and wrung George's hand with all his might.

'Not guilty of what, in Heaven's name?' asks Mr.
Warrington.

'Nay,' said the General.   'Mr. Jack, here, brought
the story.   Let him tell it.   I believe 'tis a —— lie,
with all my heart.'   And uttering this wicked expression, the General fairly walked out of the
room.

The Rev. J. Lambert looked uncommonly foolish.

'And what is this—this d—— lie, sir, that somebody
has been telling of me?' asked George, grinning at the
young clergyman.

'To question the courage of any man is always an
offence to him,' says Mr. Lambert, 'and I rejoice that
yours has been belied.'

'Who told the falsehood, sir, which you repeated?'
bawls out Mr. Warrington.   'I insist on the man's
name!'

'You forget you are bound over to keep the peace,'
says Jack.

'Curse the peace, sir!   We can go and fight in
Holland.   Tell me the man's name, I say!'

'Fair and softly, Mr. Warrington!' cries the young

parson ; ' my hearing is perfectly good.   It was not a
man who told me the story which, I confess, I im-
parted to my father.'

'What ?' asks George, the truth suddenly occurring.
' Was it that artful wicked little vixen in Bloomsbury
Square ? '

' Vixen is not the word to apply to any young lady,
George Warrington ! ' exclaims Lambert, ' much less
to the charming Miss Lydia.   She artful—the most
innocent of Heaven's creatures !   She wicked—that
angel !   With unfeigned delight that the quarrel
should be over—with devout gratitude to think that
blood consanguineous should not be shed—she spoke
in terms of the highest praise of you for declining this
quarrel, and of the deepest sympathy with you for
taking the painful but only method of averting it.'

'What method ?' demands George, stamping his
foot.

'Why, of laying an information, to be sure !' says
Mr. Jack ; on which George burst forth into language
much too violent for us to repeat here, and highly un-
complimentary to Miss Lydia.

"Don't utter such words, sir !' cried the parson—
who, as it seemed, now took his turn to be angry.
'Do not insult, in my hearing, the most charming,
the most innocent of her sex !   If she has been mistaken in her information regarding you, and doubted
your willingness to commit what, after all, is a crime
—for a crime homicide is, and of the most awful description — you, sir, have no right to blacken that
angel's character with foul words : and, innocent yourself, should respect the most innocent as she is the
most lovely of women !   O George, are you to be my
brother ? '

'I hope to have that honour,' answered George,
smiling.   He began to perceive the other's drift.

'What, then, what—though 'tis too much bliss to be hoped for by sinful man—what if she should one day be your sister? Who could see her charms without being subjugated by them? I own that I am a slave. I own that those Latin Sapphics in the September number of the *Gentleman's Magazine*, beginning "Lydiæ quondam cecinit venustæ" (with an English version by my friend Hickson of Corpus), were mine. I have told my mother what hath passed between us, and Mrs. Lambert also thinks that the most lovely of her sex has deigned to look favourably on me. I have composed a letter—she another. She proposes to wait on Miss Lydia's grandpapa this very day, and to bring me the answer, which shall make me the happiest or the most wretched of men! It was in the unrestrained intercourse of family conversation that I chanced to impart to my father the sentiments which my dear girl had uttered. Perhaps I spoke slightingly of your courage, which I don't doubt—by Heaven, I don't doubt: it may be, she has erred, too, regarding you. It may be that the fiend jealousy has been gnawing at my bosom,—and horrible suspicion!—that I thought my sister's lover found too much favour with her I would have all my own. Ah, dear George, who knows his faults? I am as one distracted with passion. Confound it, sir! What right have you to laugh at me? I would have you to know that *risu inepto*——'

'What, have you two boys made it up?' cries the General, entering at this moment, in the midst of a roar of laughter from George.

'I was giving my opinion to Mr. Warrington upon laughter, and upon his laughter in particular,' says Jack Lambert, in a fume.

'George is bound over to keep the peace, Jack! Thou canst not fight him for two years: and, between now and then, let us trust you will have made up your quarrel.   Here is dinner, boys!   We will drink absent friends, and an end to the war, and no fighting out of the profession!'

George pleaded an engagement, as a reason for running away early from his dinner ; and Jack must have speedily followed him, for when the former, after transacting some brief business at his own lodgings, came to Mr. Van den Bosch's door in Bloomsbury Square, he found the young parson already in parley with a servant there.   'His master and mistress had left town yesterday,' the servant said.

'Poor Jack ! and you had the decisive letter in your pocket ?' George asked of his future brother-in-law.

'Well, yes,'—Jack owned he had the document —'and my mother has ordered a chair, and was coming to wait on Miss Lyddy,' he whispered piteously, as the young men lingered on the steps.

George had a note, too, in his pocket for the young lady, which he had not cared to mention to Jack.   In truth, his business at home had been to write a smart note to Miss Lyddy, with a message for the gentleman who had brought her that funny story of his giving information regarding the duel !   The family being absent, George, too, did not choose to leave his note. 'If cousin Will has been the slander-bearer, I will go and make him recant,' thought George.   'Will the family soon be back?' he blandly asked.

'They are gone to visit the quality,' the servant replied.   'Here is the address on this paper;' and George read, in Miss Lydia's hand, 'The box from Madam Hocquet's to be sent by the Farnham Flying Coach : addressed to Miss Van den Bosch, at the Right Honourable the Earl of Castlewood's, Castlewood, Hants.'

'*Where?*' cried poor Jack, aghast.

'His Lordship and their Ladyships have been here often,' the servant said, with much importance. 'The families is quite intimate.'

This was very strange; for, in the course of their conversation, Lyddy had owned but to one single visit from Lady Castlewood.

'And they must be a-going to stay there some time, for Miss have took a power of boxes and gowns with her!' the man added. And the young men walked away, each crumpling his letter in his pocket.

'What was that remark you made?' asks George of Jack, at some exclamation of the latter. 'I think you said ——'

'Distraction! I am beside myself, George! I— I scarce know what I am saying,' groans the clergyman. 'She is gone to Hampshire, and Mr. Esmond is gone with her.'

'Othello could not have spoken better! and she has a pretty scoundrel in her company!' says Mr. George. 'Ha! here is your mother's chair!' Indeed, at this moment poor Aunt Lambert came swinging down Great Russell Street, preceded by her footman. ''Tis no use going farther, Aunt Lambert!' cries George. 'Our little bird has flown.'

'What little bird?'

'The bird Jack wished to pair with;—the Lyddy bird, aunt. Why, Jack, I protest you are swearing again! This morning 'twas the Sixth Commandment you wanted to break; and now ——'

'Confound it! leave me alone, Mr. Warrington, do you hear?' growls Jack, looking very savage; and away he strides far out of the reach of his mother's bearers.

'What is the matter, George?' asks the lady.

George, who has not been very well pleased with

brother Jack's behaviour all day, says : 'Brother Jack
has not a fine temper, Aunt Lambert. He informs
you all that I am a coward, and remonstrates with
me for being angry. He finds his mistress gone to
the country, and he bawls, and stamps, and swears.
O fie! Oh, Aunt Lambert, beware of jealousy!
Did the General ever make you jealous ?'

'You will make me very angry if you speak to me
in this way,' says poor Aunt Lambert, from her
chair.

'I am respectfully dumb. I make my bow. I
withdraw,' says George, with a low bow, and turns
towards Holborn.

His soul was wroth within him. He was bent on
quarrelling with somebody. Had he met Cousin
Will that night, it had gone ill with his sureties.

He sought Will at all his haunts, at Arthur's, at
his own house. There Lady Castlewood's servants
informed him that they believed Mr. Esmond had
gone to join the family in Hants. He . iot: a letter
to his cousin :—

'My dear kind Cousin William,' he said, 'you
know I am bound over, and would not quarrel with
any one, much less with a dear, truth-telling, affectionate kinsman, whom my brother insulted by
caning. But if you can find any one who says that I
prevented a meeting the other day by giving information, will you tell your informant that I think it is
not I but somebody else is the coward? And I write
to Mr. Van den Bosch by the same post, to inform
him and Miss Lyddy that I find some rascal has been
telling them lies to my discredit, and to beg them
have a care of such persons.' And, these neat letters
being despatched, Mr. Warrington dressed himself,
showed himself at the play, and took supper cheerfully
at the 'Bedford.'

In a few days George found a letter on his breakfast-table franked 'Castlewood,' and, indeed, written
by that nobleman :—

'Dear Cousin,' my Lord wrote, 'there has been so much
annoyance in our family of late, that I am sure 'tis time
our quarrels should cease. Two days since my brother
William brought me a very angry letter, signed G. Warrington, and at the same time, to my great grief and pain,
acquainted me with a quarrel that had taken place between
you, in which, to say the least, your conduct was violent.
'Tis an ill use to put good wine to—that to which you
applied good Mr. Van den Bosch's.   Sure, before an old
man, young ones should be more respectful.   I do not
deny that William's language and behaviour are often
irritating.   I know he has often tried my temper, and
that within the 24 hours.

'Ah! why should we not all live happily together?
You know, cousin, I have ever professed a sincere regard
for you—that I am a sincere admirer of the admirable
young lady to whom you are engaged, and to whom I offer
my most cordial compliments and remembrances.   I
would live in harmony with all my family where 'tis
possible—the more because I hope to introduce to it a
Countess of Castlewood.

'At my mature age, 'tis not uncommon for a man to
choose a young wife.   My Lydia (you will divine that I
am happy in being able to call mine the elegant Miss Van
den Bosch) will naturally survive me.   After soothing my
declining years, I shall not be jealous if at their close she
should select some happy man to succeed me; though I
shall envy him the possession of so much perfection and
beauty.   Though of a noble Dutch family, her rank, the
girl declares, is not equal to mine, which she confesses that
she is pleased to share. I, on the other hand, shall not be sorry
to see descendants to my house, and to have it, through my
Lady Castlewood's means, restored to something of the
splendour which it knew before two or three improvident
predecessors impaired it.   My Lydia, who is by my side,

sends you and the charming Lambert family her warmest remembrances.

'The marriage will take place very speedily here. May I hope to see you at church? My brother will not be present to quarrel with you. When I and dear Lydia announced the match to him yesterday, he took the intelligence in bad part, uttered language that I know he will one day regret, and is at present on a visit to some neighbours. The Dowager Lady Castlewood retains the house at Kensington; we having our own establishment, where you will be ever welcomed, dear cousin, by your affectionate humble servant,   CASTLEWOOD.'

From the *London Magazine* of November 1759 :—

'Saturday, October 13th, married at his seat, Castlewood, Hants, the Right Honourable Eugene, Earl of Castlewood, to the beautiful Miss Van den Bosch, of Virginia. £70,000.'

CHAPTER LXXII

(FROM THE WARRINGTON MS.) IN WHICH MY LADY IS ON THE TOP OF THE LADDER

LOOKING across the fire, towards *her* accustomed chair, who has been the beloved partner of my hearth during the last half of my life, I often ask (for middle-aged gentlemen have the privilege of repeating their jokes, their questions, their stories), whether two young people ever were more foolish and imprudent than we were, when we married, as we did, in the year of the old King's death? My son, who has taken some prodigious leaps in the heat of his fox-hunting, says he surveys the gaps and rivers which he crossed so safely over, with terror afterwards, and astonishment

at his own foolhardiness in making such desperate
ventures; and yet there is no more eager sportsman
in the two counties than Miles. He loves his amusement so much that he cares for no other. He has
broken his collar-bone, and had a hundred tumbles
(to his mother's terror); but so has his father (thinking, perhaps, of a copy of verse, or his speech at
Quarter Sessions) been thrown over his old mare's
head, who has slipped on a stone, as they were both
dreaming along a park road at four miles an hour;
and Miles's reckless sport has been the delight of his
life, as my marriage has been the blessing of mine;
and I never think of it but to thank Heaven. Mind,
I don't set up my worship as an example: I don't say
to all young folks, 'Go and marry upon twopence a
year;' or people would look very black at me at our
vestry-meetings; but my wife is known to be a
desperate match-maker; and when Hodge and Susan
appear in my justice-room with a talk of allowance,
we urge them to spend their half-crown a week at
home, add a little contribution of our own, and send
for the vicar.

Now, when I ask a question of my dear oracle, I
know what the answer will be; and hence, no doubt,
the reason why I so often consult her. I have but to
wear a particular expression of face, and my Diana
takes her reflection from it. Suppose I say, 'My
dear, don't you think the moon was made of cream-
cheese, to-night?' She will say, 'Well, papa, it did
look very like cream-cheese indeed—there's nobody
like you for droll similes.' Or, suppose I say, 'My
love, Mr. Pitt's speech was very fine, but I don't
think he is equal to what I remember his father.'
'Nobody was equal to my Lord Chatham,' says my
wife. And then one of the girls cries, 'Why, I have
often heard our papa say Lord Chatham was a

charlatan !' On which mamma says, ' How like she
is to her Aunt Hetty !'

As for Miles, Tros Tyriusve is all one to him. He
only reads the sporting announcements in the
Norwich paper. So long as there is good scent,
he does not care about the state of the country. I
believe the rascal has never read my poems, much
more my tragedies (for I mentioned Pocahontas to
him the other day, and the dunce thought she was a
river in Virginia); and with respect to my Latin
verses, how can he understand them, when I know he
can't construe Corderius ? Why, this note-book lies
publicly on the little table at my corner of the fireside, and any one may read in it who will take the
trouble of lifting my spectacles off the cover : but
Miles never hath. I insert in the loose pages cari-
catures of Miles ; jokes against him : but he never
knows nor heeds them. Only once, in place of a neat
drawing of mine, in China-ink, representing Miles
asleep after dinner, and which my friend Bunbury
would not disown, I found a rude picture of myself
going over my mare Sultana's head, and entitled
' The Squire on Horseback, or Fish out of Water.'
And the fellow began to roar with laughter, and all
the girls to titter, when I came upon the page ! My
wife said she never was in such a fright as when I went
to my book : but I can bear a joke against myself, and
have heard many, though (strange to say for one who
has lived among some of the chief wits of the age) I
never heard a good one in my life. Never mind,
Miles, though thou art not a wit, I love thee none
the worse (there never was any love lost between two
wits in a family) ; though thou hast no great beauty,
thy mother thinks thee as handsome as Apollo, or
His Royal Highness the Prince of Wales, who was
born in the very same year with thee. Indeed, she

always thinks Coates's picture of the Prince is very
like her eldest boy, and has the print in her dressing-
room to this very day.*

In that same year, with what different prospects!
my Lord Esmond, Lord Castlewood's son, likewise
appeared to adorn the world. My Lord C. and his
humble servant had already come to a coolness at that
time, and, Heaven knows! my honest Miles's godmother, at his entrance into life, brought no gold
papboats to his christening! Matters have mended
since, *laus Deo*—laus Deo, indeed! for I suspect
neither Miles nor his father would ever have been
able to do much for themselves, and by their own
wits.

Castlewood House has quite a different face now
from that venerable one which it wore in the days of
my youth, when it was covered with the wrinkles of
time, the scars of old wars, the cracks and blemishes
which years had marked on its hoary features. I love
best to remember it in its old shape, as I saw it when
young Mr. George Warrington went down at the
owner's invitation, to be present at his Lordship's
marriage with Miss Lydia Van den Bosch—'an
American lady of noble family of Holland,' as the
county paper announced her Ladyship to be. Then
the Towers stood as Warrington's grandfather the
Colonel (the Marquis, as Madam Esmond would like
to call her father) had seen them. The woods
(thinned not a little to be sure) stood, nay, some of
the self-same rooks may have cawed over them, which
the Colonel had seen threescore years back. His

* Note in a female hand : 'My son is n t a spendthrift, nor a breaker
of women's hearts, as s me gentlemen are ; but that he was exceeding
like H.R.H. when they were both babies is m st certain, the Duchess
of Ancaster having herself remarked him in St. James's Park, where
Gumbo and my poor Molly used often to take him for an airing.—
Th. W.'

picture hung in the hall, which might have been his, had he not preferred love and gratitude to wealth and worldly honour; and Mr. George Esmond Warrington (that is, Egomet Ipse who write this page down), as he walked the old place, pacing the long corridors, the smooth dew-spangled terraces, and cool darkling avenues, felt awhile as if he was one of Mr. Walpole's cavaliers with ruff, rapier, buff-coat, and gorget, and as if an Old Pretender, or a Jesuit emissary in disguise, might appear from behind any tall tree-trunk round about the mansion, or antique carved cupboard within it. I had the strangest, saddest, pleasantest old-world fancies as I walked the place : I imagined tragedies, intrigues, serenades, escaladoes, Oliver's Roundheads battering the towers, or bluff Hall's Beefeaters pricking over the plain before the castle. I was then courting a certain young lady (Madam, your ladyship's eyes had no need of spectacles then, and on the brow above them there was never a wrinkle or a silver hair), and I remember I wrote a ream of romantic description, under my Lord Castlewood's franks, to the lady who never tired of reading my letters then. She says, I only send her three lines now, when I am away in London or elsewhere. 'Tis that I may not fatigue your old eyes, my dear !

Mr. Warrington thought himself authorised to order a genteel new suit of clothes for my Lord's marriage, and with Monsieur Gumbo in attendance, made his appearance at Castlewood a few days before the ceremony. I may mention that it had been found expedient to send my faithful Sady home on board a Virginia ship. A great inflammation attacking the throat and lungs, and proving fatal in very many cases, in that year of Wolfe's expedition, had seized and well-nigh killed my poor lad, for whom his native air was pronounced to be the best cure. We parted with an abundance of tears, and Gumbo shed as many when his master went to Quebec : but he had attractions in this country and none for the military life, so he remained attached to my service. We found Castlewood House full of friends, relations, and visitors. Lady Fanny was there upon compulsion, a sulky bridesmaid. Some of the virgins of the neighbourhood also attended the young Countess. A bishop's widow herself, the Baroness Beatrix brought a holy brother-in-law of the bench from London to tie the holy knot of matrimony between Eugene, Earl of Castlewood, and Lydia Van den Bosch, spinster ; and for some time before and after the nuptials the old house in Hampshire wore an appearance of gaiety to which it had long been unaccustomed. The county families came gladly to pay their compliments to the newly-married couple. The lady's wealth was the subject of everybody's talk, and no doubt did not decrease in the telling. Those naughty stories which were rife in town, and spread by her disappointed suitors there, took some little time to travel into Hampshire ; and when they reached the country found it disposed to treat Lord Castlewood's wife with civility, and not inclined to be too curious about her behaviour in town. Suppose she had jilted this man, and laughed at the other ? It was her money they were anxious about, and she was no more mercenary than they. The Hampshire folks were determined that it was a great benefit to the county to have Castlewood House once more open, with beer in the cellars, horses in the stables, and spits turning before the kitchen fires. The new lady took her place with great dignity, and 'twas certain she had uncommon accomplishments and wit.

Was it not written, in the marriage advertisements, that her Ladyship brought her noble husband seventy thousand pounds? *On a beaucoup d'esprit* with seventy thousand pounds. The Hampshire people said this was only a small portion of her wealth. When the grandfather should fall, ever so many plums would be found on that old tree.

That quiet old man, and keen reckoner, began quickly to put the dilapidated Castlewood accounts in order, of which long neglect, poverty, and improvidence had hastened the ruin. The business of the old gentleman's life now, and for some time henceforth, was to advance, improve, mend my Lord's finances; to screw the rents up where practicable, to pare the expenses of the establishment down. He could, somehow, look to every yard of worsted lace on the footmen's coats, and every pound of beef that went to their dinner. A watchful old eye noted every flagon of beer which was fetched from the buttery, and marked that no waste occurred in the larder. The people were fewer, but more regularly paid; the liveries were not so ragged, and yet the tailor had no need to dun for his money; the gardeners and grooms grumbled, though their wages were no longer overdue: but the horses fattened on less corn, and the fruit and vegetables were ever so much more plentiful—so keenly did my Lady's old grandfather keep a watch over the household affairs, from his lonely little chamber in the turret.

These improvements, though here told in a paragraph or two, were the affairs of months and years at Castlewood; where, with thrift, order, and judicious outlay of money (however, upon some pressing occasions, my Lord might say he had none) the estate and household increased in prosperity. That it was a flourishing and economical household no one

could deny : not even the dowager lady and her two
children, who now seldom entered within Castlewood
gates, my Lady considering them in the light of
enemies—for who, indeed, would like a stepmother-
in-law ?   The little reigning Countess gave the
Dowager battle, and routed her utterly and speedily.
Though educated in the colonies, and ignorant of
polite life during her early years, the Countess Lydia
had a power of language and a strength of will that
all had to acknowledge who quarrelled with her.
The Dowager and my Lady Fanny were no match
for the young American : they fled from before her
to their jointure-house in Kensington, and no wonder
their absence was not regretted by my Lord, who
was in the habit of regretting no one whose back was
turned.   Could Cousin Warrington, whose hand his
Lordship pressed so affectionately on coming and
parting, with whom Cousin Eugene was so gay and
frank and pleasant when they were together, expect
or hope that his Lordship would grieve at his departure, at his death, at any misfortune which could
happen to him, or any souls alive ?   Cousin Warrington knew better.   Always of a sceptical turn, Mr.
W. took a grim delight in watching the peculiarities
of his neighbours, and could like this one even though
he had no courage and no heart.   Courage ?   Heart ?
What are these to you and me in the world ?   A
man may have private virtues as he may have half a
million in the funds.   What we *du monde* expect is,
that he should be lively, agreeable, keep a decent
figure, and pay his way.   Colonel Esmond, Warrington's grandfather (in whose history and dwelling-place
Mr. W. took an extraordinary interest), might once
have been owner of this house of Castlewood, and of
the titles which belonged to its possessor.   The
gentleman often looked at the Colonel's grave picture

With the agility
of a schoolboy

as it still hung in the saloon, a copy or replica of which piece Mr. Warrington fondly remembered in Virginia.

'He must have been a little touched here,' my Lord said, tapping his own tall placid forehead.

There are certain actions simple and common with some men, which others cannot understand, and deny as utter lies, or deride as acts of madness.

'I do you the justice to think, cousin,' says Mr. Warrington to his Lordship, 'that you would not give up any advantage for any friend in the world.'

'Eh! I am selfish : but am I more selfish than the rest of the world?' asks my Lord, with a French shrug of his shoulders, and a pinch out of his box. Once, in their walks in the fields, his Lordship happening to wear a fine scarlet coat, a cow ran towards him : and the ordinarily languid nobleman sprang over a stile with the agility of a schoolboy. He did not conceal his tremor, or his natural want of courage. 'I dare say you respect me no more than I respect myself, George,' he would say, in his candid way, and begin a very pleasant sardonical discourse upon the fall of man, and his faults, and shortcomings ; and wonder why Heaven had not made us all brave and tall, and handsome and rich? As for Mr. Warrington, who very likely loved to be king of his company (as some people do), he could not help liking this kinsman of his, so witty, graceful, polished, high-placed in the world—so utterly his inferior. Like the animal in Mr. Sterne's famous book, 'Do not beat me,' his Lordship's look seemed to say, 'but, if you will, you may.' No man, save a bully and coward himself, deals hardly with a creature so spiritless.

CHAPTER LXXIII
WE KEEP CHRISTMAS AT CASTLEWOOD, 1759

WE know, my dear children, from our favourite
fairy story-books, how at all christenings and marriages
some one is invariably disappointed, and vows
vengeance; and so need not wonder that good Cousin
Will should curse and rage energetically at the news
of his brother's engagement with the colonial heiress.
At first, Will fled the house, in his wrath, swearing he
would never return. But nobody, including the
swearer, believed much in Master Will's oaths; and
this unrepentant prodigal, after a day or two, came back
to the paternal house. The fumes of the marriage-
feast allured him: he could not afford to resign his
knife and fork at Castlewood table. He returned,
and drank and ate there in token of revenge. He
pledged the young bride in a bumper, and drank
perdition to her under his breath. He made responses
of smothered maledictions as her grandfather gave her
away in the chapel, and my Lord vowed to love,
honour, and cherish her. He was not the only
grumbler respecting that marriage, as Mr. Warrington
knew: he heard then, and afterwards, no end of abuse
of my Lady and her grandfather. The old gentleman's city friends, his legal adviser, the Dissenting
clergyman at whose chapel they attended on their
first arrival in England, and poor Jack Lambert, the
orthodox young divine, whose eloquence he had fondly

hoped had been exerted over her in private, were
bitter against the little lady's treachery, and each had
a story to tell of his having been enslaved, encouraged,
jilted by the young American. The lawyer, who had
had such an accurate list of all her properties, estates,
moneys, slaves, ships, expectations, was ready to vow
and swear that he believed the whole account was
false; that there was no such place as New York or
Virginia; or, at any rate, that Mr. Van den Bosch
had no land there; that there was no such thing as a
Guinea trade, and that the negroes were so many
black falsehoods invented by the wily old planter.
The Dissenting pastor moaned over his stray lambling
—if such a little, wily, mischievous monster could be
called a lamb at all. Poor Jack Lambert ruefully
acknowledged to his mamma the possession of a lock
of black hair, which he bedewed with tears and
apostrophised in quite unclerical language : and as for
Mr. William Esmond, he, with the shrieks and curses
in which he always freely indulged, even at Castlewood, under his sister-in-law's own pretty little nose,
when under any strong emotion, called Acheron to
witness, that out of that region there did not exist
such an artful young devil as Miss Lydia. He swore
that she was an infernal female Cerberus, and called
down all the wrath of this world and the next upon
his swindling rascal of a brother, who had cajoled him
with fair words, and filched his prize from him.

'Why,' says Mr. Warrington (when Will expati-
ated on these matters with him), 'if the girl is such a
she-devil as you describe her, you are all the better for
losing her. If she intends to deceive her husband,
and to give him a dose of poison, as you say, how
lucky for you you are not the man ! You ought to
thank the gods, Will, instead of cursing them for
robbing you of such a fury, and can't be better

revenged on Castlewood than by allowing him her sole possession.'

'All this was very well,' Will Esmond said; but—not unjustly, perhaps—remarked that his brother was not the less a scoundrel for having cheated him out of the fortune which he expected to get, and which he had risked his life to win, too.

George Warrington was at a loss to know how his cousin had been made so to risk his precious existence (for which, perhaps, a rope's end had been a fitting termination), on which Will Esmond, with the utmost candour, told his kinsman how the little *Cerbera* had actually caused the meeting between them, which was interrupted somehow by Sir John Fielding's men; how she was always saying that George Warrington was a coward for ever sneering at Mr. Will, and the latter doubly a poltroon for not taking notice of his kinsman's taunts; how George had run away and nearly died of fright in Braddock's expedition; and 'Deuce take me,' says Will, 'I never was more surprised, cousin, than when you stood to your ground so coolly in Tottenham Court Fields yonder, for me and my second offered to wager that you would never come!'

Mr. Warrington laughed, and thanked Mr. Will for this opinion of him.

'Though,' says he, 'cousin, 'twas lucky for me the constables came up, or you would have whipped your sword through my body in another minute. Didn't you see how clumsy I was as I stood before you? And you actually turned white and shook with anger!'

'Yes, curse me,' says Mr. Will (who turned very red this time), 'that's my way of showing my rage; and I was confoundedly angry with you, cousin! But now 'tis my brother I hate, and that little devil of a

Countess—a Countess! a pretty Countess, indeed!'
And, with another rumbling cannonade of oaths, Will
saluted the reigning member of his family.

'Well, cousin,' says George, looking him queerly
in the face, 'you let me off easily, and, I dare say, I
owe my life to you, or at any rate a whole waistcoat,
and I admire your forbearance and spirit. What a
pity that a courage like yours should be wasted as a
mere Court usher! You are a loss to His Majesty's
army. You positively are!'

'I never know whether you are joking or serious,
Mr. Warrington,' growls Will.

'I should think very few gentlemen would dare to
joke with *you*, cousin, if they had a regard for their
own lives or ears!' cries Mr. Warrington, who loved
this grave way of dealing with his noble kinsman, and
used to watch, with a droll interest, the other choking
his curses, grinding his teeth because afraid to bite,
and smothering his cowardly anger.

'And you should moderate your expressions, cousin,
regarding the dear Countess and my Lord your
brother,' Mr. Warrington resumed. 'Of you they
always speak most tenderly. Her Ladyship has told
me everything.'

'What, *everything*?' cries Will, aghast.

'As much as women ever *do* tell, cousin. She
owned that she thought you had been a little *épris*
with her. What woman can help liking a man who
has admired her?'

'Why, she hates you, and says you were wild about
her, Mr. Warrington!' says Mr. Esmond.

'*Spretæ injuria formæ*, cousin!'

'For me,—what's for me?' asks the other.

'I never did care for her, and hence, perhaps, she
does not love me. Don't you remember that case of
the wife of the Captain of the Guard?'

'Which Guard?' asks Will.

'My Lord Potiphar,' says Mr. Warrington.

'Lord Who? My Lord Falmouth is Captain of the Yeomen of the Guard, and my Lord Berkeley of the Pensioners. My Lord Hobert had 'em before. Suppose you haven't been long enough in England to know who's who, cousin!' remarks Mr. William.

But Mr. Warrington explained that he was speaking of a captain of the guard of the King of Egypt, whose wife had persecuted one Joseph for not returning her affection for him. On which Will said that, as for Egypt, he believed it was a confounded long way off; and that if Lord What-d'ye-call's wife told lies about him, it was like her sex, who, he supposed, were the same everywhere.

Now the truth is, that when he paid his marriage visit to Castlewood, Mr. Warrington had heard from the little Countess her version of the story of differences between Will Esmond and herself. And this tale differed, in some respects, though he is far from saying it is more authentic than the ingenuous narrative of Mr. Will. The lady was grieved to think how she had been deceived in her brother-in-law. She feared that his life about the Court and town had injured those high principles which all the Esmonds are known to be born with; that Mr. Will's words were not altogether to be trusted; that a loose life and pecuniary difficulties had made him mercenary, blunted his honour, perhaps even impaired the high chivalrous courage 'which we Esmonds, cousin,' the little lady said tossing her head, 'which we Esmonds must always possess—leastways, you and me, and my Lord, and my cousin Harry have it, I know!' says the Countess. 'Oh, Cousin George! and must I confess that I was led to doubt of yours, without which a man of ancient and noble family like ours

isn't worthy to be called a man ! I shall try, George,
as a Christian lady, and the head of one of the first
families in this kingdom and the whole world, to
forgive my brother William for having spoken ill of a
member of our family, though a younger branch and
by the female side, and made me for a moment doubt
of you. He did so. Perhaps he told me ever so
many bad things you had said of me.'

'I, my dear lady !' cries Mr. Warrington.

'Which he *said* you said of me, cousin, and I hope
you didn't, and heartily pray you didn't : and I can
afford to despise 'em. And he paid me his court,
that's a fact ; and so have others, and that I'm used
to ; and he might have prospered better than he did
perhaps (for I did not know my dear lord, nor come
to vally his great and eminent qualities, as I do out of
the fulness of this grateful heart now !), but, oh ! I
found William was deficient in courage, and no man
as wants that can ever have the esteem of Lydia,
Countess of Castlewood, no more he can ! He said
'twas you that wanted for spirit, cousin, and angered
me by telling me that you was always abusing of me.
But I forgive you, George, that I do ! And when I
tell you that it was he was afraid—the mean skunk !
—and actually sent for them constables to prevent
the match between you and he, you won't wonder I
wouldn't vally a feller like that—no, not that much !'
and her Ladyship snapped her little fingers. 'I say,
noblesse oblige, and a man of our family who hasn't got
courage, I don't care not this pinch of snuff for him
—there, now, I don't ! Look at our ancestors,
George, round these walls ! Haven't the Esmonds
always fought for their country and king ? Is there
one of us that, when the moment arrives, ain't ready
to show that he's an Esmond and a nobleman ? If
my eldest son was to show the white feather, " My

Lord Esmond!" I would say to him (for that's the second title in our family), "I disown your Lordship!"' And so saying, the intrepid little woman looked round at her ancestors, whose effigies, depicted by Lely and Kneller, figured round the walls of her drawing-room at Castlewood.

Over that apartment, and the whole house, domain, and village, the new Countess speedily began to rule with an unlimited sway. It was surprising how quickly she learned the ways of command ; and, if she did not adopt those methods of precedence usual in England among great ladies, invented regulations for herself, and promulgated them, and made others submit. Having been bred a Dissenter, and not being over-familiar with the Established Church service, Mr. Warrington remarked that she made a blunder or two during the office (not knowing, for example, when she was to turn her face towards the east, a custom not adopted, I believe, in other Reforming churches besides the English) ; but between Warrington's first bridal visit to Castlewood and his second, my Lady had got to be quite perfect in that part of her duty, and sailed into chapel on her cousin's arm, her two footmen bearing her Ladyship's great prayer-book behind her, as demurely as that delightful old devotee with her lacquey, in Mr. Hogarth's famous picture of 'Morning,' and as if my Lady Lydia had been accustomed to have a chaplain all her life. She seemed to patronise not only the new chaplain, but the service and the church itself, as if she had never in her own country heard a Ranter in a barn. She made the oldest established families in the country—grave baronets and their wives—worthy squires of twenty descents, who rode over to Castlewood to pay the bride and bridegroom honour—know their distance, as the phrase is, and give her the *pas.*

She got an old heraldry book; and a surprising old
maiden lady from Winton, learned in politeness and
genealogies, from whom she learned the Court
etiquette (as the old Winton lady had known it in
Queen Anne's time); and ere long she jabbered gules
and sables, bends and saltires, not with correctness
always, but with a wonderful volubility and persever-
ance. She made little progresses to the neighbouring
towns in her gilt coach and six, or to the village in
her chair, and asserted a quasi-regal right of homage
from her tenants and other clodpoles. She lectured
the parson on his divinity ; the bailiff on his farming ;
instructed the astonished housekeeper how to preserve
and pickle; would have taught the great London
footman to jump behind the carriage, only it was too
high for her little Ladyship to mount : gave the
village gossips instructions how to nurse and take care
of their children long before she had one herself; and
as for physic, Madam Esmond in Virginia was not
more resolute about her pills and draughts than Miss
Lydia, the earl's new bride. Do you remember the
story of the fisherman and the Genie, in the ' Arabian
Nights'? So one wondered with regard to this lady,
how such a prodigious genius could have been corked
down into such a little bottle as her body. When
Mr. Warrington returned to London after his first
nuptial visit, she brought him a little present for her
young friends in Dean Street, as she called them
(Theo being older, and Hetty scarce younger than
herself), and sent a trinket to one and a book to the
other—G. Warrington always vowing that Theo's
present was a doll, while Hetty's share was a nursery-
book with words of one syllable. As for Mr. Will,
her younger brother-in-law, she treated him with a
maternal gravity and tenderness, and was in the habit
of speaking of and to him with a protecting air, which

was infinitely diverting to Warrington, although Will's usual curses and blasphemies were sorely increased by her behaviour.

As for old age, my Lady Lydia had little respect for that accident in the life of some gentlemen and gentlewomen ; and, once the settlements were made in her behalf, treated the ancient Van den Bosch and his large periwig with no more ceremony than Dinah, her black attendant, whose great ears she would pinch, and whose woolly pate she would pull without scruple, upon offence given—so at least Dinah told Gumbo, who told his master. All the household trembled before my Lady the Countess ; the housekeeper, of whom even my Lord and the Dowager had been in awe ; the pampered London footmen, who used to quarrel if they were disturbed at their cards, and grumbled as they swilled the endless beer, now stepped nimbly about their business when they heard her Lady-ship's call ; even old Lockwood, who had been gate-porter for half a century or more, tried to rally his poor old wandering wits when she came into his lodge to open his window, inspect his wood-closet, and turn his old dogs out of doors. Lockwood bared his old bald head before his new mistress, turned an appealing look towards his niece, and vaguely trembled before her little Ladyship's authority. Gumbo, dressing his master for dinner, talked about Elisha (of whom he had heard the chaplain read in the morning), 'and his bald head and de boys who call 'um names, and de bars eat 'um up, and serve 'um right,' says Gumbo. But, as for my Lady, when discoursing with her cousin about the old porter, 'Pooh, pooh ! Stupid old man !' says she ; 'past his work, he and his dirty old dogs ! They are as old and ugly as those old fish in the pond !' (Here she pointed to two old monsters of carp that had been in a pond in Castlewood gardens for centuries,

according to tradition, and had their backs all covered
with a hideous grey mould.) 'Lockwood must pack
off; the workhouse is the place for him; and I shall
have a smart, good-looking, tall fellow in the lodge
that will do credit to our livery.'

'He was my grandfather's man, and served him in
the wars of Queen Anne,' interposed Mr. Warrington.
On which my Lady cried petulantly, 'O Lord!
Queen Anne's dead, I suppose, and we ain't a-going
into mourning for her.'

This matter of Lockwood was discussed at the
family dinner, when her Ladyship announced her
intention of getting rid of the old man.

'I am told,' demurely remarks Mr. Van den Bosch,
'that, by the laws, poor servants and poor folks of all
kinds are admirably provided in their old age here in
England. I am sure I wish we had such an asylum
for our folks at home, and that we were eased of the
expense of keeping our old hands.'

'If a man can't work he ought to go!' cries her
Ladyship.

'Yes, indeed, and that's a fact!' says grandpapa.

'What! an old servant?' asks my Lord.

'Mr. Van den Bosch possibly was independent of
servants when he was young,' remarks Mr. Warrington.

'Greased my own boots, opened my own shutters,
sanded and watered my own——'

'Sugar, sir?' says my Lord.

'No; floor, son-in-law!' says the old man, with a
laugh; 'though there is such tricks in grocery-stores,
saving your Ladyship's presence.'

'La, pa! what should *I* know about stores and
groceries?' cries her Ladyship.

'He! Remember stealing the sugar, and what
came on it, my dear Ladyship?' says grandpapa.

'At any rate, a handsome well-grown man in our

livery will look better than that shrivelled old porter
creature!' cries my Lady.

'No livery is so becoming as old age, madam, and
no lace as handsome as silver hairs,' says Mr. Warrington. 'What will the county say if you banish
old Lockwood?'

'Oh! if you plead for him, sir, I suppose he must
stay. Hadn't I better order a couch for him out of
my drawing-room, and send him some of the best
wine from the cellar?'

'Indeed, your Ladyship couldn't do better,' Mr.
Warrington remarked, very gravely.

And my Lord said, yawning, 'Cousin George is
perfectly right, my dear. To turn away such an old
servant as Lockwood would have an ill look.'

'You see those mouldy old carps are, after all, a
curiosity, and attract visitors,' continues Mr. Warrington gravely. 'Your Ladyship must allow this
old wretch to remain. It won't be for long. And
you may then engage the tall porter. It is very hard
on us, Mr. Van den Bosch, that we are obliged to
keep our old negros when they are past work. I
shall sell that rascal Gumbo in eight or ten years.'

'Don't tink you will, master!' says Gumbo, grinning.

'Hold your tongue, sir! He doesn't know
English ways, you see, and perhaps thinks an old
servant has a claim on his master's kindness,' says
Mr. Warrington.

The next day, to Warrington's surprise, my Lady
absolutely did send a basket of good wine to Lockwood, and a cushion for his arm-chair.

'I thought of what you said, yesterday, at night
when I went to bed; and guess you know the world
better than I do, cousin; and that it's best to keep
the old man, as you say.'

And so this affair of the porter's lodge ended, Mr.

Warrington wondering within himself at this strange little character out of the West, with her *naïveté* and simplicities, and a heartlessness that would have done credit to the most battered old dowager who ever turned trumps in St. James's.

'You tell me to respect old people! Why? I don't see nothin' to respect in the old people I know,' she said to Warrington. 'They ain't so funny, and I'm sure they ain't so handsome. Look at grand-father; look at Aunt Bernstein. They say she was a beauty once! That picture painted from her! I don't believe it nohow. No one shall tell me that I shall ever be as bad as that! When they come to that, people oughtn't to live. No, that they oughtn't.'

Now, at Christmas, Aunt Bernstein came to pay her nephew and niece a visit, in company with Mr. Warrington. They travelled at their leisure in the Baroness's own landau; the old lady being in particular good health and spirits, the weather delightfully fresh and not too cold; and, as they approached her paternal home, Aunt Beatrix told her companion a hundred stories regarding it and old days. Though often lethargic, and not seldom, it must be confessed, out of temper, the old lady would light up at times, when her conversation became wonderfully lively, her wit and malice were brilliant, and her memory supplied her with a hundred anecdotes of a bygone age and society. Sure 'tis hard with respect to Beauty, that its possessors should not have even a life-enjoyment of it, but be compelled to resign it after, at the most, some forty years' lease. As the old woman prattled of her former lovers and admirers (her auditor having much more information regarding her past career than her Ladyship knew of), I would look in her face, and, out of the ruins, try to build up in my fancy a notion of her beauty in its prime. What a homily I read there! How the courts were grown with grass, the towers broken, the doors ajar, the fine gilt saloons tarnished, and the tapestries cobwebbed and torn! Yonder dilapidated palace was all alive once with splendour and music, and those dim windows were dazzling and blazing with light! What balls and feasts were once here, what splendour and laughter! I could see lovers in waiting, crowds in admiration, rivals furious. I could imagine twilight assignations, and detect intrigues, though the curtains were close and drawn. I was often minded to say to the old woman as she talked, 'Madam, I know the story was not as you tell it, but so and so'—(I had read at home the history of her life, as my dear old grandfather had wrote it): and my fancy wandered about in her, amused and solitary, as I had walked about our fathers' house at Castlewood, meditating on departed glories, and imagining ancient times.

When Aunt Bernstein came to Castlewood, her relatives there, more, I think, on account of her own force of character, imperiousness, and sarcastic wit, than from their desire to possess her money, were accustomed to pay her a great deal of respect and deference, which she accepted as her due. She expected the same treatment from the new Countess, whom she was prepared to greet with special good-humour. The match had been of her making. 'As you, you silly creature, would not have the heiress,' she said, 'I was determined she should not go out of the family.' and she laughingly told of many little schemes for bringing the marriage about. She had given the girl a coronet and her nephew a hundred thousand pounds. Of course she should be welcome to both of them. She was delighted with the little Countess's courage and spirit in routing the Dowager and Lady Fanny. Almost always pleased with pretty people on her first introduction to them, Madam Bernstein *raffolée* of her niece Lydia's bright eyes and lovely little figure. The marriage was altogether desirable. The old man was an obstacle, to be sure, and his talk and appearance somewhat too homely. But he will be got rid of. He is old and in delicate health. 'He will want to go to America, or perhaps farther,' says the Baroness, with a shrug. 'As for the child, she had great fire and liveliness, and a Cherokee manner, which is not without its charm,' said the pleased old Baroness. 'Your brother had it—so have you, Master George! Nous la formerons, cette petite. Eugene wants character and vigour, but he is a finished gentleman, and between us we shall make the little savage perfectly presentable.'

In this way we discoursed on the second afternoon as we journeyed towards Castlewood. We lay at the 'King's Arms' at Bagshot the first night, where the Baroness was always received with profound respect, and thence drove post to Hexton, where she had written to have my Lord's horses in waiting for her : but these were not forthcoming at the inn, and after a couple of hours we were obliged to proceed with our Bagshot horses to Castlewood.

During this last stage of the journey, I am bound to say the old aunt's testy humour returned, and she scarce spoke a single word for three hours. As for her companion, being prodigiously in love at the time, no doubt he did not press his aunt for conversation, but thought unceasingly about his Dulcinea, until the coach actually reached Castlewood Common, and rolled over the bridge before the house.

The housekeeper was ready to conduct her Ladyship to her apartments. My Lord and Lady were both absent. She did not know what had kept them, the housekeeper said, leading the way.

'Not that door, my Lady!' cries the woman, as Madame de Bernstein put her hand upon the door of the room which she had always occupied. 'That's her Ladyship's room now. This way.' And our aunt followed, by no means in increased good-humour. I do not envy her maids when their mistress was displeased. But she had cleared her brow before she joined the family, and appeared in the drawing - room before supper-time with a countenance of tolerable serenity.

'How d'ye do, aunt?' was the Countess's salutation. 'I declare now, I was taking a nap when your Ladyship arrived! Hope you found your room fixed to your liking!'

Having addressed three brief sentences to the astonished old lady, the Countess now turned to her other guests, and directed her conversation to them. Mr. Warrington was not a little diverted by her behaviour, and by the appearance of surprise and wrath which began to gather over Madam Bernstein's face. '*La Petite*,' whom the Baroness proposed to 'form,' was rather a rebellious subject, apparently, and proposed to take a form of her own. Looking once or twice rather anxiously towards his wife, my Lord tried to atone for her pertness towards his aunt by profuse civility on his own part; indeed, when he so wished, no man could be more courteous or pleasing. He found a score of agreeable things to say to Madam Bernstein. He warmly congratulated Mr. Warrington on the glorious news which had come from America, and on his brother's safety. He drank a toast at supper to Captain Warrington. 'Our family is distinguishing itself, cousin,' he said; and added, looking with fond significance towards his Countess, 'I hope the happiest days are in store for us all.'

'Yes, George!' says the little lady. 'You'll write and tell Harry that we are all very much pleased with him. This action at Quebec is a most glorious action; and now we have turned the French King out of the country, shouldn't be at all surprised if we set up for ourselves in America.'

'My love, you are talking treason!' cries Lord Castlewood.

'I am talking reason, anyhow, my Lord. I've no notion of folks being kept down, and treated as children for ever!'

George! Harry! I protest I was almost as much astonished as amused. 'When my brother hears that your Ladyship is satisfied with his conduct, his happiness will be complete,' I said gravely.

Next day, when talking beside her sofa, where she chose to lie in state, the little Countess no longer called her cousin 'George,' but 'Mr. George,' as before; on which Mr. George laughingly said she had changed her language since the previous day.

'Guess I did it to tease old Madam Buzwig,' says her Ladyship. 'She wants to treat me as a child, and do the grandmother over me. I don't want no grandmothers, I don't. I'm the head of this house, and I intend to let her know it. And I've brought her all the way from London in order to tell it her, too! La! how she did look when I called you George! I might have called you George—only you had seen that little Theo first, and liked her best, I suppose.'

'Yes, I suppose I like her best,' says Mr. George.

'Well, I like you because you tell the truth. Because you was the only one of 'em in London who didn't seem to care for my money, though I was downright mad and angry with you once, and with myself too, and with that little sweetheart of yours, who ain't to be compared to me, I know she ain't.'

'Don't let us make the comparison, then!' I said, laughing.

'I suppose people must lie on their beds as they make 'em,' says she, with a little sigh. 'Dare say Miss Theo is very good, and you'll marry her and go to Virginia, and be as dull as we are here. We were talking of Miss Lambert, my Lord, and I was wishing my cousin joy. How is old Goody to-day? What a supper she did eat last night, and drink!—drink like a dragoon! No wonder she has got a headache, and keeps her room. Guess it takes her ever so long to dress herself.'

'You, too, may be feeble when you are old, and require rest and wine to warm you!' says Mr. Warrington.

'Hope I shan't be like *her* when I'm old, anyhow!' says the lady. 'Can't see why I am to respect an old woman, because she hobbles on a stick, and has shaky hands, and false teeth!' And the little heathen sank back on her couch, and showed twenty-four pearls of her own.

'La!' she adds, after gazing at both her hearers through the curled lashes of her brilliant dark eyes. 'How frightened you both look! My Lord has already given me ever so many sermons about old Goody. You are both afraid of her: and I ain't, that's all. Don't look so scared at one another! I ain't a-going to bite her head off. We shall have a battle, and I intend to win. How did I serve the Dowager, if you please, and my Lady Fanny, with their high and mighty airs, when they tried to put down the Countess of Castlewood in her own house, and laugh at the poor American girl? We had a fight, and which got the best of it, pray? Me and Goody will have another, and when it is over, you will see that we shall both be perfect friends!'

When, at this point of our conversation, the door opened, and Madam Beatrix, elaborately dressed according to her wont, actually made her appearance, I, for my part, am not ashamed to own that I felt as great a panic as ever coward experienced. My Lord, with his profoundest bows and blandest courtesies, greeted his aunt and led her to the fire, by which my Lady (who was already hoping for an heir to Castlewood) lay reclining on her sofa. She did not attempt to rise, but smiled a greeting to her venerable guest. And then, after a brief talk, in which she showed a perfect self-possession, while the two gentlemen blundered and hesitated with the most dastardly tremor, my Lord said :—'If we are to look for those pheasants, cousin, we had better go now.'

'And I and aunt will have a cosy afternoon. And you will tell me about Castlewood in the old times, won't you, Baroness?' says the new mistress of the mansion.

Oh les lâches que les hommes ! I was so frightened that I scarce saw anything, but vaguely felt that Lady Castlewood's dark eyes were following me. My Lord gripped my arm in the corridor, we quickened our paces till our retreat became a disgraceful run. We did not breathe freely till we were in the open air in the courtyard, where the keepers and the dogs were waiting.

And what happened? I protest, children, I don't know. But this is certain : if your mother had been a woman of the least spirit, or had known how to scold for five minutes during as many consecutive days of her early married life, there would have been no more humble henpecked wretch in Christendom than your father. When Parson Blake comes to dinner, don't you see how at a glance from his little

wife he puts his glass down and says, ' No, thank you,
Mr. Gumbo,' when old Gum brings him wine ?
Blake wore a red coat before he took to black, and
walked up Breed's Hill with a thousand bullets
whistling round his ears, before he ever saw *our*
Bunker Hill in Suffolk. And the fire-eater of the
43rd now dares not face a glass of old port wine !
'Tis his wife has subdued his courage. The women
can master us, and did they know their own strength
were invincible.

Well, then, what happened I know not on that
disgraceful day of panic when your father fled the
field, nor dared to see the heroines engage ; but when
we returned from our shooting, the battle was over.
America had revolted, and conquered the mother
country.

<h2 style="text-align:center">CHAPTER LXXIV</h2>

NEWS FROM CANADA

OUR Castlewood relatives kept us with them till the
commencement of the new year, and after a fortnight's absence (which seemed like an age to the
absurd and infatuated young man) he returned to the
side of his charmer. Madame de Bernstein was not
sorry to leave the home of her father. She began to
talk more freely as we got away from the place.
What passed during that interview in which the battle-
royal between her and her niece occurred, she never
revealed. But the old lady talked no more of forming
cette petite, and, indeed, when she alluded to her, spoke
in a nervous laughing way, but without any hostility
towards the young Countess. Her nephew Eugene,
she said, was doomed to be henpecked for the rest of

his days: that she saw clearly. A little order
brought into the house would do it all the good
possible. The little old vulgar American gentleman
seemed to be a shrewd person, and would act advan-
tageously as a steward. The Countess's mother was a
convict, she had heard, sent out from England, where
no doubt she had beaten hemp in most of the gaols;
but this news need not be carried to the town-crier;
and, after all, in respect to certain kind of people,
what mattered what their birth was? The young
woman would be honest for her own sake now: was
shrewd enough, and would learn English presently;
and the name to which she had a right was great
enough to get her into any society. A grocer, a
smuggler, a slave-dealer, what mattered Mr. Van den
Bosch's pursuit or previous profession? The Countess
of Castlewood could afford to be anybody's daughter,
and as soon as my nephew produced her, says the old
lady, it was our duty to stand by her.

The ties of relationship binding Madame de
Bernstein strongly to her nephew, Mr. Warrington
hoped that she would be disposed to be equally affectionate to her niece; and spoke of his visit to Mr.
Hagan and his wife, for whom he entreated her aunt's
favour. But the old lady was obdurate regarding
Lady Maria; begged that her name might never be
mentioned, and immediately went on for two hours
talking about no one else. She related a series of
anecdotes regarding her niece, which, as this book lies
open *virginibus puerisque*, to all the young people of the
family, I shall not choose to record. But this I will
say of the kind creature, that if she sinned, she was
not the only sinner of the family, and if she repented,
that others will do well to follow her example.
Hagan, 'tis known, after he left the stage, led an
exemplary life, and was remarkable for elegance and

eloquence in the pulpit. His lady adopted extreme
views, but was greatly respected in the sect which she
joined; and when I saw her last talked to me of
possessing a peculiar spiritual illumination which I
strongly suspected at the time to be occasioned by the
too free use of liquor: but I remember when she and
her husband were good to me and mine, at a period
when sympathy was needful, and many a Pharisee
turned away.

I have told how easy it was to rise and fall in my
fickle aunt's favour, and how each of us brothers, by
turns, was embraced and neglected. My turn of glory
had been after the success of my play. I was introduced to the town-wits; held my place in their
company tolerably well; was pronounced to be pretty
well-bred by the macaronis and people of fashion, and
might have run a career amongst them had my purse
been long enough; had I chose to follow that life;
had I not loved at that time a pair of kind eyes better
than the brightest orbs of the Gunnings or Chudleighs,
or all the painted beauties of the Ranelagh ring.
Because I was fond of your mother, will it be believed,
children, that my tastes were said to be low, and
deplored by my genteel family? So it was, and I know
that my godly Lady Warrington and my worldly
Madam Bernstein both laid their elderly heads together and lamented my way of life.

'Why, with his name, he might marry anybody,'
says meek Religion, who had ever one eye on heaven
and one on the main chance. 'I meddle with no
man's affairs, and admire genius,' says Uncle, 'but it
is a pity you consort with those poets and authors, and
that sort of people, and that, when you might have
had a lovely creature, with a hundred thousand
pounds, you let her slip and make up to a country girl
without a penny-piece.'

'But if I had promised her, uncle?' says I.

'Promise, promise! these things are matters of arrangement and prudence, and demand a careful look-out. When you first committed yourself with little Miss Lambert, you had not seen the lovely American lady whom your mother wished you to marry, as a good mother naturally would. And your duty to your mother, nephew—your duty to the Fifth Commandment, would have warranted your breaking with Miss L., and fulfilling your excellent mother's intentions regarding Miss——what was the Countess's Dutch name? Never mind. A name is nothing; but a plum, Master George, is something to look at! Why, I have my dear little Miley at a dancing-school with Miss Barwell, Nabob Barwell's daughter, and I don't disguise my wish that the children may contract an attachment which may endure through their lives! I tell the Nabob so. We went from the House of Commons one dancing-day and saw them. 'Twas beautiful to see the young things walking a minuet together! It brought tears into my eyes, for I have a feeling heart, George, and I love my boy!'

'But if I prefer Miss Lambert, uncle, with twopence to her fortune, to the Countess, with her hundred thousand pounds?'

'Why, then, sir, you have a singular taste, that's all,' says the old gentleman, turning on his heel and leaving me. And I could perfectly understand his vexation at my not being able to see the world as he viewed it.

Nor did my Aunt Bernstein much like the engagement which I had made, or the family with which I passed so much of my time. Their simple ways wearied, and perhaps annoyed, the old woman of the world, and she no more relished their company than a certain person (who is not so black as he is painted)

likes holy water. The old lady chafed at my for
ever dangling at my sweetheart's lap. Having risen
mightily in her favour, I began to fall again : and
once more Harry was the favourite, and his brother,
Heaven knows, not jealous.

He was now our family hero. He wrote us brief
letters from the seat of war where he was engaged,
Madam Bernstein caring little at first about the
letters or the writer, for they were simple, and the
facts he narrated not over interesting. We had
early learned in London the news of the action on
the glorious first of August at Minden, where Wolfe's
old regiment was one of the British six which helped
to achieve the victory on that famous day. At the
same hour, the young General lay in his bed, in sight
of Quebec, stricken down by fever, and perhaps rage
and disappointment, at the check which his troops had
just received.

Arriving in the St. Lawrence in June, the fleet
which brought Wolfe and his army had landed them
on the last day of the month on the Island of Orleans,
opposite which rises the great cliff of Quebec. After
the great action in which his General fell, the dear
brother who accompanied the chief wrote home to me
one of his simple letters, describing his modest share
in that glorious day, but added nothing to the many
descriptions already wrote of the action of the 13th
of September, save only I remembered he wrote, from
the testimony of a brother aide-de-camp who was by
his side, that the General never *spoke at all* after receiving his death-wound, so that the phrase which has
been put into the mouth of the dying hero may be
considered as no more authentic than an oration of
Livy or Thucydides.

From his position on the island, which lies in the
great channel of the river to the north of the town,

the General was ever hungrily on the look-out for a chance to meet and attack his enemy. Above the city and below it he landed,—now here and now there ; he was bent upon attacking wherever he saw an opening. 'Twas surely a prodigious fault on the part of the Marquis of Montcalm, to accept a battle from Wolfe on equal terms, for the British General had no artillery, and when we had made our famous scalade of the heights, and were on the plains of Abraham, we were a little nearer the city, certainly, but as far off as ever from being within it.

The game that was played between the brave chiefs of those two gallant little armies, and which lasted from July until Mr. Wolfe won the crowning hazard in September, must have been as interesting a match as ever eager players engaged in. On the very first night after the landing (as my brother has narrated it) the sport began. At midnight the French sent a flaming squadron of fire-ships down upon the British ships which were discharging their stores at Orleans. Our seamen thought it was good sport to tow the fire-ships clear of the fleet, and ground them on the shore, where they burned out.

As soon as the French commander heard that our ships had entered the river, he marched to Beauport in advance of the city and there took up a strong position. When our stores and hospitals were established, our General crossed over from his island to the left shore, and drew nearer to his enemy. He had the ships in the river behind him, but the whole country in face of him was in arms. The Indians in the forest seized our advanced parties as they strove to clear it, and murdered them with horrible tortures. The French were as savage as their Indian friends. The Montmorenci river rushed between Wolfe and the enemy.   He could neither attack these nor the city behind them.

Bent on seeing whether there was no other point at which his foe might be assailable, the General passed round the town of Quebec and skirted the left shore beyond.   Everywhere it was guarded, as well as in his immediate front, and having run the gauntlet of the batteries up and down the river, he returned to his post at Montmorenci.   On the right of the French position, across the Montmorenci river, which was fordable at low tide, was a redoubt of the enemy. He would have that.   Perhaps, to defend it, the French chief would be forced out from his lines, and a battle be brought on.   Wolfe determined to play these odds.   He would fetch over the body of his army from the island of Orleans, and attack from the St. Lawrence.   He would time his attack, so that, at shallow water, his lieutenants, Murray and Townsend, might cross the Montmorenci, and, at the last day of July, he played this desperate game.

He first, and General Monckton, his second in command (setting out from Point Levi, which he occupied), crossed over the St. Lawrence from their respective stations, being received with a storm of shot and artillery as they rowed to the shore.   No sooner were the troops landed than they rushed at the French redoubt without order, were shot down before it in great numbers, and were obliged to fall back.   At the preconcerted signal the troops on the other side of the Montmorenci advanced across the river in perfect order.   The enemy even evacuated the redout, and fell back to their lines; but from these the assailants were received with so fierce a fire that an impression on them was hopeless, and the General had to retreat.

That battle of Montmorenci (which my brother

Harry and I have fought again many a time over our
wine) formed the dismal burthen of the first despatch
from Mr. Wolfe which reached England, and plunged
us all in gloom. What more might one expect of a
commander so rash? What disasters might one not
foretell? Was ever scheme so wild as to bring three
great bodies of men across broad rivers, in the face
of murderous batteries, merely on the chance of
inducing an enemy, strongly intrenched and guarded,
to leave his position and come out and engage us?
'Twas the talk of the town. No wonder grave
people shook their heads, and prophesied fresh
disaster. The General, who took to his bed after
this failure, shuddering with fever, was to live barely
six weeks longer, and die immortal! How is it, and
by what, and whom, that Greatness is achieved?
Is Merit—is Madness the patron? Is it Frolic or
Fortune? Is it Fate that awards successes and
defeats? Is it the Just Cause that ever wins? How
did the French gain Canada from the savage, and we
from the French, and after which of the conquests
was the right time to sing Te Deum? We are
always for implicating Heaven in our quarrels, and
causing the gods to intervene whatever the *nodus* may
be. Does Broughton, after pummelling and beating
Slack, lift up a black eye to Jove and thank him for
the victory? And if ten thousand boxers are to be
so heard, why not one? And if Broughton is to be
grateful, what is Slack to be?

'By the list of disabled officers (many of whom are of
rank) you may perceive, sir, that the army is much
weakened. By the nature of this river, the most
formidable part of the armament is deprived of the power
of acting, yet we have almost the whole force of Canada
to oppose. In this situation there is such a choice of

difficulties, that I own myself at a loss how to determine. The affairs of Great Britain, I know, require the most vigorous measure; but then the courage of a handful of brave men should be exerted only where there is some hope of a favourable event. The Admiral and I have examined the town with a view to a general assault : and he would readily join in this or any other measure for the public service ; but I cannot propose to him an undertaking of so dangerous a nature, and promising so little success. . . I found myself so ill, and am still so weak, that I begged the general officers to consult together for the public utility. They are of opinion that they should try by conveying up a corps of 4000 or 5000 men (which is nearly the whole strength of the army, after the points of Levi and Orleans are put in a proper state of defence) to draw the enemy from their present position, and bring them to an action. I have acquiesced in their proposal, and we are preparing to put it into execution.'

So wrote the General (of whose noble letters it is clear *our* dear scribe was not the author or secretary) from his headquarters at Montmorenci Falls on the 2nd day of September : and on the 14th of October following, the Rodney cutter arrived with the sad news in England. The attack had failed, the chief was sick, the army dwindling, the menaced city so strong that assault was almost impossible ; 'the only chance was to fight the Marquis of Montcalm upon terms of less disadvantage than attacking his intrenchments, and, if possible, to draw him from his present position.' Would the French chief, whose great military genius was known in Europe, fall into such a snare? No wonder there were pale looks in the city at the news, and doubt and gloom wheresoever it was known.

Three days after this first melancholy intelligence, came the famous letters announcing that wonderful consummation of fortune with which Mr. Wolfe's

wonderful career ended. If no man is to be styled
happy till his death, what shall we say of this one?
His end was so glorious, that I protest not even his
mother nor his mistress ought to have deplored it, or
at any rate have wished him alive again. I know it
is a hero we speak of; and yet I vow I scarce know
whether in the last act of his life I admire the result
of genius, invention, and daring, or the boldness of a
gambler winning surprising odds. Suppose his ascent
discovered a half-hour sooner, and his people, as they
would have been assuredly, beaten back? Suppose the
Marquis of Montcalm not to quit his intrenched lines
to accept that strange challenge? Suppose these
points—and none of them depend upon Mr. Wolfe at
all—and what becomes of the glory of the young
hero, of the great Minister who discovered him, of the
intoxicated nation which rose up frantic with self-
gratulation at the victory? I say, what fate is it, that
shapes our ends, or those of nations? In the many
hazardous games which my Lord Chatham played, he
won this prodigious one. And as the greedy British
hand seized the Canadas, it let fall the United States
out of its grasp.

To be sure this wisdom *d'après coup* is easy. We
wonder at this man's rashness now the deed is done,
and marvel at the other's fault. What generals some
of us are upon paper; what repartees come to our
mind when the talk is finished; and, the game over,
how well we see how it should have been played!
Writing of an event at a distance of thirty years, 'tis
not difficult now to criticise and find fault. But at
the time when we first heard of Wolfe's glorious deeds
upon the plains of Abraham—of that army marshalled
in darkness and carried silently up the midnight river
—of those rocks scaled by the intrepid leader and his
troops—of that miraculous security of the enemy, of

his present acceptance of our challenge to battle, and of his defeat on the open plain by the sheer valour of his conqueror—we were all intoxicated in England by the news. The whole nation rose up and felt itself the stronger for Wolfe's victory. Not merely all men engaged in the battle, but those at home who had condemned its rashness, felt themselves heroes. Our spirit rose as that of our enemy faltered. Friends embraced each other when they met. Coffee-houses and public places were thronged with people eager to talk the news. Courtiers rushed to the King and the great Minister by whose wisdom the campaign had been decreed. When he showed himself, the people followed him with shouts and blessings. People did not deplore the dead warrior, but admired his *euthanasia*. Should James Wolfe's friends weep and wear mourning, because a chariot had come from the skies to fetch him away? Let them watch with wonder, and see him departing, radiant; rising above us superior. To have a friend who had been near or about him was to be distinguished. Every soldier who fought with him was a hero. In our fond little circle I know 'twas a distinction to be Harry's brother. We should not in the least wonder but that he, from his previous knowledge of the place, had found the way up the heights which the British army took, and pointed it out to his General. His promotion would follow as a matter of course. Why, even our Uncle Warrington wrote letters to bless Heaven and congratulate me and himself upon the share Harry had had in the glorious achievement. Our aunt Beatrix opened her house and received company upon the strength of the victory. I became a hero from my likeness to my brother. As for Parson Sampson, he preached such a sermon that his auditors (some of whom had been warned by his reverence of the coming discourse) were with difficulty

restrained from huzzaing the orator, and were mobbed
as they left the chapel. 'Don't talk to me, madam,
about grief,' says General Lambert to his wife, who,
dear soul, was for allowing herself some small indul-
gence of her favourite sorrow on the day when
Wolfe's remains were gloriously buried at Greenwich.
'If our boys could come by such deaths as James's,
you know you wouldn't prevent them from being
shot, but would scale the Abraham heights to see the
thing done ! Wouldst thou mind dying in the arms
of victory, Charley ?' he asks of the little hero from
the Chartreux. 'That I wouldn't,' says the little
man ; 'and the Doctor gave us a holiday, too.'

Our Harry's promotion was ensured after his share
in the famous battle, and our aunt announced her intention of purchasing a company for him.

CHAPTER LXXV

THE COURSE OF TRUE LOVE

HAD your father, young folks, possessed the
commonest share of prudence, not only would this
chapter of his history never have been written, but
you yourselves would never have appeared in the
world to plague him in a hundred ways : to shout and
laugh in the passages when he wants to be quiet at his
books ; to wake him when he is dozing after dinner,
as a healthy country gentleman should ; to mislay his
spectacles for him, and steal away his newspaper when
he wants to read it ; to ruin him with tailors' bills,
mantua-makers' bills, tutors' bills, as you all of you
do ; to break his rest of nights when you have the impudence to fall ill, and when he would sleep undisturbed, but that your silly mother will never be quiet

for half-an-hour ; and when Joan can't sleep, what
use, pray, is there in Darby putting on his nightcap ?
Every trifling ailment that any one of you has had,
has scared her so that I protest I have never been
tranquil ; and, were I not the most long-suffering
creature in the world, would have liked to be rid of
the whole pack of you.   And now, forsooth, that you
have grown out of childhood, long petticoats, chicken-
pox, small-pox, whooping-cough, scarlet fever, and the
other delectable accidents of puerile life, what must
that unconscionable woman propose but to arrange
the south rooms as a nursery for possible grandchildren,
and set up the Captain with a wife, and make him
marry early because we did ! He is too fond, she says,
of Brooks's and Goosetree's when he is in London.
She has the perversity to hint that, though an entrée
to Carlton House may be very pleasant, 'tis very
dangerous for a young gentleman : and she would
have Miles live away from temptation, and sow his
wild oats, and marry, as we did.   Marry ! my dear
creature, we had no business to marry at all ! By the
laws of common prudence and duty, I ought to have
backed out of my little engagement with Miss Theo
(who would have married somebody else), and taken
a rich wife. Your Uncle John was a parson and
couldn't fight ; poor Charley was a boy at school ; and
your grandfather was too old a man to call me to
account with sword and pistol. I repeat there never
was a more foolish match in the world than ours, and
our relations were perfectly right in being angry with
us.   What are relations made for, indeed, but to be
angry and find fault ? When Hester marries, do you
mind, Master George, to quarrel with her if she does
not take a husband of your selecting. When George
has got his living, after being senior wrangler and
fellow of his college, Miss Hester, do you toss up your

little nose at the young lady he shall fancy. As for
you, my little Theo, I can't part with *you*.* You
must not quit your old father ; for he likes you to play
Haydn to him, and peel his walnuts after dinner.

Whilst they had the blessing (forsooth!) of meeting, and billing and cooing every day, the two young
people, your parents, went on in a fool's paradise, little
heeding the world round about them, and all its
tattling and meddling. Rinaldo was as brave a warrior
as ever slew Turk, but you know he loved dangling
in Armida's garden. Pray, my Lady Armida, what did
you mean by flinging your spells over me in youth, so
that not glory, not fashion, not gaming-tables, not the
society of men of wit in whose way I fell, could keep
me long from your apron-strings, or out of reach of
your dear simple prattle ? Pray, my dear, what used
we to say to each other during those endless hours of
meeting ? I never went to sleep after dinner then.
Which of us was so witty ? Was it I or you ? And
how came it our conversations were so delightful ? I
remember that year I did not even care to go and see
my Lord Ferrers tried and hung, when all the world
was running after his Lordship. The King of
Prussia's capital was taken : had the Austrians and
Russians been encamped round the Tower there could
scarce have been more stir in London : yet Miss Theo
and her young gentleman felt no inordinate emotion
of pity or indignation. What to us was the fate of
Leipzig or Berlin ? The truth is, that dear old house

* On the blank leaf opposite this paragraph is written, in a large
girlish hand :—
    'I never intend to go.—THEODOSIA.'
    'Nor I.—HESTER.'
    They both married, as I see by the note in the family Bible : Miss
Theodosia Warrington to Joseph Clinton, son of the Rev. Joseph Blake,
and himself subsequently Master of Rodwell Regis Grammar School ;
and Miss Hester Mary, in 1804, to Captain F. Handyman, R. N.—ED.

in Dean Street was an enchanted garden of delights.
I have been as idle since, but never as happy. Shall
we order the post-chaise, my dear, leave the children
to keep house ; and drive up to London and see if the
old lodgings are still to be let? And you shall sit at
your old place in the window, and wave a little handkerchief as I walk up the street. Say what we did
was imprudent. Would we not do it over again? My
good folks, if Venus had walked into the room and
challenged the apple, I was so infatuated, I would have
given it your mother. And had she had the choice,
she would have preferred her humble servant in a thread-
bare coat to my Lord Clive with all his diamonds.

Once, to be sure, and for a brief time in that year,
I had a notion of going on the highway in order to
be caught and hung as my Lord Ferrers ; or of
joining the King of Prussia, and requesting some
of His Majesty's enemies to knock my brains out ;
or of enlisting for the India service, and performing
some desperate exploit which should end in my bodily
destruction. Ah me! that was indeed a dreadful
time! Your mother scarce dares speak of it now,
save in a whisper of terror ; or think of it—it was
such cruel pain. She was unhappy years after on the
anniversary of the day, until one of you was born on
it. Suppose we had been parted : what had come to
us? What had my lot been without her? As I think
of that possibility, the whole world is a blank. I do
not say were we parted now. It has pleased God to
give us thirty years of union. We have reached the
autumn season. Our successors are appointed and
ready ; and that one of us who is first called away,
knows the survivor will follow ere long. But we
were actually parted in our youth ; and I tremble to
think what *might* have been, had not a dearest friend
brought us together.

Unknown to myself, and very likely meaning only
my advantage, my relatives in England had chosen to
write to Madam Esmond in Virginia, and represent
what they were pleased to call the folly of the
engagement I had contracted. Every one of them
sang the same song: and I saw the letters, and
burned the whole cursed pack of them years afterwards when my mother showed them to me at home
in Virginia. Aunt Bernstein was forward with her
advice. A young person with no wonderful good
looks, of no family, with no money :—was ever such
an imprudent connection, and ought it not for dear
George's sake to be broken off? She had several
eligible matches in view for me. With my name
and prospects, 'twas a shame I should throw myself
away on this young lady; her sister ought to
interpose—and so forth.

My Lady Warrington must write, too, and in her
peculiar manner. Her Ladyship's letter was garnished
with Scripture texts. She dressed her worldliness out
in phylacteries. She pointed out how I was living in
an unworthy society of player-folks, and the like
people, who she could not say were absolutely
without religion (Heaven forbid!), but who were
deplorably worldly. She would not say an artful
woman had *inveigled me for her daughter*, having
in vain tried to captivate my younger brother. She
was far from saying any harm of the young woman
I had selected; but at the least this was certain, Miss
L. had no fortune or expectations, and her parents
might naturally be anxious to compromise me.
She had taken counsel, &c. &c. She had sought for
guidance where it was, &c. Feeling what her *duty*
was, she had determined to speak. Sir Miles, a man
of excellent judgment in the affairs of this world
(though he knew and sought a better), fully agreed

with her in opinion, nay, desired her to write, and
entreat her sister to interfere, that the ill-advised
match should not take place.

And who besides must put a little finger into the
pie but the new Countess of Castlewood? She wrote
a majestic letter to Madam Esmond, and stated, that
having been placed by Providence at the head of the
Esmond family, it was her duty to communicate with
her kinswoman and warn her to break off this
marriage.   I believe the three women laid their
heads together previously ; and, packet after packet,
sent off their warnings to the Virginian lady.

One raw April morning, as Corydon goes to pay
his usual duty to Phyllis, he finds, not his charmer
with her dear smile as usual ready to welcome him,
but Mrs. Lambert, with very red eyes, and the
General as pale as death.   'Read this, George
Warrington!' says he, as his wife's head drops
between her hands ; and he puts a letter before
me, of which I recognised the handwriting.   I can
hear now the sobs of the good Aunt Lambert, and
to this day the noise of fire-irons stirring a fire in
a room overhead gives me a tremor.   I heard such a
noise that day in the girls' room where the sisters
were together.   Poor gentle child !   Poor Theo !

'What can I do after this, George, my poor boy ?'
asks the General, pacing the room with desperation in
his face.

I did not quite read the whole of Madam Esmond's
letter, for a kind of sickness and faintness came over
me ; but I fear I could say some of it now by heart.
Its style was good, and its actual words temperate
enough, though they only implied that Mr. and
Mrs. Lambert had inveigled me into the marriage ;
that they knew such an union was unworthy of me ;
that (as Madam E. understood) they had desired a

similar union for her younger son, which project, not
unluckily for him, perhaps, was given up when it was
found that Mr. Henry Warrington was not the in-
heritor of the Virginian property.   If Mr. Lambert
was a man of spirit and honour, as he was represented
to be, Madam Esmond scarcely supposed that, after
her representations, he would persist in desiring this
match.   She would not lay commands upon her son,
whose temper she knew ; but for the sake of Miss
Lambert's own reputation and comfort, she urged
that the dissolution of the engagement should come
from *her* family, and not from the just unwillingness
of Rachel Esmond Warrington of Virginia.

'God help us, George !' the General said, 'and give
us all strength to bear this grief, and these charges
which it has pleased your mother to bring !   They
are hard, but they don't matter now.   What is of
most importance, is to spare as much sorrow as we
can to my poor girl.   I know you love her so well,
that you will help me and her mother to make the
blow as tolerable as we may to that poor gentle heart.
Since she was born she has never given pain to a soul
alive, and 'tis cruel that she should be made to suffer.'
And as he spoke he passed his hand across his dry
eyes.

'It was my fault, Martin !   It was my fault !' weeps
the poor mother.

'Your mother spoke us fair, and gave her promise,'
said the father.

'And do you think I will withdraw mine ?' cried
I ; and protested, with a thousand frantic vows, what
they knew full well, 'that I was bound to Theo before
Heaven, and that nothing should part me from
her.'

'She herself will demand the parting.   She is a
good girl, God help me ! and a dutiful.   She will not

have her father and mother called schemers, and
treated with scorn. Your mother knew not, very
likely, what she was doing, but 'tis done. You may
see the child, and she will tell you as much. Is Theo
dressed, Molly? I brought the letter home from my
office last evening after you were gone. The women
have had a bad night. She knew at once by my face
that there was bad news from America. She read the
letter quite firmly. She said she would like to see you
and say Good-bye. Of course, George, you will give
me your word of honour not to try and see her afterwards. As soon as my business will let me we will
get away from this, but mother and I think we are
best all together. 'Tis you, perhaps, had best go.
But give me your word, at any rate, that you will not
try and see her. We must spare her pain, sir! We
must spare her pain!' And the good man sat down in
such deep anguish himself that I, who was not yet
under the full pressure of my own grief, actually felt
his, and pitied it. It could not be that the dear lips I
had kissed yesterday were to speak to me only once
more. We were all here together: loving each other,
sitting in the room where we met every day; my
drawing on the table by her little work-box: she
was in the chamber upstairs; she must come down
presently.

Who is this opens the door? I see her sweet face.
It was like our little Mary's when we thought she
would die of the fever. There was even a smile upon
her lips. She comes up and kisses me. 'Good-bye,
dear George!' she says. Great Heaven! An old
man sitting in this room,—with my wife's work-box
opposite, and she but five minutes away, my eyes grow
so dim and full that I can't see the book before me.
I am three-and-twenty years old again. I go through
every stage of that agony. I once had it sitting in my

own post-chaise, with my wife actually by my side. Who dared to sully her sweet love with suspicion? Who had a right to stab such a soft bosom? Don't you see my ladies getting their knives ready, and the poor child baring it? My wife comes in. She has been serving out tea or tobacco to some of her pensioners. 'What is it makes you look so angry, papa?' she says. 'My love!' I say, 'it is the thirteenth of April.' A pang of pain shoots across her face, followed by a tender smile. She has under-gone the martyrdom, and in the midst of the pang comes a halo of forgiveness. I can't forgive; not until my days of dotage come, and I cease remember-ing anything. 'Hal will be home for Easter; he will bring two or three of his friends with him from Cam-bridge,' she says. And straightway she falls to de-vising schemes for amusing the boys. When is she ever occupied, but with plans for making others happy?

A gentleman sitting in spectacles before an old ledger, and writing down pitiful remembrances of his own condition, is a quaint and ridiculous object. My corns hurt me, I know, but I suspect my neighbour's shoes pinch him too. I am not going to howl much over my own grief, or enlarge at any great length on this one. Many another man, I dare say, has had the light of his day suddenly put out, the joy of his life extinguished, and has been left to darkness and vague torture. I have a book I tried to read at this time of grief—'Howel's Letters'—and when I come to the part about Prince Charles in Spain, up starts the whole tragedy alive again. I went to Brighthelmstone, and there, at the inn, had a room facing the east, and saw the sun get up ever so many mornings, after blank nights of wakefulness, and smoked my pipe of Virginia in his face. When I am in that place by

chance, and see the sun rising now, I shake my fist at
him, thinking, O orient Phœbus, what horrible grief
and savage wrath have you not seen me suffer!
Though my wife is mine ever so long, I say I am
angry just the same. Who dared, I want to know,
to make us suffer so? I was forbidden to see her. I
kept my promise, and remained away from the house:
that is, after that horrible meeting and parting. But
at night I would go and look at her window, and
watch the lamp burning there; I would go to the
Chartreux (where I knew another boy), and call for
her brother, and gorge him with cakes and half-
crowns. I would meanly have her elder brother to
dine, and almost kiss him when he went away. I used
to breakfast at a coffee-house in Whitehall, in order
to see Lambert go to his office; and we would salute
each other sadly, and pass on without speaking.
Why did not the women come out? They never did.
They were practising on her, and persuading her to
try and forget me. Oh, the weary weary days! Oh,
the maddening time! At last a doctor's chariot used
to draw up before the General's house every day.
Was she ill? I fear I was rather glad she was ill.
My own suffering was so infernal, that I greedily
wanted her to share my pain. And would she not?
What grief of mine has it not felt, that gentlest and
most compassionate of hearts? What pain would it
not suffer to spare mine a pang?

I sought that Doctor out. I had an interview with
him. I told my story, and laid bare my heart to him,
with an outburst of passionate sincerity which won
his sympathy. My confession enabled him to understand his young patient's malady; for which his drugs
had no remedy or anodyne. I had promised not to
see her, or to go to her: I had kept my promise. I had
promised to leave London: I had gone away. Twice,

thrice I went back and told my sufferings to him.
He would take my fee now and again, and always
receive me kindly, and let me speak. Ah, how I
clung to him! I suspect he must have been unhappy
once in his own life, he knew so well and gently how
to succour the miserable.

He did not tell me how dangerously, though he
did not disguise from me how gravely and seriously,
my dearest girl had been ill. I told him everything
—that I would marry her and brave every chance and
danger; that, without her, I was a man utterly
wrecked and ruined, and cared not what became of
me. My mother had once consented, and had now
chosen to withdraw her consent, when the tie between
us had been, as I held, drawn so closely together, as
to be paramount to all filial duty.

'I think, sir, if your mother heard you, and saw
Miss Lambert, she would relent,' said the Doctor.
Who was my mother to hold me in bondage; to claim
a right of misery over me; and to take this angel out
of my arms?

'He could not,' he said, 'be a message-carrier
between young ladies who were pining and young
lovers on whom the sweethearts' gates were shut: but
so much he would venture to say, that he had seen
me, and was prescribing for me, too.' Yes, he *must*
have been unhappy once, himself. I saw him, you
may be sure, on the very day when he had kept his
promise to me. He said she seemed to be comforted by
hearing news of me.

'She bears her suffering with an angelical sweetness. I prescribe Jesuit's bark, which she takes; but
I am not sure the hearing of you has not done more
good than the medicine.' The women owned afterwards that they had never told the General of the
Doctor's new patient.

I know not what wild expressions of gratitude I poured out to the good Doctor for the comfort he brought me. His treatment was curing two unhappy sick persons. 'Twas but a drop of water, to be sure ; but then a drop of water to a man raging in torment. I loved the ground he trod upon, blessed the hand that took mine, and had felt *her* pulse. I had a ring with a pretty cameo head of a Hercules upon it. 'Twas too small for his finger, nor did the good old man wear such ornaments. I made him hang it to his watch-chain, in hopes that she might see it, and recognise that the token came from me. How I fastened upon Spencer at this time (my friend of the Temple, who also had an unfortunate love-match), and walked with him from my apartments to the Temple, and he back with me to Bedford Gardens, and our talk was for ever about our women ! I dare say I told everybody of my grief. My good landlady and Betty the house-maid pitied me. My son Miles, who, for a wonder, has been reading in my MS., says, ' By Jove, sir, I didn't know you and my mother were took in this kind of way. The year I joined, I was hit very bad myself. An infernal little jilt that threw me over for Sir Craven Oaks of our regiment. I thought I should have gone crazy.' And he gives a melancholy whistle, and walks away.

The General had to leave London presently on one of his military inspections, as the Doctor casually told me ; but having given my word that I would not seek to present myself at his house, I kept it, availing myself, however, as you may be sure, of the good physician's leave to visit him, and have news of his dear patient. His accounts of her were far from encouraging. 'She does not rally,' he said. ' We must get her back to Kent again, or to the sea.' I did not know then that the poor child had begged and prayed so piteously not to be moved, that her parents, divining, perhaps, the reason of her desire to linger in London, and feeling that it might be dangerous not to humour her, had yielded to her entreaty, and consented to remain in town.

At last one morning I came, pretty much as usual, and took my place in my doctor's front parlour, whence his patients were called in their turn to his consulting-room. Here I remained, looking heedlessly over the books on the table and taking no notice of any person in the room, which speedily emptied itself of all, save me and one lady who sat with her veil down. I used to stay till the last, for Osborn, the Doctor's man, knew my business, and that it was not my own illness I came for.

When the room was empty of all save me and the lady, she puts out two little hands, cries in a voice which made me start, 'Don't you know me, George?' And the next minute I have my arms round her, and kissed her as heartily as ever I kissed in my life, and gave way to a passionate outgush of emotion the most refreshing, for my parched soul had been in rage and torture for six weeks past, and this was a glimpse of heaven.

Who was it, children? You think it was your mother whom the Doctor had brought to me? No. It was Hetty.

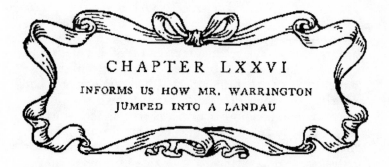

CHAPTER LXXVI

INFORMS US HOW MR. WARRINGTON
JUMPED INTO A LANDAU

THE emotion at the first surprise and greeting over, the little maiden began at once.

'So you are come at last to ask after Theo, and you feel very sorry that your neglect has made her so ill? For six weeks she has been unwell, and you have never asked a word about her! Very kind of you, Mr. George, I'm sure!'

'Kind!' gasps out Mr. Warrington.

'I suppose you call it kind to be with her every day and all day for a year, and then to leave her without a word?'

'My dear, you know my promise to your father?' I reply.

'Promise!' says Miss Hetty, shrugging her shoulders. 'A very fine promise, indeed, to make my darling ill, and then suddenly one fine day to say, "Good-bye, Theo," and walk away for ever. I suppose gentlemen make these promises, because they wish to keep 'em. *I* wouldn't trifle with a poor child's heart, and leave her afterwards, if I were a man. What has she ever done to you, but be a fool and too fond of you? Pray, sir, by what right do you take her away from all of us, and then desert her, because an old woman in America don't approve of her? She was happy with us before you came. She loved her sister—there never was such a sister—until she saw you. And now, because your mamma thinks

168

her young gentleman might do better, you must leave her forsooth !'

'Great powers, child !' I cried, exasperated at this wrong-headedness. 'Was it I that drew back ? Is it not I that am forbidden your house ; and did not your father require, on my honour, that I should not see her ?'

'Honour ! And you are the men who pretend to be our superiors ; and it is we who are to respect you and admire you ! I declare, George Warrington, you ought to go back to your schoolroom in Virginia again ; have your black nurse to tuck you up in bed, and ask leave from your mamma when you might walk out. Oh, George ! I little thought that my sister was giving her heart away to a man who hadn't the spirit to stand by her ; but, at the first difficulty, left her ! When Doctor Heberden said he was attending you, I determined to come and see you, and you do look very ill, that I am glad to see ; and I suppose it's your mother you are frightened of. But I shan't tell Theo that you are unwell. *She* hasn't left off caring for you. *She* can't walk out of a room, break her solemn engagements, and go into the world the next day as if nothing had happened ! That is left for men, our superiors in courage and wisdom ; and to desert an angel—yes, an angel ten thousand times too good for you ; an angel who used to love me till she saw you, and who was the blessing of life and of all of us—is what you call honour ? Don't tell me, sir ! I despise you all ! You are our betters, are you ? We are to worship and wait on you, I suppose ? *I* don't care about your wit, and your tragedies, and your verses; and I think they are often very stupid. *I* won't sit up at nights copying your manuscripts, nor watch hour after hour at a window wasting my time and neglecting everybody

because I want to see your worship walk down the
street with your hat cocked! If you are going away,
and welcome, give me back my sister, I say! Give
me back my darling of old days, who loved every one
of us, till she saw you. And you leave her because
your mamma thinks she can find somebody richer for
you! Oh, you brave gentleman! Go and marry
the person your mother chooses, and let my dear
die here deserted!'

'Great heavens, Hetty!' I cry, amazed at the
logic of the little woman. 'Is it I who wish to leave
your sister? Did I not offer to keep my promise,
and was it not your father who refused me, and made
me promise never to try and see her again? What
have I but my word, and my honour?'

'Honour, indeed! You keep your word to him,
and you break it to her! Pretty honour! If I were
a man I would soon let you know what I thought of
your honour! Only I forgot—you are bound to
keep the peace and mustn't—— Oh, George, George!
Don't you see the grief I am in? I am distracted,
and scarce know what I say. You must not leave
my darling. They don't know it at home. They
don't think so: but I know her best of all, and she
will die if you leave her. Say you won't! Have pity
upon me, Mr. Warrington, and give me my dearest
back!' Thus the warm-hearted distracted creature
ran from anger to entreaty, from scorn to tears.
Was my little doctor right in thus speaking of the
case of her dear patient? Was there no other remedy
than that which Hetty cried for? Have not others
felt the same cruel pain of amputation, undergone the
same exhaustion and fever afterwards, lain hopeless of
anything save death, and yet recovered after all, and
limped through life subsequently? Why, but that
love is selfish, and does not heed other people's griefs

and passions, or that ours was so intense and special
that we deemed no other lovers could suffer like
ourselves ;—here in the passionate young pleader for
her sister, we might have shown an instance, that a
fond heart could be stricken with the love malady
and silently suffer it, live under it, recover from it.
What had happened in Hetty's own case ?   Her sister
and I, in our easy triumph and fond confidential
prattle, had many a time talked over that matter, and
egotists as we were, perhaps drawn a secret zest and
security out of her less fortunate attachment.   'Twas
like sitting by the fireside, and hearing the winter
howling without ; 'twas like walking by the *mari
magno*, and seeing the ship tossing at sea.   We clung
to each other only the more closely, and, wrapped in
our own happiness, viewed other's misfortunes with
complacent pity.   Be the truth as it may ;—grant
that we might have been sundered, and after a while
survived the separation, so much my sceptical old age
may be disposed to admit.   Yet, at that time, I was
eager enough to share my ardent little Hetty's terrors
and apprehensions, and willingly chose to believe that
the life dearest to me in the world would be sacrificed
if separated from mine.   Was I wrong ?   I would
not say as much now.   I may doubt about myself (or
not doubt, I know), but of her, never ; and Hetty
found in me quite a willing sharer in her alarms and
terrors.   I was for imparting some of these to our
Doctor ; but the good gentleman shut my mouth.
' Hush,' says he, with a comical look of fright.   ' I
must hear none of this.   If two people who happen
to know each other, chance to meet and talk in my
patient's room, I cannot help myself ; but as for
match-making and love-making, I am your humble
servant !   What will the General do when he comes
back to town ?   He will have me behind Montagu

House as sure as I am a live doctor, and alive I wish to remain, my good sir!' and he skips into his carriage, and leaves me there meditating. 'And you and Miss Hetty must have no meetings here again, mind you that,' he had said previously.

Oh, no! Of course we would have none! We are gentlemen of honour, and so forth, and our word is our word. Besides, to have seen Hetty, was not that an inestimable boon, and would we not be for ever grateful? I am so refreshed with that *drop of water* I have had, that I think I can hold out for ever so long a time now. I walk away with Hetty to Soho, and never once thought of arranging a new meeting with her. But the little emissary was more thoughtful, and she asks me whether I go to the Museum now to read? And I say, 'Oh, yes, sometimes, my dear; but I am too wretched for reading now; I cannot see what is on the paper. I do not care about my books. Even "Pocahontas" is wearisome to me. I——' I might have continued ever so much farther, when, 'Nonsense!' she says, stamping her little foot. 'Why, I declare, George, you are more stupid than Harry!'

'How do you mean, my dear child?' I ask.

'When do you go? You go away at three o'clock. You strike across on the road to Tottenham Court. You walk through the village, and return by the Green Lane that leads back towards the new hospital. You know you do! If you walk for a week there, it can't do you any harm. Good morning, sir! You'll please not follow me any further.' And she drops me a curtsey, and walks away with a veil over her face.

That Green Lane, which lay to the north of the new hospital, is built all over with houses now. In *my* time, when good old George the Second was yet

King, 'twas a shabby rural outlet of London ; so dangerous, that the City folks who went to their villas and junketing-houses at Hampstead and the outlying villages, would return in parties of nights, and escorted by waiters with lanthorns, to defend them from the footpads who prowled about the town outskirts. Hampstead and Highgate churches, each crowning its hill, filled up the background of the view which you saw as you turned your back to London ; and one, two, three days Mr. George Warrington had the pleasure of looking upon this landscape, and walking back in the direction of the new hospital. Along the lane were sundry small houses of entertainment ; and I remember at one place, where they sold cakes and beer, at the sign of the ' Protestant Hero,' a decent woman smiling at me on the third or fourth day, and curtseying in her clean apron, as she says, ' It appears the lady don't come, sir ! Your honour had best step in, and take a can of my cool beer.'

At length, as I am coming back through Tottenham Road, on the 25th of May—O day to be marked with the whitest stone !—a little way beyond Mr. Whitfield's Tabernacle, I see a landau before me, and on the box-seat by the driver is my young friend Charley, who waves his hat to me, and calls out, ' George, George ! ' I ran up to the carriage, my knees knocking together so that I thought I should fall by the wheel ; and inside I see Hetty, and by her my dearest Theo, propped with a pillow. How thin the little hand had become since last it was laid in mine ! The cheeks were flushed and wasted, the eyes strangely bright, and the thrill of the voice when she spoke a word or two, smote me with a pang, I know not of grief or joy was it, so intimately were they blended.

' I am taking her an airing to Hampstead,' says

Hetty demurely. 'The doctor says the air will do
her good.'

'I have been ill, but I am better now, George,'
says Theo. There came a great burst of music from
the people in the chapel hard by, as she was speaking.
I held her hand in mine. Her eyes were looking into
mine once more. It seemed as if we had never been
parted.

I can never forget the tune of that psalm. I have
heard it all through my life. My wife has touched
it on her harpsichord, and her little ones have warbled
it. Now, do you understand, young people, why I
love it so? Because 'twas the music played at our
amoris redintegratio. Because it sang hope to me, at
the period of my existence the most miserable. Yes,
the most miserable : for that dreary confinement of
Duquesne had its tendernesses and kindly associations
connected with it ; and many a time in after days I
have thought with fondness of the poor Biche and my
tipsy gaoler ; and the *réveillée* of the forest birds and
military music of my prison.

Master Charley looks down from his box-seat upon
his sister and me engaged in beatific contemplation,
and Hetty listening too, to the music. 'I think I
should like to go and hear it. And that famous Mr.
Whitfield, perhaps he is going to preach this very day !
Come in with me, Charley—and George can drive
for half-an-hour with dear Theo towards Hampstead
and back.'

Charley did not seem to have any very strong
desire for witnessing the devotional exercises of good
Mr. Whitfield and his congregation, and proposed that
George Warrington should take Hetty in ; but Het
was not to be denied. 'I will never help you in
another exercise as long as you live, sir,' cries Miss
Hetty, 'if you don't come on,'—while the youth

clambered down from his box-seat, and they entered
the temple together.

Can any moralist, bearing my previous promises in
mind, excuse me for jumping into the carriage and
sitting down once more by my dearest Theo?
Suppose I did break 'em? Will he blame me much?
Reverend sir, you are welcome. I broke my promise;
and if you would not do as much, good friend, you
are welcome to your virtue. Not that I for a moment
suspect my own children will ever be so bold as to
think of having hearts of their own, and bestowing
them according to their liking. No, my young
people, you will let papa choose for you; be hungry
when he tells you; be thirsty when he orders; and
settle your children's marriages afterwards.

And now of course you are anxious to hear what
took place when papa jumped into the landau by the
side of poor little mamma, propped up by her pillows.
'I am come to your part of the story, my dear,' says
I, looking over to my wife as she is plying her
needles.

'To what, pray?' says my lady. 'You should skip
all that part, and come to the grand battles, and your
heroic defence of——'

'Of Fort Fiddle-de-dee in the year 1778, when I
pulled off Mr. Washington's epaulet, gouged General
Gates's eye, cut off Charles Lee's head, and pasted it
on again!'

'Let us hear all about the fighting,' say the boys.
Even the Captain condescends to own he will listen
to any military details, though only from a militia
officer.

'Fair and softly, young people! Everything in its
turn. I am not yet arrived at the war. I am only a
young gentleman, just stepping into a landau, by the
side of a young lady whom I promised to avoid. I

am taking her hand, which, after a little ado, she leaves in mine. Do you remember how hot it was, the little thing, how it trembled, and how it throbbed and jumped a hundred and twenty in a minute? And as we trot on towards Hampstead, I address Miss Lambert in the following terms——'

'Ah, ah, ah!' say the girls in a chorus with Mademoiselle, their French governess, who cries, 'Nous écoutons maintenant. La parole est à vous, Monsieur le Chevalier!'

Here we have them all in a circle: mamma is at her side of the fire, papa at his; Mademoiselle Eléonore, at whom the Captain looks rather sweetly (eyes off, Captain!); the two girls, listening like— like *nymphas discentes* to Apollo, let us say; and John and Tummas (with obtuse ears), who are bringing in tea-trays and urns.

'Very good,' says the Squire, pulling out the MS., and waving it before him. 'We are going to tell your mother's secrets and mine.'

'I am sure you may, papa,' cries the house matron. 'There's nothing to be ashamed of.' And a blush rises over her kind face.

'But before I begin, young folks, permit me two or three questions.'

'Allons, toujours des questions!' says Mademoiselle, with a shrug of her pretty shoulders. (Florac has recommended her to us, and I suspect the little Chevalier has himself an eye upon this pretty Mademoiselle de Blois.)

To the questions, then.

CHAPTER LXXVII
AND HOW EVERYBODY GOT OUT AGAIN

'IF you, Captain Miles Warrington, have the honour
of winning the good graces of a lady—of ever so many
ladies—of the Duchess of Devonshire, let us say, of
Mrs. Crew, of Mrs. Fitzherbert, of the Queen of
Prussia, of the goddess Venus, of Mademoiselle
Hillisberg of the Opera—never mind of whom in
fine. If you win a lady's good graces, do you always
go to the mess and tell what happened?'

'Not such a fool, Squire!' says the Captain,
surveying his side-curl in the glass.

'Have you, Miss Theo, told your mother every
word you said to Mr. Joe Blake, junior, in the
shrubbery, this morning?'

'Joe Blake, indeed!' cries Theo, junior.

'And you, Mademoiselle? That scented billet
which came to you under Sir Thomas's frank, have
you told us all the letter contains? Look how she
blushes! As red as the curtain, on my word! No,
Mademoiselle, we all have our secrets' (says the
Squire, here making his best French bow). 'No,
Theo, there was nothing in the shrubbery—only nuts,
my child! No, Miles, my son, we don't tell all,
even to the most indulgent of fathers—and if I tell
what happened in a landau on the Hampstead Road,
on the 25th of May, 1760, may the Chevalier
Ruspini pull out every tooth in my head!'

'Pray tell, papa!' cries mamma; 'or, as Jobson,
who drove us, is in your service now, perhaps you

will have him in from the stables! I insist upon
your telling!'

'What is, then, this mystery?' asks Mademoiselle in her pretty French accent, of my wife.

'Eh, ma fille!' whispers the lady. 'Thou wouldst
ask me what I said? I said "Yes!"—behold all I said.'
And so 'tis my wife has peached, and not I; and this
was the sum of our conversation, as the carriage, all
too swiftly as I thought, galloped towards Hampstead,
and flew back again. Theo had not agreed to fly in
the face of her honoured parents—no such thing.
But we would marry no other person; no, not if we
lived to be as old as Methuselah; no, not the Prince
of Wales himself would she take. Her heart she had
given away with her papa's consent—nay, order—it
was not hers to resume. So kind a father must relent
one of these days; and, if George would keep his
promise—were it now, or were it in twenty years, or
were it in another world, she knew she should never
break hers.

Hetty's face beamed with delight when, my little
interview over, she saw Theo's countenance wearing
a sweet tranquillity. All the doctor's medicine has
not done her so much good, the fond sister said. The
girls went home after their act of disobedience. I
gave up the place which I had held during a brief
period of happiness by my dear invalid's side. Hetty
skipped back into her seat, and Charley on to his box.
He told me, in after days, that it was a very dull
stupid sermon he had heard. The little chap was too
orthodox to love dissenting preachers' sermons.

Hetty was not the only one of the family who remarked her sister's altered countenance and improved
spirits. I am told that on the girls' return home,
their mother embraced both of them, especially the
invalid, with more than common ardour of affection.

"My child, the country air has done you all the good in the world"

'There was nothing like a country ride,' Aunt Lambert said, 'for doing her dear Theo good. She had been on the road to Hampstead, had she? She must have another ride to-morrow. Heaven be blessed, my Lord Wrotham's horses were at their orders three or four times a week, and the sweet child might have the advantage of them!' As for the idea that Mr.

Warrington might have happened to meet the children
on their drive, Aunt Lambert never once entertained
it,—at least spoke of it.   I leave anybody who is
interested in the matter to guess whether Mrs.
Lambert could by any possibility have supposed that
her daughter and her sweetheart could ever have come
together again.   Do women help each other in love-
perplexities ?   Do women scheme, intrigue, make
little plans, tell little fibs, provide little amorous
opportunities, hang up the rope-ladder, coax, wheedle,
mystify the guardian or Abigail, and turn their attention away while Strephon and Chloe are billing and
cooing in the twilight, or whisking off in the post-
chaise to Gretna Green?   My dear young folks,
some people there are of this nature ; and some kind
souls who have loved tenderly and truly in their own
time, continue ever after to be kindly and tenderly
disposed towards their young successors, when they
begin to play the same pretty game.

Miss Prim doesn't.   If _she_ hears of two young
persons attached to each other, it is to snarl at them
for fools, or to imagine of them all conceivable evil.
Because she has a hump-back herself, she is for biting
everybody else's.   I believe if she saw a pair of turtles
cooing in a wood, she would turn her eyes down, or
fling a stone to frighten them; but I am speaking,
you see, young ladies, of your grandmother, Aunt
Lambert, who was one great syllabub of human kindness ; and, besides, about the affair at present under
discussion, how am I ever to tell whether she knew
anything regarding it or not ?

So, all she says to Theo on her return home is, ' My
child, the country air has done you all the good in
the world, and I hope you will take another drive to-
morrow, and another, and another, and so on.'

' Don't you think, papa, the ride has done the child

most wonderful good, and must not she be made to go out in the air?' Aunt Lambert asks of the General, when he comes in for supper.

Yes, sure, if a coach and six will do his little Theo good, she shall have it, Lambert says, or he will drag the landau up Hampstead Hill himself, if there are no horses; and so the good man would have spent, freely, his guineas, or his breath, or his blood, to give his child pleasure. He was charmed at his girl's altered countenance; she picked a bit of chicken with appetite; she drank a little negus, which he made for her; indeed it did seem to be better than the kind doctor's best medicine, which hitherto, God wot, had been of little benefit. Mamma was gracious and happy. Hetty was radiant and rident. It was quite like an evening at home at Oakhurst. Never for months past, never since that fatal cruel day, that no one spoke of, had they spent an evening so delightful.

But, if the other women chose to coax and cajole the good simple father, Theo herself was too honest to continue for long even that sweet and fond delusion. When, for the third or fourth time, he comes back to the delightful theme of his daughter's improved health, and asks, 'What has done it? Is it the country air? is it the Jesuit's bark? is it the new medicine?'

'Can't you think, dear, what it is?' she says, laying a hand upon her father's, with a tremor in her voice, perhaps, but eyes that are quite open and bright.

'And what is it, my child?' asks the General.

'It is because I have seen him again, papa!' she says.

The other two women turned pale, and Theo's heart, too, begins to palpitate, and her cheek to whiten, as she continues to look in her father's scared face.

'It was not wrong to see him,' she continues, more quickly; 'it would have been wrong not to tell you.'

'Great God!' groans the father, drawing his hand back, and with such a dreadful grief in his countenance, that Hetty runs to her almost swooning sister, clasps her to her heart, and cries out rapidly, 'Theo knew nothing of it, sir! It was my doing—it was all my doing!'

Theo lies on her sister's neck, and kisses it twenty, fifty times.

'Women, women! are you playing with my honour?' cries the father, bursting out with a fierce exclamation.

Aunt Lambert sobs wildly, 'Martin! Martin!' 'Don't say a word to her!' again calls out Hetty, and falls back herself staggering towards the wall, for Theo has fainted on her shoulder.

I was taking my breakfast next morning, with what appetite I might, when my door opens, and my faithful black announces, 'General Lambert.' At once I saw, by the General's face, that the yesterday's transaction was known to him. 'Your accomplices did not confess,' the General said, as soon as my servant had left us, 'but sided with you against their father—a proof how desirable clandestine meetings are. It was from Theo herself I heard that she had seen you.'

'Accomplices, sir!' I said (perhaps not unwilling to turn the conversation from the real point at issue). 'You know how fondly and dutifully your young people regard their father. If they side against you in this instance, it must be because justice is against you. A man like you is not going to set up *sic volo sic jubeo* as the sole law in his family!'

'Psha, George!' cries the General. 'For though we are parted, God forbid I should desire that we

should cease to love each other. I had your promise
that you would not seek to see her.'

'Nor did I go to her, sir,' I said, turning red, no
doubt; for though this was truth, I own it was
untrue.

'You mean she was brought to you?' says Theo's
father, in great agitation. 'Is it behind Hester's
petticoat that you will shelter yourself? What a fine
defence for a gentleman!'

'Well, I won't screen myself behind the poor child,'
I replied. 'To speak as I did was to make an attempt
at evasion, and I am ill-accustomed to dissemble. I
did not infringe the letter of my agreement, but I
acted against the spirit of it. From this moment I
annul it altogether.'

'You break your word given to me!' cries Mr.
Lambert.

'I recall a hasty promise made on a sudden at a
moment of extreme excitement and perturbation.
No man can be for ever bound by words uttered at
such a time; and, what is more, no man of honour or
humanity, Mr. Lambert, would try to bind him.'

'Dishonour to *me!* sir,' exclaims the General.

'Yes, if the phrase is to be shuttlecocked between
us!' I answered hotly. 'There can be no question
about love, or mutual regard, or difference of age,
when that word is used: and were you my own father
—and I love you better than a father, Uncle Lambert,
—I would not bear it! What have I done? I have
seen the woman whom I consider my wife before God
and man, and if she calls me I will see her again. If
she comes to me, here is my home for her, and the half
of the little I have. 'Tis you, who have no right,
having made me the gift, to resume it. Because my
mother taunts you unjustly, are you to visit Mrs.
Esmond's wrong upon this tender innocent creature?

You profess to love your daughter, and you can't bear a little wounded pride for her sake. Better she should perish away in misery, than an old woman in Virginia should say that Mr. Lambert had schemed to marry one of his daughters. Say that to satisfy what you call honour and I call selfishness, we part, we break our hearts well nigh, we rally, we try to forget each other, we marry elsewhere? Can any man be to my dear as I have been? God forbid! Can any woman be to me what she is? You shall marry her to the Prince of Wales to-morrow, and it is a cowardice and treason. How can we, how can you, undo the promises we have made to each other before Heaven? You may part us! and she will die as surely as if she were Jephthah's daughter. Have you made any vow to Heaven to compass her murder? Kill her if you conceive your promise so binds you: but this I swear, that I am glad you have come, so that I may here formally recall a hasty pledge which I gave, and that, call me when she will, I will come to her!'

No doubt this speech was made with the flurry and agitation belonging to Mr. Warrington's youth, and with the firm conviction that death would infallibly carry off one or both of the parties, in case their worldly separation was inevitably decreed. Who does not believe his first passion eternal? Having watched the world since and seen the rise, progress, and—alas, that I must say it!—decay of other amours, I may smile now as I think of my own youthful errors and ardours; but, if it be a superstition, I had rather hold it; I had rather think that neither of us could have lived with any other mate, and that, of all its innumerable creatures, Heaven decreed these special two should be joined together.

'We must come, then, to what I had fain have

spared myself,' says the General, in reply to my outbreak; 'to an unfriendly separation. When I meet you, Mr. Warrington, I must know you no more. I must order—and they will not do other than obey me—my family and children not to recognise you when they see you, since you will not recognise in your intercourse with me the respect due to my age, the courtesy of gentlemen. I had hoped so far from your sense of honour, and the idea I had formed of you, that, in my present great grief and perplexity, I should have found you willing to soothe and help me as far as you might—for, God knows, I have need of everybody's sympathy. But, instead of help, you fling obstacles in my way. Instead of a friend—a gracious Heaven pardon me!— I find in you an enemy! An enemy to the peace of my home and the honour of my children, sir! And as such I shall treat you, and know how to deal with you, when you molest me!'

And, waving his hand to me, and putting on his hat, Mr. Lambert hastily quitted my apartment.

I was confounded, and believed, indeed, there was war between us. The brief happiness of yesterday was clouded over and gone, and I thought that never since the day of the first separation had I felt so exquisitely unhappy as now, when the bitterness of quarrel was added to the pangs of parting, and I stood not only alone but friendless. In the course of one year's constant intimacy I had come to regard Lambert with a reverence and affection which I had never before felt for any mortal man except my dearest Harry. That his face should be turned from me in anger was as if the sun had gone out of my sphere, and all was dark around me. And yet I felt sure that in withdrawing the hasty promise I had made not to see Theo, I was acting rightly—that my fidelity to her, as hers now to me, was paramount to all other ties of duty or obedience, and that, ceremony or none, I was hers, first and before all. Promises were passed between us, from which no parent could absolve either; and all the priests in Christendom could no more than attest and confirm the sacred contract which had tacitly been ratified between us.

I saw Jack Lambert by chance that day, as I went mechanically to my not unusual haunt, the library of the new Museum; and with the impetuousness of youth, and eager to impart my sorrow to some one, I took him out of the room and led him about the gardens, and poured out my grief to him. I did not much care for Jack (who in truth was somewhat of a prig, and not a little pompous and wearisome with his Latin quotations) except in the time of my own sorrow, when I would fasten upon him or any one; and having suffered himself in his affair with the little American, being *haud ignarus mali* (as I knew he would say), I found the college gentleman ready to compassionate another's misery. I told him, what has here been represented at greater length, of my yesterday's meeting with his sister; of my interview with his father in the morning; of my determination at all hazards never to part with Theo. When I found from the various quotations from the Greek and Latin authors which he uttered that he leaned to my side in the dispute, I thought him a man of great sense, clung eagerly to his elbow, and bestowed upon him much more affection than he was accustomed at other times to have from me. I walked with him up to his father's lodgings in Dean Street; saw him enter at the dear door; surveyed the house from without with a sickening desire to know from its exterior appearance how my beloved fared within; and called for a bottle at the coffee-house where I

waited Jack's return. I called him brother when I
sent him away. I fondled him as the condemned
wretch at Newgate hangs about the gaoler or the
parson, or any one who is kind to him in his misery.
I drank a whole bottle of wine at the coffee-house—
by the way, Jack's Coffee-House was its name—
called another. I thought Jack would never come
back.

He appeared at length with rather a scared face;
and, coming to my box, poured out for himself two
or three bumpers from my second bottle, and then
fell to his story, which, to me at least, was not a
little interesting. My poor Theo was keeping her
room, it appeared, being much agitated by the occurrences of yesterday; and Jack had come home in
time to find dinner on table; after which his good
father held forth upon the occurrences of the morning,
being anxious and able to speak more freely, he said,
because his eldest son was present and Theodosia was
not in the room. The General stated what had
happened at my lodgings between me and him. He
bade Hester be silent, who indeed was as dumb as a
mouse, poor thing! he told Aunt Lambert (who was
indulging in that madefaction of pocket-handkerchiefs
which I have before described), and with something
like an imprecation, that the women were all against
him, and pimps (he called them) for one another; and
frantically turning round to Jack, asked what was his
view in the matter?

To his father's surprise and his mother's and sister's
delight, Jack made a speech on my side. He ruled
with me (citing what ancient authorities I don't know),
that the matter had gone out of the hands of the parents
on either side; that having given their consent, some
months previously, the elders had put themselves out
of court. Though he did not hold with a great,

a respectable, he might say a host of divines, those sacramental views of the marriage-ceremony—for which there was a great deal to be said—yet he held it, if possible, even more sacredly than they; conceiving that though marriages were made before the civil magistrate, and without the priest, yet they were, before Heaven, binding and indissoluble.

'It is not merely, sir,' says Jack, turning to his father, 'those whom I, John Lambert, Priest, have joined, let no man put asunder; it is those whom *God* has joined let no man separate.' (Here he took off his hat, as he told the story to me.) 'My views are clear upon the point, and surely these young people were joined, or permitted to plight themselves to each other by the consent of you, the priest of your own family. My views, I say, are clear, and I will lay them down at length in a series of two or three discourses which, no doubt, will satisfy you. Upon which,' says Jack, 'my father said, "I am satisfied already, my dear boy," and my lively little Het (who has much archness) whispers to me, "Jack, mother and I will make you a dozen shirts, as sure as eggs is eggs."'

'Whilst we were talking,' Mr. Lambert resumed, 'my sister Theodosia made her appearance, I must say very much agitated and pale, kissed our father, and sat down at his side, and took a sippet of toast —(my dear George, this port is excellent, and I drink your health)—and took a sippet of toast and dipped it in his negus.

'"You should have been here to hear Jack's sermon!" says Hester. "He has been preaching most beautifully."

'"Has he?" asks Theodosia, who is too languid and weak, poor thing, much to care for the exercises of eloquence, or the display of authorities, such as

I must own,' says Jack, 'it was given to me this afternoon to bring forward.

'"He has talked for three-quarters of an hour by Shrewsbury clock," says my father, though I certainly had not talked so long or half so long *by my own watch*. "And his discourse has been you, my dear," says papa, playing with Theodosia's hand.

'"Me, papa?"

'"You and—and Mr. Warrington—and—and George, my love," says papa. Upon which' (says Mr. Jack) 'my sister came closer to the General, and laid her head upon him, and wept upon his shoulder.

'"This is different, sir," says I, "to a passage I remember in Pausanias."

'"In Pausanias? Indeed!" said the General. "And pray, who was he?"

'I smiled at my father's simplicity in exposing his ignorance before his children. "When Ulysses was taking away Penelope from her father, the King hastened after his daughter and bridegroom, and besought his darling to return. Whereupon it is related, Ulysses offered her her choice,—whether she would return, or go on with him? Upon which the daughter of Icarius covered her face with her veil. For want of a veil my sister has taken refuge in your waistcoat, sir," I said, and we all laughed; though my mother vowed that if such a proposal had been made to *her*, or Penelope had been a girl of spirit, she would have gone home with her father that instant.

'"But I am not a girl of any spirit, dear mother!" says Theodosia, still *in gremio patris*. I do not remember that this habit of caressing was frequent in my own youth,' continues Jack. 'But after some more discourse, Brother Warrington! I bethought me of you, and left my parents insisting upon Theodosia returning to bed. The late transactions have, it appears, weakened and agitated her much. I myself have experienced, in my own case, how full of *solliciti timoris* is a certain passion ; how it racks the spirits ; and I make no doubt, if carried far enough, or indulged to the extent to which women (who have little philosophy) will permit it to go—I make no doubt, I say, is ultimately injurious to the health. My service to you, brother !'

From grief to hope, how rapid the change was ! What a flood of happiness poured into my soul, and glowed in my whole being ! Landlord, more port ! Would honest Jack have drunk a binful I would have treated him ; and, to say truth, Jack's sympathy was large in this case, and it had been generous all day. I decline to score the bottles of port : and place to the fabulous computations of interested waiters, the amount scored against me in the reckoning. Jack was my dearest, best of brothers. My friendship for him I swore should be eternal. If I could do him any service, were it a bishopric, by George ! he should have it. He says I was interrupted by the watchman rhapsodising verses beneath the loved one's window. I know not. I know I awoke joyfully and rapturously, in spite of a racking headache, the next morning.

Nor did I know the extent of my happiness quite, or the entire conversion of my dear noble enemy of the previous morning. It must have been galling to the pride of an elder man to have to yield to representations and objections couched in language so little dutiful as that I had used towards Mr. Lambert. But the true Christian gentleman, retiring from his talk with me, mortified and wounded by my asperity of remonstrance, as well as by the pain which he saw his beloved daughter suffer, went thoughtfully and

sadly to his business, as he subsequently told me, and
in the afternoon (as his custom not unfrequently was)
into a church which was open for prayers. And it
was here, on his knees, submitting his case in the
quarter whither he frequently, though privately, came
for guidance and comfort, that it seemed to him that
his child was right in her persistent fidelity to me, and
himself wrong in demanding her utter submission.
Hence Jack's cause was won almost before he began
to plead it; and the brave gentle heart, which could
bear no rancour, which bled at inflicting pain on those
it loved, which even shrank from asserting authority
or demanding submission, was only too glad to return
to its natural pulses of love and affection.

CHAPTER LXXVIII

PYRAMUS AND THISBE

IN examining the old papers at home, years afterwards,
I found, docketed and labelled with my mother's
well-known neat handwriting, 'From London, April,
1760. My son's dreadful letter.'

When it came to be mine I burnt the document,
not choosing that that story of domestic grief and
disunion should remain amongst our family annals
for future Warringtons to gaze on, mayhap, and
disobedient sons to hold up as examples of foregone
domestic rebellions. For similar reasons, I have
destroyed the paper which my mother despatched
to me at this time of tyranny, revolt, annoyance,
and irritation.

Maddened by the pangs of separation from my
mistress, and not unrightly considering that Mrs.
Esmond was the prime cause of the greatest grief

and misery which had ever befallen me in the world,
I wrote home to Virginia a letter, which might have
been more temperate, it is true, but in which I
endeavoured to maintain the extremest respect and
reticence. I said I did not know by what motives
she had been influenced, but that I held her answerable for the misery of my future life, which she had
chosen wilfully to mar and render wretched. She
had occasioned a separation between me and a
virtuous and innocent young creature, whose own
hopes, health, and happiness were cast down for
ever by Mrs. Esmond's interference. The deed
was done, as I feared, and I would offer no comment
upon the conduct of the perpetrator, who was
answerable to God alone; but I did not disguise
from my mother that the injury which she had
done me was so dreadful and mortal that her life
or mine could never repair it; that the tie of my
allegiance was broken towards her, and that I never
could be, as heretofore, her dutiful and respectful
son.

Madam Esmond replied to me in a letter of very
great dignity (her style and correspondence were
extraordinarily elegant and fine). She uttered not a
single reproach or hard word, but coldly gave me to
understand that it was before that awful tribunal of
God she had referred the case between us, and asked
for counsel: that, in respect of her own conduct, as a
mother, she was ready, in all humility, to face it.
Might I, as a son, be equally able to answer for myself, and to show, when the Great Judge demanded
the question of me, whether I had done my own duty,
and honoured my father and mother! *O popoi!* My
grandfather has quoted in his Memoir a line of Homer,
showing how in our troubles and griefs the gods are
always called in question. When our pride, our

avarice, our interest, our desire to domineer, are
worked upon, are we not for ever pestering Heaven
to decide in their favour ? In our great American
quarrel, did we not on both sides appeal to the skies as
to the justice of our causes, sing *Te Deum* for victory,
and boldly express our confidence that the right should
prevail ? Was America right because she was victorious ?
Then I suppose Poland was wrong because she was
defeated !—How am I wandering into this digression
about Poland, America, and what not, and all the
while thinking of a little woman now no more, who
appealed to Heaven and confronted it with a thousand
texts out of its own book, because her son wanted to
make a marriage not of her liking ! We appeal, we
imprecate, we go down on our knees, we demand
blessings, we shriek out for sentence according to law ;
the great course of the great world moves on ; we
pant and strive, and struggle ; we hate ; we rage ;
we weep passionate tears ; we reconcile ; we race and
win ; we race and lose ; we pass away, and other little
strugglers succeed ; our days are spent ; our night
comes, and another morning rises, which shines on us
no more.

My letter to Madam Esmond, announcing my
revolt and disobedience (perhaps I myself was a little
proud of the composition of that document), I showed
in duplicate to Mr. Lambert, because I wished him to
understand what my relations to my mother were, and
how I was determined, whatever of threats or quarrels
the future might bring, never for my own part to consider my separation from Theo as other than a forced
one. Whenever I could see her again I would. My
word given to her was *in secula seculorum*, or binding
at least as long as my life should endure. I implied
that the girl was similarly bound to me, and her poor
father knew indeed as much. He might separate us ;

as he might give her a dose of poison, and the gentle obedient creature would take it and die ; but the death or separation would be his doing : let him answer them. Now he was tender about his children to weakness, and could not have the heart to submit any one of them—this one especially—to torture. We had tried to part : we could not. He had endeavoured to separate us : it was more than was in his power. The bars were up, but the young couple—the maid within and the knight without—were loving each other all the same. The wall was built, but Pyramus and Thisbe were whispering on either side. In the midst of all his grief and perplexity, Uncle Lambert had plenty of humour, and could not but see that his *rôle* was rather a sorry one. Light was beginning to show through that lime and rough plaster of the wall : the lovers were getting their hands through, then their heads through—indeed, it was wall's best business to retire.

I forget what happened stage by stage and day by day ; nor, for the instruction of future ages, does it much matter. When my descendants have love-scrapes of their own, they will find their own means of getting out of their troubles. I believe I did not go back to Dean Street, but that practice of driving in the open air was considered most healthful for Miss Lambert. I got a fine horse, and rode by the side of her carriage. The old woman at Tottenham Court came to know both of us quite well, and nod and wink in the most friendly manner when we passed by. I fancy the old goody was not unaccustomed to interest herself in young couples, and has dispensed the hospitality of her roadside cottage to more than one pair.

The doctor and the country air effected a prodigious cure upon Miss Lambert. Hetty always attended as

duenna, and sometimes of his holiday, Master Charley
rode my horse, when I got into the carriage. What
a deal of love-making Miss Hetty heard!—with what
exemplary patience she listened to it! I do not say
she went to hear the Methodist sermons any more, but
'tis certain that when we had a closed carriage she
would very kindly and considerately look out of the
window. Then, what heaps of letters there were!—
what running to and fro! Gumbo's bandy legs were
for ever on the trot from my quarters to Dean Street;
and, on my account or her own, Mrs. Molly, the girls'
maid, was for ever bringing back answers to Bloomsbury. By the time when the autumn leaves began to
turn pale, Miss Theo's roses were in full bloom again,
and my good Doctor Heberden's cure was pronounced
to be complete. What else happened during this
blessed period? Mr. Warrington completed his great
tragedy of ' Pocahontas,' which was not only accepted
by Mr. Garrick this time (his friend Doctor Johnson
having spoken not unfavourably of the work), but
my friend and cousin, Hagan, was engaged by the
manager to perform the part of the hero, Captain
Smith. Hagan's engagement was not made before it
was wanted. I had helped him and his family with
means disproportioned, perhaps, to my power, especially considering my feud with Madam Esmond, whose
answer to my angry missive of April came to me
towards autumn, and who wrote back from Virginia
with war for war, controlment for controlment.
These menaces, however, frightened me little: my
poor mother's thunder could not reach me; and my
conscience, or casuistry, supplied me with other inter-
pretations for her texts of Scripture, so that her oracles
had not the least weight with me in frightening me
from my purpose. How my new loves speeded I
neither informed her, nor any other members of my

maternal or paternal family, who, on both sides, had been bitter against my marriage. Of what use wrangling with them? It was better *carpere diem* and its sweet loves and pleasures, and to leave the railers to grumble, or the seniors to advise, at their ease.

Besides Madam Esmond I had, it must be owned, in the frantic rage of my temporary separation, addressed notes of wondrous sarcasm to my uncle Warrington, to my aunt Madame de Bernstein, and to my Lord or Lady of Castlewood (I forget to which individually), thanking them for the trouble which they had taken in preventing the dearest happiness of my life, and promising them a corresponding gratitude from their obliged relative. Business brought the jovial Baronet and his family to London somewhat earlier than usual, and Madame de Bernstein was never sorry to get back to Clarges Street and her cards. I saw them. They found me perfectly well. They concluded the match was broken off, and I did not choose to undeceive them. The Baroness took heart at seeing how cheerful I was, and made many sly jokes about my philosophy, and my prudent behaviour as a man of the world. She was, as ever, bent upon finding a rich match for me: and I fear I paid many compliments at her house to a rich young soap-boiler's daughter from Mile End, whom the worthy Baroness wished to place in my arms.

'You court her with infinite wit and esprit, my dear,' says my pleased kinswoman, 'but she does not understand half you say, and the other half, I think, frightens her. This *ton de persiflage* is very well in our society, but you must be sparing of it, my dear nephew, amongst these *roturiers*.'

Miss Badge married a young gentleman of royal

dignity, though shattered fortunes, from a neighbouring island ; and I trust Mrs. Mackshane has ere this
pardoned my levity. There was another person besides Miss at my aunt's house, who did not understand my *persiflage* much better than Miss herself ;
and that was a lady who had seen James the Second's
reign, and who was alive and as worldly as ever in
King George's. I loved to be with her : but that
my little folks have access to this volume, I could
put down a hundred stories of the great old folks
whom she had known in the great old days—of
George the First and his ladies, of St. John and
Marlborough, of his reigning Majesty and the late
Prince of Wales, and the causes of the quarrel
between them—but my modest muse pipes for boys
and virgins. Son Miles does not care about Court
stories, or if he doth, has a fresh budget from Carlton
House, quite as bad as the worst of our old Baroness.
No, my dear wife, thou hast no need to shake thy
powdered locks at me ! Papa is not going to
scandalise his nursery with old-world gossip, nor bring
a blush over our chaste bread and butter.

But this piece of scandal I cannot help. My aunt
used to tell it with infinite gusto ; for, to do her
justice, she hated your would-be-good people, and
sniggered over the faults of the self-styled righteous
with uncommon satisfaction. In her later days she
had no hypocrisy, at least ; and in so far was better
than some white-washed—— Well, to the story.
My Lady Warrington, one of the tallest and the most
virtuous of her sex, who had goodness for ever on her
lips and ' Heaven in her eye,' like the woman in Mr.
Addison's tedious tragedy (which has kept the stage,
from which some others, which shall be nameless, have
disappeared), had the world in her other eye, and an
exceedingly shrewd desire of pushing herself in it.

What does she do when my marriage with your ladyship yonder was supposed to be broken off, but attempt
to play off on me those arts which she had tried on
my poor Harry with such signal ill success, and
which failed with me likewise! It was not the
Beauty—Miss Flora was for my master—(and what
a master! I protest I take off my hat at the idea
of such an illustrious connection!)—it was Dora,
the Muse, was set upon me to languish at me and to
pity me, and to read even my godless tragedy, and
applaud me and console me. Meanwhile, how was
the Beauty occupied? Will it be believed that my
severe aunt gave a great entertainment to my Lady
Yarmouth, presented her boy to her, and placed poor
little Miles under her Ladyship's august protection?
That, so far, is certain; but can it be that she sent
her daughter to stay at my Lady's house, which our
gracious lord and master daily visited, and with the
views which old Aunt Bernstein attributed to her?
' But for that fit of apoplexy, my dear,' Bernstein said,
' that aunt of yours intended there should have been a
Countess in her own right in the Warrington family!' *
My neighbour and kinswoman, my Lady Claypool, is
dead and buried. Grow white, ye daisies upon Flora's
tomb! I can see my pretty Miles, in a gay little
uniform of the Norfolk Militia, led up by his parent
to the lady whom the king delighted to honour, and
the good-natured old Jezebel laying her hand upon the
boy's curly pate. I am accused of being but a lukewarm Royalist; but sure I can contrast those times
with ours, and acknowledge the difference between
the late Sovereign and the present, who, born a Briton,

* Compare Walpole's letters in Mr. Cunningham's excellent new
edition. See the story of the supper at N. House, to show what great
noblemen would do for a king's mistress, and the pleasant account of the
waiting for the Prince of Wales before Holland House.—ED.

has given to every family in the empire an example of decorum and virtuous life.*

Thus my life sped in the pleasantest of all occupation ; and, being so happy myself, I could afford to be reconciled to those who, after all, had done me no injury, but rather added to the zest of my happiness by the brief obstacle which they had placed in my way. No specific plans were formed, but Theo and I knew that a day would come when we need say farewell no more. Should the day befall a year hence—ten years hence—we were ready to wait. Day after day we discussed our little plans with Hetty for our confidante. On our drives we spied out pretty cottages that we thought might suit young people of small means ; we devised all sorts of delightful schemes and childish economics. We were Strephon and Chloe to be sure. A cot and a brown loaf should content us ! Gumbo and Molly should wait upon us (as indeed they have done from that day until this). At twenty who is afraid of being poor ? Our trials would only confirm our attachment. The 'sweet sorrow' of every day's parting but made the morrow's meeting more delightful ; and when we separated we ran home and wrote each other those precious letters, which we and other young gentlemen and ladies write under such circumstances ; but though my wife has them all in a great tin sugar-box in the closet in her bedroom, and, I own, I myself have looked at them once, and even thought some of them pretty,—I hereby desire my heirs and executors to burn them all unread, at our demise ; specially desiring my son the Captain (to whom I know the perusal of MSS. is not pleasant) to perform this duty. Those secrets whispered to the penny-post, or delivered between Molly and Gumbo,

* The Warrington MS. is dated 1793.—Ed.

were intended for us alone, and no ears of our
descendants shall overhear them.

We heard in successive brief letters how our dear
Harry continued with the army, as General Amherst's
aide-de-camp, after the death of his own glorious
General. By the middle of October there came news
of the capitulation of Montreal and the whole of
Canada, and a brief postscript in which Hal said he
would ask for leave now, and must go and see the old
lady at home, who wrote *as sulky as a bare*, Captain
Warrington remarked. I could guess why, though
the claws could not reach me. I had written pretty
fully to my brother how affairs were standing with
me in England.

Then on the 25th October comes the news that
His Majesty has fallen down dead at Kensington, and
that George the Third reigned over us. I feared we
grieved but little. What do those care for the
Atridæ whose hearts are strung only to *erota mounon?*
A modest, handsome, brave new Prince, we gladly
accept the common report that he is endowed with
every virtue ; and we cry huzzay with the loyal
crowd that hails his accession : it could make little
difference to us, as we thought, simple young sweethearts, whispering our little love-stories in our
corner.

But who can say how great events affect him ?
Did not our little Charley, at the Chartreux, wish
impiously for a new king immediately, because on His
Gracious Majesty's accession Doctor Crusius gave his
boys a holiday ? He and I, and Hetty, and Theo
(Miss Theo was strong enough to walk many a delightful mile now), heard the heralds proclaim his new
Majesty before Savile House in Leicester Fields, and a
pickpocket got the watch and chain of a gentleman
hard by us, and was caught and carried to Bridewell,

all on account of His Majesty's accession. Had the King not died, the gentleman would not have been in the crowd : the chain would not have been seized ; the thief would not have been caught and soundly whipped ; in this way many of us, more or less remotely, were implicated in the great change which ensued, and even we humble folks were affected by it presently.

As thus. My Lord Wrotham was a great friend of the august family of Savile House, who knew and esteemed his many virtues. Now, of all living men, my Lord Wrotham knew and loved best his neighbour and old fellow-soldier, Martin Lambert, declaring that the world contained few better gentlemen. And my Lord Bute, being all potent, at first, with His Majesty, and a nobleman, as I believe, very eager at the commencement of his brief and luckless tenure of power to patronise merit wherever he could find it, was strongly prejudiced in Mr. Lambert's favour by the latter's old and constant friend.

My (and Harry's) old friend Parson Sampson, who had been in and out of gaol I don't know how many times of late years, and retained an ever-enduring hatred for the Esmonds of Castlewood, and as lasting a regard for me and my brother, was occupying poor Hal's vacant bed at my lodgings at this time (being, in truth, hunted out of his own by the bailiffs). I liked to have Sampson near me, for a more amusing Jack-friar never walked in cassock ; and, besides, he entered into all my rhapsodies about Miss Theo : was never tired (so he vowed) of hearing me talk of her ; admired ' Pocahontas ' and ' Carpezan ' with, I do believe, an honest enthusiasm ; and could repeat whole passages of those tragedies with an emphasis and effect that Barry or Cousin Hagan himself could not surpass. Sampson was the go-between between

Lady Maria and such of her relations as had not disowned her ; and, always in debt himself, was never
more happy than in drinking a pot, or mingling his
tears with his friends in similar poverty. His
acquaintance with pawnbrokers' shop was prodigious.
He could procure more money, he boasted, on an
article than any gentleman of his cloth. He never
paid his own debts, to be sure, but he was ready to
forgive his debtors. Poor as he was, he always found
means to love and help his needy little sister, and a
more prodigal, kindly, amiable rogue never probably
grinned behind bars. They say that I love to have
parasites about me. I own to have had a great liking
for Sampson, and to have esteemed him much better
than probably much better men.

When he heard how my Lord Bute was admitted
into the Cabinet, Sampson vowed and declared that
his Lordship—a great lover of the drama, who had
been to see 'Carpezan,' who had admired it, and who
would act the part of the King very finely in it—he
vowed, by George ! that my Lord must give me a
place worthy of my birth and merits. He insisted
upon it that I should attend his Lordship's levée. I
wouldn't ? The Esmonds were all as proud as
Lucifer ; and, to be sure, my birth was as good as
that of any man in Europe. Where was my Lord
himself when the Esmonds were lords of great
counties, warriors, and Crusaders ? Where were
they ? Beggarly Scotchmen, without a rag to their
backs—by George ! tearing raw fish in their islands.
But now the times were changed. The Scotchmen
were in luck. Mum's the word ! ' I don't envy him,'
says Sampson, ' but he shall provide for you and my
dearest, noblest, heroic Captain ! He SHALL, by
George !' would my worthy parson roar out. And
when, in the month after his accession, His Majesty

ordered the play of 'Richard III.' at Drury Lane, my
chaplain cursed, vowed, swore, but he would have
him to Covent Garden to see 'Carpezan' too. And
now, one morning, he bursts into my apartment,
where I happened to lie rather late, waving the newspaper in his hand, and singing 'Huzzay!' with all
his might.

'What is it, Sampson?' says I. 'Has my brother
got his promotion?'

'No, in truth: but some one else has. Huzzay!
Huzzay! His Majesty has appointed Major-General
Martin Lambert to be Governor and Commander-in-
Chief of the Island of Jamaica.'

I started up. Here was news indeed! Mr.
Lambert would go to his government: and who
would go with him? I had been supping with some
genteel young fellows at the 'Cocoatree.' The
rascal Gumbo had a note for me from my dear
mistress on the night previous, conveying the same
news to me, and had delayed to deliver it. Theo
begged me to see her at the old place at midday the
next day without fail.*

There was no little trepidation in our little council
when we reached our place of meeting. Papa had
announced his acceptance of the appointment, and his
speedy departure. He would have a frigate given
him, and *take his family with him*. Merciful powers!
and were we to be parted? My Theo's old deathly
paleness returned to her. Aunt Lambert thought she
would have swooned; one of Mrs. Goodison's girls
had a bottle of salts, and ran up with it from the
work-room. 'Going away? Going away in a frigate,
Aunt Lambert? Going to tear her away from me?

* In the Warrington MS. there is not a word to say what the 'old
place' was. Perhaps some obliging reader of *Notes and Queries* will be
able to inform me, and who Mrs. Goodison was.—ED.

Great God! Aunt Lambert, I shall die!' She was better when mamma came up from the work-room with the young lady's bottle of salts. You see the women used to meet me: knowing dear Theo's delicate state, how could they refrain from compassionating her? But the General was so busy with his levées and his waiting on Ministers, and his outfit, and the settlement of his affairs at home, that they never happened to tell him about our little walks and meetings: and even when orders for the outfit of the ladies were given, Mrs. Goodison, who had known and worked for Miss Molly Benson as a school-girl (she remembered Miss Esmond of Virginia perfectly, the worthy lady told me, and a dress she made for the young lady to be presented at Her Majesty's Ball)— 'even when the outfit was ordered for the three ladies,' says Mrs. Goodison demurely, 'why, I thought I could do no harm in completing the order.'

Now I need not say in what perturbation of mind Mr. Warrington went home in the evening to his lodgings, after the discussion with the ladies of the above news. No, or at least a very few, more walks; no more rides to dear dear old Hampstead or beloved Islington; no more fetching and carrying of letters for Gumbo and Molly! The former blubbered so, that Mr. Warrington was quite touched by his fidelity, and gave him a crown-piece to go to supper with the poor girl, who turned out to be his sweetheart. What, you too unhappy, Gumbo, and torn from the maid you love? I was ready to mingle with him tear for tear.

What a solemn conference I had with Sampson that evening! He knew my affairs, my expectations, my mother's anger. Psha! that was far off, and he knew some excellent liberal people (of the order of Melchisedec) who would discount the other. The

General would not give his consent? Sampson
shrugged his broad shoulders and swore a great
roaring oath. My mother would not relent? What
then? A man was a man, and to make his own way
in the world, he supposed. He is only a churl who
won't play for such a stake as that, and lose or win,
by George! shouts the chaplain, over a bottle of
Burgundy at the 'Bedford Head,' where we dined.
I need not put down our conversation. We were
two of us, and I think there was only one mind
between us. Our talk was of a Saturday night. . . .

I did not tell Theo, nor any relative of hers, what
was being done. But when the dear child faltered
and talked, trembling, of the coming departure, I
bade her bear up and vowed all would be well, so confidently, that she, who ever has taken her alarms and
joys from my face (I wish, my dear, it were sometimes
not so gloomy), could not but feel confidence; and
placed (with many fond words that need not here be
repeated) her entire trust in me—murmuring those
sweet words of Ruth that must have comforted
myriads of tender hearts in my dearest maiden's
plight; that whither I would go she would go, and
that my people should be hers. At last, one day, the
General's preparations being made, the trunks en-
cumbering the passages of the dear old Dean Street
lodging, which I shall love as long as I shall remember
at all—one day, almost the last of his stay, when the
good man (his Excellency we called him now) came
home to his dinner—a comfortless meal enough it
was in the present condition of the family—he looked
round the table at the place where I had used to sit
in happy old days, and sighed out—'I wish, Molly,
George was here.'

'Do you, Martin?' says Aunt Lambert, flinging
into his arms.

'Yes, I do; but I don't wish you to choke me, Molly,' he says. 'I love him dearly. I may go away and never see him again, and take his foolish little sweetheart along with me. I suppose you will write to each other, children? I can't prevent that, you know; and until he changes his mind, I suppose Miss Theo won't obey papa's orders, and get him out of her foolish little head. Wilt thou, Theo?'

'No, dearest, dearest, best papa!'

'What! more embraces and kisses! What does all this mean?'

'It means that—that George is in the drawing-room,' says mamma.

'Is he? My dearest boy!' cries the General. 'Come to me—come in!' And when I entered he held me to his heart and kissed me.

I confess at this I was so overcome that I fell down on my knees before the dear good man, and sobbed on his own.

'God bless you, my dearest boy!' he mutters hurriedly. 'Always loved you as a son—haven't I, Molly? Broke my heart nearly when I quarrelled with you about this little—What!—odds marrow-bones!—all down on your knees! Mrs Lambert, pray what is the meaning of all this?'

'Dearest, dearest papa! I will go with you all the same!' whimpers one of the kneeling party. 'And I will wait—oh! as long as ever my dearest father wants me!'

'In Heaven's name!' roars the General, 'tell me what has happened?'

What had happened was, that George Esmond Warrington and Theodosia Lambert had been married in Southwark that morning, their banns having been duly called in the church of a certain friend of the Reverend Mr. Sampson.

"In heaven's name!" roars the General,
"tell me what has happened?"

CHAPTER LXXIX
CONTAINING BOTH COMEDY AND TRAGEDY

WE, who had been active in the guilty scene of the
morning, felt trebly guilty when we saw the effect
which our conduct had produced upon him, whom, of
all others, we loved and respected. The shock to the
good man was strange, and pitiful to us to witness who
had administered it. The child of his heart had deceived and disobeyed him—I declare I think, my dear,
now, we would not or could not do it over again ;—
his whole family had entered into a league against him.
Dear kind friend and father ! We know thou hast
pardoned our wrong—in the heaven where thou
dwellest amongst purified spirits who learned on earth
how to love and pardon ! To love and forgive were
easy duties with that man. Beneficence was natural
to him, and a sweet smiling humility ; and to wound
either was to be savage and brutal, as to torture a child,
or strike blows at a nursing woman. The deed done,
all we guilty ones grovelled in the earth, before the
man we had injured. I pass over the scenes of forgiveness, of reconciliation, of common worship together, of final separation when the good man departed
to his government, and the ship sailed away before us,
leaving me and Theo on the shore. We stood there
hand in hand horribly abashed, silent, and guilty. My
wife did not come to me till her father went : in the
interval between the ceremony of our marriage and
his departure, she had remained at home, occupying
her old place by her father, and bed by her sister's
side : he as kind as ever, but the women almost speech-

less among themselves; Aunt Lambert, for once,
unkind and fretful in her temper; and little Hetty
feverish and strange, and saying, ' I wish we were
gone. I wish we were gone.' Though admitted to
the house, and forgiven, I slunk away during those
last days, and only saw my wife for a minute or two
in the street, or with her family. She was not mine
till they were gone. We went to Winchester and
Hampton for what may be called our wedding. It
was but a dismal business. For a while we felt utterly
lonely : and of our dear father as if we had buried
him, or drove him to the grave by our undutiful-
ness.

I made Sampson announce our marriage in the
papers. (My wife used to hang down her head before
the poor fellow afterwards.) I took Mrs. Warrington
back to my old lodgings in Bloomsbury, where there
was plenty of room for us, and our modest married life
began. I wrote home a letter to my mother in
Virginia, informing her of no particulars, but only
that Mr. Lambert being about to depart for his
government, I considered myself bound in honour to
fulfil my promise towards his dearest daughter; and
stated that I intended to carry out my intention of
completing my studies for the Bar, and qualifying
myself for employment at home, or in our own or any
other colony. My good Mrs. Mountain answered
this letter, by desire of Madam Esmond, she said, who
thought that for the sake of peace my communications
had best be conducted that way. I found my relatives
in a fury which was perfectly amusing to witness.
The butler's face, as he said ' Not at home,' at my
uncle's house in Hill Street, was a bland tragedy that
might have been studied by Garrick when he sees
Banquo. My poor little wife was on my arm, and
we were tripping away laughing at the fellow's *accueil*,

when we came upon my Lady in a street stoppage in her chair. I took off my hat and made her the lowest possible bow. I affectionately asked after my dear cousins. 'I—I wonder you dare look me in the face !' Lady Warrington gasped out. 'Nay, don't deprive me of *that* precious privilege!' says I. 'Move on, Peter,' she screams to her chairman. 'Your Lady-ship would not impale your husband's own flesh and blood?' says I. She rattles up the glass of her chair in a fury. I kiss my hand, take off my hat and per-form another of my very finest bows.

Walking shortly afterwards in Hyde Park with my dearest companion, I met my little cousin exercising on horseback with a groom behind him. As soon as he sees us, he gallops up to us, the groom pounding afterwards and bawling out, 'Stop, Master Miles, stop !' 'I am not to speak to my cousin,' says Miles, 'but telling you to send my love to Harry is not speaking to you, is it? Is that my new cousin? I'm not told not to speak to her. I'm Miles, cousin, Sir Miles Warrington Baronet's son, and you are very pretty !' 'Now, *duee* now, Master Miles,' says the groom, touching his hat to us; and the boy trots away laughing and looking at us over his shoulder. 'You see how my relations have determined to treat me,' I say to my partner. 'As if I married you for your relations !' says Theo, her eyes beaming joy and love into mine. Ah ! how happy we were ! how brisk and pleasant the winter ! How snug the kettle by the fire (where the abashed Sampson sometimes came and made the punch); how delightful the night at the theatre, for which our friends brought us tickets of admission, and where we daily expected our new play of ' Pocahontas' would rival the successes of all former tragedies.

The fickle old aunt of Clarges Street, who re-ceived me on my first coming to London with my

wife, with a burst of scorn, mollified presently, and
as soon as she came to know Theo (whom she
had pronounced to be an insignificant little country-
faced chit), fell utterly in love with her, and would
have her to tea and supper every day when there was
no other company. 'As for company, my dears,' she
would say, 'I don't ask you. You are no longer du
monde. Your marriage has put that entirely out of
the question.' So she would have had us come to
amuse her, and go in and out by the back-stairs. My
wife was fine lady enough to feel only amused at this
reception; and I must do the Baroness's domestics
the justice to say that, had we been duke and duchess,
we could not have been received with more respect.
Madame de Bernstein was very much tickled and
amused with my story of Lady Warrington and
the chair. I acted it for her, and gave her
anecdotes of the pious Baronet's lady and her
daughters, which pleased the mischievous lively old
woman.

The Dowager Countess of Castlewood, now
established in her house at Kensington, gave us that
kind of welcome which genteel ladies extend to their
poorer relatives. We went once or twice to her
ladyship's drums at Kensington; but losing more
money at cards, and spending more money in coach-
hire than I liked to afford, we speedily gave up those
entertainments, and, I dare say, were no more missed
or regretted than other people in the fashionable world,
who are carried by death, debt, or other accident out
of the polite sphere. My Theo did not in the least
regret this exclusion. She had made her appearance
at one of these drums, attired in some little ornaments
which her mother left behind her, and by which the
good lady set some store; but I thought her own
white neck was a great deal prettier than these poor

"Here is my friend Mr. Reynolds
that shall paint you"

twinkling stones; and there were dowagers, whose
wrinkled old bones blazed with rubies and diamonds,
which, I am sure, they would gladly have exchanged
for her modest *parure* of beauty and freshness. Not
a soul spoke to her—except, to be sure, Beau Lothair,
a friend of Mr. Will's, who prowled about Bloomsbury afterwards, and even sent my wife a billet. I
met him in Covent Garden shortly after, and promised

to break his ugly face if ever I saw it in the neighbourhood of my lodgings, and Madam Theo was molested
no further.

The only one of our relatives who came to see us
(Madame de Bernstein never came; she sent her
coach for us sometimes, or made inquiries regarding
us by her woman or her major-domo) was our poor
Maria, who, with her husband, Mr. Hagan, often
took a share of our homely dinner. Then we had
friend Spencer from the Temple, who admired our
Arcadian felicity, and gently asked our sympathy for
his less fortunate loves; and twice or thrice the
famous Doctor Johnson came in for a dish of Theo's
tea. A dish? a pailful! 'And a pail the best thing
to feed him, sar!' says Mr. Gumbo indignantly: for
the Doctor's appearance was not pleasant, nor his
linen particularly white. He snorted, he grew red,
and sputtered in feeding; he flung his meat about,
and bawled out in contradicting people: and annoyed
my Theo, whom he professed to admire greatly, by
saying, every time he saw her, 'Madam, you do not
love me; I see by your manner you do not love me;
though I admire you, and come here for your sake.
Here is my friend Mr. Reynolds that shall paint you:
he has no ceruse in his paint-box that is as brilliant
as your complexion.' And so Mr. Reynolds, a most
perfect and agreeable gentleman, would have painted
my wife: but I knew what his price was, and did not
choose to incur that expense. I wish I had now, for
the sake of the children, that they might see what
yonder face was like some five-and-thirty years ago.
To me, madam, 'tis the same now as ever; and your
ladyship is always young!

What annoyed Mrs. Warrington with Doctor
Johnson more than his contradictions, his sputterings,
and his dirty nails, was, I think, an unfavourable

opinion which he formed of my new tragedy. Hagan once proposed that he should read some scenes from it after tea.

'Nay, sir, conversation is better,' says the Doctor. 'I can read for myself, or hear you at the theatre. I had rather hear Mrs. Warrington's artless prattle than your declamation of Mr. Warrington's decasyllables. Tell us about your household affairs, madam, and whether his Excellency your father is well, and whether you made the pudden and the butter sauce. The butter sauce was delicious!' (He loved it so well that he had kept a large quantity in the bosom of a very dingy shirt.) 'You made it as though you loved me. You helped me as though you loved me, though you don't.'

'Faith, sir, you are taking some of the present away with you in your waistcoat,' says Hagan, with much spirit.

'Sir, you are rude!' bawls the Doctor. 'You are unacquainted with the first principles of politeness, which is courtesy before ladies. Having received a university education I am surprised that you have not learnt the rudiments of politeness. I respect Mrs. Warrington. I should never think of making personal remarks about her guests before her!'

'Then, sir,' says Hagan fiercely, 'why did you speak of my theatre?'

'Sir, you are saucy!' roars the Doctor.

'De te fabula,' says the actor. 'I think it is your waistcoat that is saucy. Madam, shall I make some punch in the way we make it in Ireland?'

The Doctor, puffing, and purple in the face, was wiping the dingy shirt with a still more dubious pocket-handkerchief, which he then applied to his forehead. After this exercise, he blew a hyperborean whistle as if to blow his wrath away. 'It *is* de me, sir—though, as a young man, perhaps you need not have told me so.'

'I drop my point, sir ! If you have been wrong, I am sure I am bound to ask your pardon for setting you so !' says Mr. Hagan, with a fine bow.

'Doesn't he look like a god ?' says Maria, clutching my wife's hand : and indeed Mr. Hagan did look like a handsome young gentleman. His colour had risen ; he had put his hand to his breast with a noble air : Chamont or Castalio could not present himself better.

'Let me make you some lemonade, sir ; my papa has sent us a box of fresh limes. May we send you some to the Temple ?'

'Madam, if they stay in your house, they will lose their quality and turn sweet,' says the Doctor. 'Mr. Hagan, you are a young saucebox, that's what you are ! Ho ! ho ! It is I have been wrong.'

'O my Lord, my Polidore !' bleats Lady Maria, when she was alone in my wife's drawing-room :—

'" Oh, I could hear thee talk forever thus,
    Eternally admiring,—fix and gaze
    On those dear eyes, for every glance they send
    Darts through my soul, and fills my heart with rapture !"

Thou knowest not, my Theo, what a pearl and paragon of a man my Castalio is ; my Chamont, my —O dear me, child, what a pity it is that in your husband's tragedy he should have to take the horrid name of Captain Smith !'

Upon this tragedy not only my literary hopes, but much of my financial prospects were founded. My brother's debts discharged, my mother's drafts from home duly honoured, my own expenses paid, which, though moderate, were not inconsiderable,—pretty nearly the whole of my patrimony had been spent,

and this auspicious moment I must choose for my
marriage! I could raise money on my inheritance:
that was not impossible, though certainly costly. My
mother could not leave her eldest son without a maintenance, whatever our quarrels might be. I had
health, strength, good wits, some friends, and reputation—above all, my famous tragedy, which the
manager had promised to perform, and upon the
proceeds of this I counted for my present support.
What becomes of the arithmetic of youth? How do
we then calculate that a hundred pounds is a maintenance, and a thousand a fortune? How did I dare
play against Fortune with such odds? I succeeded,
I remember, in convincing my dear General, and he
left home convinced that his son-in-law had for the
present necessity at least a score of hundred pounds at
his command. He and his dear Molly had begun life
with less, and the ravens had somehow always fed
them. As for the women, the question of poverty
was one of pleasure to those sentimental souls, and
Aunt Lambert, for her part, declared it would be
wicked and irreligious to doubt of a provision being
made for her children. Was the righteous ever forsaken? Did the just man ever have to beg his bread?
She knew better than that! ' No, no, my dears!
I am not going to be afraid on *that* account, I warrant
you! Look at me and my General! '

Theo believed all I said and wished to believe myself. So we actually began life upon a capital of Five
Acts, and about three hundred pounds of ready money
in hand!

Well, the time of the appearance of the famous
tragedy drew near, and my friends canvassed the town
to get a body of supporters for the opening night. I
am ill at asking favours from the great ; but when
my Lord Wrotham came to London, I went, with

Theo in my hand, to wait on his Lordship, who received us kindly, out of regard for his old friend, her father—though he good-naturedly shook a finger at me (at which my little wife hung down her head) for having stole a march on the good General. However, he would do his best for her father's daughter; hoped for a success; said he had heard great things of the piece; and engaged a number of places for himself and his friends. But this patron secured, I had no other. '*Mon cher*, at my age,' says the Baroness, 'I should bore myself to death at a tragedy: but I will do my best; and I will certainly send my people to the boxes. Yes! Case in his best black looks like a nobleman; and Brett in one of my gowns has a *faux air de moi* which is quite distinguished. Put down my name for two in the front boxes. Good-bye, my dear. *Bonne chance!*' The Dowager Countess presented compliments (on the back of the nine of clubs), had a card-party that night, and was quite sorry she and Fanny could not go to my tragedy. As for my uncle and Lady Warrington, they were out of the question. After the affair of the sedan chair I might as well have asked Queen Elizabeth to go to Drury Lane. These were all my friends—that host of aristocratic connections about whom poor Sampson had bragged; and on the strength of whom the manager, as he said, had given Mr. Hagan his engagement! 'Where was my Lord Bute? Had I not promised his Lordship should come?' he asks snappishly, taking snuff (how different from the brisk, and engaging, and obsequious little manager of six months ago!) — 'I promised Lord Bute should come?'

'Yes,' says Mr. Garrick, 'and Her Royal Highness the Princess of Wales and His Majesty too.'

Poor Sampson owned that he, buoyed up by vain

hopes, had promised the appearance of these august personages.

The next day, at rehearsal, matters were worse still, and the manager in a fury.

'Great Heavens, sir!' says he, 'into what a pretty *guetapens* have you led me? Look at that letter, sir! —read that letter!' And he hands me one :—

'My DEAR SIR' (said the letter),—' I have seen his Lordship, and conveyed to him Mr. Warrington's request that he would honour the tragedy of "Pocahontas" by his presence. His Lordship is a patron of the drama, and a magnificent friend of all the liberal arts : but he desires me to say that he cannot think of attending himself, much less of asking his Gracious Master to witness the performance of a play, a principal part in which is given to an actor who has made a clandestine marriage with a daughter of one of His Majesty's nobility.

'Your well-wisher,

'SAUNDERS M'DUFF.

'Mr. D. GARRICK,

'At the Theatre Royal in Drury Lane.'

My poor Theo had a nice dinner waiting for me after the rehearsal. I pleaded fatigue as the reason for looking so pale : I did not dare to convey to her this dreadful news.

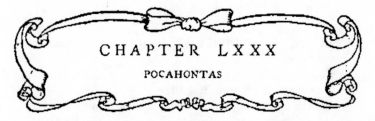

CHAPTER LXXX

POCAHONTAS

THE English public, not being so well acquainted
with the history of Pocahontas as we of Virginia,
who still love the memory of that simple and kindly
creature, Mr. Warrington, at the suggestion of his
friends, made a little ballad about this Indian princess,
which was printed in the magazines a few days before
the appearance of the tragedy. This proceeding,
Sampson and I considered to be very artful and ingenious. 'It is like ground-bait, sir,' says the
enthusiastic parson, 'and you will see the fish rise in
multitudes, on the great day!' He and Spencer declared that the poem was discussed and admired at
several coffee-houses in their hearing, and that it had
been attributed to Mr. Mason, Mr. Cowper of the
Temple, and even to the famous Mr. Gray. I believe
poor Sam had himself set abroad these reports; and,
if Shakspeare had been named as the author of the
tragedy, would have declared 'Pocahontas' to be one
of the poet's best performances. I made acquaintance
with brave Captain Smith, as a boy, in my grandfather's library at home, where I remember how I
would sit at the good old man's knees, with my
favourite volume on my own, spelling out the exploits
of our Virginian hero. I loved to read of Smith's
travels, sufferings, captivities, escapes, not only in
America, but Europe. I become a child again almost
as I take from the shelf before me in England the
familiar volume, and all sorts of recollections of my
early home come crowding over my mind. The old
grandfather would make pictures for me of Smith

doing battle with the Turks on the Danube, or led
out by our Indian savages to death. Ah, what a
terrific fight was that in which he was engaged with
the three Turkish champions, and how I used to delight over the story of his combat with Bonny
Molgro, the last and most dreadful of the three!
What a name Bonny Molgro was, and with what a
prodigious turban, scimitar, and whiskers we represented him! Having slain and taken off the heads
of his first two enemies, Smith and Bonny Molgro
met, falling to (says my favourite old book) ' with
their battle-axes, whose piercing bills made sometimes
the one, sometimes the other to have scarce sense to
keep their saddles : especially the Christian received
such a wound that he lost his battle-axe, whereat the
supposed conquering Turke had a great shout from
the rampires. Yet, by the readinesse of his horse, and
his great judgment and dexteritie, he not only avoided
the Turke's blows, but, having drawn his falchion, so
pierced the Turke under the cutlets, through back
and body, that though hee alighted from his horse, he
stood not long, ere *hee* lost his head *as the rest had
done.* In reward for which deed, Duke Segismundus
gave him 3 Turke's head in a shield for armes and
300 Duckats yeerely for a pension.' Disdaining time
and place (with that daring which is the privilege of
poets) in my tragedy, Smith is made to perform similar
exploits on the banks of our Potemac and James's
River. Our ' ground-bait ' verses ran thus :—

POCAHONTAS.

Wearied arm and broken sword
  Wage in vain the desperate fight :
Round him press a countless horde ;
  He is but a single knight.

Hark ! a cry of triumph shrill
  Through the wilderness resounds,
  As, with twenty bleeding wounds,
Sinks the warrior, fighting still.

Now they heap the fatal pyre,
  And the torch of death they light :
Ah ! 'tis hard to die of fire !
  Who will shield the captive knight ?
Round the stake with fiendish cry
  Wheel and dance the savage crowd,
  Cold the victim's mien and proud,
And his breast is bared to die.

Who will shield the fearless heart ?
  Who avert the murderous blade ?
From the throng, with sudden start,
  See, there springs an Indian maid.
Quick she stands before the knight,
  ' Loose the chain, unbind the ring,
  I am daughter of the King,
And I claim the Indian right ! '

Dauntlessly aside she flings
  Lifted axe and thirsty knife :
Fondly to his heart she clings,
  And her bosom guards his life !
In the woods of Powhattan,
  Still 'tis told, by Indian fires,
  How a daughter of their sires
Saved the captive Englishman.

I need not describe at length the plot of my tragedy,
as my children can take it down from the shelves any
day and peruse it for themselves. Nor shall I, let me
add, be in a hurry to offer to read it again to my
young folks, since Captain Miles and the parson both
chose to fall asleep last Christmas, when, at mamma's

request, I read aloud a couple of acts. But any person having a moderate acquaintance with plays and novels can soon, out of the above sketch, fill out a picture to his liking. An Indian king; a lovely princess, and her attendant, in love with the British captain's servant; a traitor in the English fort; a brave Indian warrior, himself entertaining an unhappy passion for Pocahontas; a medicine-man and priest of the Indians (very well played by Palmer), capable of every treason, stratagem, and crime, and bent upon the torture and death of the English prisoner; these, with the accidents of the wilderness, the war dances and cries (which Gumbo had learned to mimic very accurately from the red people at home), and the arrival of the English fleet, with allusions to the late glorious victories in Canada, and the determination of Britons ever to rule and conquer in America, some of us not unnaturally thought might contribute to the success of our tragedy.

But I have mentioned the ill omens which preceded the day; the difficulties which a peevish, and jealous, and timid management threw in the way of the piece, and the violent prejudice which was felt against it in *certain high quarters*. What wonder then, I ask, that 'Pocahontas' should have turned out not to be a victory? I laugh to scorn the malignity of the critics who found fault with the performance. Pretty critics, forsooth, who said that 'Carpezan' was a masterpiece, whilst *a far superior and more elaborate work* received only their sneers! I insist on it that Hagan acted his part so admirably that *a certain actor and manager of the theatre* might well be jealous of him; and that, but for the cabal made outside, the piece would have succeeded. The order had been given that the play could not succeed; so at least Sampson declared to me. 'The house swarmed with Macs, by George, and they should have the galleries washed with brim-

stone,' the honest fellow swore, and always vowed
that Mr. Garrick himself would not have had the
piece succeed for the world; and was never in such a
rage as during that grand scene in the second act,
where Smith (poor Hagan) being bound to the stake,
Pocahontas comes and saves him, and when the whole
house was thrilling with applause and sympathy.

Anybody who has curiosity sufficient may refer to
the published tragedy (in the octavo form, or in the
subsequent splendid quarto edition of my Collected
Works, and Poems Original and Translated), and
say whether the scene is without merit, whether the
verses are not elegant, the language rich and noble?
One of the causes of the failure was my actual *fidelity
to history*. I had copied myself at the Museum, and
tinted neatly, a figure of Sir Walter Raleigh in a frill
and beard; and (my dear Theo giving some of her
mother's best lace for the ruff) we dressed Hagan
accurately after this drawing, and no man could look
better. Miss Pritchard as Pocahontas, I dressed too
as a Red Indian, having seen enough of *that* costume
in my own experience at home. Will it be believed
that the house tittered when she first appeared?
They got used to her, however, but just at the
moment when she rushes into the prisoner's arms, and
a number of people were actually in tears, a fellow in
the pit bawls out, 'Bedad! here's the Belle Savage
kissing the Saracen's Head;' on which an impertinent
roar of laughter sprang up in the pit, breaking out
with fitful explosions during the remainder of the
performance. As the wag in Mr. Sheridan's amusing
'Critic' admirably says about the morning guns, the
playwrights were not content with one of them, but
must fire two or three; so with this wretched pot-
house joke of the Belle Savage (the ignorant people
not knowing that Pocahontas herself was the very

Belle Sauvage from whom the tavern took its name !).
My friend of the pit repeated it *ad nauseam* during
the performance, and as each new character appeared,
saluted him by the name of some tavern—for instance,
the English governor (with a long beard) he called
the 'Goat and Boots ;' his lieutenant (Barker), whose
face certainly was broad, the 'Bull and Mouth,' and
so on !   And the curtain descended amidst a shrill
storm of whistles and hisses, which especially assailed
poor Hagan, every time he opened his lips.   Sampson
saw Master Will in the green boxes, with some pretty
acquaintances of his, and had no doubt that the
treacherous scoundrel was one of the ringleaders in
the conspiracy.   'I would have flung him over into
the pit,' the faithful fellow said (and Sampson was
man enough to execute his threat), 'but I saw a
couple of Mr. Nadab's followers prowling about the
lobby, and was obliged to sheer off.'   And so the eggs
we had counted on selling at market were broken,
and our poor hopes lay shattered before us !
   I looked in at the house from the stage before the
curtain was lifted, and saw it pretty well filled,
especially remarking Mr. Johnson in the front boxes,
in a laced waistcoat, having his friend Mr. Reynolds
by his side ; the latter could not hear, and the former
could not see, and so they came good-naturedly *à
deux* to form an opinion of my poor tragedy.   I could
see Lady Maria (I knew the hood she wore) in the
lower gallery, where she once more had the opportunity of sitting and looking at her beloved actor
performing a principal character in a piece.   As for
Theo, she fairly owned that, unless I ordered her,
she had rather not be present, nor had I any such
command to give, for, if things went wrong, I knew
that to see her suffer would be intolerable pain to
myself, and so acquiesced in her desire to keep away.

Being of a pretty equanimous disposition, and, as I
flatter myself, able to bear good or evil fortune without disturbance ; I myself, after taking a light dinner
at the ' Bedford,' went to the theatre a short while
before the commencement of the play, and proposed
to remain there, until the defeat or victory was
decided. I own now, I could not help seeing which
way the fate of the day was likely to turn. There
was something gloomy and disastrous in the general
aspect of all things around. Miss Pritchard had the
headache : the barber who brought home Hagan's
wig had powdered it like a wretch ; amongst the
gentlemen and ladies in the green-room, I saw none
but doubtful faces : and the manager (a very flippant,
not to say impertinent gentleman, in my opinion, and
who himself on that night looked as dismal as a mute
at a funeral) had the insolence to say to me, ' For
Heaven's sake, Mr. Warrington, go and get a glass
of punch at the " Bedford," and don't frighten us all
here by your dismal countenance !' 'Sir,' says I, ' I
have a right, for five shillings, to comment upon your
face, but I never gave you any authority to make
remarks upon mine.' ' Sir,' says he in a pet, ' I most
heartily wish I had never seen your face at all !'
' Yours, sir !' said I, ' has often amused me greatly ;
and when painted for Abel Drugger is exceedingly
comic '—and indeed I have always done Mr. G.
the justice to think that in low comedy he was
unrivalled.

I made him a bow, and walked off to the coffee-
house, and for five years after never spoke a word to
the gentleman. When he apologised to me, at a
nobleman's house where we chanced to meet, I
said I had utterly forgotten the circumstance to which
he alluded, and that, on the first night of a play, no
doubt, author and manager were flurried alike. And

added, 'After all, there is no shame in not being
made for the theatre. Mr. Garrick—you were.' A
compliment with which he appeared to be as well
pleased as I intended he should.

Fidus Achates ran over to me at the end of the
first act to say that all things were going pretty well ;
though he confessed to the titter in the house upon
Miss Pritchard's first appearance dressed exactly like
an Indian princess.

'I cannot help it, Sampson,' said I (filling him a
bumper of good punch), 'if Indians are dressed so.'

'Why,' says he, 'would you have had Caractacus
painted blue like an ancient Briton, or Bonduca with
nothing but a cow-skin?'—And indeed it may be
that the fidelity to history was the cause of the
ridicule cast on my tragedy, in which case I, for one,
am not ashamed of its defeat.

After the second act, my aide-de-camp came from
the field with dismal news indeed. I don't know
how it is that, nervous before action,* in disaster I
become pretty cool and cheerful. 'Are things going
ill?' says I. I call for my reckoning, put on my
hat, and march to the theatre as calmly as if I was
going to dine at the Temple ; fidus Achates walking
by my side, pressing my elbow, kicking the link-
boys out of the way, and crying, 'By George, Mr.
Warrington, you are a man of spirit—a Trojan, sir!'
So, there were men of spirit in Troy ; but, alas! fate
was too strong for them.

At any rate, no man can say that I did not bear
my misfortune with calmness : I could no more
help the clamour and noise of the audience than a
captain can help the howling and hissing of the

* The writer seems to contradict himself here, having just boasted of
possessing a pretty equanimous disposition. He was probably mistaken
in his own estimate of himself, as other folks have been besides.—ED.

storm in which his ship goes down. But I was determined that the rushing waves and broken masts should *impavidum ferient*, and flatter myself that I bore my calamity without flinching. 'Not Regulus, my dear madam, could step into his barrel more coolly,' Sampson said to my wife. 'Tis unjust to say of men of the parasitic nature that they are unfaithful in misfortune. Whether I was prosperous or poor, the wild parson was equally true and friendly, and shared our crust as eagerly as ever he had partaken of our better fortune.

I took my place on the stage, whence I could see the actors of my poor piece, and a portion of the audience who condemned me. I suppose the performers gave me a wide berth out of pity for me. I must say that I think I was as little moved as any spectator; and that no one would have judged from my mien that I was the unlucky hero of the night.

But my dearest Theo, when I went home, looked so pale and white, that I saw from the dear creature's countenance that the knowledge of my disaster had preceded my return. Spencer, Sampson, Cousin Hagan, and Lady Maria were to come after the play, and congratulate the author, God wot! (Poor Miss Pritchard was engaged to us likewise, but sent word that I must understand that she was a great deal too unwell to sup that night.) My friend the gardener of Bedford House had given my wife his best flowers to decorate her little table. There they were; the poor little painted standards—and the battle lost! I had borne the defeat well enough, but as I looked at the sweet pale face of the wife across the table, and those artless trophies of welcome which she had set up for her hero, I confess my courage gave way, and my heart felt a pang almost as keen as any that ever has smitten it.

Our meal, it may be imagined, was dismal enough, nor was it rendered much gayer by the talk we strove to carry on. Old Mrs. Hagan was, luckily, very ill at this time; and her disease, and the incidents connected with it, a great blessing to us. Then we had His Majesty's approaching marriage, about which there was a talk. (How well I remember the most futile incidents of the day: down to a tune which a carpenter was whistling by my side at the playhouse, just before the dreary curtain fell!) Then we talked about the death of good Mr. Richardson, the author of 'Pamela' and 'Clarissa,' whose works we all admired exceedingly. And as we talked about 'Clarissa,' my wife took on herself to wipe her eyes once or twice, and say, faintly, 'You know, my love, mamma and I could never help crying over that dear book. Oh, my dearest dearest mother' (she adds), 'how I wish she could be with me now!' This was an occasion for more open tears, for of course a young lady may naturally weep for her absent mother. And then we mixed a gloomy bowl with Jamaica limes, and drank to the health of his Excellency the Governor: and then, for a second toast, I filled a bumper, and, with a smiling face, drank to 'our better fortune!'

This was too much. The two women flung themselves into each other's arms, and irrigated each other's neck-handkerchiefs with tears. 'O Maria! Is not— is not my George good and kind?' sobs Theo. 'Look at my Hagan—how great, how god-like he was in his part!' gasps Maria. 'It was a beastly cabal which threw him over—and I could plunge this knife into Mr. Garrick's black heart—the odious little wretch!' and she grasps a weapon at her side. But throwing it presently down the enthusiastic creature rushes up to her lord and master, flings her arms round him, and embraces him in the presence of the little company.

I am not sure whether some one else did not do likewise. We were all in a state of extreme excitement and enthusiasm. In the midst of grief, Love the consoler appears amongst us, and soothes us with such fond blandishments and tender caresses, that one scarce wishes the calamity away. Two or three days afterwards, on our birthday, a letter was brought me in my study, which contained the following lines :—

FROM POCAHONTAS.

Returning from the cruel fight
How pale and faint appears my knight !
He sees me anxious at his side ;
' Why seek, my love, your wounds to hide ?
Or deem your English girl afraid
To emulate the Indian maid ?'

Be mine my husband's grief to cheer,
In peril to be ever near ;
Whate'er of ill or woe betide,
To bear it clinging at his side ;
The poisoned stroke of fate to ward,
His bosom with my own to guard ;
Ah ! could it spare a pang to his,
It could not know a purer bliss !
'Twould gladden as it felt the smart,
And thank the hand that flung the dart !

I do not say the verses are very good, but that I like them as well as if they were—and that the face of the writer (whose sweet young voice I fancy I can hear as I hum the lines), when I went into her drawing-room after getting the letter, and when I saw her blushing and blessing me—seemed to me more beautiful than any I can fancy out of heaven.

CHAPTER LXXXI

RES ANGUSTA DOMI

I HAVE already described my present feelings as an elderly gentleman, regarding that rash jump into matrimony, which I persuaded my dear partner to take with me when we were both scarce out of our teens. As a man and a father—with a due sense of the necessity of mutton-chops, and the importance of paying the baker—with a pack of rash children round about us who might be running off to Scotland to-morrow, and pleading papa's and mamma's example for their impertinence,—I know that I ought to be very cautious in narrating this early part of the married life of George Warrington, Esquire, and Theodosia his wife—to call out *mea culpa*, and put on a demure air, and sitting in my comfortable easy-chair here, profess to be in a white sheet and on the stool of repentance, offering myself up as a warning to imprudent and hot-headed youth.

But, truth to say, that married life, regarding which my dear relatives prophesied so gloomily, has disappointed all those prudent and respectable people. It has had its trials: but I can remember them without bitterness—its passionate griefs, of which time, by God's kind ordinance, has been the benign consoler—its days of poverty, which we bore, who endured it, to the wonder of our sympathising relatives looking on—its precious rewards and

blessings, so great that I scarce dare to whisper
them to this page; to speak of them, save with
awful respect and to One Ear, to which are
offered up the prayers and thanks of all men. To
marry without a competence is wrong and dangerous,
no doubt, and a crime against our social codes; but
do not scores of thousands of our fellow-beings commit the crime every year with no other trust but in
Heaven, health, and their labour? Are young people
entering into the married life not to take hope into
account, nor dare to begin their housekeeping until
the cottage is completely furnished, the cellar and
larder stocked, the cupboard full of plate, and the
strong box of money? The increase and multiplica-
tion of the world would stop, were the laws which
regulate the genteel part of it to be made universal.
Our gentlefolks tremble at the brink in their silk
stockings and pumps, and wait for whole years,
until they find a bridge or a gilt barge to carry
them across; our poor do not fear to wet their
bare feet, plant them in the brook, and trust to
fate and strength to bear them over. Who would
like to consign his daughter to poverty? Who
would counsel his son to undergo the countless risks
of poor married life, to remove the beloved girl from
comfort and competence, and subject her to debt,
misery, privation, friendlessness, sickness, and the
hundred gloomy consequences of the *res angusta
domi*? I look at my own wife and ask her pardon
for having imposed a task so fraught with pain and
danger upon one so gentle. I think of the trials
she endured, and am thankful for them and for that
unfailing love and constancy with which God blessed
her and strengthened her to bear them all. On this
question of marriage I am not a fair judge: my own
was so imprudent and has been so happy, that I must

THE VIRGINIANS

not dare to give young people counsel. I have
endured poverty, but scarcely ever found it otherwise
than tolerable : had I not undergone it, I never
could have known the kindness of friends, the
delight of gratitude, the surprising joys and con-
solations which sometimes accompany the scanty
meal and narrow fire, and cheer the long day's
labour. This at least is certain, in respect of the
lot of the decent poor, that a great deal of
superfluous pity is often thrown away upon it.
Good-natured fine folks, who sometimes stepped out
of the sunshine of their riches into our narrow
obscurity, were blinded, as it were, whilst we
could see quite cheerfully and clearly : they stumbled
over obstacles which were none to us : they were
surprised at the resignation with which we drank
small beer, and that we could heartily say grace
over such very cold mutton.

The good General, my father-in-law, had married
his Molly, when he was a subaltern of a foot
regiment, and had a purse scarce better filled than
my own. They had had their ups and downs of
fortune. I think (though my wife will never confess
to this point) they had married, as people could do in
their young time, without previously asking papa's
and mamma's leave. * At all events, they were so
well pleased with their own good luck in matrimony,
that they did not grudge their children's, and were by
no means frightened at the idea of any little hardships
which we in the course of our married life might be
called upon to undergo. And I suppose when I made
my own pecuniary statements to Mr. Lambert, I was
anxious to deceive both of us. Believing me to be
master of a couple of thousand pounds he went to

* The editor has looked through Burn's *History of the Fleet Marriages*
without finding the names of Martin Lambert and Mary Benson.

Jamaica quite easy in his mind as to his darling
daughter's comfort and maintenance, at least for
some years to come. After paying the expenses of
his family's outfit the worthy man went away not
much richer than his son-in-law : and a few trinkets,
and some lace of Aunt Lambert's, with twenty new
guineas in a purse which her mother and sisters made
for her, were my Theo's marriage portion. But in
valuing my stock, I chose to count as a good debt a
sum which my honoured mother never could be got
to acknowledge up to the day when the resolute old
lady was called to pay the last debt of all. The sums
I had disbursed for her, she urged, were spent for the
improvement and maintenance of the estate which
was to be mine at her decease. What money she
could spare was to be for my poor brother, who
had nothing, who would never have spent his own
means had he not imagined himself to be *sole heir* of
the Virginian property, *as he would have been*—the
good lady took care to emphasise this point in many
of her letters—but for a half-hour's accident of
birth. He was now distinguishing himself in the
service of his king and country. To purchase his
promotion was his mother's, *she should suppose* his
brother's duty ! When I had finished my bar-
studies and my *dramatic amusements*, Madam Esmond
informed me that I was welcome to return home and
take that place in our colony to which my birth
entitled me. This statement she communicated to
me more than once through Mountain, and before the
news of my marriage had reached her.

There is no need to recall her expressions of
maternal indignation when she was informed of the
step I had taken. On the pacification of Canada, my
dear Harry asked for leave of absence, and dutifully
paid a visit to Virginia. He wrote, describing his

reception at home, and the splendid entertainments
which my mother made in honour of her son. Castlewood, which she had not inhabited since our departure
for Europe, was thrown open again to our friends of
the colony; and the friend of Wolfe, and the soldier
of Quebec, was received by all our acquaintance with
every becoming honour. Some dismal quarrels, to be
sure, ensued, because my brother persisted in maintaining his friendship with Colonel Washington, of Mount
Vernon, whose praises Harry was never tired of singing. Indeed I allow the gentleman every virtue;
and in the struggles which terminated so fatally for
England a few years since, I can admire as well as
his warmest friends, General Washington's glorious
constancy and success.

If these battles between Harry and our mother
were frequent, as, in his letters, he described them
to be, I wondered, for my part, why he should continue at home? One reason naturally suggested
itself to my mind, which I scarcely liked to communicate to Mrs. Warrington; for we had both
talked over our dear little Hetty's romantic attachment
for my brother, and wondered that he had never
discovered it. I need not say, I suppose, that my
gentleman had found some young lady at home
more to his taste than our dear Hester, and hence
accounted for his prolonged stay in Virginia.

Presently there came, in a letter from him, not
a full confession, but an admission of this interesting
fact. A person was described, not named—a being
all beauty and perfection, like other young ladies
under similar circumstances. My wife asked to see
the letter: I could not help showing it, and handed
it to her, with a very sad face. To my surprise she
read it, without exhibiting any corresponding sorrow
of her own.

'I have thought of this before, my love,' I said. 'I feel with you for your disappointment regarding poor Hetty.'

'Ah! poor Hetty,' says Theo, looking down at the carpet.

'It would never have done,' says I.

'No—they would not have been happy,' sighs Theo.

'How strange he never should have found out her secret!' I continued.

She looked me full in the face with an odd expression.

'Pray, what does that look mean?' I asked.

'Nothing, my dear—nothing! only I am not surprised!' says Theo, blushing.

'What,' I ask, 'can there be another?'

'I am sure I never said so, George,' says the lady hurriedly. 'But if Hetty has overcome her childish folly, ought we not all to be glad? Do you gentlemen suppose that you only are to fall in love and grow tired, indeed?'

'What!' I say, with a strange commotion of my mind. 'Do you mean to tell me, Theo, that you ever cared for any one but me?'

'Oh, George,' she whimpers, 'when I was at school, there was—there was one of the boys of Doctor Backhouse's school, who sat in the loft next to us; and I thought he had lovely eyes, and I was so shocked when I recognised him behind the counter at Mr. Grigg the mercer's, when I went to buy a cloak for baby, and I wanted to tell you, my dear, and I didn't know how!'

I went to see this creature with the lovely eyes, having made my wife describe the fellow's dress to me, and I saw a little bandy-legged wretch in a blue camlet coat, with his red hair tied with a dirty ribbon, about whom I forbore generously even to reproach my wife; nor will she ever know that I have looked at the fellow, until she reads the confession in this page. If our wives saw us as we are, I thought, would they love us as they do? Are we as much mistaken in them, as they in us? I look into one candid face at least, and think it never has deceived me.

Lest I should encourage my young people to an imitation of my own imprudence, I will not tell them with how small a capital Mrs. Theo and I commenced life. The unfortunate tragedy brought us nothing; though the reviewers, since its publication of late, have spoken not unfavourably as to its merits, and Mr. Kemble himself has done me the honour to commend it. Our kind friend Lord Wrotham was for having the piece published by subscription, and sent me a bank-note, with a request that I would let him have a hundred copies for his friends; but I was always averse to that method of levying money, and preferring my poverty *sine dote*, locked up my manuscript, with my poor girl's verses inserted at the first page. I know not why the piece should have given such offence at court, except for the fact that an actor who had run off with an earl's daughter performed a principal part in the play; but I was told that sentiments which I had put into the mouths of some of the Indian characters (who were made to declaim against ambition, the British desire of rule, and so forth) were pronounced dangerous and unconstitutional; so that the little hope of Royal favour, which I might have had, was quite taken away from me.

What was to be done? A few months after the failure of the tragedy, as I counted up the remains of my fortune (the calculation was not long or difficult), I came to the conclusion that I must beat a retreat out of my pretty apartments in Bloomsbury, and so gave warning to our good landlady, informing her that my wife's health required that we should have lodgings in the country. But we went no farther than Lambeth, our faithful Gumbo and Molly following us : and here, though as poor as might be, we were waited on by a maid and a lacquey in livery, like any folks of condition. You may be sure kind relatives cried out against our extravagance ; indeed, are they not the people who find our faults out for us, and proclaim them to the rest of the world ?

Returning home from London one day, whither I had been on a visit to some booksellers, I recognised the family arms and livery on a grand gilt chariot which stood before a public-house near to our lodgings. A few loitering inhabitants were gathered round the splendid vehicle, and looking with awe at the footmen, resplendent in the sun, and quaffing blazing pots of beer. I found my Lady Castlewood sitting opposite to my wife in our little apartment (whence we had a very bright pleasant prospect of the river, covered with barges and wherries, and the ancient towers and trees of the Archbishop's place and garden, and Mrs. Theo, who has a very droll way of describing persons and scenes, narrated to me all the particulars of her Ladyship's conversation, when she took her leave.

'I have been here this ever-so-long,' says the Countess, 'gossiping with Cousin Theo, while you have been away at the coffee - house, I dare say, making merry with your friends, and drinking your punch and coffee. Guess she must find it rather lonely here, with nothing to do but work them little caps, and hem them frocks. Never mind, dear ; reckon you'll soon have a companion who will amuse you when Cousin George is away at his coffee-house! What a nice lodging you have got here, I do declare ! Our

new house which we have took is twenty times as big,
and covered with gold from top to bottom : but I
like this quite as well. Bless you ! being rich is no
better than being poor. When we lived to Albany,
and I did most all the work myself, scoured the rooms,
biled the kettle, helped the wash, and all, I was just
as happy as I am now. We only had one old negro
to keep the store. Why don't you sell Gumbo,
Cousin George ? He ain't no use here idling and
dawdling about, and making love to the servant-girl.
Fogh ! guess they ain't particular, these English
people !' So she talked, rattling on with perfect
good-humour, until her hour for departure came ;
when she produced a fine repeating watch, and said it
was time for her to pay a call upon Her Majesty at
Buckingham House. 'And mind you come to us,
George,' says her Ladyship, waving a little parting
hand out of the gilt coach. 'Theo and I have
settled all about it.'

'Here, at least,' said I, when the laced footmen
had clambered up behind the carriage, and our magnificent little patroness had left us ;—'here is one
who is not afraid of our poverty, nor ashamed to remember her own.'

'Ashamed !' said Theo, resuming her lilliputian
needlework. 'To do her justice, she would make
herself at home in any kitchen or palace in the world.
She has given me and Molly twenty lessons in housekeeping. She says, when she was at home to Albany,
she roasted, baked, swept the house, and milked the
cow.' (Madam Theo pronounced the word cow
archly in our American way, and imitated her Ladyship's accent very divertingly.)

'And she has no pride,' I added. 'It was good-
natured of her to ask us to dine with her and my
Lord. When will Uncle Warrington ever think of

offering us a crust again, or a glass of his famous beer?'

'Yes, it was not ill-natured to invite us,' says Theo slily. 'But, my dear, you don't know all the conditions!' And then my wife, still imitating the Countess's manner, laughingly informed me what these conditions were. 'She took out her pocket-book, and told me,' says Theo, 'what days she was engaged abroad and at home. On Monday she received a Duke and a Duchess, with several other members of my Lord's house, and their ladies. On Tuesday came more earls, two bishops, and an ambassador. "Of course you won't come on them days?" says the Countess. "Now you are so poor, you know that fine company ain't no good for you. Lord bless you! father never dines on our company days! he don't like it; he takes a bit of cold meat anyways." On which,' says Theo, laughing, 'I told her that Mr. Warrington did not care for any but the best of company, and proposed that she should ask us on some day when the Archbishop of Canterbury dined with her, and his Grace must give us a lift home in his coach to Lambeth. And she is an economical little person, too,' continues Theo. '"I thought of bringing with me some of my baby's caps and things, which his Lordship has outgrown 'em, but they may be wanted again, you know, my dear." And so we lose that addition to our wardrobe,' says Theo, smiling, 'and Molly and I must do our best without her Ladyship's charity. "When people are poor, they are poor," the Countess said, with her usual outspoken-ness, "and must get on the best they can. What we shall do for that poor Maria, goodness only knows! we can't ask her to see us as we can you, though you are so poor : but an earl's daughter to marry a play-actor! La, my dear, it's dreadful : His Majesty and

the Princess have both spoken of it! Every other
noble family in this kingdom as has ever heard of it,
pities us; though I have a plan for helping those poor
unhappy people, and have sent down Simons, my
groom of the chambers, to tell them on it." This
plan was, that Hagan, who had kept almost all his
terms at Dublin College, should return thither and
take his degree, and enter into holy orders, "when
we will provide him with a chaplaincy at home,
you know," Lady Castlewood added.' And I may
mention here, that this benevolent plan was executed a
score of months later; when I was enabled myself to
be of service to Mr. Hagan, who was one of the
kindest and best of our friends during our own time of
want and distress. Castlewood then executed his
promise loyally enough, got orders and a colonial
appointment for Hagan, who distinguished himself
both as a soldier and preacher, as we shall presently
hear; but not a guinea did his Lordship spare to aid
either his sister or his kinsman in their trouble. I
never asked him, thank Heaven, to assist me in my
own; though, to do him justice, no man could express
himself more amiably, and with a joy which I believe
was quite genuine, when my days of poverty were
ended.

As for my Uncle Warrington, and his virtuous wife
and daughters, let me do them justice likewise, and
declare that, throughout my period of trial, their
sorrow at my poverty was consistent and unvarying.
I still had a few acquaintances who saw them, and of
course (as friends will) brought me a report of their
opinions and conversation; and I never could hear
that my relatives had uttered one single good word
about me or my wife. They spoke even of my
tragedy as a crime—I was accustomed to hear that
sufficiently maligned—of the author as a miserable

reprobate, for ever reeling about Grub Street in rags
and squalor. They held me out no hand of help.
My poor wife might cry in her pain, but they had no
twopence to bestow upon her. They went to church
a half-dozen times in the week. They subscribed
to many public charities. Their tribe was known
eighteen hundred years ago, and will flourish as long
as men endure. They will still thank Heaven that
they are not as other folks are ; and leave the wounded
and miserable to other succour.

I don't care to recall the dreadful doubts and
anxieties which began to beset me : the plan after plan
which I tried, and in which I failed, for procuring
work and adding to our dwindling stock of money. I
bethought me of my friend Mr. Johnson, and when I
think of the eager kindness with which he received
me, am ashamed of some pert speeches which I own
to have made regarding his manners and behaviour. I
told my story and difficulties to him, the circumstance
of my marriage, and the prospects before me. He
would not for a moment admit they were gloomy, or,
si male nunc, that they would continue to be so. I had
before me the chances, certainly very slender, of a
place in England ; the inheritance which must be
mine in the course of nature, or at any rate would fall
to the heir I was expecting. I had a small stock of
money for present actual necessity—a possibility,
' though, to be free with you, sir ' (says he) ' after the
performance of your tragedy, I doubt whether nature
has endowed you with those peculiar qualities which
are necessary for achieving a remarkable literary
success'—and finally a submission to the maternal rule,
and a return to Virginia, where plenty and a home
were always ready for me. ' Why, sir ! ' he cried,
' such a sum as you mention would have been a
fortune to me when I began the world, and my friend

Mr. Goldsmith would set up a coach and six on it.
With youth, hope, to-day, and a couple of hundred
pounds in cash — no young fellow need despair.
Think, sir, you have a year at least before you, and
who knows what may chance between now and then.
Why, sir, your relatives here may provide for you, or
you may succeed to your Virginian property, or you
may come into a fortune!' I did not in the course
of that year, but he did. My Lord Bute gave Mr.
Johnson a pension, which set all Grub Street in a fury
against the recipient, who, to be sure, had published
his own not very flattering opinion upon pensions
and pensioners.

Nevertheless, he did not altogether discourage my
literary projects, promised to procure me work from
the booksellers, and faithfully performed that kind
promise. 'But,' says he, 'sir, you must not appear
amongst them *in formâ pauperis*. Have you never a
friend's coach in which we can ride to see them?
You must put on your best-laced hat and waistcoat;
and we must appear, sir, as if you were doing *them* a
favour.' This stratagem answered, and procured me
respect enough at the first visit or two: but when the
booksellers knew that I wanted to be paid for my
work, their backs refused to bend any more, and they
treated me with a familiarity which I could ill stomach.
I overheard one of them, who had been a footman, say,
'Oh, it's Pocahontas, is it? let him wait.' And he
told his boy to say as much to me. 'Wait, sir!' says
I, fuming with rage and putting my head into his
parlour. 'I'm not accustomed to waiting, but I have
heard you are.' And I strode out of the shop into
Pall Mall in a mighty fluster.

And yet Mr. D. was in the right. I came to him,
if not to ask a favour, at any rate to propose a bargain,
and surely it was my business to wait his time and

convenience. In more fortunate days I asked the
gentleman's pardon, and the kind author of the 'Muse
in Livery' was instantly appeased.

I was more prudent, or Mr. Johnson more fortunate, in an application elsewhere, and Mr. Johnson
procured me a little work from the booksellers in
translating from foreign languages, of which I happen
to know two or three. By a hard day's labour I could
earn a few shillings; so few that a week's work would
hardly bring me a guinea: and that was flung to me
with insolent patronage by the low hucksters who
employed me. I can put my finger upon two or
three magazine articles written at this period,* and
paid for with a few wretched shillings, which papers
as I read them awaken in me the keenest pangs of
bitter remembrance. I recall the doubts and fears
which agitated me, see the dear wife nursing her
infant and looking up into my face with hypocritical
smiles that vainly try to mask her alarm: the struggles
of pride are fought over again: the wounds under
which I smarted, reopen. There are some acts of injustice committed against me which I don't know how
to forgive; and which, whenever I think of them,
awaken in me the same feelings of revolt and indignation. The gloom and darkness gather over me—till
they are relieved by a reminiscence of that love and
tenderness which through all gloom and darkness have
been my light and consolation.

* Mr. George Warrington, of the Upper Temple, says he remembers
a book containing his grandfather's book-plate, in which were pasted
various extracts from reviews and newspapers in an old type, and lettered
outside *Les Chaînes de l'Esclavage*. These were no doubt the contribu-
tions above mentioned; but the volume has not been found, either in the
town-house or in the library at Warrington Manor. The editor, by the
way, is not answerable for a certain inconsistency, which may be remarked
in the narrative. The writer says, p. 229, that he speaks 'without bitterness' of past times, and presently falls into a fury with them. The same
manner of forgiving our enemies is not uncommon in the present century.

CHAPTER LXXXII
MILES'S MOIDORE

LITTLE Miles made his appearance in this world within a few days of the gracious Prince who commands his regiment. Illuminations and cannonading saluted the Royal George's birth, multitudes were admitted to see him as he lay behind a gilt railing at the Palace with noble nurses watching over him. Few nurses guarded the cradle of our little prince: no courtiers, no faithful retainers saluted it, except our trusty Gumbo and kind Molly, who to be sure loved and admired the little heir of my poverty as loyally as our hearts could desire. Why was our boy not named George like the other paragon just mentioned, and like his father? I gave him the name of a little scapegrace of my family, a name which many generations of Warringtons had borne likewise; but my poor little Miles's love and kindness touched me at a time when kindness and love were rare from those of my own blood, and Theo and I agreed that our child should be called after that single little friend of my paternal race.

We wrote to acquaint our royal parents with the auspicious event, and bravely inserted the child's birth in the *Daily Advertiser*, and the place, Church Street, Lambeth, where he was born. 'My dear,' says Aunt Bernstein, writing to me in reply to my announcement, 'how could you point out to all the world that you live in such a *trou* as that in which you have buried yourself? I kiss the little mamma, and send a remembrance for the child.' This remembrance was a fine silk coverlid, with a lace edging fit for a prince. It was not very useful : the price of the lace would have served us much better, but Theo and Molly were delighted with the present, and my eldest son's cradle had a cover as fine as any nobleman's.

Good Doctor Heberden came over several times to visit my wife, and see that all things went well. He knew and recommended to us a surgeon in the vicinage, who took charge of her : luckily, my dear patient needed little care, beyond that which our landlady and her own trusty attendant could readily afford her. Again our humble precinct was adorned with the gilded apparition of Lady Castlewood's chariot wheels ; she brought a pot of jelly, which she thought Theo might like, and which, no doubt, had been served at one of her Ladyship's banquets on a previous day. And she told us of all the ceremonies at Court, and of the splendour and festivities attending the birth of the august heir to the Crown. Our good Mr. Johnson happened to pay me a visit on one of those days when my Lady Countess's carriage flamed up to our little gate. He was not a little struck by her magnificence, and made her some bows, which were more respectful than graceful. She called me cousin very affably, and helped to transfer the present of jelly from her silver dish into our crockery pan with much benignity. The Doctor tasted the sweetmeat, and pronounced it to be excellent. 'The great, sir,' says he, 'are fortunate in every way. They can engage the most skilful practitioners of the culinary art, as they can assemble the most amiable wits round their table. If, as you think, sir, and from the appearance of the dish your suggestion at least is plausible, this sweetmeat may have appeared already at his Lordship's table, it has been there in good company. It has quivered under the eyes of celebrated beauties, it has been tasted by ruby lips, it has divided the attention of the distinguished company, with fruits, tarts, and creams, which I make no doubt were like itself, delicious.' And so saying, the good Doctor absorbed a considerable portion of Lady Castlewood's benefaction; though as regards the epithet delicious I am bound to say, that my poor wife, after tasting the jelly, put it away from her as not to her liking; and Molly, flinging up her head, declared it was mouldy.

My boy enjoyed at least the privilege of having an earl's daughter for his godmother; for this office was performed by his cousin, our poor Lady Maria, whose kindness and attention to the mother and the infant were beyond all praise; and who, having lost her own solitary chance for maternal happiness, yearned over our child in a manner not a little touching to behold. Captain Miles is a mighty fine gentleman, and his uniforms of the Prince's Hussars as splendid as any that ever bedizened a soldier of fashion; but he hath too good a heart, and is too true a gentleman, let us trust, not to be thankful when he remembers that his own infant limbs were dressed in some of the little garments which had been prepared for the poor player's child. Sampson christened him in that very chapel in Southwark, where our marriage ceremony had been performed. Never were the words of the Prayer-book more beautifully and impressively read than by the celebrant of the service; except at its end, when his voice failed him, and he and the rest of the little congregation were fain to wipe their eyes. 'Mr. Garrick himself, sir,' says Hagan, 'could not have read those words so nobly. I am sure little innocent never entered the world accompanied by wishes and benedictions more tender and sincere.'

And now I have not told how it chanced that the

Captain came by his name of Miles. A couple of days before his christening, when as yet I believe it was intended that our firstborn should bear his father's name, a little patter of horse's hoofs comes galloping up to our gate ; and who should pull at the bell but young Miles, our cousin ? I fear he had disobeyed his parents when he galloped away on that undutiful journey.

'You know,' says he, 'Cousin Harry gave me my little horse : and I can't help liking you, because you are so like Harry, and because they are always saying things of you at home, and it's a shame : and I have brought my whistle and coral that my godmamma Lady Suckling gave me, for your little boy ; and if you're so poor, Cousin George, here's my gold moidore, and it's worth ever so much, and it's no use to me, because I mayn't spend it, you know.'

We took the boy up to Theo in her room (he mounted the stair in his little tramping boots, of which he was very proud) ; and Theo kissed him, and thanked him ; and his moidore has been in her purse from that day.

My mother, writing through her ambassador as usual, informed me of her royal surprise and displeasure on learning that my son had been christened Miles—a name not known, at least in the Esmond family. I did not care to tell the reason at the time ; but when, in after years, I told Madam Esmond how my boy came by his name, I saw a tear roll down her wrinkled cheek, and I heard afterwards that she had asked Gumbo many questions about the boy who gave his name to *our* Miles : our Miles Gloriosus of Pall Mall, Valenciennes, Almack's, Brighton.

CHAPTER LXXXIII
TROUBLES AND CONSOLATIONS

IN our early days at home, when Harry and I used to
be so undutiful to our tutor, who would have thought
that Mr. Esmond Warrington of Virginia would turn
bear-leader himself? My mother (when we came
together again) never could be got to speak directly
of this period of my life; but would allude to it as
'that terrible time, my love, which I can't bear to
think of,' 'those dreadful years when there was
difference between us,' and so forth, and though my
pupil, a worthy and grateful man, sent me out to
Jamestown several barrels of that liquor by which his
great fortune was made, Madam Esmond spoke of
him as 'your friend in England,' 'your wealthy
Lambeth friend,' &c., but never by his name; nor
did she ever taste a drop of his beer. We brew our own
too at Warrington Manor, but our good Mr. Foker
never fails to ship to Ipswich every year a couple of
butts of his entire. His son is a young sprig of fashion,
and has married an earl's daughter; the father is a very
worthy and kind gentleman, and it is to the luck of making his acquaintance that I owe the receipt of some of the
most welcome guineas that ever I received in my life.

It was not so much the sum, as the occupation and
hope given me by the office of Governor, which I
took on myself, which were then so precious to me.
Mr. F.'s Brewery (the site has since been changed)
then stood near to Pedlar's Acre in Lambeth: and

247

the surgeon who attended my wife in her confinement, likewise took care of the wealthy brewer's
family. He was a Bavarian, originally named
Voelker. Mr. Lance, the surgeon, I suppose, made
him acquainted with my name and history. The
worthy doctor would smoke many a pipe of Virginia
in my garden, and had conceived an attachment for
me and my family. He brought his patron to my
house : and when Mr. F. found that I had a smatter-
ing of his language, and could sing ' Prinz Eugen,
the noble Ritter ' (a song that my grandfather had
brought home from the Marlborough wars), the
German conceived a great friendship for me : his lady
put her chair and her chariot at Mrs. Warrington's
service : his little daughter took a prodigious fancy to
our baby (and to do him justice, the Captain, who is
as ugly a fellow now as ever wore a queue,* was
beautiful as an infant) : and his son and heir, Master
Foker, being much maltreated at Westminster School
because of his father's profession of brewer, the parents
asked if I would take charge of him ; and paid me a
not insufficient sum for superintending his education.

Mr. F. was a shrewd man of business, and as he
and his family really interested themselves in me and
mine, I laid all my pecuniary affairs pretty unre-
servedly before him ; and my statement, he was
pleased to say, augmented the respect and regard
which he felt for me. He laughed at our stories of
the aid which my noble relatives had given me—my
aunt's coverlid, my Lady Castlewood's mouldy jelly,
Lady Warrington's contemptuous treatment of us.
But he wept many tears over the story of little Miles's
moidore ; and as for Sampson and Hagan, ' I wow,'
says he, ' dey shall have as much beer als ever dey can

---

* The very image of the Squire at thirty, everybody says so.—M.W.
(*Note in the MS.*)

drink.' He sent his wife to call upon Lady Maria, and treated her with the utmost respect and obsequiousness, whenever she came to visit him. It was with Mr. Foker that Lady Maria stayed when Hagan went to Dublin to complete his college terms ; and the good brewer's purse also ministered to our friend's wants and supplied his outfit.

When Mr. Foker came fully to know my own affairs and position, he was pleased to speak of me with terms of enthusiasm, and as if my conduct showed some extraordinary virtue. I have said how my mother saved money for Harry, and how the two were in my debt. But when Harry spent money, he spent it fancying it to be his ; Madam Esmond never could be made to understand she was dealing hardly with me—the money was paid and gone, and there was an end of it. Now, at the end of '62, I remember Harry sent over a considerable remittance for the purchase of his promotion, begging me at the same time to remember that he was in my debt, and to draw on his agents if I had any need. He did not know how great the need was, or how my little capital had been swallowed.

Well, to take my brother's money would delay his promotion, and I naturally did not draw on him, though I own I was tempted ; nor, knowing my dear General Lambert's small means, did I care to impoverish him by asking for supplies. These simple acts of forbearance my worthy brewer must choose to consider as instances of exalted virtue. And what does my gentleman do but write privately to my brother in America, lauding me and my wife as the most admirable of human beings, and call upon Madame de Bernstein, who never told me of his visit, indeed, but who, I perceived about this time, treated us with singular respect and gentleness, that surprised me in one whom I could not but consider as selfish and worldly. In after days I remember asking him how he had gained admission to the Baroness? He laughed : ' De Baroness !' says he. ' I knew de Baron when he was a *walet* at Munich, and I was a brewer-apprentice.' I think our family had best not be too curious about our uncle the Baron.

Thus, the part of my life which ought to have been most melancholy was in truth made pleasant by many friends, happy circumstances, and strokes of lucky fortune. The bear I led was a docile little cub, and danced to my piping very readily. Better to lead him about, than to hang round booksellers' doors, or wait the pleasure or caprice of managers ! My wife and I, during our exile, as we may call it, spent very many pleasant evenings with these kind friends and bene-factors. Nor were we without intellectual enjoy-ments : Mrs. Foker and Mrs. Warrington sang finely together ; and sometimes, when I was in the mood, I read my own play of ' Pocahontas ' to this friendly audience, in a manner better than Hagan's own, Mr. Foker was pleased to say.

After that little escapade of Miles Warrington, junior, I saw nothing of him, and heard of my paternal relatives but rarely. Sir Miles was assiduous at Court (as I believe he would have been at Nero's), and I laughed one day when Mr. Foker told me that he had heard on 'Change 'that they were going to make my uncle a Beer.'—' A Beer ?' says I in wonder.—' Can't you understand de vort, ven I say it ?' says the testy old gentleman. ' Vell, vell, a Lort !' Sir Miles indeed was the obedient humble servant of the Minister, whoever he might be. I am surprised he did not speak English with a Scotch accent during the first favourite's brief reign. I saw him and his wife coming from Court, when Mrs. Claypool was presented to Her

Majesty on her marriage. I had my little boy on my
shoulder. My uncle and aunt stared resolutely at me
from their gilt coach window. The footmen looked
blank over their nosegays. Had I worn the Fairy's
cap and been invisible, my father's brother could not
have passed me with less notice.

We did not avail ourselves much, or often, of that
queer invitation of Lady Castlewood, to go and drink
tea and sup with her Ladyship, when there was no
other company. Old Van den Bosch, however
shrewd his intellect and great his skill in making a
fortune, was not amusing in conversation, except to
his daughter, who talked household and City matters,
bulling and bearing, raising and selling farming-stock,
and so forth, quite as keenly and shrewdly as her
father. Nor was my Lord Castlewood often at home
or much missed by his wife when absent, or very
much at ease in the old father's company. The
Countess told all this to my wife in her simple way.
'Guess,' says she, 'my Lord and father don't pull well
together nohow. Guess my Lord is always wanting
money, and father keeps the key of the box : and
quite right too. If he could have the fingering of all
our money, my Lord would soon make away with it,
and then what's to become of our noble family ? We
pay everything, my dear, except play debts, and them
we won't have nohow. We pay cooks, horses, wine-
merchants, tailors, and everybody—and lucky for them,
too—reckon my Lord wouldn't pay 'em ! And we
always take care that he has a guinea in his pocket,
and goes out like a real nobleman. What that man
do owe to us : what he did before we come—gracious
goodness only knows ! Me and father does our best
to make him respectable : but it's no easy job, my
dear. La ! he'd melt the plate, only father keeps the
key of the strong-room ; and when we go to Castle-

wood, my father travels with me, and papa is armed too, as well as the people.'

'Gracious heavens!' cries my wife, 'your Ladyship does not mean to say, you suspect your own husband of a desire to———'

'To what? Oh no, nothing of course! And I would trust our brother Will with untold money, wouldn't I? As much as I'd trust the cat with the cream-pan! I tell you, my dear, it's not all pleasure being a woman of rank and fashion : and if I have bought a countess's coronet, I have paid a good price for it—that I have!'

And so had my Lord Castlewood paid a large price for having his estate freed from incumbrances, his houses and stables furnished, and his debts discharged. He was the slave of the little wife and her father. No wonder the old man's society was not pleasant to the poor victim, and that he gladly slunk away from his own fine house, to feast at the club when he had money, or at least to any society save that which he found at home. To lead a bear, as I did, was no very pleasant business to be sure ; to wait in a book-seller's ante-room until it should please his honour to finish his dinner and give me audience, was sometimes a hard task for a man of my name and with my pride ; but would I have exchanged my poverty against Castlewood's ignominy, or preferred his miserable dependence to my own? At least I earned my wage such as it was ; and no man can say that I ever flattered my patrons or was servile to them ; or indeed, in my dealings with them, was otherwise than sulky, overbearing, and, in a word, intolerable.

Now there was a certain person with whom Fate had thrown me into a life-partnership, who bore *her* poverty with such a smiling sweetness and easy grace, that niggard Fortune relented before her, and, like some savage Ogre in the fairy tales, melted at the constant goodness and cheerfulness of that uncomplaining, artless, innocent creature. However poor she was, all who knew her saw that here was a fine lady ; and the little tradesmen and humble folks round about us treated her with as much respect as the richest of our neighbours. 'I think, my dear,' says good-natured Mrs. Foker, when they rode out in the latter's chariot, 'you look like the mistress of the carriage, and I only as your maid.' Our landladies adored her ; the tradesfolk executed her little orders as eagerly as if a duchess gave them, or they were to make a fortune by waiting on her. I have thought often of the lady in 'Comus,' and how, through all the rout and rabble, she moves, entirely serene and pure.

Several times, as often as we chose indeed, the good-natured parents of my young bear lent us their chariot to drive abroad or to call on the few friends we had. If I must tell the truth, we drove once to the 'Protestant Hero' and had a syllabub in the garden there ; and the hostess would insist upon calling my wife her Ladyship during the whole afternoon. We also visited Mr. Johnson, and took tea with him (the ingenious Mr. Goldsmith was of the company) ; the Doctor waited upon my wife to her coach. But our most frequent visits were to Aunt Bernstein, and I promise you I was not at all jealous because my aunt presently professed to have a wonderful liking for Theo.

This liking grew so that she would have her most days in the week, or to stay altogether with her, and thought that Theo's child and husband were only plagues to be sure, and hated us in the most amusing way for keeping her favourite from her. Not that my wife was unworthy of anybody's favour ; but her many forced absences, and the constant difficulty of intercourse with her, raised my aunt's liking for a while to a sort of passion. She poured in notes like love-letters ; and her people were ever about our kitchen. If my wife did not go to her, she wrote heartrending appeals, and scolded me severely when I saw her ; and, the child being ill once (it hath pleased Fate to spare our Captain to be a prodigious trouble to us, and a wholesome trial for our tempers), Madam Bernstein came three days running to Lambeth ; vowed there was nothing the matter with the baby ; —nothing at all;—and that we only pretended his illness, in order to vex her.

The reigning Countess of Castlewood was just as easy and affable with her old aunt, as with other folks great and small. 'What *air* you all about, scraping and bowing to that old woman, I can't tell noways!' her Ladyship would say. 'She a fine lady ! Nonsense ! She ain't no more fine than any other lady : and I guess I'm as good as any of 'em with their high heels and their grand airs ! She a beauty once ! Take away her wig, and her rouge, and her teeth ; and what becomes of your beauty, I'd like to know ! Guess you'd put it all in a band-box, and there would be nothing left but a shrivelled old woman !' And indeed the little homilist only spoke too truly. All beauty must at last come to this complexion ; and decay, either under ground or on the tree. Here was old age, I fear, without reverence. Here were grey hairs, that were hidden, or painted. The world was still here, and she tottering on it, and clinging to it with her crutch. For fourscore years she had moved on it, and eaten of the tree, forbidden and permitted. She had had beauty, pleasure, flattery : but what secret rages, disappointments, defeats, humiliations ! what thorns under the roses ! what stinging bees in the fruit! 'You are not a beauty, my dear,' she would say to my wife : 'and may thank your stars that you are not.' (If she contradicted herself in her talk, I suppose the rest of us occasionally do the like.) 'Don't tell me that your husband is pleased with your face, and you want no one else's admiration! We all do. Every woman would rather be beautiful, than be anything else in the world— ever so rich, or ever so good, or have all the gifts of the fairies! Look at that picture, though I know 'tis but a bad one, and that stupid vapouring Kneller could not paint my eyes, nor my hair, nor my complexion. What a shape I had then—and look at me now, and this wrinkled old neck! Why have we such a short time of our beauty? I remember Mademoiselle de l'Enclos at a much greater age than mine, quite fresh and well-conserved. We can't hide our ages. They are wrote in Mr. Collins's books for us. I was born in the last year of King James's reign. I am not old yet. I am but seventy-six. But what a wreck, my dear : and isn't it cruel that our time should be so short?'

Here my wife has to state the incontrovertible proposition, that the time of all of us is short here below.

'Ha!' cries the Baroness. 'Did not Adam live near a thousand years, and was not Eve beautiful all the time? I used to perplex Mr. Tusher with that —poor creature! What have we done since, that our lives are so much lessened, I say?'

'Has your life been so happy that you would prolong it ever so much more?' asks the Baroness's auditor. 'Have you, who love wit, never read Dean Swift's famous description of the deathless people in "Gulliver"? My papa and my husband say 'tis one of the finest and most awful sermons ever wrote. It were better not to live at all, than to live without love ; and I'm sure,' says my wife, putting her handkerchief to her eyes, 'should anything happen to my dearest George, I would wish to go to heaven that moment.'

'Who loves me in heaven ? I am quite alone, child—that is why I had rather stay here,' says the Baroness, in a frightened and rather piteous tone. 'You are kind to me, God bless your sweet face ! Though I scold, and have a frightful temper, my servants will do anything to make me comfortable, and get up at any hour of the night, and never say a cross word in answer. I like my cards still. Indeed, life would be a blank without 'em. Almost everything is gone except that. I can't eat my dinner now, since I lost those last two teeth. Everything goes away from us in old age. But I still have my cards —thank Heaven, I still have my cards !' And here she would begin to doze : waking up, however, if my wife stirred or rose, and imagining that Theo was about to leave her. 'Don't go away, I can't bear to be alone. I don't want you to talk. But I like to see your face, my dear ! It is much pleasanter than that horrid old Brett's, that I have had scowling about my bedroom these ever so long years.'

'Well, Baroness ! still at your cribbage ?' (We may fancy a noble Countess interrupting a game at cards between Theo and Aunt Bernstein.) 'Me and my Lord Esmond have come to see you ! Go and shake hands with grand-aunt, Esmond, and tell her Ladyship that your Lordship's a good boy !'

'My Lordship's a good boy,' says the child. (Madam Theo used to act these scenes for me in a very lively way.)

'And if he is, I guess he don't take after his father,' shrieks out Lady Castlewood. She chose to fancy that Aunt Bernstein was deaf, and always bawled at the old lady.

'Your Ladyship chose my nephew for better or for worse,' says Aunt Bernstein, who was now always very much flurried in the presence of the young Countess.

'But he is a precious deal worse than ever I thought he was. I am speaking of your pa, Ezzy. If it wasn't for your mother, my son, Lord knows what would become of you! We are a-going to see his little Royal Highness. Sorry to see your Ladyship not looking quite so well to-day. We can't always remain young; and la! how we *do* change as we grow old! Go up and kiss that lady, Ezzy. She has got a little boy, too. Why, bless us! have you got the child downstairs?' Indeed, Master Miles was down below, for special reasons accompanying his mother on her visits to Aunt Bernstein sometimes; and our aunt desired the mother's company so much, that she was actually fain to put up with the child. 'So you have got the child here? Oh, you sly-boots!' says the Countess. 'Guess you come after the old lady's money. La bless you! Don't look so frightened. She can't hear a single word I say. Come, Ezzy. Good-bye, aunt!' And my Lady Countess rustles out of the room.

Did Aunt Bernstein hear her or not? Where was the wit for which the old lady had been long famous? and was that fire put out, as well as the brilliancy of her eyes? With other people she was still ready enough, and unsparing of her sarcasms. When the Dowager of Castlewood and Lady Fanny visited her (these exalted ladies treated my wife with perfect in-difference and charming good-breeding)—the Baroness, in their society, was stately, easy, and even command-ing. She would mischievously caress Mrs. Warring-

ton before them ; in her absence, vaunt my wife's
good-breeding ; say that her nephew had made a
foolish match perhaps, but that I certainly had taken
a charming wife. 'In a word, I praise you so to
them, my dear,' says she, 'that I think they would
like to tear your eyes out.' But before the little
American 'tis certain that she was uneasy and
trembled. She was so afraid, that she actually did not
dare to deny her the door ; and, the Countess's back
turned, did not even abuse her. However much they
might dislike her, my ladies did not tear out Theo's
eyes. Once they drove to our cottage at Lambeth,
where my wife happened to be sitting at the open
window, holding her child on her knee, and in full
view of her visitors. A gigantic footman strutted
through our little garden, and delivered their Ladyships' visiting tickets at our door. Their hatred hurt
us no more than their visit pleased us. When next
we had the loan of our friend the brewer's carriage, Mrs.
Warrington drove to Kensington, and Gumbo handed
over to the giant our cards in return for those which
his noble mistresses had bestowed on us.

The Baroness had a coach, but seldom thought of
giving it to us ; and would let Theo and her maid and
baby start from Clarges Street in the rain, with a
faint excuse that she was afraid to ask her coachman
to take his horses out. But, twice on her return
home, my wife was frightened by rude fellows on the
other side of Westminster Bridge ; and I fairly told
my aunt that I should forbid Mrs. Warrington to go
to her, unless she could be brought home in safety ;
so grumbling Jehu had to drive his horses through
the darkness. He grumbled at my shillings : he
did not know how few I had. Our poverty wore
a pretty decent face. My relatives never thought
of relieving it, nor I of complaining before them. I

don't know how Sampson got a windfall of guineas ; but, I remember, he brought me six once ; and they were more welcome than any money I ever had in my life. He had been looking into Mr. Miles's crib, as the child lay asleep ; and, when the parson went away, I found the money in the baby's little rosy hand. Yes, love is best of all. I have many such benefactions registered in my heart—precious welcome fountains springing up in desert places, kind friendly lights cheering our despondency and gloom.

This worthy divine was willing enough to give as much of his company as she chose to Madame de Bernstein, whether for cards or theology. Having known her Ladyship for many years now, Sampson could see, and averred to us, that she was breaking fast ; and as he spoke of her evidently increasing infirmities, and of the probability of their fatal termination, Mr. S. would discourse to us in a very feeling manner of the necessity for preparing for a future world ; of the vanities of this, and of the hope that in another there might be happiness for all repentant sinners.

'I have been a sinner for one,' says the chaplain, bowing his head, 'God knoweth, and I pray him to pardon me. I fear, sir, your aunt, the Lady Baroness, is not in such a state of mind as will fit her very well for the change which is imminent. I am but a poor weak wretch, and no prisoner in Newgate could confess that more humbly and heartily. Once or twice of late, I have sought to speak on this matter with her Ladyship, but she has received me very roughly. "Parson," says she, "if you come for cards 'tis mighty well, but I will thank you to spare me your sermons." What can I do, sir ? I have called more than once of late, and Mr. Case hath told me his lady was unable to see me.' In fact Madam Bernstein told my

wife, whom she never refused, as I said, that the poor
chaplain's *ton* was unendurable, and as for his theology,
' Haven't I been a Bishop's wife ? ' says she, ' and do
I want this creature to teach me ? '

The old lady was as impatient of doctors as of
divines ; pretending that my wife was ailing, and
that it was more convenient for our good Doctor
Heberden to visit her in Clarges Street than to travel
all the way to our Lambeth lodgings, we got
Dr. H. to see Theo at our aunt's house, and prayed
him if possible to offer his advice to the Baroness : we
made Mrs. Brett, her woman, describe her ailments, and
the Doctor confirmed our opinion that they were
most serious, and might speedily end. She would
rally briskly enough of some evenings, and entertain
a little company ; but of late she scarcely went
abroad at all. A somnolence, which we had remarked
in her, was attributable in part to opiates which she
was in the habit of taking ; and she used these
narcotics to smother habitual pain. One night, as we
two sat with her (Mr. Miles was weaned by this time,
and his mother could leave him to the charge of our
faithful Molly), she fell asleep over her cards. We
hushed the servants who came to lay out the supper-
table (she would always have this luxurious, nor could
any injunction of ours or the Doctor's teach her
abstinence), and we sat a while as we had often done
before, waiting in silence till she should arouse from
her doze.

When she awoke, she looked fixedly at me for a
while, fumbled with the cards, and dropped them
again in her lap, and said, ' Henry, have I been long
asleep ? ' I thought at first that it was for my
brother she mistook me ; but she went on quickly,
and with eyes fixed as upon some very far distant
object, and said, ' My dear, 'tis of no use, I am not

good enough for you. I love cards and play, and
Court ; and oh, Harry, you don't know all !' Here
her voice changed, and she flung her head up.
' His father married Anne Hyde, and sure the Esmond
blood is as good as any that's not Royal. Mamma,
you must please to treat me with more respect. Vos
sermons me fatiguent ; entendez vous ?—faites place
à mon Altesse Royale : mesdames, me connaissez-
vous ? je suis la——' Here she broke out into
frightful hysterical shrieks and laughter, and as we
ran up to her alarmed, ' Oui, Henri,' she says, ' il a
juré de m'épouser, et les princes tiennent parole—
n'est-ce pas ? Oh oui ! ils tiennent parole ; si non,
tu le tueras, cousin ; tu le—ah ! que je suis folle !'
And the pitiful shrieks and laughter recommenced.
Ere her frightened people had come up to her
summons, the poor thing had passed out of this mood
into another ; but always labouring under the same
delusion—that I was the Henry of past times, who
had loved her and had been forsaken by her, whose
bones were lying far away by the banks of the
Potomac. My wife and the women put the poor
lady to bed as I ran myself for medical aid. She
rambled, still talking wildly, through the night, with
her nurses and the surgeon sitting by her. Then she
fell into a sleep, brought on by more opiate. When
she awoke, her mind did not actually wander ; but
her speech was changed, and one arm and side were
paralysed.

'Tis needless to relate the progress and termination
of her malady, or watch that expiring flame of life as it
gasps and flickers. Her senses would remain with
her for awhile (and then she was never satisfied unless
Theo was by her bedside), or again her mind would
wander, and the poor decrepit creature, lying upon
her bed, would imagine herself young again, and

speak incoherently of the scenes and incidents of her early days. Then she would address me as Henry again, and call upon me to revenge some insult or slight, of which (whatever my suspicions might be) the only record lay in her insane memory. 'They have always been so,' she would murmur: 'they never loved man or woman but they forsook them. Je me vengerai, oh oui, je me vengerai! I know them all: I know them all: and I will go to my Lord Stair with the list. Don't tell me! His religion can't be the right one. I will go back to my mother's, though she does not love me. She never did. Why don't you, mother? Is it because I am too wicked? Ah! pitié! pitié! O mon père! I will make my confession'—and here the unhappy paralysed lady made as if she would move in her bed.

Let us draw the curtain round it. I think with awe still of those rapid words, uttered in the shadow of the canopy, as my pallid wife sits by, her Prayer-book on her knee; as the attendants move to and fro noiselessly; as the clock ticks without, and strikes the fleeting hours; as the sun fails upon the Kneller picture of Beatrix in her beauty, with the blushing cheeks, the smiling lips, the wavering auburn tresses, and the eyes which seem to look towards the dim figure moaning in the bed. I could not for a while understand why our aunt's attendants were so anxious that we should quit it. But towards evening a servant stole in, and whispered her woman; and then Brett, looking rather disturbed, begged us to go downstairs, as the—as the Doctor was come to visit the Baroness. I did not tell my wife, at the time, who 'the Doctor' was; but as the gentleman slid by us, and passed upstairs, I saw at once that he was a Catholic ecclesiastic. When Theo next saw our poor lady, she was speechless; she never recognised any one about her,

and so passed unconsciously out of life. During her
illness her relatives had called assiduously enough,
though she would see none of them save us. But
when she was gone, and we descended to the lower
rooms after all was over, we found Castlewood with
his white face, and my Lady from Kensington, and
Mr. Will, already assembled in the parlour. They
looked greedily at us as we appeared. They were
hungry for the prey.

When our aunt's will was opened, we found it was
dated five years back, and everything she had was left
to her dear nephew, Henry Esmond Warrington of
Castlewood in Virginia, 'in affectionate love and remembrance of the name which he bore.' The property was not great. Her revenue had been derived
from pensions from the Crown as it appeared (for
what services I cannot say), but the pensions of course
died with her, and there were only a few hundred
pounds, besides jewels, trinkets, and the furniture of
the house in Clarges Street, of which all London
came to the sale. Mr. Walpole bid for her portrait,
but I made free with Harry's money so far as to buy
the picture in : and it now hangs over the mantelpiece
of the chamber in which I write. What with jewels,
laces, trinkets, and old china which she had gathered
—Harry became possessed of more than four thousand
pounds by his aunt's legacy. I made so free as to lay
my hand upon a hundred, which came, just as my
stock was reduced to twenty pounds ; and I procured
bills for the remainder, which I forwarded to Captain
Henry Esmond in Virginia. Nor should I have
scrupled to take more (for my brother was indebted
to me in a much greater sum), but he wrote me there
was another wonderful opportunity for buying an
estate and negroes in our neighbourhood at home ;
and Theo and I were only too glad to forego our

little claim, so as to establish our brother's fortune.
As to mine, poor Harry at this time did not know the
state of it.   My mother had never informed him that
she had ceased remitting to me.   She helped him with
a considerable sum, the result of her savings, for the
purchase of his new estate ; and Theo and I were most
heartily thankful at his prosperity.

And how strange ours was !   By what curious good
fortune, as our purse was emptied, was it filled again !
I had actually come to the end of our stock, when
poor Sampson brought me his six pieces—and with
these I was enabled to carry on, until my half-year's
salary, as young Mr. Foker's Governor, was due : then
Harry's hundred, on which I laid *main basse,* helped us
over three months (we were behindhand with our
rent, or the money would have lasted six good weeks
longer) : and when this was pretty near expended,
what should arrive but a bill of exchange for a couple
of hundred pounds from Jamaica, with ten thousand
blessings from the dear friends there, and fond scolding from the General that we had not sooner told him
of our necessity—of which he had only heard through
our friend Mr. Foker, who spoke in such terms of
Theo and myself as to make our parents more than
ever proud of their children.   Was my quarrel with
my mother irreparable ?   Let me go to Jamaica.
There was plenty there for all, and employment
which his Excellency as Governor would immediately
procure for me.   'Come to us !' writes Hetty.
'Come to us !' writes Aunt Lambert.   'Have my
children been suffering poverty, and we rolling in our
Excellency's coach, with guards to turn out whenever
we pass ?   Has Charley been home to you for ever so
many holidays, from the Chartreux, and had ever so
many of my poor George's half-crowns in his pocket,
I dare say ?' (this was indeed the truth, for where

was he to go for holidays but to his sister? and was there any use in telling the child how scarce half-crowns were with us?) 'And you always treating him with such goodness, as his letters tell me, which are brimful of love for George and little Miles! Oh, how we long to see Miles!' wrote Hetty and her mother; 'and *as for his godfather*' (writes Het), 'who has been good to my dearest and her child, I promise him a kiss whenever I see him!'

Our young benefactor was never to hear of our family's love and gratitude to him. That glimpse of his bright face over the railings before our house at Lambeth, as he rode away on his little horse, was the last we ever were to have of him. At Christmas a basket comes to us, containing a great turkey, and three brace of partridges, with a card, and '*shot by M. W.*' wrote on one of them. And on receipt of this present, we wrote to thank the child, and gave him our sister's message.

To this letter there came a reply from Lady Warrington, who said she was bound to inform me, that in visiting me her child had been guilty of *disobedience*, and that she learned his visit to me now for the first time. Knowing *my* views regarding *duty to my parents* (which I had exemplified *in my marriage*), she could not wish her son to adopt them. And fervently hoping that I might be brought to see the errors *of my present course*, she took leave *of this most unpleasant subject*, subscribing herself, &c. &c. And we got this pretty missive as sauce for poor Miles's turkey, which was our family feast for New Year's day. My Lady Warrington's letter choked our meal, though Sampson and Charley rejoiced over it.

Ah me! Ere the month was over, our little friend was gone from amongst us. Going out shooting, and dragging his gun through a hedge after him, the trigger caught in a bush, and the poor little man was brought home to his father's house, only to live a few days and expire in pain and torture. Under the yew-trees yonder, I can see the vault which covers him, and where my bones one day no doubt will be laid. And over our pew at church my children have often wistfully spelt the touching epitaph in which Miles's heartbroken father has inscribed his grief and love for his only son.

CHAPTER LXXXIV

IN WHICH HARRY SUBMITS TO THE COMMON LOT

HARD times were now over with me, and I had to battle with poverty no more. My little kinsman's death made a vast difference in my worldly prospects. I became next heir to a good estate. My uncle and his wife were not likely to have more children. 'The woman is capable of committing any crime to disappoint you,' Sampson vowed; but, in truth, my Lady Warrington was guilty of no such treachery. Cruelly smitten by the stroke which fell upon them, Lady Warrington was taught by her religious advisers to consider it as a chastisement of Heaven, and submit to the Divine Will. 'Whilst your son lived, your heart was turned away from the better world' (her clergyman told her), 'and your Ladyship thought too much of this. For your son's advantage you desired rank and title. You asked and might have obtained an earthly coronet. Of what avail is it now, to one who has but a few years to pass upon earth—of what importance compared to the heavenly crown, for which you are an assured candidate?' The accident caused no little sensation. In the chapels of that enthusiastic sect, towards which, after her son's death, she now more than ever inclined, many sermons were preached bearing reference to the event. Far be it from me to question the course which the bereaved mother pursued, or to regard with other than respect and sympathy any unhappy soul seeking that refuge whither sin and grief and disappointment fly for consolation. Lady Warrington even tried a reconciliation with myself. A year after her loss, being in London, she signified that she would see me, and I waited on her; and she gave me, in her usual didactic way, a homily upon my position and her own. She marvelled at the decree of Heaven, which had permitted, and how dreadfully punished! her poor child's disobedience to her—a disobedience by which I was to profit. (It appeared my poor little man had disobeyed orders, and gone out with his gun, unknown to his mother.) She hoped that, should I ever succeed to the property, though the Warringtons were, thank Heaven, a long-lived family, except in my own father's case, whose life had been curtailed by the excesses of a very ill-regulated youth,—but should I ever succeed to the family estate and honours, she hoped, she prayed, that my present course of life might be altered; that I should part from my unworthy associates; that I should discontinue all connection with the horrid theatre and its licentious frequenters; that I should turn to that quarter where only peace was to be had; and to those sacred duties which she feared—she very much feared—that I had neglected. She filled her exhortation with Scripture language, which I do not care to imitate. When I took my leave she gave me a packet of sermons for Mrs. Warrington, and a little book of hymns by Miss Dora, who has been eminent in that society of which she and her mother became avowed professors subsequently, and who, after the Dowager's death, at Bath, three years since, married young Mr. Juffles, a celebrated preacher. The poor lady forgave me then, but she could not bear the sight of our boy. We lost our second child, and then my aunt and her daughter came eagerly enough to the poor suffering mother, and even invited us hither. But my uncle was now almost every day in our house. He would sit for hours looking at our boy. He brought him endless toys and sweetmeats. He begged that the child might call him Godpapa. When we felt our own grief, (which at times still, and after the lapse of five-and-twenty years, strikes me as keenly as on the day when we first lost our little one)—when I felt my own grief I knew how to commiserate his. But my wife could pity him before she knew what it was to lose a child of her own. The mother's anxious heart had already divined the pang which was felt by the sorrow-stricken father ; mine, more selfish, has only learned pity from experience, and I was reconciled to my uncle by my little baby's coffin.

The poor man sent his coach to follow the humble funeral, and afterwards took out little Miles, who prattled to him unceasingly, and forgot any grief he might have felt in the delights of his new black clothes, and the pleasures of the airing. How the innocent talk of the child stabbed the mother's heart ! Would we ever wish that it should heal of that wound ? I know her face so well that, to this day, I can tell when, sometimes, she is thinking of the loss of that little one. It is not a grief for a parting so long ago ; it is a communion with a soul we love in heaven.

We came back to our bright lodgings in Bloomsbury soon afterwards, and my young bear, whom I could no longer lead, and who had taken a prodigious friendship for Charley, went to the Chartreux School, where his friend took care that he had no more beating than was good for him, and where (in consequence of the excellence of his private tutor, no doubt) he took and kept a good place. And he liked the school so much, that he says, if ever he has a son, he shall be sent to that seminary.

Now, I could no longer lead my bear, for this reason, that I had other business to follow. Being fully reconciled to us, I do believe, for Mr. Miles's sake, my uncle (who was such an obsequious supporter of Government, that I wonder the Minister ever gave him anything, being perfectly sure of his vote) used his influence in behalf of his nephew and heir; and I had the honour to be gazetted as one of His Majesty's Commissioners for licensing hackney-coaches, a post I filled, I trust, with credit, until a quarrel with the Minister (to be mentioned in its proper place) deprived me of *that* one. I took my degree also at the Temple, and appeared in Westminster Hall in my gown and wig. And, this year, my good friend, Mr. Foker, having business at Paris, I had the pleasure of accompanying him thither, where I was received *à bras ouverts* by my dear American preserver, Monsieur de Florac, who introduced me to his noble family, and to even more of the polite society of the capital than I had leisure to frequent; for I had too much spirit to desert my kind patron Foker, whose acquaintance lay chiefly amongst the bourgeoisie, especially with Monsieur Santerre, a great brewer of Paris, a scoundrel who hath since distinguished himself in blood and not beer. Mr. F. had need of my services as interpreter, and I was too glad that he should command them, and to be able to pay back some of the kindness which he had rendered to me. Our ladies, meanwhile, were residing at Mr. Foker's new villa at Wimbledon, and were pleased to say that they were amused with the 'Parisian letters' which I sent to them through my distinguished friend Mr. Hume, then of the Embassy, and which subsequently have been published in a neat volume.

Whilst I was tranquilly discharging my small official duties in London, those troubles were commencing which were to end in the great separation between our colonies and the mother country. When Mr. Grenville proposed his Stamp duties, I said to my wife that the Bill would create a mighty discontent at home, for we were ever anxious to get as much as we could from England, and. pay back as little; but assuredly I never anticipated the prodigious anger which the scheme created. It was with us as with families or individuals. A pretext is given for a quarrel; the real cause lies in long bickerings and previous animosities. Many foolish exactions and petty tyrannies, the habitual insolence of Englishmen towards all foreigners, all colonists, all folk who dare to think their rivers as good as our Abana and Pharpar; the natural spirit of men outraged by our imperious domineering spirit, set Britain and her colonies to quarrel; and the astonishing blunders of the system adopted in England brought the quarrel to an issue, which I, for one, am not going to deplore. Had I been in Virginia instead of London, 'tis very possible I should have taken the provincial side, if out of mere opposition to that resolute mistress of Castlewood, who might have driven me into revolt, as England did the Colonies. Was the Stamp Act the cause of the revolution?—a tax no greater than that cheerfully paid in England. Ten years earlier, when the French were within our territory, and we were imploring succour from home, would the colonies have rebelled at the payment of this tax? Do not most people consider the tax-gatherer their

natural enemy?   Against the British in America
there were arrayed thousands and thousands of the
high-spirited and brave, but there were thousands
more who found their profit in the quarrel, or had
their private reasons for engaging in it.   I protest I
don't know now whether mine were selfish or
patriotic, or which side was the right, or whether
both were not?   I am sure we in England had
nothing to do but to fight the battle out; and,
having lost the game, I do vow and believe that, after
the first natural soreness, the loser felt no rancour.

What made brother Hal write home from Virginia,
which he seemed exceedingly loth to quit, such
flaming patriotic letters?   My kind best brother was
always led by somebody; by me when we were
together (he had such an idea of my wit and wisdom,
that if I said the day was fine, he would ponder over
the observation as though it was one of the sayings of
the Seven Sages), by some other wiseacre when I
was away.   Who inspired these flaming letters, this
boisterous patriotism, which he sent to us in London?
'He is rebelling against Madam Esmond,' said I.
'He is led by some colonial person—by that lady,
perhaps,' hinted my wife.   Who 'that lady' was Hal
never had told us; and, indeed, besought me never
to allude to the delicate subject in my letters to him;
'for Madam wishes to see 'em all, and I wish to say
nothing *about you know what* until the proper
moment,' he wrote.   No affection could be greater
than that which his letters showed.   When he heard
(from the informant whom I have mentioned) that
in the midst of my own extreme straits I had retained
no more than a hundred pounds out of his aunt's
legacy, he was for mortgaging the estate which he
had just bought; and had more than one quarrel with
his mother in my behalf, and spoke his mind with a

great deal more frankness than I should ever have ventured to show. Until her angry recriminations (when she charged him with ingratitude, after having toiled and saved so much and so long for him) the poor fellow did not know that our mother had cut off my supplies, to advance his interests; and by the time this news came to him his bargains were made, and I was fortunately quite out of want.

Every scrap of paper which we ever wrote, our thrifty parent at Castlewood taped and docketed and put away. We boys were more careless about our letters to one another: I especially, who perhaps chose rather to look down upon my younger brother's literary performances; but my wife is not so supercilious, and hath kept no small number of Harry's letters, as well as those of the angelic being whom we were presently to call sister.

'To think whom he has chosen, and whom he might have had! Oh, 'tis cruel!' cries my wife, when we got that notable letter in which Harry first made us acquainted with the name of his charmer.

'She was a very pretty little maid when I left home, she may be a perfect beauty now,' I remarked, as I read over the longest letter Harry ever wrote on private affairs.

'But is she to compare to my Hetty?' says Mrs. Warrington.

'We agreed that Hetty and Harry were not to be happy together, my love,' say I.

Theo gives her husband a kiss. 'My dear, I wish they had tried,' she says, with a sigh. 'I was afraid lest—lest Hetty should have led him, you see; and I think she hath the better head. But, from reading this, it appears that the new lady has taken command of poor Harry,' and she hands me the letter :—

'My dearest George hath been prepared by previous letters to understand how a certain lady has made a conquest of my heart, which I have given away in exchange for something infinitely more valuable, *namely, her own*. She is at my side as I write this letter, and if there is no bad spelling such as you often used to laugh at, 'tis because I have my pretty dictionary at hand, which makes no fault in the longest word, nor *in anything* else I know of : being of opinion that she is *perfection*.

'As Madam Esmond saw all your letters, I writ you not to give any hint of a certain delicate matter—but now *'tis no secret*, and is known to all the country. Mr. George is not the only one of our family who has made a secret marriage, and been scolded by his mother. As a dutifu younger brother I *have followed his example ;* and now I may tell you how this mighty event came about.

'I had not been at home long before I saw *my fate was accomplisht*. I will not tell you how beautiful Miss Fanny Mountain had grown since I had been away in Europe. She saith, "You *never will think so*," and I am glad, as she is the only thing in life I would grudge to my dearest brother.

'That neither Madam Esmond nor my *other* mother (as Mountain is now) should have seen our mutual attachment, is a wonder—only to be accounted for by supposing that love makes other folks blind. Mine for my Fanny was increased by seeing what the treatment was she had from Madam Esmond, who indeed was very rough and haughty with her, which my love bore with a sweetness perfectly angelic (this I will say, though she will order me not to write any such nonsense). She was scarce better treated than a servant of the house—indeed our negroes can talk much more free before Madam Esmond than ever my Fanny could.

'And yet my Fanny says she doth not regret Madam's unkindness, as without it I possibly never should have been what I am to her. Oh, dear brother ! when I remember how great your goodness hath been, how, in my own want, you paid my debts, and rescued me out of prison ; how you have been living in poverty which never need have occurred but for my fault ; how you might have paid yourself back my just debt to you and would not, preferring my advantage to your own comfort, indeed I am lost at the thought of such goodness ; and ought I not to be thankful to Heaven that hath given me such a wife and such a brother !

'When I writ to you requesting you to send me my aunt's legacy money, for which indeed I had the most profitable and urgent occasion, I had no idea that you were yourself suffering poverty. That you, the head of our family, should condescend to be governor to a brewer's son !—that you should have to write for booksellers (except in so far as your own genius might prompt you), never once entered my mind, until Mr. Foker's letter came to us, and this would never have been shown—for Madam kept it secret—had it not been for the difference which sprang up between us.

'Poor Tom Diggle's estate and negroes being for sale, owing to Tom's losses and extravagance at play, and his father's debts before him—Madam Esmond saw here was a great opportunity of making a provision for me, and that with six thousand pounds for the farm and stock, I should be put in possession of as pretty a property as falls to most younger sons in this country. It lies handy enough to Richmond, between Kent and Hanover Court House— the mansion nothing for elegance compared to ours at Castlewood, but the land excellent and the people extraordinary healthy.

'Here was a second opportunity, Madam Esmond said, such as never might again befall. By the sale of my commissions and her own savings I might pay more than half of the price of the property, and get the rest of the money on mortgage ; though here, where money is scarce to procure, it would have been difficult and dear. At this juncture, with our new relative, Mr. Van den Bosch, bidding against us (his agent is wild that we should have bought the property over him), my aunt's legacy most

opportunely fell in. And now I am owner of a good
house and negroes in my native country, shall be called,
no doubt, to our House of Burgesses, and hope to see my
dearest brother and family under my own roof-tree. To
sit at my own fireside, to ride my own horses to my own
hounds, is better than going a-soldiering, now war is
over, and there are no French to fight. Indeed, Madam
Esmond made a condition that I should leave the army,
and live at home, when she brought me her £1750 of
savings. She had lost one son, she said, who chose to
write play-books, and live in England—let the other stay
with her at home.

'But after the purchase of the estate was made, and my
papers for selling out were sent home, my mother would
have had me marry a person of *her* choosing, but by no
means of mine. You remember Miss Betsy Pitts at
Williamsburg? She is in nowise improved by having had
her face dreadfully scarred with small-pock, and though
Madam Esmond saith the young lady hath every virtue, I
own her virtues did not suit me. Her eyes do not look
straight; she hath one leg shorter than another; and oh,
brother! didst thou never remark Fanny's ankles when we
were boys? *Neater I never saw at the Opera.*

'Now, when 'twas agreed that I should leave the army,
a certain dear girl (canst thou guess her name?) one day,
when we were private, burst into tears of such happiness,
that I could not but feel immensely touched by her
sympathy.

'"Ah!" says she, "do you think, sir, that the idea of
the son of my revered benefactress going to battle doth
not inspire me with terror? Ah, Mr. Henry! do you
imagine I have no heart? When Mr. George was with
Braddock, do you fancy we did not pray for him? And
when you were with Mr. Wolfe—oh!"

'Here the dear creature hid her eyes in her handkerchief, and had hard work to prevent her mamma, who
came in, from seeing that she was crying. But my dear
Mountain declares that, though she might have fancied,
might have prayed in secret for such a thing (she owns to

that now), she never imagined it for one moment. Nor, indeed, did my good mother, who supposed that Sam Lintot, the apothecary's lad at Richmond, was Fanny's flame—an absurd fellow that I near kicked into James River.

'But when the commission was sold, and the estate bought, what does Fanny do but fall into a deep melancholy? I found her crying, one day, in her mother's room, where the two ladies had been at work trimming hats for my negroes.

'"What! crying, miss?" says I. "Has my mother been scolding you?"

'"No," says the dear creature. "Madam Esmond has been kind to-day."

'And her tears drop down on a cockade which she is sewing on to a hat for Sady, who is to be head groom.

'"Then why, miss, are those dear eyes so red?" say I.

'"Because I have the toothache," she says, "or because—because I am a fool." Here she fairly bursts out. "Oh, Mr. Harry! oh, Mr. Warrington! You are going to leave us, and 'tis as well. You will take your place in your country, as becomes you. You will leave us poor women in our solitude and dependence. You will come to visit us from time to time. And when you are happy, and honoured, and among your gay companions, you will remember your——"

'Here she could say no more, and hid her face with one hand as I, I confess, seized the other.

'"Dearest, sweetest Miss Mountain!" says I. "Oh, could I think that the parting from me has brought tears to those lovely eyes! Indeed, I fear, I should be almost happy! Let them look upon your——"

'"Oh, sir!" cries my charmer. "Oh, Mr. Warrington! consider who I am, sir, and who you are! Remember the difference between us! Release my hand, sir! What would Madam Esmond say if—if——"

'If what, I don't know, for here our mother was in the room.

'"What would Madam Esmond say?" she cries out.

"She would say that you are an ungrateful, artful, false little——."

' " Madam ! " says I.

' " Yes, an ungrateful, artful, false little wretch ! " cries out my mother. " For shame, miss ! What would Mr. Lintot say if he saw you making eyes at the Captain ? And for you, Harry, I will have you bring none of your garrison manners hither. This is a Christian family, sir, and you will please to know that my house is not intended for captains and their misses ! "

' " Misses, mother ! " says I. " Gracious powers, do you ever venture for to call Miss Mountain by such a name ? Miss Mountain, the purest of her sex ! "

' " The purest of her sex ! Can I trust my own ears ? " asks Madam, turning very pale.

' " I mean that if a man would question her honour, I would fling him out of window," says I.

' " You mean that you—your mother's son—are actually paying honourable attentions to this young person ? "

' " He would never dare to offer any other ! " cries my Fanny ; " nor any woman but you, madam, to think so ! "

' " Oh ! I didn't know, miss ! " says mother, dropping her a fine curtsey, " I didn't know the honour you were doing our family ! You propose to marry with us, do you ? Do I understand Captain Warrington aright, that he intends to offer me Miss Mountain as a daughter-in-law ? "

' " 'Tis to be seen, madam, that I have no protector, or you would not insult me so ! " cries my poor victim.

' " I should think the apothecary protection sufficient ! " says our mother.

' " I don't, mother ! " I bawl out, for I was very angry ; " and if Lintot offers her any liberty, I'll brain him with his own pestle ! "

' " Oh ! if Lintot has withdrawn, sir, I suppose I must be silent. But I did not know of the circumstance. He came hither, as I supposed, to pay court to Miss : and we all thought the match equal, and I encouraged it."

' " He came because I had the toothache ! " cries my

darling. (And indeed she had *a dreadful bad* tooth. And he took it out for her, and there is no end to the suspicions and calumnies of women.)

'"What more natural than that he should marry my housekeeper's daughter—'twas a very suitable match!" continues Madam, taking snuff. "But I confess," she adds, going on, "I was not aware that you intended to jilt the apothecary for my son!"

'"Peace, for Heaven's sake; peace, Mr. Warrington!" cries my angel.

'"Pray, sir, before you fully make up your mind, had you not better look round the rest of my family?" says Madam. "Dinah is a fine tall girl, and not very black; Cleopatra is promised to Ajax the blacksmith, to be sure; but then we could break the marriage, you know. If with an apothecary, why not with a blacksmith? Martha's husband has run away, and——"

'Here, dear brother, I own I broke out a-swearing. I can't help it; but at times, when a man is angry, it *do* relieve him immensely. I'm blest but I should have gone wild, if it hadn't been for them oaths.

'"Curses, blasphemy, ingratitude, disobedience," says mother, leaning now on her tortoiseshell stick, and then waving it—something like a queen in a play. "These are my rewards!" says she. "O Heaven, what have I done, that I should merit this awful punishment? and does it please you to visit the sins of my fathers upon me? Where do my children inherit their pride? When I was young, had I any? When my papa bade me marry, did I refuse? Did I ever think of disobeying? No, sir. My fault hath been, and I own it, that my love was centred upon you, perhaps to the neglect of your elder brother." (Indeed, brother, there was some truth in what Madam said.) "I turned from Esau, and I clung to Jacob. And now I have my reward, I have my reward! I fixed my vain thoughts on this world and its distinctions. To see my son advanced in worldly rank was my ambition. I toiled, and spared, that I might bring him worldly wealth. I took unjustly from my eldest son's portion, that my

younger might profit. And oh ! that I should live to see
him seducing the daughter of my own housekeeper under
my own roof, and replying to my just anger with oaths
and blasphemies ! "

' " I try to seduce no one, madam," I cried out. " If I
utter oaths and blasphemies, I beg your pardon ; but you
are enough to provoke a saint to speak 'em. I won't have
this young lady's character assailed—no, not by my own
mother nor any mortal alive. No, dear Miss Mountain !
If Madam Esmond chooses to say that my designs on you
are dishonourable,—let this undeceive her ! " And, as I
spoke, I went down on my knees, seizing my adorable
Fanny's hand. " And if you will accept this heart and
hand, miss," says I, " they are yours for ever."

' " *You*, at least, I knew, sir," says Fanny with a noble
curtsey, " never said a word that was disrespectful to me,
or entertained any doubt of my honour. And I trust it is
only Madam Esmond, in the world, who can have such an
opinion of me. After what your Ladyship hath said of
me, of course I can stay no longer in your house."

' " Of course, madam, I never intended you should ;
and the sooner you leave it the better," cries our mother.

' " If you are driven from my mother's house, mine,
miss, is at your service," says I, making her a low bow.
" It is nearly ready now. If you will take it and stay in
it for ever, it is yours ! And as Madam Esmond insulted
your honour, at least let me do all in my power to make
a reparation ! " I don't know what more I exactly said,
for you may fancy I was not a little flustered and excited
by the scene. But here Mountain came in, and my
dearest Fanny, flinging herself into her mother's arms,
wept upon her shoulder ; whilst Madam Esmond, sitting
down in her chair, looked at us as pale as a stone. Whilst
I was telling my story to Mountain (who, poor thing, had
not the least idea, not she, that Miss Fanny and I had the
slightest inclination for one another), I could hear our
mother once or twice still saying, " I am punished for
my crime ! "

' Now, what our mother meant by her crime I did not

know at first, or indeed take much heed of what she said ;
for you know her way, and how, when she is angry, she
always talks sermons. But Mountain told me afterwards,
when we had some talk together, as we did at the tavern,
whither the ladies presently removed with their bag and
baggage—for not only would they not stay at Madam's
house after the language she used, but my mother
determined to go away likewise. She called her servants
together, and announced her intention of going home
instantly to Castlewood ; and I own to you 'twas with a
horrible pain I saw the family coach roll by, with six
horses, and ever so many of the servants on mules and on
horseback, as I and Fanny looked through the blinds of
the tavern.

'After the words Madam used to my spotless Fanny,
'twas impossible that the poor child or her mother should
remain in our house : and indeed M. said that she would
go back to her relations in England : and, a ship bound
homewards lying in James River, she went and bargained
with the captain about a passage, so bent was she upon
quitting the country, and so little did *she* think of making
a match between me and my angel. But the cabin was
mercifully engaged by a North Carolina gentleman and
his family, and before the next ship sailed (which bears
this letter to my dearest George) they have agreed to stop
with me. Almost all the ladies in this neighbourhood
have waited on them. When the marriage takes place, I
hope Madam Esmond will be reconciled. My Fanny's
father was a British officer ; and, sure, ours was no more.
Some day, please Heaven, we shall visit Europe, and the
places where *my wild oats* were sown, and where I committed so many extravagances from which my dear brother
rescued me.

'The ladies send you their affection and duty, and to my
sister. We hear His Excellency General Lambert is much
beloved in Jamaica : and I shall write to our dear friends
there *announcing my happiness*. My dearest brother will
participate in it, and I am ever his grateful and affectionate
                                                    'H. E. W.

'*P.S.*—Till Mountain told me, I had no more notion than the *ded* that Madam E. had actially stopt your allowances; besides making you pay for ever so much—near upon £1000 Mountain says—for goods, &c., provided for the Virginian proparty. Then there was all the charges of me *out of prison*, which *I. O. U. with all my hart.* Draw upon me, please, dearest brother—*to any amount*—adressing me to care of ·Messrs. Horn and Sandon, Williamsburg, *privit;* who remitt by present occasion a bill for £225, payable by their London agents on demand. *Please don't acknolledge this in answering:* as there's no good in *botharing women with accounts:* and with the extra £5 by a capp or what she likes for my dear sister, and a toy for my nephew from *Uncle Hal.'*

The conclusion to which we came on the perusal of this document was, that the ladies had superintended the style and spelling of my poor Hal's letter, but that the postscript was added without their knowledge. And I am afraid we argued that the Virginian Squire was under female domination—as Hercules, Samson, and *fortes multi* had been before him.

CHAPTER LXXXV

INVENI PORTUM

WHEN my mother heard of my acceptance of a place
at home, I think she was scarcely well pleased. She
may have withdrawn her supplies in order to starve me
into a surrender, and force me to return with my
family to Virginia, and to dependence under her. We
never, up to her dying day, had any explanation on
the pecuniary dispute between us. She cut off my
allowances: I uttered not a word; but managed to
live without her aid. I never heard that she repented
of her injustice, or acknowledged it, except from
Harry's private communication to me. In after days,
when we met, by a great gentleness in her behaviour,
and an uncommon respect and affection shown to my
wife, Madam Esmond may have intended I should
understand her tacit admission that she had been
wrong; but she made no apology, nor did I ask one.
Harry being provided for (whose welfare I could not
grudge), all my mother's savings and economical
schemes went to my advantage, who was her heir.
Time was when a few guineas would have been more
useful to me than hundreds which might come to me
when I had no need; but when Madam Esmond and
I met, the period of necessity was long passed away;
I had no need to scheme ignoble savings, or to grudge
the doctor his fee: I had plenty, and she could but
bring me more. No doubt she suffered in her own

mind to think that my children had been hungry, and
she had offered them no food ; and that strangers had
relieved the necessity from which her proud heart had
caused her to turn aside. Proud ? Was she prouder
than I ? A soft word of explanation between us might
have brought about a reconciliation years before it
came : but I would never speak, nor did she. When
I commit a wrong, and know it subsequently, I love
to ask pardon ; but 'tis as a satisfaction to my own
pride, and to myself I am apologising for having been
wanting to myself. And hence, I think (out of regard
to that personage of *ego*), I scarce ever could degrade
myself to do a meanness. How do men feel whose
whole lives (and many men's lives are) are lies, schemes,
and subterfuges ? What sort of company do they keep
when they are alone ? Daily in life I watch men
whose every smile is an artifice, and every wink is an
hypocrisy. Doth such a fellow wear a mask in his
own privacy, and to his own conscience ? If I choose
to pass over an injury, I fear 'tis not from a Christian
and forgiving spirit : 'tis because I can afford to remit
the debt, and disdain to ask a settlement of it. One
or two sweet souls I have known in my life (and perhaps tried) to whom forgiveness is no trouble,—a plant
that grows naturally, as it were, in the soil. I know
how to remit, I say, not forgive. I wonder are we
proud men proud of being proud ?

So I showed not the least sign of submission towards
my parent in Virginia yonder, and we continued for
years to live in estrangement, with occasionally a brief
word or two (such as the announcement of the birth
of a child, or what not) passing between my wife and
her. After our first troubles in America about the
Stamp Act, troubles fell on me in London likewise.
Though I have been on the Tory side in our quarrel
(as indeed upon the losing side in most controversies),

having no doubt that the Imperial Government had a full right to levy taxes in the colonies, yet at the time of the dispute I must publish a pert letter to a member of the House of Burgesses in Virginia, in which the question of the habitual insolence of the mother country to the colonies was so freely handled, and sentiments were uttered so disagreeable to persons in power, that I was deprived of my place as hackney-coach licenser, to the terror and horror of my uncle, who never could be brought to love people in disgrace. He had grown to have an extreme affection for my wife as well as my little boy ; but towards myself, personally, entertained a kind of pitying contempt which always infinitely amused me. He had a natural scorn and dislike for poverty, and a corresponding love for success and good fortune. Any opinion departing at all from the regular track shocked and frightened him, and all truth-telling made him turn pale. He must have had originally some warmth of heart and genuine love of kindred : for, spite of the dreadful shocks I gave him, he continued to see Theo and the child (and me too, giving me a mournful recognition when we met); and though broken-hearted by my free-spokenness, he did not refuse to speak to me as he had done at the time of our first differences, but looked upon me as a melancholy lost creature, who was past all worldly help or hope. Never mind, I must cast about for some new scheme of life ; and the repayment of Harry's debt to me at this juncture enabled me to live at least for some months, or even years to come. O strange fatuity of youth ! I often say. How was it that we dared to be so poor and so little cast down ?

At this time His Majesty's Royal uncle of Cumberland fell down and perished in a fit ; and, strange to say, his death occasioned a remarkable change in my fortune. My poor Sir Miles Warrington never missed

any Court ceremony to which he could introduce
himself. He was at all the drawing-rooms, christenings, balls, funerals of the Court. If ever a prince
or princess was ailing, his coach was at their door:
Leicester Fields, Carlton House, Gunnersbury, were
all the same to him, and nothing must satisfy him now
but going to the stout Duke's funeral. He caught a
great cold and an inflammation of the throat from standing bareheaded at this funeral in the rain; and one
morning, before almost I had heard of his illness, a
lawyer waits upon me at my lodgings in Bloomsbury,
and salutes me by the name of Sir George Warrington.

Poverty and fear of the future were over now.
We laid the poor gentleman by the side of his little
son, in the family churchyard where so many of his
race repose. Little Miles and I were the chief
mourners. An obsequious tenantry bowed and
curtseyed before us, and did their utmost to conciliate
my honour and my worship. The Dowager and her
daughter withdrew to Bath presently; and I and my
family took possession of the house, of which I have
been master for thirty years. Be not too eager, O
my son! Have but a little patience, and I too shall
sleep under yonder yew-trees, and the people will be
tossing up their caps for Sir Miles.

The records of a prosperous country life are easily
and briefly told. The steward's books show what
rents were paid and forgiven, what crops were raised,
and in what rotation. What visitors came to us, and
how long they stayed: what pensioners my wife had,
and how they were doctored and relieved, and how
they died: what year I was sheriff, and how often the
hounds met near us: all these are narrated in our
house-journals, which any of my heirs may read who
choose to take the trouble. We could not afford the

fine mansion in Hill Street, which my predecessor had occupied ; but we took a smaller house, in which, however, we spent more money. We made not half the show (with liveries, equipages, and plate) for which my uncle had been famous ; but our beer was stronger, and my wife's charities were perhaps more costly than those of the Dowager Lady Warrington. No doubt she thought there was no harm in spoiling the Philistines ; for she made us pay unconscionably for the goods she left behind her in our country-house, and I submitted to most of her extortions with un-utterable good-humour. What a value she imagined the potted plants in her green-houses bore ! What a price she set upon that horrible old spinet she left in her drawing-room ! And the framed pieces of worsted-work, performed by the accomplished Dora and the lovely Flora, had they been masterpieces of Titian or Vandyck, to be sure my Lady Dowager could hardly have valued them at a higher price. But though we paid so generously, though we were, I may say without boast, far kinder to our poor than ever she had been, for a while we had the very worst reputation in the county, where all sorts of stories had been told to my discredit. I thought I might perhaps succeed to my uncle's seat in Parliament, as well as to his landed property ; but I found, I knew not how, that I was voted to be a person of very dangerous opinions. I would not bribe. I would not coerce my own tenants to vote for me in the election of '68. A gentleman came down from Whitehall with a pocket-book full of bank-notes ; and I found that I had no chance against my competitor.

Bon Dieu ! Now that we were at ease in respect of worldly means—now that obedient tenants bowed and curtseyed as we went to church ; that we drove to visit our friends, or to the neighbouring towns, in

the great family coach with the four fat horses ; did
we not often regret poverty, and the dear little cottage
at Lambeth, where Want was ever prowling at the
door ? Did I not long to be bear-leading again, and
vow that translating for booksellers was not such
very hard drudgery ? When we went to London, we
made sentimental pilgrimages to all our old haunts.
I dare say my wife embraced all her landladies. You
may be sure we asked all the friends of those old times
to share the comforts of our new home with us. The
Reverend Mr. Hagan and his lady visited us more
than once. His appearance in the pulpit at B——
(where he preached very finely, as we thought) caused
an awful scandal there. Sampson came too, another
unlucky Levite, and was welcome as long as he would
stay among us. Mr. Johnson talked of coming, but
he put us off once or twice. I suppose our house was
dull. I know that I myself would be silent for days,
and fear that my moodiness must often have tried the
sweetest-tempered woman in the world who lived with
me. I did not care for field sports. The killing one
partridge was so like killing another, that I wondered
how men could pass days after days in the pursuit of that
kind of slaughter. Their fox-hunting stories would
begin at four o'clock, when the table-cloth was
removed, and last till supper-time. I sat silent, and
listened : day after day I fell asleep : no wonder I was
not popular with my company.

What admission is this I am making ? Here was
the storm over, the rocks avoided, the ship in port, and
the sailor not over-contented ! Was Susan I had
been sighing for during the voyage, not the beauty I
expected to find her ? In the first place, Susan and
all the family can look in her William's log-book, and
so, madam, I am not going to put my secrets down
there. No, Susan, I never had secrets from thee. I

never cared for another woman. I have seen more beautiful, but none that suited me as well as your Ladyship. I have met Mrs. Carter and Miss Mulso, and Mrs. Thrale and Madam Kaufmann, and the angelical Gunnings, and her Grace of Devonshire, and a host of beauties who were not angelic by any means ; and I was not dazzled by them. Nay, young folks, I may have led your mother a weary life, and been a very Bluebeard over her, but then I had no other heads in the closet. Only, the first pleasure of taking possession of our kingdom over, I own I began to be quickly tired of the crown. When the Captain wears it, His Majesty will be a very different Prince. He can ride a-hunting five days in the week, and find the sport amusing. I believe he would hear the same sermon at church fifty times, and not yawn more than I do at the first delivery. But sweet Joan, beloved Baucis ! being thy faithful husband and true lover always, thy Darby is rather ashamed of having been testy so often ; and, being arrived at the consummation of happiness, Philemon asks pardon for falling asleep so frequently after dinner. There came a period of my life when, having reached the summit of felicity, I was quite tired of the prospect I had there : I yawned in Eden, and said, 'Is this all ? What, no lions to bite ? no rain to fall ? no thorns to prick you in the rose-bush when you sit down ? —only Eve, for ever sweet and tender, and figs for breakfast, dinner, supper, from week's end to week's end ! ' Shall I make my confessions ? Hearken ! Well, then, if I must make a clean breast of it.

. . . .

[Here three pages are torn out of Sir George Warrington's MS. book, for which the Editor is sincerely sorry.]

NO, A SOLDIER CANNOT SUP WITH MY COMPANY

The Virginians Vol. II, p. LXXXV.

I know the theory and practice of the Roman
Church; but, being bred of another persuasion (and
sceptical and heterodox regarding that), I can't help
doubting the other, too, and wondering whether
Catholics, in their confessions, confess all? Do we
Protestants ever do so; and has education rendered
those other fellow-men so different from us? At
least, amongst us, we are not accustomed to suppose
Catholic priests or laymen more frank and open than
ourselves. Which brings me back to my question,—
does any man confess all? Does yonder dear creature
know all my life, who has been the partner of it for
thirty years; who, whenever I have told her a sorrow,
has been ready with the best of her gentle power to
soothe it; who has watched when I did not speak, and
when I was silent has been silent herself, or with the
charming hypocrisy of woman has worn smiles and an
easy appearance so as to make me imagine she felt no
care, or would not even ask to disturb her lord's secret
when he seemed to indicate a desire to keep it private?
Oh the dear hypocrite! Have I not watched her
hiding the boys' peccadilloes from papa's anger?
Have I not known her cheat out of her housekeeping
to pay off their little extravagances; and talk to me
with an artless face, as if she did not know that our
revered Captain had had dealings with the gentlemen
of Duke's Place, and our learned collegian, at the end
of his terms, had very pressing reasons for sporting
his oak (as the phrase is) against some of the University
tradesmen? Why, from the very earliest days, thou
wise woman, thou wert for ever concealing something
from me,—this one stealing jam from the cupboard;
that one getting into disgrace at school; that naughty
rebel (put on the caps, young folks, according to the
fit) flinging an inkstand at mamma in a rage, whilst I
was told the gown and the carpet were spoiled by

accident. We all hide from one another. We have
all secrets. We are all alone. We sin by ourselves,
and, let us trust, repent too. Yonder dear woman
would give her foot to spare mine a twinge of the
gout ; but, when I have the fit, the pain is in my
slipper. At the end of the novel or the play, the
hero and heroine marry or die, and so there is an end
of them as far as the poet is concerned, who huzzays
for his young couple till the postchaise turns the
corner ; or fetches the hearse and plumes, and shovels
them underground. But when Mr. Random and Mr.
Thomas Jones are married, is all over ? Are there no
quarrels at home ? Are there no Lady Bellastons
abroad ? are there no constables to be outrun ? no
temptations to conquer us, or be conquered by us ?
The Sirens sang after Ulysses long after his marriage,
and the suitors whispered in Penelope's ear, and he
and she had many a weary day of doubt and care, and
so have we all. As regards money I was put out of
trouble by the inheritance I made : but does not
Atra Cura sit behind baronets as well as *equites ?*
My friends in London used to congratulate me on my
happiness. Who would not like to be master of a
good house and a good estate ? But can Gumbo shut
the hall-door upon blue devils, or lay them always in
a red sea of claret ? Does a man sleep the better who
has four-and-twenty hours to doze in ? Do his
intellects brighten after a sermon from the dull old
vicar ; a ten minutes' cackle and flattery from the
village apothecary ; or the conversation of Sir John
and Sir Thomas with their ladies, who come ten
moonlight muddy miles to eat a haunch, and play a
rubber ? 'Tis all very well to have tradesmen bowing
to your carriage-door, room made for you at quarter-
sessions, and my lady wife taken down the second or
the third to dinner : but these pleasures fade—nay,

have their inconveniences. In our part of the country,
for seven years after we came to Warrington Manor,
our two what they called best neighbours were my
Lord Tutbury and Sir John Mudbrook. We are of
an older date than the Mudbrooks, consequently,
when we dined together, my Lady Tutbury always
fell to my lot, who was deaf and fell asleep after
dinner ; or if I had Lady Mudbrook, she chattered
with a folly so incessant and intense, that even my
wife could hardly keep her complacency (consummate
hypocrite as her Ladyship is), knowing the rage with
which I was fuming at the other's clatter. I come to
London. I show my tongue to Doctor Heberden.
I pour out my catalogue of complaints. 'Psha, my
dear Sir George !' says the unfeeling physician.
'Headaches, languor, bad sleep, bad temper——'
('Not bad temper : Sir George has the sweetest
temper in the world, only he is sometimes a little
melancholy,' says my wife.) 'Bad sleep, bad temper,'
continues the implacable Doctor. 'My dear lady,
his inheritance has been his ruin, and a little poverty
and a great deal of occupation would do him all the
good in life.'

No, my brother Harry ought to have been the
squire, with remainder to my son Miles, of course.
Harry's letters were full of gaiety and good spirits.
His estate prospered ; his negroes multiplied ; his
crops were large ; he was a member of our House of
Burgesses ; he adored his wife : could he but have a
child his happiness would be complete. Had Hal
been master of Warrington Manor-house in my
place, he would have been beloved through the whole
country ; he would have been steward at all the races,
the gayest of all the jolly huntsmen, the *bien venu* at
all the mansions round about, where people scarce
cared to perform the ceremony of welcome at sight of

my glum face. As for my wife, all the world liked her, and agreed in pitying her. I don't know how the report got abroad, but 'twas generally agreed that I treated her with awful cruelty, and that for jealousy I was a perfect Bluebeard. Ah me! And so it is true that I have had many dark hours; that I pass days in long silence; that the conversation of fools and whipper-snappers makes me rebellious and peevish, and that, when I feel contempt, I sometimes don't know how to conceal it, or I should say did not. I I hope as I grow older I grow more charitable. Because I do not love bawling and galloping after a fox, like the Captain yonder, I am not his superior; but in this respect, humbly own that he is mine. He has perceptions which are denied me; enjoyments which I cannot understand. Because I am blind the world is not dark. I try now and listen with respect when Squire Codgers talks of the day's run. I do my best to laugh when Captain Rattleton tells his garrison stories. I step up to the harpsichord with old Miss Humby (our neighbour from Beccles) and try and listen as she warbles her ancient ditties. I play whist laboriously. Am I not trying to do the duties of life? and I have a right to be garrulous and egotistical, because I have been reading Montaigne all the morning.

I was not surprised, knowing by what influences my brother was led, to find his name in the list of Virginia burgesses who declared that the sole right of imposing taxes on the inhabitants of this colony is now, and ever has been, legally and constitutionally vested in the House of Burgesses, and called upon the other colonies to pray for the Royal interposition in favour of the violated rights of America. And it was now, after we had been some three years settled in our English home, that a correspondence between us and Madam Esmond began to take place. It was my wife who (upon some pretext such as women always know how to find) reestablished the relations between us. Mr. Miles must need have the small-pox, from which he miraculously recovered without losing any portion of his beauty ; and on this recovery the mother writes her prettiest little wheedling letter to the grandmother of the fortunate babe. She coaxes her with all sorts of modest phrases and humble offerings of respect and goodwill. She narrates anecdotes of the precocious genius of the lad (what hath subsequently happened, I wonder, to stop the growth of that gallant young officer's brains ?), and she must have sent over to his grandmother a lock of the darling boy's hair, for the old lady, in her reply, acknowledged the receipt of some such present. I wonder, as it came from England, they allowed it to pass our custom-house at Williamsburg. In return for these peace-offerings and smuggled tokens of submission, comes a tolerably gracious letter from my lady of Castlewood. She inveighs against the dangerous spirit pervading the colony : she laments to think that her unhappy son is consorting with people who, she fears, will be no better than rebels and traitors. She does not wonder, considering *who his friends and advisers are.* How can a wife taken from an *almost menial situation* be expected to sympathise with persons of rank and dignity who have the honour of the Crown at heart ? If evil times were coming for the monarchy (for the folks in America appeared to be disinclined to pay taxes, and required that everything should be done for them without cost), she remembered how to monarchs in misfortune the Esmonds—her father the Marquis especially—had ever been faithful. She knew not what opinions (though she might judge from my *new-fangled* Lord Chatham) were in fashion in England.

She prayed, at least, she might hear that *one* of her
sons was not on the side of *rebellion*. When we
came, in after days, to look over old family papers in
Virginia, we found ' Letters from my daughter Lady
Warrington,' neatly tied up with a ribbon. My Lady
Theo insisted I should not open them ; and the truth,
I believe, is, that they were so full of praises of her
husband that she thought my vanity would suffer from
reading them.

When Madam began to write, she gave us brief
notices of Harry and his wife. ' The two women,'
she wrote, ' still govern everything with my poor boy
at Fannystown (as he chooses to call his house).
They must save money there, for I hear but a *shabby
account* of their manner of entertaining. The *Mount
Vernon gentleman* continues to be his great friend, and
he votes in the House of Burgesses very much as *his
guide* advises him. Why he should be so sparing of
his money I cannot understand: I heard, of five
negroes who went with his equipages to my Lord
Bottetourt's, only two had shoes to their feet. I had
reasons to save, having sons for whom I wished to
provide, but he hath no children, wherein he certainly
is spared from much grief, though, no doubt, Heaven
in its wisdom means our good by the trials which,
through our children, it causes us to endure. His
mother-in-law,' she added in one of her letters, ' has
been ailing. Ever since his marriage, my poor Henry
has been the creature of these two artful women, and
they rule him entirely. Nothing, my dear daughter,
is more contrary to common sense and to Holy
Scripture than this. Are we not told, *Wives, be
obedient to your husbands ?* Had Mr. Warrington lived,
I should have endeavoured to follow up that sacred
precept, holding that nothing so becomes a woman as
humility and obedience.'

Presently we had a letter sealed with black, and announcing the death of our dear good Mountain, for whom I had a hearty regret and affection, remembering her sincere love for us as children. Harry deplored the event in his honest way, and with tears which actually blotted his paper. And Madam Esmond, alluding to the circumstance, said : ' My late housekeeper, Mrs. Mountain, as soon as she found her illness was fatal, sent to me requesting a last interview on her death-bed, intending, doubtless, to pray my forgiveness for her treachery towards me. I sent her word that I could forgive her *as a Christian*, and heartily hope (though I confess I doubt it) that she had a due sense of her crime towards me. But our meeting, I considered, was of no use, and could only occasion unpleasantness between us. If she repented, *though at the eleventh hour*, it was not too late, and I sincerely trusted that she was now doing so. And, would you believe her lamentable and hardened condition ?' she sent me word through Dinah, my woman, whom I despatched to her with medicines for *her soul's and her body's health*, that she had nothing to repent of as far as regarded her conduct to me, and she wanted to be left alone ! Poor Dinah distributed the medicine to my negroes, and our people took it *eagerly*— whilst Mrs. Mountain, left to herself, succumbed to the fever. Oh the perversity of human kind ! This poor creature was *too proud* to take my remedies, and is now beyond the reach of cure and physicians. You tell me your little Miles is subject to fits of cholic. *My* remedy, and I will beg you to let me know if effectual, is,' &c. &c.—and here followed the prescription which thou didst not take, O my son, my heir, and my pride ! because thy fond mother had *her* mother's favourite powder, on which in his infantine troubles our first-born was dutifully nurtured. Did words not exactly consonant with truth pass between the ladies in their correspondence? I fear my Lady Theo was not altogether candid : else how to account for a phrase in one of Madam Esmond's letters, who said, 'I am glad to hear the powders have done the dear child good! They are, if not on a first, on a second or third application, *almost infallible*, and have been the blessed means of relieving many persons round me, both infants and adults, white and coloured. I send my grandson an Indian bow and arrows. Shall these old eyes never behold him at Castlewood, I wonder, and is Sir George so busy with his books and his politics that he can't afford a few months to his mother in Virginia? I am much alone now. My son's chamber is just as he left it : the same books are in the presses : his little hanger and fowling-piece over the bed, and my father's picture over the mantelpiece. I never allow anything to be altered in his room or his brother's. I fancy the children playing near me sometimes, and that I can see my dear father's head as he dozes in his chair. Mine is growing almost as white as my father's. Am I never to behold my children ere I go hence? The Lord's will be done!'

CHAPTER LXXXVI

AT HOME

SUCH an appeal as this of our mother would have softened hearts much less obdurate than ours ; and we talked of a speedy visit to Virginia, and of hiring all the 'Young Rachel's' cabin accommodation. But our child must fall ill, for whom the voyage would be dangerous, and from whom the mother of course could not part ; and the 'Young Rachel' made her voyage without us that year. Another year there was another difficulty, in my worship's first attack of the gout (which occupied me a good deal, and afterwards certainly cleared my wits and enlivened my spirits) ; and now came another much sadder cause for delay in the sad news we received from Jamaica. Some two years after our establishment at the Manor, our dear General returned from his government, a little richer in the world's goods than when he went away, but having undergone a loss for which no wealth could console him, and after which, indeed, he did not care to remain in the West Indies. My Theo's poor mother—the most tender and affectionate friend (save one) I have ever had—died abroad of the fever. Her last regret was that she should not be allowed to live to see our children and ourselves in prosperity.

'She sees us, though we do not see her ; and she thanks you, George, for having been good to her children,' her husband said.

He, we thought, would not be long ere he joined her. His love for her had been the happiness and

business of his whole life. To be away from her
seemed living no more. It was pitiable to watch the
good man as he sat with us. My wife, in her air and
in many tones and gestures, constantly recalled her
mother to the bereaved widower's heart. What
cheer we could give him in his calamity we offered;
but, especially, little Hetty was now, under Heaven,
his chief support and consolation. She had refused
more than one advantageous match in the island,
the General told us; and on her return to England,
my Lord Wrotham's heir laid himself at her feet.
But she loved best to stay with her father, Hetty
said. As long as he was not tired of her she cared
for no husband.

'Nay,' said we, when this last great match was
proposed, 'let the General stay six months with us at
the Manor here, and you can have him at Oakhurst
for the other six.'

But Hetty declared her father never could bear
Oakhurst again now that her mother was gone; and
she would marry no man for his coronet and money
—not she! The General, when we talked this
matter over, said gravely that the child had no
desire for marrying, owing possibly to some disappointment in early life, of which she never spoke;
and we, respecting her feelings, were for our parts
equally silent. My brother Lambert had by this
time a college living near to Winchester, and a wife
of course to adorn his parsonage. We professed but
a moderate degree of liking for this lady, though we
made her welcome when she came to us. *Her* idea
regarding our poor Hetty's determined celibacy was
different to that which I had. This Mrs. Jack was a
chatterbox of a woman, in the habit of speaking her
mind very freely, and of priding herself excessively on
her skill in giving pain to her friends.

'My dear Sir George,' she was pleased to say, '*I*
have often and often told our dear Theo that *I*
wouldn't have a pretty sister in my house to make tea
for Jack when I was upstairs, and always to be at
hand when I was wanted in the kitchen or nursery,
and always to be dressed neat and in her best when I
was very likely making pies or puddings or looking
to the children. I have every confidence in Jack,
of course. I should like to see him look at another
woman, indeed! And so I have in Jemima: but
they don't come together in *my* house when *I'm*
upstairs—that I promise you! And so I told my
sister Warrington.'

'Am I to understand,' says the General, 'that
you have done my Lady Warrington the favour to
warn her against her sister, my daughter Miss
Hester?'

'Yes, pa, of course I have. A duty is a duty, and
a woman is a woman, and a man's a man, as I know
very well. Don't tell me! He *is* a man. Every
man is a man, with all his sanctified airs!'

'You yourself have a married sister, with whom
you were staying when my son Jack first had the
happiness of making your acquaintance?' remarks the
General.

'Yes, of course I have a married sister, every one
knows that, and I have been as good as a mother to
her children, that I have!'

'And am I to gather from your conversation that
your attractions proved a powerful temptation for
your sister's husband?'

'La, General! I don't know how you can go for
to say I ever said any such a thing!' cries Mrs. Jack,
red and voluble.

'Don't you perceive, my dear madam, that it
is you who have insinuated as much, not only

regarding yourself, but regarding my own two daughters?'

'Never, never, never, as I'm a Christian woman! And it's most cruel of you to say so, sir. And I *do* say a sister is best out of the house, that I do! And as Theo's time is coming I warn her, that's all.'

'Have you discovered, my good madam, whether my poor Hetty has stolen any of the spoons? When I came to breakfast this morning, my daughter was alone, and there must have been a score of pieces of silver on the table.'

'La, sir! who ever said a word about spoons? Did *I* ever accuse the poor dear? If I did, may I drop down dead at this moment on this hearth-rug! And I ain't used to be spoke to in this way. And me and Jack have both remarked it; and I've done my duty, that I have.' And here Mrs. Jack flounces out of the room, in tears.

'And has the woman had the impudence to tell you this, my child?' asks the General, when Theo (who is a little delicate) comes to the tea-table.

'She has told me every day since she has been here. She comes into my dressing-room to tell me. She comes to my nursery, and says, "Ah, *I* wouldn't have a sister prowling about my nursery, that I wouldn't." Ah, how pleasant it is to have amiable and well-bred relatives, say I.'

'Thy poor mother has been spared this woman,' groans the General.

'Our mother would have made her better, papa,' says Theo, kissing him.

'Yes, dear.' And I see that both of them are at their prayers.

But this must be owned, that to love one's relatives is not always an easy task; to live with one's neighbours is sometimes not amusing. From Jack

Theo knelt down
to ask her blessing.

Lambert's demeanour next day, I could see that his
wife had given him her version of the conversation.
Jack was sulky, but not dignified. He was angry,
but his anger did not prevent his appetite. He
preached a sermon for us which was entirely stupid.
And little Miles, once more in sables, sat at his
grandfather's side, his little hand placed in that of the
kind old man.

Would he stay and keep house for us during our
Virginian trip? The housekeeper should be put
under the full domination of Hetty. The butler's
keys should be handed over to him; for Gumbo, not
I thought with an over good grace, was to come with
us to Virginia: having, it must be premised, united
himself with Mrs. Molly in the bonds of matrimony,
and peopled a cottage in my park with sundry tawny
Gumbos. Under the care of our good General and
his daughter we left our house then; we travelled to
London, and thence to Bristol, and our obsequious
agent there had the opportunity of declaring that he
should offer up prayers for our prosperity, and of
vowing that children so beautiful as ours (we had an
infant by this time to accompany Miles) were never
seen on any ship before. We made a voyage without
accident. How strange the feeling was as we landed
from our boat at Richmond! A coach and a host of
negroes were there in waiting to receive us; and
hard by a gentleman on horseback, with negroes in
our livery, too, who sprang from his horse and rushed
up to embrace us. Not a little charmed were both
of us to see our dearest Hal. He rode with us to our
mother's door. Yonder she stood on the steps to
welcome us: and Theo knelt down to ask her
blessing.

Harry rode in the coach with us as far as our
mother's house; but would not, as he said, spoil sport

by entering with us. 'She sees me,' he owned, 'and
we are pretty good friends; but Fanny and she are
best apart; and there is no love lost between 'em, I
can promise you. Come over to me at the tavern,
George, when thou art free. And to-morrow I shall
have the honour to present her sister to Theo. 'Twas
only from happening to be in town yesterday that I
heard the ship was signalled, and waited to see you.
I have sent a negro boy home to my wife, and she'll
be here to pay her respects to my Lady Warrington.'
And Harry, after this brief greeting, jumped out of
the carriage, and left us to meet our mother alone.

Since I parted from her I had seen a great deal of
fine company, and Theo and I had paid our respects to
the King and Queen at St. James's; but we had seen
no more stately person than this who welcomed us, and
raising my wife from her knee, embraced her and led
her into the house. 'Twas a plain wood-built place,
with a gallery round, as our Virginian houses are; but
if it had been a palace, with a little empress inside, our
reception could not have been more courteous. There
was old Nathan, still the major-domo, a score of kind
black faces of blacks grinning welcome. Some whose
names I remembered as children were grown out of
remembrance, to be sure, to be buxom lads and lasses;
and some I had left with black pates were grizzling
now with snowy polls: and some who were born since
my time were peering at doorways with their great
eyes and little naked feet. It was, 'I'm little Sip,
Master George!' and 'I'm Dinah, Sir George!' and
'I'm Master Miles's boy!' says a little chap in a new
livery and boots of nature's blacking. Ere the day
was over the whole household had found a pretext for
passing before us, and grinning and bowing and making us welcome. I don't know how many repasts were
served to us. In the evening my Lady Warrington

had to receive all the gentry of the little town, which
she did with perfect grace and good-humour, and I
had to shake hands with a few old acquaintances—old
enemies I was going to say; but I had come into a
fortune and was no longer a naughty prodigal. Why,
a drove of fatted calves was killed in my honour!
My poor Hal was of the entertainment, but gloomy
and crestfallen. His mother spoke to him, but it was
as a queen to a rebellious prince, her son, who was not
yet forgiven. We two slipped away from the company, and went up to the rooms assigned to me: but
there, as we began a free conversation, our mother,
taper in hand, appeared with her pale face. Did I
want anything? Was everything quite as I wished
it? She had peeped in at the dearest children, who
were sleeping like cherubs. How she did caress them,
and delight over them! How she was charmed with
Miles's dominating airs, and the little Theo's smiles
and dimples! 'Supper is just coming on the table,
Sir George. If you like our cookery better than the
tavern, Henry, I beg you to stay.' What a different
welcome there was in the words and tone addressed
to each of us! Hal hung down his head, and followed
to the lower room. A clergyman begged a blessing
on the meal. He touched with not a little art and
eloquence upon our arrival at home, upon our safe
passage across the stormy waters, upon the love and
forgiveness which awaited us in the mansions of the
Heavenly Parent when the storms of life were
over.

Here was a new clergyman, quite unlike some
whom I remembered about us in earlier days, and I
praised him, but Madam Esmond shook her head.
She was afraid his principles were very dangerous: she
was afraid others had adopted those dangerous principles. Had I not seen the paper signed by the

burgesses and merchants at Williamsburg the year before—the Lees, Randolphs, Bassets, Washingtons, and the like, and oh, my dear, that I should have to say it, our name, that is, your brother's (by what influence I do not like to say), and this unhappy Mr. Belman's who begged a blessing last night?

If there had been quarrels in our little colonial society when I left home, what were these to the feuds I found raging on my return? We had sent the Stamp Act to America, and been forced to repeal it. Then we must try a new set of duties on glass, paper, and what not, and repeal that Act too, with the exception of a duty on tea. From Boston to Charleston the tea was confiscated. Even my mother, loyal as she was, gave up her favourite drink; and my poor wife would have had to forego hers, but we had brought a quantity for our private drinking on board ship, which had paid four times as much duty at home. Not that I for my part would have hesitated about paying duty. The home Government must have some means of revenue, or its pretensions to authority were idle. They say the colonies were tried and tyrannised over : I say the home Government was tried and tyrannised over. ('Tis but an affair of argument and history, now : we tried the question, and were beat ; and the matter is settled as completely as the conquest of Britain by the Normans.) And all along, from conviction, I trust, I own to have taken the British side of the quarrel. In that brief and unfortunate experience of war which I had had in my early life, the universal cry of the army and well-affected persons was, that Mr. Braddock's expedition had failed, and defeat and disaster had fallen upon us in consequence of the remissness, the selfishness, and the rapacity of many of the very people for whose defence against the French arms had been taken up.

The colonists were for having all done for them, and for doing nothing. They made extortionate bargains with the champions who came to defend them ; they failed in contracts ; they furnished niggardly supplies ; they multiplied delays until the hour for beneficial action was past, and until the catastrophe came which never need have occurred but for their ill-will. What shouts of joy were there, and what ovations for the great British Minister who had devised and effected the conquest of Canada ! Monsieur de Vaudreuil said justly that that conquest was the signal for the defection of the North American colonies from their allegiance to Great Britain ; and my Lord Chatham, having done his best to achieve the first part of the scheme, contributed more than any man in England towards the completion of it. The colonies were insurgent, and he applauded their rebellion. What scores of thousands of waverers must he have encouraged into resistance ! It was a general who says to an army in revolt, 'God save the King ! My men, you have a right to mutiny !' No wonder they set up his statue in this town, and his picture in t'other ; whilst here and there they hanged Ministers and Governors in effigy. To our Virginian town of Williamsburg, some wiseacres must subscribe to bring over a portrait of my Lord, in the habit of a Roman orator speaking in the Forum, to be sure, and pointing to the palace of Whitehall, and the special window out of which Charles I. was beheaded ! Here was a neat allegory, and a pretty compliment to a British statesman ! I hear, however, that my Lord's head was painted from a bust, and so was taken off without his knowledge.

Now my country is England, not America or Virginia : and I take, or rather took, the English side of the dispute. My sympathies had always been with

home, where I was now a squire and a citizen : but
had my lot been to plant tobacco, and live on the
banks of James River or Potomac, no doubt my
opinions had been altered.   When, for instance, I
visited my brother at his new house and plantation, I
found him and his wife as staunch Americans as we
were British.   We had some words upon the matter
in dispute,—who had not in those troublesome times ?
—but our argument was carried on without rancour ;
even my new sister could not bring us to that, though
she did her best when we were together, and in the
curtain lectures, which I have no doubt she inflicted
on her spouse, like a notable housewife as she was.
But we trusted each other so entirely that even
Harry's duty towards his wife would not make him
quarrel with his brother.   He loved me from old time,
when my word was law with him ; he still protested
that he and every Virginian gentleman of his
side was loyal to the Crown.   War was not declared
as yet, and gentlemen of different opinions were
courteous enough to one another.   Nay, at our public
dinners and festivals, the health of the King was still
ostentatiously drunk : and the Assembly of every
colony, though preparing for Congress, though
resisting all attempts at taxation on the part of the
home authorities, was loud in its expressions of regard
for the King our father, and pathetic in its appeals to
that paternal sovereign to put away evil counsellors
from him, and listen to the voice of moderation and
reason.   Up to the last, our Virginian gentry were a
grave, orderly, aristocratic folk, with the strongest
sense of their own dignity and station.   In later days,
and nearer home, we have heard of fraternisation and
equality.   Amongst the great folks of our Old World
I have never seen a gentleman standing more on his
dignity and maintaining it better than Mr. Washing-

ton : no—not the King against whom he took arms.
In the eyes of all the gentry of the French Court,
who gaily joined in the crusade against us, and so
took their revenge for Canada, the great American
chief always appeared as *anax andron*, and they
allowed that his better could not be seen in Versailles
itself.

Though they were quarrelling with the Governor,
the gentlemen of the House of Burgesses still maintained amicable relations with him, and exchanged
dignified courtesies. When my Lord Bottetourt
arrived, and held his court at Williamsburg in no
small splendour and state, all the gentry waited upon
him, Madam Esmond included. And at his death,
Lord Dunmore, who succeeded him, and brought a
fine family with him, was treated with the utmost
respect by our gentry privately, though publicly the
House of Assembly and the Governor were at
war.

Their quarrels are a matter of history, and
concern me personally only so far as this, that our
burgesses being convened for the 1st of March in
the year after my arrival in Virginia, it was agreed that
we should all pay a visit to our capital, and our duty
to the Governor. Since Harry's unfortunate marriage
Madam Esmond had not performed this duty, though
always previously accustomed to pay it ; but now that
her eldest son was arrived in the colony, my mother
opined that we must certainly wait upon his Excellency
the Governor, nor were we sorry, perhaps, to get
away from our little Richmond to enjoy the gaieties of
the provincial capital. Madam engaged, and at a great
price, the best house to be had at Richmond for herself
and her family. Now I was rich, her generosity was
curious. I had more than once to interpose (her old
servants likewise wondering at her new way of life),

and beg her not to be so lavish. But she gently said, in former days she had occasion to save, which now existed no more. Harry had enough, sure, with such a wife as he had taken out of the housekeeper's room. If she chose to be a little extravagant now, why should she hesitate? She had not her dearest daughter and grandchildren with her every day (she fell in love with all three of them, and spoiled them as much as they were capable of being spoiled). Besides, in former days I certainly could not accuse her of too much *extravagance*, and this I think was almost the only allusion she made to the pecuniary differences between us. So she had her people dressed in their best, and her best wines, plate, and furniture from Castlewood by sea at no small charge, and her dress in which she had been married in George the Second's reign, and we all flattered ourselves that our coach made the greatest figure of any except his Excellency's, and we engaged Signor Formicalo, his Excellency's major-domo, to superintend the series of feasts that were given in my honour ; and more flesh-pots were set a-stewing in our kitchens in one month, our servants said, than had been known in the family since the young gentlemen went away. So great was Theo's influence over my mother, that she actually persuaded her, that year, to receive our sister Fanny, Hal's wife, who would have stayed upon the plantation rather than face Madam Esmond. But trusting to Theo's promise of amnesty, Fanny (to whose house we had paid more than one visit) came up to town, and made her curtsey to Madam Esmond, and was forgiven. And rather than be forgiven in that way, I own, for my part, that I would prefer perdition or utter persecution.

'You know these, my dear?' says Madam Esmond, pointing to her fine silver sconces. 'Fanny hath often cleaned them when she was with me at Castle-

wood. And this dress, too, Fanny knows, I dare say?
Her poor mother had the care of it. I always had
the greatest confidence in her.'

Here there is wrath flashing from Fanny's eyes,
which our mother, who has forgiven her, does not
perceive—not she!

'Oh, she was a treasure to me!' Madam resumes.
'I never should have nursed my boys through their
illnesses but for your mother's admirable care of them.
Colonel Lee, permit me to present you to my
daughter, my Lady Warrington. Her Ladyship is a
neighbour of your relatives the Bunburys at
home. Here comes his Excellency. Welcome, my
Lord!'

And our princess performs before his Lordship one
of those curtseys of which she was not a little proud;
and I fancy I see some of the company venturing to
smile.

'By George, madam,' says Mr. Lee, 'since Count
Borulawski, I have not seen a bow so elegant as your
ladyship's.'

'And pray, sir, who was Count Borulawski?' asks
Madam.

'He was a nobleman high in favour with his Polish
Majesty,' replies Mr. Lee. 'May I ask you, madam,
to present me to your distinguished son?'

'This is Sir George Warrington,' says my mother,
pointing to me.

'Pardon me, madam. I meant Captain Warrington, who was by Mr. Wolfe's side when he died. I
had been contented to share his fate, so I had been
near him.'

And the ardent Lee swaggers up to Harry, and
takes his hand with respect, and pays him a compliment or two, which makes me, at least, pardon him
for his late impertinence: for my dearest Hal walks

gloomily through his mother's rooms, in his old uniform of the famous corps which he has quitted.

We had had many meetings, which the stern mother could not interrupt, and in which that instinctive love which bound us to one another, and which nothing could destroy, had opportunity to speak. Entirely unlike each other in our pursuits, our tastes, our opinions—his life being one of eager exercise, active sport, and all the amusements of the field, while mine is to dawdle over books and spend my time in languid self-contemplation—we have, nevertheless, had such a sympathy as almost passes the love of women. My poor Hal confessed as much to me, for his part, in his artless manner, when we went away without wives or womankind, except a few negroes left in the place, and passed a week at Castle-wood together.

The ladies did not love each other. I know enough of my Lady Theo, to see after a very few glances whether or not she takes a liking to another of her amiable sex. All my powers of persuasion or command fail to change the stubborn creature's opinion. Had she ever said a word against Mrs. This or Miss That? Not she! Has she been otherwise than civil? No, assuredly! My Lady Theo is polite to a beggar-woman, treats her kitchen-maids like duchesses, and murmurs a compliment to the dentist for his elegant manner of pulling her tooth out. She would black my boots, or clean the grate, if I ordained it (always looking like a duchess the while); but as soon as I say to her, 'My dear creature, be fond of this lady, or t'other!' all obedience ceases; she executes the most refined curtseys; smiles and kisses even to order; but performs that mysterious undefinable freemasonic signal, which passes between women, by which each knows that the other hates her. So, with regard to

Fanny, we had met at her house, and at others. I
remembered her affectionately from old days, I fully
credited poor Hal's violent protests and tearful oaths,
that, by George, it was our mother's persecution which
made him marry her. He couldn't stand by and see
a poor thing tortured as she was, without coming to
her rescue ; no, by heavens, he couldn't ! I say I
believed all this ; and had for my sister-in-law a genuine
compassion, as well as an early regard ; and yet I had
no love to give her : and, in reply to Hal's passionate
outbreaks in praise of her beauty and worth, and eager
queries to me whether I did not think her a perfect
paragon, I could only answer with faint compliments
or vague approval, feeling all the while that I was disappointing my poor ardent fellow, and cursing inwardly
that revolt against flattery and falsehood into which I
sometimes frantically rush. Why should I not say,
' Yes, dear Hal, thy wife is a paragon; her singing is
delightful, her hair and shape are beautiful ; ' as I might
have said by a little common stretch of politeness ?
Why could I not cajole this or that stupid neighbour
or relative, as I have heard Theo do a thousand times,
finding all sorts of lively prattle to amuse them, whilst
I sit before them dumb and gloomy ? I say it was a
sin not to have more words to say in praise of Fanny.
We ought to have praised her, we ought to have liked
her. My Lady Warrington certainly ought to have
liked her, for she can play the hypocrite, and I cannot.
And there was this young creature—pretty, graceful,
shaped like a nymph, with beautiful black eyes—and
we cared for them no more than for two gooseberries !
At Warrington my wife and I, when we pretended to
compare notes, elaborately complimented each other
on our new sister's beauty. What lovely eyes !—Oh,
yes ! What a sweet little dimple on her chin !—*Ah
oui !* What wonderful little feet !—Perfectly Chinese !

where should we in London get slippers small enough
for her ?　And, these compliments exhausted, we knew
that we did not like Fanny the value of one penny-
piece ; we knew that we disliked her ; we knew that
we ha——　Well, what hypocrites women are !　We
heard from many quarters how eagerly my brother
had taken up the new anti-English opinion, and what
a champion he was of so-called American rights and
freedom.　'It is her doing, my dear,' says I to my
wife.　'If I had said so much, I am sure you would
have scolded me,' says my Lady Warrington, laughing : and I did straightway begin to scold her, and say
it was most cruel of her to suspect our new sister ;
and what earthly right had we to do so ?　But I say
again, I know Madam Theo so well, that when once
she has got a prejudice against a person in her little
head, not all the King's horses nor all the King's men
will get it out again.　I vow nothing would induce
her to believe that Harry was not henpecked—
nothing.

Well, we went to Castlewood together without the
women, and stayed at the dreary, dear old place, where
we had been so happy, and I, at least, so gloomy.　It
was winter, and duck time, and Harry went away to
the river, and shot dozens and scores and bushels of
canvas-backs, whilst I remained in my grandfather's
library amongst the old mouldering books which I
loved in my childhood—which I see in a dim vision
still resting on a little boy's lap, as he sits by an old
white-headed gentleman's knee.　I read my books ; I
slept in my own bed and room—religiously kept, as
my mother told me, and left as on the day when I
went to Europe.　Hal's cheery voice would wake me,
as of old.　Like all men who love to go a-field, he
was an early riser : he would come and wake me, and
sit on the foot of the bed and perfume the air with his

morning pipe, as the house negroes laid great logs on
the fire. It was a happy time! Old Nathan had
told me of cunning crypts where ancestral rum and
claret were deposited. We had had cares, struggles,
battles, bitter griefs, and disappointments; we were
boys again as we sat there together. I am a boy now
even, as I think of the time.

That unlucky tea-tax, which alone of the taxes
lately imposed upon the colonies the home Government was determined to retain, was met with defiance
throughout America. 'Tis true we paid a shilling in
the pound at home, and asked only threepence from
Boston or Charleston; but, as a question of principle,
the impost was refused by the provinces, which indeed
ever showed a most spirited determination to pay as
little as they could help. In Charleston, the tea-
ships were unloaded, and the cargoes stored in cellars.
From New York and Philadelphia, the vessels were
turned back to London. In Boston (where there
was an armed force, whom the inhabitants were
perpetually mobbing), certain patriots, painted and
disguised as Indians, boarded the ships, and flung the
obnoxious cargoes into the water. The wrath of our
white Father was kindled against this city of Mohocks
in masquerade. The notable Boston Port Bill was
brought forward in the British House of Commons:
the port was closed, and the Custom House removed
to Salem. The Massachusetts Charter was annulled;
and—in just apprehension that riots might ensue, in
dealing with the perpetrators of which the colonial
courts might be led to act partially—Parliament
decreed that persons indicted for acts of violence and
armed resistance might be sent home, or to another
colony, for trial. If such acts set all America in a
flame, they certainly drove all well-wishers of our
country into a fury. I might have sentenced Master

Miles Warrington, at five years old, to a whipping,
and he would have cried, taken down his little small-
clothes, and submitted : but suppose I offered (and he
richly deserving it) to chastise Captain Miles of the
Prince's Dragoons ?   He would whirl my paternal
cane out of my hand, box my hair-powder out of
my ears.   Lord a-mercy !   I tremble at the very
idea of the controversy !   He would *assert his independence*, in a word ! and if, I say, I think the
home Parliament had a right to levy taxes in the
colonies, I own that we took means most captious,
most insolent, most irritating, and, above all, most
impotent, to assert our claim.

My Lord Dunmore, our Governor of Virginia,
upon Lord Bottetourt's death, received me into
some intimacy soon after my arrival in the colony,
being willing to live on good terms with all our
gentry.   My mother's severe loyalty was no secret
to him ; indeed, she waved the King's banner in all
companies, and talked so loudly and resolutely, that
Randolph and Patrick Henry himself were struck
dumb before her.   It was Madam Esmond's celebrated
reputation for loyalty (his Excellency laughingly told
me) which induced him to receive her eldest son to
grace.

'I have had the worst character of you from home,'
his Lordship said.   'Little birds whisper to me, Sir
George, that you are a man of the most dangerous
principles.   You are a friend of Mr. Wilkes and
Alderman Beckford.   I am not sure you have not
been at Medmenham Abbey.   You have lived with
players, poets, and all sorts of wild people.   I have
been warned against you, sir, and I find you——'

'Not so black as I have been painted,' I interrupted
his Lordship with a smile.

'Faith,' says my Lord, 'if I tell Sir George

Warrington that he seems to me a very harmless quiet gentleman, and that 'tis a great relief to me to talk to him amidst these loud politicians; these lawyers with their perpetual noise about Greece and Rome; these Virginian squires who are for ever professing their loyalty and respect, whilst they are shaking their fists in my face—I hope nobody over-hears us,' says my Lord, with an arch smile, 'and nobody will carry my opinions home.'

His Lordship's ill opinion having been removed by a better knowledge of me, our acquaintance daily grew more intimate; and, especially between the ladies of his family and my own, a close friendship arose—between them and my wife at least. Hal's wife, received kindly at the little provincial Court, as all ladies were, made herself by no means popular there by the hot and eager political tone which she adopted. She assailed all the Government measures with indiscriminating acrimony. Were they lenient? She said the perfidious British Government was only preparing a snare, and biding its time until it could forge heavier chains for unhappy America. Were they angry? Why did not every American citizen rise, assert his rights as a freeman, and serve every British governor, officer, soldier, as they had treated the East India Company's tea? My mother, on the other hand, was pleased to express her opinions with equal frankness, and, indeed, to press her advice upon his Excellency with a volubility which may have fatigued that representative of the Sovereign. Call out the militia; send for fresh troops from New York, from home, from anywhere; lock up the Capitol! (this advice was followed, it must be owned) and send every one of the ringleaders amongst those wicked burgesses to prison! was Madam Esmond's daily counsel to the Governor by word and letter.

And if not only the burgesses, but the burgesses' wives could have been led off to punishment and captivity, I think this Brutus of a woman would scarce have appealed against the sentence.

CHAPTER LXXXVII

THE LAST OF 'GOD SAVE THE KING'

WHAT perverse law of Fate is it that ever places me in a minority? Should a law be proposed to hand over this realm to the Pretender of Rome, or the Grand Turk, and submit it to the new sovereign's religion, it might pass, as I should certainly be voting against it. At home in Virginia, I found myself disagreeing with everybody as usual. By the Patriots I was voted (as indeed I professed myself to be) a Tory; by the Tories I was presently declared to be a dangerous Republican. The time was utterly out of joint. O cursed spite! Ere I had been a year in Virginia, how I wished myself back by the banks of Waveney! But the aspect of affairs was so troublous, that I could not leave my mother, a lone lady, to face possible war and disaster, nor would she quit the country at such a juncture, nor should a man of spirit leave it. At his Excellency's table, and over his Excellency's plentiful claret, that point was agreed on by numbers of the well-affected, that vow was vowed over countless brimming bumpers. No; it was *statue signum, signifer!* We Cavaliers would all rally round it; and at these times, our Governor talked like the bravest of the brave.

Now, I will say, of all my Virginian acquaintance, Madam Esmond was the most consistent. Our gentlefolks had come in numbers to Williamsburg;

and a great number of them proposed to treat her Excellency the Governor's lady to a ball, when the news reached us of the Boston Port Bill. Straightway the House of Burgesses adopts an indignant protest against this measure of the British Parliament, and decrees a solemn day of fast and humiliation throughout the country, and of solemn prayer to Heaven to avert the calamity of Civil War. Meanwhile the invitation to my Lady Dunmore having been already given and accepted, the gentlemen agreed that their ball should take place on the appointed evening, and then sackcloth and ashes should be assumed some days afterwards.

'A ball!' says Madam Esmond. 'I go to a ball which is given by a set of rebels who are going publicly to insult His Majesty a week afterwards! I will die sooner!' And she wrote to the gentlemen who were stewards for the occasion to say, that viewing the dangerous state of the country, she, for her part, could not think of attending a ball.

What was her surprise then, the next time she went abroad in her chair, to be cheered by a hundred persons, white and black, and shouts of 'Huzzah, madam!' 'Heaven bless your Ladyship!' They evidently thought her patriotism had caused her determination not to go to the ball.

Madam, that there should be no mistake, puts her head out of the chair, and cries out 'God save the King!' as loud as she can. The people cried 'God save the King!' too. Everybody cried 'God save the King!' in those days. On the night of that entertainment, my poor Harry, as a Burgess of the House, and one of the givers of the feast, donned his uniform red coat of Wolfe's (which he so soon was to exchange for another colour) and went off with Madam Fanny to the ball. My Lady Warrington and her humble servant, as being strangers in the country, and English people as it were, were permitted by Madam to attend the assembly, from which she of course absented herself. I had the honour to dance a country-dance with the lady of Mount Vernon, whom I found a most lively, pretty, and amiable partner; but am bound to say that my wife's praises of her were received with a very grim acceptance by my mother, when Lady Warrington came to recount the events of the evening. Could not Sir George Warrington have danced with my Lady Dunmore or her daughters, or with anybody but Mrs. Washington; to be sure the Colonel thought so well of himself and his wife, that no doubt he considered her the grandest lady in the room; and she who remembered him a road surveyor at a guinea a day! Well, indeed! there was no measuring the pride of these provincial upstarts, and as for this gentleman, my Lord Dunmore's partiality for him had evidently turned his head. I do not know about Mr. Washington's pride, I know that my good mother never could be got to love him or anything that was his.

She was no better pleased with him for going to the ball, than with his conduct three days afterwards, when the day of fast and humiliation was appointed, and when he attended the service which our new clergyman performed. She invited Mr. Belman to dinner that day, and sundry colonial authorities. The clergyman excused himself: Madam Esmond tossed up her head, and said he might do as he liked. She made a parade of a dinner; she lighted her house up at night, when all the rest of the city was in darkness and gloom; she begged Mr. Hardy, one of his Excellency's aides-de-camp, to sing 'God save the King,' to which the people in the street outside listened, thinking that it might be a part of some

religious service which Madam was celebrating; but
then she called for 'Britons, strike home!' which the
simple young gentleman, just from Europe, began to
perform, when a great yell arose in the street, and a
large stone, flung from some rebellious hand, plumped
into the punch-bowl before me, and scattered it and its
contents about our dining-room.

My mother went to the window nothing daunted.
I can see her rigid little figure now, as she stands with
a tossed-up head, outstretched frilled arms, and the
twinkling stars for a background, and sings in chorus,
'Britons, strike home! strike home!' The crowd in
front of the palings shout and roar, 'Silence! for
shame! go back!' but she will not go back, not she.
'Fling more stones, if you dare!' says the brave little
lady; and more might have come, but some gentlemen issuing out of the 'Raleigh Tavern' interpose
with the crowd. 'You mustn't insult a lady,'
says a voice I think I know. 'Huzzah, Colonel!
Hurrah, Captain! God bless your honour!' say the
people in the street. And thus the enemies are
pacified.

My mother, protesting that the whole disturbance
was over, would have had Mr. Hardy sing another
song; but he gave a sickly grin, and said, 'He really
did not like to sing to such accompaniments,' and the
concert for that evening was ended; though I am
bound to say that some scoundrels returned at night,
frightened my poor wife almost out of wits, and broke
every single window in the front of our tenement.
'Britons, strike home!' was a little too much;
Madam should have contented herself with 'God save
the King.' Militia were drilled, bullets were cast,
supplies of ammunition got ready, cunning plans for
disappointing the Royal ordinances devised and carried
out; but, to be sure, 'God save the King' was the

cry everywhere, and in reply to my objections to the gentlemen-patriots, 'Why, you are scheming for a separation; you are bringing down upon you the inevitable wrath of the greatest power in the world!' —the answer to me always was, 'We mean no separation at all; we yield to no men in loyalty; we glory in the name of Britons,' and so forth, and so forth. The powder-barrels were heaped in the cellar, the train was laid, but Mr. Fawkes was persistent in his dutiful petitions to King and Parliament, and meant no harm, not he! 'Tis true when I spoke of the power of our country, I imagined she would exert it; that she would not expect to overcome three millions of fellow-Britons on their own soil with a few battalions, a half-dozen generals from Bond Street, and a few thousand bravos hired out of Germany. As if we wanted to insult the thirteen colonies as well as to subdue them, we must set upon them these hordes of Hessians, and the murderers out of the Indian wigwams. Was our great quarrel not to be fought without *tali auxilio* and *istis defensoribus?* Ah! 'tis easy, now we are worsted, to look over the map of the great empire wrested from us, and show how we ought not to have lost it. Long Island ought to have exterminated Washington's army; he ought never to have come out of Valley Forge except as a prisoner. The South was ours after the battle of Camden but for the inconceivable meddling of the Commander-in-Chief at New York, who paralysed the exertions of the only capable British General who appeared during the war, and sent him into that miserable *cul-de-sac* at York Town, whence he could only issue defeated and a prisoner. Oh, for a week more! a day more, an hour more of darkness or light! In reading over our American campaigns from their unhappy commencement to their inglorious end, now that we are able to see the enemy's movements and condition as well as our own, I fancy we can see how an advance, a march, might have put enemies into our power who had no means to withstand it, and changed the entire issue of the struggle. But it was ordained by Heaven, and for the good, as we can now have no doubt, of both empires, that the great Western Republic should separate from us : and the gallant soldiers who fought on her side, their indomitable Chief above all, had the glory of facing and overcoming, not only veterans amply provided and inured to war, but wretchedness, cold, hunger, dissensions, treason within their own camp, where all must have gone to rack but for the pure unquenchable flame of patriotism that was for ever burning in the bosom of the heroic leader. What a constancy, what a magnanimity, what a surprising persistence against fortune ! Washington before the enemy was no better nor braver than hundreds that fought with him or against him (who has not heard the repeated sneers against ' Fabius ' in which his factious captains were accustomed to indulge?); but Washington the Chief of a nation in arms, doing battle with distracted parties ; calm in the midst of conspiracy ; serene against the open foe before him and the darker enemies at his back ; Washington inspiring order and spirit into troops hungry and in rags; stung by ingratitude, but betraying no anger, and ever ready to forgive ; in defeat invincible, magnanimous in conquest, and never so sublime as on that day when he laid down his victorious sword and sought his noble retirement : —here indeed is a character to admire and revere ; a life without a stain, a fame without a flaw. *Quando invenies parem?* In that more extensive work, which I have planned and partly written on the subject of this great war, I hope I have done justice to the

character of its greatest leader.* And this from the
sheer force of respect which his eminent virtues ex-
torted. With the young Mr. Washington of my
own early days I had not the honour to enjoy much
sympathy : though my brother, whose character is
much more frank and affectionate than mine, was
always his fast friend in early times, when they were
equals, as in latter days when the General, as I do
own and think, was all mankind's superior.

I have mentioned that contrariety in my disposition, and, perhaps, in my brother's, which somehow
placed us on wrong sides in the quarrel which ensued,
and which from this time forth raged for five years,
until the mother-country was fain to acknowledge
her defeat. Harry should have been the Tory and I
the Whig. Theoretically my opinions were very
much more liberal than those of my brother, who,
especially after his marriage, became what our Indian
Nabobs call a Bahadoor—a person ceremonious, stately,
and exacting respect. When my Lord Dunmore, for
instance, talked about liberating the negroes, so as to
induce them to join the King's standard, Hal was for
hanging the Governor and the Black Guards (as he
called them) whom his Excellency had crimped. ' If
you gentlemen are fighting for freedom,' says I, ' sure
the negroes may fight too.' On which Harry roars
out, shaking his fist, ' Infernal villains, if I meet any
of 'em, they shall die by this hand !' And my mother

* And I trust that in the opinions I have recorded regarding him, I
have shown that I also can be just and magnanimous towards those who
view me personally with no favour. For my brother Hal being at
Mount Vernon, and always eager to bring me and his beloved Chief on
good terms, showed his Excellency some of the early sheets of my history.
General Washington (who read but few books, and had not the slightest
pretensions to literary taste) remarked, ' If you *will* have my opinion, my
dear General, I think Sir George's projected work, from the specimen I
have of it, is certain to offend both parties.'—G. E. W.

agreed that this idea of a negro insurrection was the
most abominable and parricidal notion which had ever
sprung up in her unhappy country. She at least was
more consistent than brother Hal. She would have
black and white obedient to the powers that be :
whereas Hal only could admit that freedom was the
right of the latter colour.

As a proof of her argument, Madam Esmond, and
Harry too, would point to an instance in our own family
in the person of Mr. Gumbo. Having got his freedom
from me, as a reward for his admirable love and
fidelity to me when times were hard, Gumbo, on his
return to Virginia, was scarce a welcome guest in his
old quarters, amongst my mother's servants. He was
free, and they were not : he was, as it were, a centre
of insurrection. He gave himself no small airs of
protection and consequence amongst them ; bragging
of his friends in Europe ('at home,' as he called it),
and his doings there ; and for a while bringing the
household round about him to listen to him and
admire him, like the monkey who had seen the world.
Now Sady, Hal's boy, who went to America of his
own desire, was not free. Hence jealousies between
him and Mr. Gum ; and battles, in which they both
practised the noble art of boxing and butting, which
they had learned at Marybone Gardens and Hockley-
in-the-Hole. Nor was Sady the only jealous person ;
almost all my mother's servants hated Signor Gumbo
for the airs which he gave himself ; and, I am sorry
to say, that our faithful Molly, his wife, was as jealous
as his old fellow-servants. The blacks could not
pardon her for having demeaned herself so far as to
marry one of their kind. She met with no respect,
could exercise no authority, came to her mistress with
ceaseless complaints of the idleness, knavery, lies,
stealing of the black people ; and finally with a story

of jealousy against a certain Dinah, or Diana, who, I heartily trust, was as innocent as her namesake, the moonlight visitant of Endymion. Now, on the article of morality, Madam Esmond was a very Draconess; and a person accused was a person guilty. She made charges against Mr. Gumbo to which he replied with asperity. Forgetting that he was a free gentleman, my mother now ordered Gumbo to be whipped, on which Molly flew at her Ladyship, all her wrath at her husband's infidelity vanishing at the idea of the indignity put upon him : there was a rebellion in our house at Castlewood. A quarrel took place between me and my mother, as I took my man's side. Hal and Fanny sided with her, on the contrary ; and in so far the difference did good, as it brought about some little intimacy between madam and her younger children. This little difference was speedily healed; but it was clear that the Standard of Insurrection must be removed out of our house ; and we determined that Mr. Gumbo and his lady should return to Europe.

My wife and I would willingly have gone with them, God wot, for our boy sickened and lost his strength, and caught the fever in our swampy country; but at this time she was expecting to lie in (of our son Henry), and she knew, too, that I had promised to stay in Virginia. It was agreed that we should send the two back ; but when I offered Theo to go, she said her place was with her husband ;—her father and Hetty at home would take care of our children ; and she scarce would allow me to see a tear in her eyes whilst she was making her preparations for the departure of her little ones. Dost thou remember the time, madam, and the silence round the work-tables, as the piles of little shirts are made ready for the voyage ? And the stealthy visits to the children's chambers whilst they are asleep and yet with you? and the terrible time of parting, as our barge with the servants and children rows to the ship, and you stand on the shore? Had the Prince of Wales been going on that voyage, he could not have been better provided. Where, sirrah, is the Tompion watch your grandmother gave you? and how did you survive the boxes of cakes which the good lady stowed away in your cabin?

The ship which took out my poor Theo's children returned with the Reverend Mr. Hagan and my Lady Maria on board, who meekly chose to resign her rank, and was known in the colony (which was not to be a colony very long) only as Mrs. Hagan. At the time when I was in favour with my Lord Dunmore, a living falling vacant in Westmoreland county, he gave it to our kinsman, who arrived in Virginia time enough to christen our boy Henry, and to preach some sermons on the then gloomy state of affairs, which Madam Esmond pronounced to be prodigious fine. I think my Lady Maria won Madam's heart by insisting on going out of the room after her. 'My father, your brother, was an earl, 'tis true,' says she; 'but you know your Ladyship is a marquis's daughter, and I never can think of taking precedence of you!' So fond did Madam become of her niece, that she even allowed Hagan to read plays—my own humble compositions amongst others—and was fairly forced to own that there was merit in the tragedy of 'Pocahontas,' which our parson delivered with uncommon energy and fire.

Hal and his wife came but rarely to Castlewood and Richmond when the chaplain and his lady were with us. Fanny was very curt and rude with Maria, used to giggle and laugh strangely in her company, and repeatedly remind her of her age, to our mother's

astonishment, who would often ask was there any
cause of quarrel between her niece and her daughter-
in-law? I kept my own counsel on these occasions,
and was often not a little touched by the meekness
with which the elder lady bore her persecutions.
Fanny loved to torture her in her husband's presence
(who, poor fellow, was also in a happy ignorance
about his wife's early history), and the other bore her
agony wincing as little as might be. I sometimes
would remonstrate with Madam Harry, and ask her
was she a Red Indian that she tortured her victims
so? 'Have not I had torture enough in my time?'
says the young lady, and looked as though she was
determined to pay back the injuries inflicted on
her.

'Nay,' says I, 'you were bred in our wigwam, and
I don't remember anything but kindness!'

'Kindness!' cries she. 'No slave was ever treated
as I was. The blows which wound most often are
those which never are aimed. The people who hate
us are not those we have injured.'

I thought of little Fanny in our early days, silent,
smiling, willing to run and do all our biddings for us,
and I grieved for my poor brother, who had taken this
sly creature into his bosom.

CHAPTER LXXXVIII
YANKEE DOODLE COMES TO TOWN

ONE of the uses to which we put America in the days of our British dominion was to make it a refuge for our sinners. Besides convicts and assigned servants whom we transported to our colonies, we discharged on their shores scapegraces and younger sons, for whom dissipation, despair, and bailiffs made the old country uninhabitable. And as Mr. Cook, in his voyages, made his newly discovered islanders presents of English animals (and other specimens of European civilisation), we used to take care to send samples of our *black sheep* over to the colonies, there to browse as best they might, and propagate their precious breed. I myself was perhaps a little guilty in this matter, in busying myself to find a living in America for the worthy Hagan, husband of my kins-woman,—at least was guilty in so far as this, that as we could get him no employment in England, we were glad to ship him to Virginia, and give him a colonial pulpit-cushion to thump. He demeaned himself there as a brave honest gentleman, to be sure ; he did his duty thoroughly by his congregation, and his King too ; and in so far did credit to my small patronage. Madam Theo used to urge this when I confided to her my scruples of conscience on this subject, and show, as her custom was, and is, that my conduct in this, as in all other matters, was dictated by the highest principles of morality and honour. But would I have given Hagan our living at home, and selected him and his wife to minister to our parish? I fear not. I never had a doubt of our cousin's sincere repentance; but I think I was secretly glad when she went to work it out in the wilderness. And I say this, acknowledging my pride and my error. Twice, when I wanted them most, this kind Maria aided me with her sympathy and friendship. She bore her own distresses courageously, and soothed those of others with admirable affection and devotion. And yet I, and some of mine (not Theo), *would* look down upon her. Oh, for shame, for shame on our pride.

My poor Lady Maria was not the only one of our family who was to be sent out of the way to American wildernesses. Having borrowed, stolen, cheated at home, until he could cheat, borrow, and steal no more, the Honourable William Esmond, Esquire, was accommodated with a place at New York; and his noble brother and Royal master heartily desired that they might see him no more. When the troubles began, we heard of the fellow and his doings in his new habitation. Lies and mischief were his *avant-couriers* wherever he travelled. My Lord Dunmore informed me that Mr. Will declared publicly, that our estate of Castlewood was only ours during his brother's pleasure; that his father, out of consideration for Madam Esmond, his Lordship's half-sister, had given her the place for life, and that he, William, was in negotiation with his brother, the present Lord Castlewood, for the purchase of the reversion of the estate! We had the deed of gift in our strong-room at Castlewood, and it was furthermore registered in due form at Williamsburg; so that we were easy on that score. But the intention was everything; and Hal and I promised, as soon as ever we met Mr. William, to get from him a confirmation of this pretty story. What

Madam Esmond's feelings and expressions were when she heard it, I need scarcely here particularise. 'What! my father, the Marquis of Esmond, was a liar, and I am a cheat, am I?' cries my mother. 'He will take my son's property at my death, will he?' And she was for writing, not only to Lord Castlewood in England, but to His Majesty himself at St. James's, and was only prevented by my assurances that Mr. Will's lies were notorious amongst all his acquaintance, and that we could not expect, in our own case, that he should be so inconsistent as to tell the truth. We heard of him presently as one of the loudest amongst the Loyalists in New York, as Captain, and presently Major, of a corps of volunteers who were sending their addresses to the well-disposed in all the other colonies, and announcing their perfect readiness to die for the mother-country.

We could not lie in a house without a whole window, and closing the shutters of that unlucky mansion we had hired at Williamsburg, Madam Esmond left our little capital, and my family returned to Richmond, which also was deserted by the members of the (dissolved) Assembly. Captain Hal and his wife returned pretty early to their plantation; and I, not a little annoyed at the course which events were taking, divided my time pretty much between my own family and that of our Governor, who professed himself very eager to have my advice and company. There were the strongest political differences, but as yet no actual personal quarrel. Even after the dissolution of our House of Assembly (the members of which adjourned to a tavern, and there held that famous meeting where, I believe, the idea of a Congress of all the colonies was first proposed), the gentlemen who were strongest in opposition remained good friends with his Excellency, partook of his hospitality, and joined him in excursions or pleasure. The session over, the gentry went home and had meetings in their respective counties; and the Assemblies in most of the other provinces having been also abruptly dissolved, it was agreed everywhere that a General Congress should be held. Philadelphia, as the largest and most important city on our continent, was selected as the place of meeting; and those celebrated conferences began, which were but the angry preface of war. We were still at God save the King; we were still presenting our humble petitions to the throne; but when I went to visit my brother Harry at Fanny's Mount (his new plantation lay not far from ours, but with Rappahannock between us, and towards Mattaponey river), he rode out on business one morning, and I in the afternoon happened to ride too, and was told by one of the grooms that Master was gone towards 'Willis's Ordinary;' in which direction, thinking no harm, I followed. And upon a clear place not far from 'Willis's,' as I advance out of the wood, I come on Captain Hal on horseback, with three or four and thirty countrymen round about him, armed with every sort of weapon, pike, scythe, fowling-piece, and musket; and the Captain, with two or three likely young fellows as officers under him, was putting the men through their exercise.

As I rode up a queer expression comes over Hal's face. 'Present arms!' says he (and the army tries to perform the salute as well as they could). 'Captain Cade, this is my brother, Sir George Warrington.'

'As a relation of yours, *Colonel*,' says the individual addressed as captain, 'the gentleman is welcome,' and he holds out a hand accordingly.

'And—and a true friend to Virginia,' says Hal, with a reddening face.

'Yes, please God! gentlemen,' say I, on which

the regiment gives a hearty huzzay for the Colonel and
his brother. The drill over, the officers, and the men
too, were for adjourning to 'Willis's' and taking some
refreshment, but Colonel Hal said he could not drink
with them that afternoon, and we trotted homewards
together.

'So, Hal, the cat's out of the bag !' I said.

He gave me a hard look. 'I guess there's wilder
cats in it. It must come to this, George. I say, you
mustn't tell Madam,' he adds.

'Good God !' I cried, 'do you mean that with
fellows such as those I saw yonder, you and your
friends are going to make fight against the greatest
nation and the best army in the world ?'

'I guess we shall get an awful whipping,' says Hal,
'and that's the fact. But then, George,' he added,
with his sweet kind smile, 'we are young, and a
whipping or two may do us good. Won't it do us
good, Dolly, you old slut ?' and he gives a playful
touch with his whip to an old dog of *all trades*, that
was running by him.

I did not try to urge upon him (I had done so in
vain many times previously) our British side of the
question, the side which appears to me to be the best.
He was accustomed to put off my reasons by saying,
'All mighty well, brother ; you speak as an Englishman, and have cast in your lot with your country, as
I have with mine.' To this argument I own there is
no answer, and all that remains for the disputants is to
fight the matter out, when the strongest is in the
right. Which had the right in the wars of the last
century ? The King or the Parliament ? The side
that was uppermost was the right, and on the whole
much more humane in their victory than the
Cavaliers would have been had they won. Nay,
suppose we Tories had won the day in America : how

frightful and bloody that triumph would have been! What ropes and scaffolds one imagines, what noble heads laid low! A strange feeling this, I own : I was on the Loyalist side, and yet wanted the Whigs to win. My brother Hal, on the other hand, who distinguished himself greatly with his regiment, never allowed a word of disrespect against the enemy whom he opposed. 'The officers of the British army,' he used to say, 'are gentlemen : at least, I have not heard that they are very much changed since my time. There may be scoundrels and ruffians amongst the enemy's troops ; I dare say we could find some such amongst our own. Our business is to beat His Majesty's forces, not to call them names ; any rascal can do that.' And, from a name which Mr. Lee gave my brother, and many of his rough horsemen did not understand, Harry was often called 'Chevalier Baird' in the Continental army. He was a knight, indeed, without fear and without reproach.

As for the argument, 'What could such people as those you were drilling do against the British army?' Hal had a confident answer. 'They can beat them,' says he, 'Mr. George, that's what they can do.'

'Great Heavens!' I cry, 'do you mean with your company of Wolfe's you would hesitate to attack five hundred such?'

'With my company of the 67th I would go anywhere, and agree with you, that at this present moment I know more of soldiering than they ;—but place me on that open ground where you found us, armed as you please, and half-a-dozen of my friends, with rifles, in the woods round about me : which would get the better? You know best, Mr. Braddock's aide-de-camp.'

There was no arguing with such a determination as this. 'Thou knowest my way of thinking, Hal,'

I said; 'and having surprised you at your work, I
must tell my Lord what I have seen.'

'Tell him, of course. You have seen our
county militia exercising. You will see as much
in every colony from here to the St. Lawrence
or Georgia. As I am an old soldier, they have
elected me colonel. What more natural? Come,
brother, let us trot on; dinner will be ready,
and Mrs. Fan does not like me to keep it waiting.'
And so we made for his house, which was open, like
all the houses of our Virginian gentlemen, and where
not only every friend and neighbour, but every
stranger and traveller, was sure to find a welcome.

'So, Mrs. Fan,' I said, 'I have found out what
game my brother has been playing.'

'I trust the Colonel will have plenty of sport ere
long,' says she, with a toss of her head.

My wife thought Harry had been hunting, and I
did not care to undeceive her, though what I had
seen and he had told me made me naturally very
anxious.

CHAPTER LXXXIX
A COLONEL WITHOUT A REGIMENT

WHEN my visit to my brother was concluded, and my wife and young child had returned to our maternal house at Richmond, I made it my business to go over to our Governor, then at his country-house, near Williamsburg, and confer with him regarding these open preparations for war, which were being made not only in our own province, but in every one of the colonies, as far as we could learn. Gentlemen with whose names history has since made all the world familiar were appointed from Virginia as Delegates to the General Congress about to be held in Philadelphia. In Massachusetts the people and the Royal troops were facing each other almost in open hostility: in Maryland and Pennsylvania we flattered ourselves that a much more loyal spirit was prevalent: in the Carolinas and Georgia the mother-country could reckon upon staunch adherents, and a great majority of the inhabitants: and it never was to be supposed that our own Virginia would forego its ancient loyalty. We had but few troops in the province, but its gentry were proud of their descent from the Cavaliers of the old times: and round about our Governor were swarms of loud and confident Loyalists who were only eager for the moment when they might draw the sword, and scatter the rascally rebels before them. Of course, in these meetings, I

was forced to hear many a hard word against my poor
Harry. His wife, all agreed (and not without good
reason, perhaps), had led him to adopt these extreme
anti-British opinions which he had of late declared ;
and he was infatuated by his attachment to the gentleman of Mount Vernon, it was farther said, whose
opinions my brother always followed, and who, day
by day, was committing himself farther in the
dreadful and desperate course of resistance. 'This
is your friend,' the people about his Excellency said,
'this is the man you favoured, who has had your special
confidence, and who has repeatedly shared your
hospitality !' It could not but be owned much of
this was true: though what some of our eager
Loyalists called treachery, was indeed rather a proof
of the longing desire Mr. Washington and other
gentlemen had, not to withdraw from their allegiance
to the Crown, but to remain faithful, and exhaust the
very last chance of reconciliation, before they risked
the other terrible alternative of revolt and separation.
Let traitors arm, and villains draw the parricidal
sword ! We at least would remain faithful ; the
unconquerable power of England would be exerted,
and the misguided and ungrateful provinces punished
and brought back to their obedience. With what
cheers we drank His Majesty's health after our
banquets ! We would die in defence of his rights ;
we would have a Prince of his Royal house to come
and govern his ancient dominions ! In consideration
of my own and my excellent mother's loyalty, my
brother's benighted conduct should be forgiven. Was
it yet too late to secure him by offering him a
good command ? Would I not intercede with him,
who, it was known, had a great influence over him ?
In our Williamsburg councils we were alternately in
every state of exaltation and triumph, of hope, of fury

against the rebels, of anxious expectancy of home
succour, of doubt, distrust, and gloom.

I promised to intercede with my brother ; and wrote
to him, I own, with but little hope of success, repeating,
and trying to strengthen the arguments which I had
many a time used in our conversations. My mother,
too, used her authority ; but from this, I own, I
expected little advantage. She assailed him, as her
habit was, with such texts of Scripture as she thought
bore out her own opinion, and threatened punishment to
him. She menaced him with the penalties which must
fall upon those who were disobedient to the powers
that be. She pointed to his elder brother's example ;
and hinted, I fear, at his subjection to his wife, the
very worst argument she could use in such a controversy. She did not show me her own letter to
him ; possibly she knew I might find fault with the
energy of some of the expressions she thought proper
to employ ; but she showed me his answer, from which
I gathered what the style and tenour of her argument
had been. And if Madam Esmond brought Scripture to her aid, Mr. Hal, to my surprise, brought
scores of texts to bear upon her in reply, and addressed
her in a very neat, temperate, and even elegant composition, which I thought his wife herself was scarcely
capable of penning. Indeed, I found he had enlisted the
services of Mr. Belman, the new Richmond clergyman, who had taken up strong opinions on the Whig
side, and who preached and printed sermons against
Hagan (who, as I have said, was of our faction), in
which I fear Belman had the best of the dispute.

My exhortations to Hal had no more success than
our mother's. He did not answer my letters. Being
still farther pressed by the friends of the Government, I wrote over most imprudently to say I would
visit him at the end of the week at Fanny's Mount ;

but on arriving, I only found my sister, who received me with perfect cordiality, but informed me that Hal was gone into the country, ever so far towards the Blue Mountains to look at some horses, and was to be away—she did not know how long he was to be away!

I knew then there was no hope. 'My dear,' I said, 'as far as I can judge from the signs of the times, the train that has been laid these years must have a match put to it before long. Harry is riding away. God knows to what end.'

'The Lord prosper the righteous cause, Sir George,' says she.

'Amen, with all my heart. You and he speak as Americans; I as an Englishman. Tell him from me, that when anything in the course of nature shall happen to our mother, I have enough for me and mine in England, and shall resign all our land here in Virginia to him.'

'You don't mean that, George?' she cries, with brightening eyes. 'Well, to be sure, it is but right and fair,' she presently added. 'Why should you, who are the eldest but by an hour, have everything,—a palace and lands in England—the plantation here—the title—and children—and my poor Harry none? But 'tis generous of you all the same—leastways handsome and proper, and I didn't expect it of you : and you don't take after your mother in this, Sir George, that you don't nohow. Give my love to sister Theo!' And she offers me a cheek to kiss, ere I ride away from her door. With such a woman as Fanny to guide him, how could I hope to make a convert of my brother?

Having met with this poor success in my enterprise, I rode back to our Governor, with whom I agreed that it was time to arm in earnest, and prepare ourselves against the shock that certainly was at hand.

He and his whole Court of Officials were not a little
agitated and excited ; needlessly savage, I thought, in
their abuse of the wicked Whigs, and loud in their
shouts of Old England for ever ; but they were all
eager for the day when the contending parties could
meet hand to hand, and they could have an opportunity of riding those wicked Whigs down.   And
I left my Lord, having received the thanks of his
Excellency in Council, and engaged to do my best
endeavours to raise a body of men in defence of the
Crown.   Hence the corps, called afterwards the
Westmoreland Defenders, had its rise, of which I
had the honour to be appointed Colonel, and which
I was to command when it appeared in the field.
And that fortunate event must straightway take
place, as soon as the county knew that a gentleman
of my station and name would take the command of
the force.   The announcement was duly made in the
Government *Gazette*, and we filled in our officers
readily enough ; but the recruits, it must be owned,
were slow to come in, and quick to disappear.
Nevertheless, friend Hagan eagerly came forward
to offer himself as chaplain.   Madam Esmond gave
us our colours, and progressed about the country
engaging volunteers ; but the most eager recruiter
of all was my good old tutor, little Mr. Dempster,
who had been out as a boy on the Jacobite side in
Scotland, and who went specially into the Carolinas,
among the children of his banished old comrades,
who had worn the white cockade of Prince Charles,
and who most of all showed themselves in this contest
still loyal to the Crown.

Hal's expedition in search of horses led him not
only so far as the Blue Mountains in our colony, but
thence on a long journey to Annapolis and Baltimore ;
and from Baltimore to Philadelphia, to be sure ; where

a second General Congress was now sitting, attended
by our Virginian gentlemen of the last year. Meanwhile, all the almanacs tell what had happened.
Lexington had happened, and the first shots were fired
in the war which was to end in the independence of my
native country. We still protested of our loyalty to
His Majesty; but we stated our determination to die
or be free; and some twenty thousand of our loyal
petitioners assembled round about Boston with arms
in their hands, and cannon, to which they had helped
themselves out of the Government stores. Mr.
Arnold had begun that career which was to end so
brilliantly, by the daring and burglarious capture of
two forts, of which he forced the doors. Three
generals from Bond Street, with a large reinforce-
ment, were on their way to help Mr. Gage out of his
ugly position at Boston. Presently the armies were
actually engaged; and our British generals commenced their career of conquest and pacification in
the colonies by the glorious blunder of Breed's
Hill. Here they fortified themselves, feeling themselves not strong enough for the moment to
win any more glorious victories over the rebels;
and the two armies lay watching each other whilst
Congress was deliberating at Philadelphia who should
command the forces of the confederated colonies.

We all know on whom the most fortunate choice
of the nation fell. Of the Virginian regiments which
marched to join the new General-in-Chief, one was
commanded by Henry Esmond Warrington, Esq., late
a Captain in His Majesty's service; and by his side
rode his little wife, of whose bravery we often subsequently heard. I was glad, for one, that she had
quitted Virginia; for, had she remained after her
husband's departure, our mother would infallibly have
gone over to give her battle; and I was thankful, at

least, that that incident of civil war was spared to our family and history.

The rush of our farmers and country-folk was almost all directed towards the new northern army; and our people were not a little flattered at the selection of a Virginian gentleman for the principal command. With a thrill of wrath and fury the provinces heard of the blood drawn at Lexington; and men yelled denunciations against the cruelty and wantonness of the bloody British invader. The invader was but doing his duty, and was met and resisted by men in arms, who wished to prevent him from helping himself to his own; but people do not stay to weigh their words when they mean to be angry; the colonists had taken their side; and, with what I own to be a natural spirit and ardour, were determined to have a trial of strength with the braggart domineering mother-country. Breed's Hill became a mountain, as it were, which all men of the American continent might behold, with Liberty, Victory, Glory, on its flaming summit. These dreaded troops could be withstood, then, by farmers and ploughmen. These famous officers could be out-generalled by doctors, lawyers, and civilians! Granted that Britons could conquer all the world;—here were their children who could match and conquer Britons! Indeed, I don't know which of the two deserves the palm, either for bravery or vainglory. We are in the habit of laughing at our French neighbours for boasting, gasconading, and so forth; but for a steady self-esteem and indomitable confidence in our own courage, greatness, magnanimity;—who can compare with Britons, except their children across the Atlantic?

The people round about us took the people's side for the most part in the struggle, and, truth to say, Sir George Warrington found his regiment of West-

moreland Defenders but very thinly manned at the
commencement, and woefully diminished in numbers
presently, not only after the news of battle from the
north, but in consequence of the behaviour of my Lord
our Governor, whose conduct enraged no one more
than his own immediate partisans, and the loyal
adherents of the Crown throughout the colony. That
he would plant the King's standard, and summon all
loyal gentlemen to rally round it, had been a measure
agreed in countless meetings, and applauded over
thousands of bumpers. I have a pretty good memory,
and could mention the name of many a gentleman,
now a smug officer of the United States Government,
whom I have heard hiccup out a prayer that he might
be allowed to perish under the folds of his country's
flag ; or roar a challenge to the bloody traitors absent
with the rebel army. But let bygones be bygones.
This, however, is matter of public history, that his
Lordship, our Governor, a peer of Scotland, the
Sovereign's representative in his Old Dominion, who
so loudly invited all the lieges to join the King's
standard, was the first to put it in his pocket, and fly
to his ships out of reach of danger. He would not
leave them, save as a pirate at midnight to burn and
destroy. Meanwhile, we loyal gentry remained on
shore, committed to our cause, and only subject to
greater danger in consequence of the weakness and
cruelty of him who ought to have been our leader.
It was the beginning of June, our orchards and gardens
were all blooming with plenty and summer ; a week
before I had been over at Williamsburg, exchanging
compliments with his Excellency, devising plans for
future movements by which we should be able to make
good head against rebellion, shaking hands heartily at
parting, and *vincere aut mori* the very last words upon
all our lips. Our little family was gathered at Rich-

mond, talking over, as we did daily, the prospect of
affairs in the north, the quarrels between our own
Assembly and his Excellency, by whom they had been
afresh convened, when our ghostly Hagan rushes into
our parlour, and asks, 'Have we heard the news of the
Governor ? '

'Has he dissolved the Assembly again, and put that
scoundrel Patrick Henry in irons ?' asks Madam
Esmond.

'No such thing !   His Lordship with his lady and
family have left their palace privately at night.   They
are on board a man-of-war off York, whence my Lord
has sent a despatch to the Assembly, begging them to
continue their sitting, and announcing that he himself had only quitted his Government House out of
fear of the fury of the people.'

What was to become of the sheep, now the
shepherd had run away ?   No entreaties could be
more pathetic than those of the gentlemen of the
House of Assembly, who guaranteed their Governor
security if he would but land, and implored him to
appear amongst them, if but to pass bills and transact
the necessary business.   No: the man-of-war was
his seat of Government, and my Lord desired his
House of Commons to wait upon him there.   This
was erecting the King's standard with a vengeance.
Our Governor had left us; our Assembly perforce
ruled in his stead; a rabble of people followed the
fugitive Viceroy on board his ships.   A mob of negroes
deserted out of the plantations to join this other
deserter.   He and his black allies landed here and
there in darkness, and emulated the most lawless
of our opponents in their alacrity at seizing and
burning.   He not only invited runaway negroes, but
he sent an ambassador to Indians with entreaties to
join his standard.   When he came on shore it was

to burn and destroy ; when the people resisted, as at
Norfolk and Hampton, he retreated and betook himself to his ships again.

Even my mother, after that miserable flight of our
chief, was scared at the aspect of affairs, and doubted
of the speedy putting down of the rebellion. The
arming of the negroes was, in her opinion, the most
cowardly blow of all. The loyal gentry were ruined,
and robbed, many of them, of their only property.
A score of our worst hands deserted from Richmond
and Castlewood, and fled to our courageous Governor's
fleet ; not all of them, though some of them, were
slain, and a couple hung by the enemy for plunder
and robbery perpetrated whilst with his Lordship's
precious army. Because her property was wantonly
injured and His Majesty's chief officer an imbecile,
would Madam Esmond desert the cause of Royalty
and Honour ? My good mother was never so
prodigiously dignified, and loudly and enthusiastically loyal, as after she heard of our Governor's
lamentable defection. The people round about her,
though most of them of quite a different way of
thinking, listened to her speeches without unkindness. Her oddities were known far and wide through
our province ; where, I am afraid, many of the wags
amongst our young men were accustomed to smoke
her, as the phrase then was, and draw out her stories
about the Marquis her father, about the splendour of
her family, and so forth. But, along with her
oddities, her charities and kindness were remembered,
and many a rebel, as she called them, had a sneaking
regard for the pompous little Tory lady.

As for the Colonel of the Westmoreland Defenders,
though that gentleman's command dwindled utterly
away after the outrageous conduct of his chief, yet I
escaped from some very serious danger which might

have befallen me and mine in consequence of some
disputes which I was known to have had with my
Lord Dunmore. Going on board his ship after he
had burnt the stores at Hampton, and issued the
proclamation calling the negroes to his standard, I
made so free as to remonstrate with him in regard to
both measures; I implored him to return to Williamsburg, where hundreds of us, thousands, I hoped, would
be ready to defend him to the last extremity; and
in my remonstrance used terms so free, or rather, as
I suspect, indicated my contempt for his conduct so
clearly by my behaviour, that his Lordship flew into
a rage, said I was a ——— rebel, like all the rest of them,
and ordered me under arrest there on board his own
ship. In my quality of Militia officer (since the
breaking out of the troubles I commonly used a red
coat, to show that I wore the King's colour), I begged
for a court-martial immediately; and turning round
to two officers who had been present during our
altercation, desired them to remember all that had
passed between his Lordship and me. These gentlemen were no doubt of my way of thinking as to the
chief's behaviour, and our interview ended in my
going ashore unaccompanied by a guard. The story
got wind amongst the Whig gentry, and was improved
in the telling. I had spoken out my mind manfully
to the Governor; no Whig could have uttered sentiments more liberal. When riots took place in
Richmond, and many of the Loyalists remaining
there were in peril of life and betook themselves to
the ships, my mother's property and house were never
endangered, nor her family insulted. We were still
at the stage when a reconciliation was fondly thought
possible. 'Ah! if all the Tories were like you,' a
distinguished Whig has said to me, 'we and the
people at home should soon come together again.'

This, of course, was before the famous Fourth of
July, and that declaration which rendered reconcile-
ment impossible. Afterwards, when parties grew
more rancorous, motives much less creditable were
assigned for my conduct, and it was said I chose to
be a Liberal Tory because I was a cunning fox, and
wished to keep my estate whatever way things went.
And this, I am bound to say, is the opinion regarding
my humble self which has obtained in very high
quarters at home, where a profound regard for my own
interest has been supposed not uncommonly to have
occasioned my conduct during the late unhappy
troubles.

There were two or three persons in the world (for
I had not told my mother how I was resolved to cede
to my brother all my life-interest in our American
property) who knew that I had no mercenary motives
in regard to the conduct I pursued. It was not worth
while to undeceive others; what were life worth, if a
man were forced to put himself *à la piste* of all the
calumnies uttered against him? And I do not quite
know to this present day, how it happened that my
mother, that notorious Loyalist, was left for several
years quite undisturbed in her house at Castlewood, a
stray troop or company of Continentals being occasionally quartered upon her. I do not know for certain, I
say, how this piece of good fortune happened, though
I can give a pretty shrewd guess as to the cause of it.
Madam Fanny, after a campaign before Boston, came
back to Fanny's Mount, leaving her Colonel. My
modest Hal, until the conclusion of the war, would
accept no higher rank, believing that in command of
a regiment he could be more useful than in charge of
a division. Madam Fanny, I say, came back, and it
was remarkable after her return how her old asperity
towards my mother seemed to be removed, and what

an affection she showed for her and all the property.
She was great friends with the Governor and some of
the most influential gentlemen of the new Assembly :—
Madam Esmond was harmless, and for her son's sake,
who was bravely battling for his country, her errors
should be lightly visited :—I know not how it was,
but for years she remained unharmed, except in respect
of heavy Government requisitions, which of course
she had to pay, and it was not until the red-coats
appeared about our house, that much serious evil came
to it.

CHAPTER XC

IN WHICH WE BOTH FIGHT AND RUN AWAY

WHAT was the use of a Colonel without a regiment?
The Governor and Council who had made such a
parade of thanks in endowing me with mine, were
away out of sight, skulking on board ships, with an
occasional piracy and arson on shore. My Lord
Dunmore's black allies frightened away those of his
own blood ; and besides these negroes whom he had
summoned around him in arms, we heard that he had
sent an envoy among the Indians of the South, and
that they were to come down in numbers and tomahawk our people into good behaviour. 'And these
are to be our allies !' I say to my mother, exchanging
ominous looks with her, and remembering, with a
ghastly distinctness, that savage whose face glared
over mine, and whose knife was at my throat when
Florac struck him down on Braddock's field. We
put our house of Castlewood into as good a state of
defence as we could devise ; but, in truth, it was more
of the red men and the blacks than of the rebels we

were afraid. I never saw my mother lose courage but once, and then when she was recounting to us the particulars of our father's death in a foray of Indians more than forty years ago. Seeing some figures one night moving in front of our house, nothing could persuade the good lady but that they were savages, and she sank on her knees crying out, 'The Lord have mercy upon us! The Indians—the Indians!'

My Lord's negro allies vanished on board his ships, or where they could find pay and plunder; but the painted heroes from the South never made their appearance, though I own to have looked at my mother's grey head, my wife's brown hair, and our little one's golden ringlets, with a horrible pang of doubt lest these should fall the victims of ruffian war. And it was we who fought with such weapons, and enlisted these allies! But that I *dare* not (so to speak) be setting myself up as interpreter of Providence, and pointing out the special finger of Heaven (as many people are wont to do), I would say our employment of these Indians, and of the German mercenaries, brought their own retribution with them in this war. In the field, where the mercenaries were attacked by the Provincials, they yielded, and it was triumphing over them that so raised the spirit of the Continental army; and the murder of one woman (Miss M'Crea) by a half-dozen drunken Indians, did more harm to the Royal cause than the loss of a battle or the destruction of regiments.

Now, the Indian panic over, Madam Esmond's courage returned: and she began to be seriously and not unjustly uneasy at the danger which I ran myself, and which I brought upon others by remaining in Virginia.

'What harm can they do me,' says she, 'a poor woman? If I have one son a Colonel without a regiment, I have another with a couple of hundred Continentals behind him in Mr. Washington's camp. If the Royalists come, they will let me off for your sake ; if the rebels appear, I shall have Harry's passport. I don't wish, sir, I don't like, that your delicate wife, and this dear little baby should be here, and only increase the risk of all of us ! We must have them away to Boston or New York. Don't talk about defending me ! Who will think of hurting a poor harmless old woman ? If the rebels come, I shall shelter behind Mrs. Fanny's petticoats, and shall be much safer without you in the house than in it.' This she said in part, perhaps, because 'twas reasonable ; more so because she would have me and my family out of the danger ; and danger or not, for her part she was determined to remain in the land where her father was buried, and she was born. She was living *backwards*, so to speak. She had seen the new generation, and blessed them, and bade them farewell. She belonged to the past, and old days and memories.

While we were debating about the Boston scheme, comes the news that the British have evacuated that luckless city altogether, never having ventured to attack Mr. Washington in his camp at Cambridge (though he lay there for many months without powder at our mercy) ; but waiting until he procured ammunition, and seized and fortified Dorchester heights, which commanded the town, out of which the whole British army and colony was obliged to beat a retreat. That the King's troops won the battle at Bunker's Hill, there is no more doubt than that they beat the French at Blenheim ; but through the war their chiefs seem constantly to have been afraid of assaulting intrenched Continentals afterwards ; else why, from July to March, hesitate to strike an almost defenceless enemy? Why the hesitation at Long Island, when the Continental army was in our hand? Why that astonishing timorousness of Howe before Valley Forge, where the relics of a force starving, sickening, and in rags, could scarcely man the lines, which they held before a great, victorious, and perfectly appointed army?

As the hopes and fears of the contending parties rose and fell, it was curious to mark the altered tone of the partisans of either. When the news came to us in the country of the evacuation of Boston every little Whig in the neighbourhood made his bow to Madam, and advised her to a speedy submission. She did not carry her loyalty quite so openly as heretofore, and flaunt her flag in the faces of the public, but she never swerved. Every night and morning in private poor Hagan prayed for the Royal Family in our own household, and on Sundays any neighbours were welcome to attend the service, where my mother acted as a very emphatic clerk, and the prayer for the High Court of Parliament under our Most Religious and Gracious King was very stoutly delivered. The brave Hagan was a parson without a living, as I was a Militia Colonel without a regiment. Hagan had continued to pray stoutly for King George in Williamsburg, long after his Excellency our Governor had run away : but on coming to church one Sunday to perform his duty, he found a corporal's guard at the church door, who told him that the Committee of Safety had put another divine in his place, and he was requested to keep a quiet tongue in his head. He told the man to 'lead him before their chiefs' (our honest friend always loved tall words and tragic attitudes); and accordingly was marched through the streets to the Capitol, with a chorus of white and coloured blackguards at the skirts of his gown ; and had an interview with Mr. Henry and the new State officers, and confronted the robbers, as he said, in their den. Of course he was for making an heroic speech before these gentlemen (and was one of many men who perhaps would have no objection to be made martyrs, so that they might be roasted *coram populo*, or tortured in a full house), but Mr. Henry was determined to give him no such chance. After keeping Hagan three or four hours waiting in an ante-room in the company of negroes, when the worthy divine entered the new chief magistrate's room with an undaunted mien, and began a prepared speech with—'Sir, by what authority am I, a minister of the—' 'Mr. Hagan,' says the other, interrupting him, 'I am too busy to listen to speeches. And as for King George, he has henceforth no more authority in this country than King Nebuchadnezzar. Mind you that, and hold your tongue, if you please ! Stick to King John, sir, and King Macbeth ; and if you will send round your benefit-tickets, all the Assembly shall come and hear you. Did you ever see Mr. Hagan, on the boards, when you was in London, General ?' And, so saying, Henry turns round upon Mr. Washington's second in command, General Lee, who was now come into Virginia upon State affairs, and our shamefaced good Hagan was bustled out of the room, reddening and almost crying with shame. After this event we thought that Hagan's ministrations were best confined to us in the country, and removed the worthy pastor from his restive lambs in the city.

The selection of Virginians to the very highest civil and military appointments of the new Government bribed and flattered many of our leading people, who but for the outrageous conduct of our Government

might have remained faithful to the Crown, and made
good head against the rising rebellion. But, although
we Loyalists were gagged and muzzled, though the
Capitol was in the hands of the Whigs, and our
vaunted levies of loyal recruits so many Falstaff's
regiments, for the most part, the faithful still kept in-
telligences with one another in the colony, and with
our neighbours ; and though we did not rise, and
though we ran away, and though, in examination
before committees, justices, and so forth, some of our
frightened people gave themselves Republican airs,
and vowed perdition to kings and nobles ; yet we knew
each other pretty well, and—according as the chances
were more or less favourable to us, the master more
or less hard—we concealed our colours, showed our
colours, half showed our colours, or downright aposta-
tised for the nonce, and cried 'Down with King
George!' Our negroes bore about, from house to
house, all sorts of messages and tokens. Endless
underhand plots and schemes were engaged in by
those who could not afford the light. The battle
over, the neutrals come and join the winning side,
and shout as loudly as the patriots. The runaways
are not counted. Will any man tell me that the
signers and ardent well-wishers of the Declaration of
Independence were not in a minority of the nation,
and that the minority did not win ? We knew that
a part of the defeated army of Massachusetts was
about to make an important expedition southward,
upon the success of which the very greatest hopes
were founded ; and I, for one, being anxious to make
a movement as soon as there was any chance of
activity, had put myself in communication with the
ex-Governor Martin, of North Carolina, whom I proposed to join, with three or four of our Virginian
gentlemen, officers of that notable corps of which we

only wanted privates. We made no particular mystery
about our departure from Castlewood ; the affairs of
Congress were not going so well yet that the new
Government could afford to lay any particular stress
or tyranny upon persons of a doubtful way of thinking.
Gentlemen's houses were still open ; and in our
Southern fashion we would visit our friends for months
at a time. My wife and I, with our infant and a
fitting suite of servants, took leave of Madam Esmond
on a visit to a neighbouring plantation. We went
thence to another friend's house, and then to another,
till finally we reached Wilmington, in North Carolina,
which was the point at which we expected to stretch
a hand to the succours which were coming to meet
us.

Ere our arrival, our brother Carolinian Royalists
had shown themselves in some force. Their encounters with the Whigs had been unlucky. The
poor Highlanders had been no more fortunate in their
present contest in favour of King George, than when
they had drawn their swords against him in their own
country. We did not reach Wilmington until the
end of May, by which time we found Admiral Parker's
squadron there, with General Clinton and five British
regiments on board, whose object was a descent upon
Charleston.

The General, to whom I immediately made myself
known, seeing that my regiment consisted of Lady
Warrington, our infant, whom she was nursing, and
three negro servants, received us at first with a very
grim welcome. But Captain Horner of the 'Sphinx'
frigate, who had been on the Jamaica station, and received, like all the rest of the world, many kindnesses
from our dear Governor there, when he heard that
my wife was General Lambert's daughter, eagerly
received her on board, and gave up his best cabin to

our service; and so we were refugees, too, like my
Lord Dunmore, having waved our flag, to be sure,
and pocketed it, and slipped out at the back door.
From Wilmington we bore away quickly to Charleston,
and in the course of the voyage and our delay in the
river, previous to our assault on the place, I made
some acquaintance with Mr. Clinton which increased
to a further intimacy. It was the King's birthday
when we appeared in the river: we determined it
was a glorious day for the commencement of the
expedition.

It did not take place for some days after, and I leave
out, purposely, all descriptions of my Andromache
parting from her Hector, going forth on this expedition. In the first place, Hector is perfectly well
(though a little gouty), nor has any rascal of a Pyrrhus
made a prize of his widow: and in times of war and
commotion, are not such scenes of woe and terror,
and parting, occurring every hour? I can see the
gentle face yet over the bulwark, as we descend the
ship's side into the boats, and the smile of the infant
on her arm. What old stories, to be sure! Captain
Miles, having no natural taste for poetry, you have
forgot the verses, no doubt, in Mr. Pope's ' Homer,'
in which you are described as parting with your heroic
father; but your mother often read them to you as a
boy, and keeps the gorget I wore on that day some-
where amongst her dressing-boxes now.

My second venture at fighting was no more lucky
than my first. We came back to our ships that
evening thoroughly beaten. The madcap Lee, whom
Clinton had faced at Boston, now met him at
Charleston. Lee, and the gallant garrison there,
made a brilliant and most successful resistance. The
fort on Sullivan's Island, which we attacked, was a
nut we could not crack. The fire of all our frigates

was not strong enough to pound its shell; the passage by which we moved up to the assault of the place was not fordable, as those officers found—Sir Henry at the head of them, who was always the first to charge—who attempted to wade it.   Death by shot, by drowning, by catching my death of cold, I had braved before I returned to my wife; and our frigate being aground for a time and got off with difficulty, was agreeably cannonaded by the enemy until she got off her bank.

A small incident in the midst of this unlucky struggle was the occasion of a subsequent intimacy which arose between me and Sir Harry Clinton, and bound me to that most gallant officer during the period in which it was my fortune to follow the war. Of his qualifications as a leader there may be many opinions : I fear to say, regarding a man I heartily respect and admire, there ought only to be one.   Of his personal bearing and his courage there can be no doubt; he was always eager to show it; and whether at the final charge on Breed's Hill, when at the head of the rallied troops he carried the Continental lines, or here before Sullivan's Fort, or a year later at Fort Washington, when, standard in hand, he swept up the height, and entered the fort at the head of the storming column, Clinton was always foremost in the race of battle, and the King's service knew no more admirable soldier.

We were taking to the water from our boats, with the intention of forcing a column to the fort, through a way which our own guns had rendered practicable, when a shot struck a boat alongside of us, so well aimed, as actually to put three-fourths of the boat's crew *hors de combat*, and knocked down the officer steering, and the flag behind him.   I could not help crying out, ' Bravo ! well aimed !' for no ninepins ever went down more helplessly than these poor fellows before the round shot. Then the General, turning round to me, says rather grimly, 'Sir, the behaviour of the enemy seems to please you!' 'I am pleased, sir,' says I, 'that my countrymen, yonder, should fight as becomes our nation.' We floundered on towards the fort in the midst of the same amiable attentions from small arms and great, until we found the water was up to our breasts and deepening at every step, when we were fain to take to our boats again and pull out of harm's way. Sir Henry waited upon my Lady Warrington on board the 'Sphinx' after this, and was very gracious to her, and mighty facetious regarding the character of the humble writer of the present Memoir, whom his Excellency always described as a rebel at heart. I pray my children may live to see or engage in no great revolutions,—such as that, for instance, raging in the country of our miserable French neighbours. Save a very very few indeed, the actors in those great tragedies do not bear to be scanned too closely; the chiefs are often no better than ranting quacks; the heroes ignoble puppets: the heroines anything but pure. The prize is not always to the brave. In our revolution it certainly did fall, for once and for a wonder, to the most deserving: but who knows his enemies now? His great and surprising triumphs were not in those rare engagements with the enemy where he obtained a trifling mastery; but over Congress; over hunger and disease; over lukewarm friends, or smiling foes in his own camp, whom his great spirit had to meet, and master. When the struggle was over, and our impotent chiefs who had conducted it began to squabble and accuse each other in their own defence before the nation,—what charges and counter-charges were brought; what pretexts of delay were urged; what piteous excuses were put forward that this fleet arrived too late ; that that regiment mistook its orders ; that these cannon-balls would not fit those guns : and so to the end of the chapter ! Here was a general who beat us with *no* shot at times, and no powder, and no money ; and *he* never thought of a convention ; *his* courage never capitulated ! Through all the doubt and darkness, the danger and long tempest of the war, I think it was only the American leader's indomitable soul that remained entirely steady.

Of course our Charleston expedition was made the most of, and pronounced a prodigious victory by the enemy, who had learnt (from their parents, perhaps) to cry victory if a corporal's guard were surprised, as loud as if we had won a pitched battle. Mr. Lee rushed back to New York, the conqueror of conquerors, trumpeting his glory, and by no man received with more eager delight than by the Commander-in-Chief of the American army. It was my dear Lee and my dear General between them, then ; and it hath always touched me in the history of our early Revolution to note that simple confidence and admiration with which the General-in-Chief was wont to regard officers under him, who had happened previously to serve with the King's army. So the Mexicans of old looked and wondered when they first saw an armed Spanish horseman ! And this mad flashy braggart (and another Continental General, whose name and whose luck afterwards were sufficiently notorious) you may be sure took advantage of the modesty of the Commander-in-Chief, and advised, and blustered, and sneered, and disobeyed orders ; daily presenting fresh obstacles (as if he had not enough otherwise !) in the path over which only Mr. Washington's astonishing endurance could have enabled him to march.

Whilst we were away on our South Carolina expedition, the famous Fourth of July had taken place, and we and the thirteen United States were parted for ever. My own native State of Virginia had also distinguished itself by announcing that all men are equally free ; that all power is vested in the people, who have an inalienable right to alter, reform, or abolish their form of government *at pleasure*, and that the idea of an hereditary first magistrate is unnatural and absurd ! Our General presented me with this document fresh from Williamsburg, as we were sailing northward by the Virginia capes, and, amidst not a little amusement and laughter, pointed out to me the faith to which, from the Fourth inst. inclusive, I was bound. There was no help for it ; I was a Virginian—my godfathers had promised and vowed, in my name, that all men were equally free (including, of course, the race of poor Gumbo), that the idea of a monarchy is absurd, and that I had the right to alter my form of government *at pleasure*. I thought of Madam Esmond at home, and how she would look when these articles of faith were brought her to subscribe : how would Hagan receive them ? He demolished them in a sermon, in which all the logic was on his side ; but the U.S. Government has not, somehow, been affected by the discourse ; and when he came to touch upon the point that all men being free, therefore Gumbo and Sady, and Nathan, had assuredly a right to go to Congress : 'Tut, tut ! my good Mr. Hagan,' says my mother, 'let us hear no more of this nonsense ; but leave such wickedness and folly to the rebels !'

By the middle of August we were before New York, whither Mr. Howe had brought his army that had betaken itself to Halifax after its inglorious expulsion from Boston. The American Commander-

in-Chief was at New York, and a great battle inevitable ; and I looked forward to it with an inexpressible
feeling of doubt and anxiety, knowing that my
dearest brother and his regiment formed part of the
troops whom we must attack, and could not but
overpower. Almost the whole of the American army
came over to fight on a small island, where every
officer on both sides knew that they were to be
beaten, and whence they had not a chance of escape.
Two frigates, out of a hundred we had placed so as
to command the enemy's intrenched camp and point
of retreat across East River to New York, would
have destroyed every bark in which he sought to fly,
and compelled him to lay down his arms on shore.
He fought : his hasty levies were utterly overthrown ;
some of his generals, his best troops, his artillery
taken ; the remnant huddled into their intrenched
camp after their rout, the pursuers entering it with
them. The victors were called back ; the enemy
was then pent up in a corner of the island, and could
not escape. 'They are at our mercy, and are ours
to-morrow,' says the gentle General. Not a ship
was set to watch the American force ; not a sentinel
of ours could see a movement in their camp. A
whole army crossed under our eyes in one single
night to the mainland without the loss of a single
man ; and General Howe was suffered to remain in
command after this feat, and to complete his glories
of Long Island and Breed's Hill, at Philadelphia ! A
friend, to be sure, crossed in the night to say the
enemy's army was being ferried over, but he fell upon
a picket of Germans : they could not understand
him : their commander was boozing or asleep. In
the morning, when the spy was brought to some one
who could comprehend the American language, the
whole Continental force had crossed the East River,

and our empire over thirteen colonies had slipped away.

The opinions I had about our chief were by no means uncommon in the army ; though, perhaps, wisely kept secret by gentlemen under Mr. Howe's immediate command. Am I more unlucky than other folks, I wonder ? or why are my imprudent sayings carried about more than my neighbours ? My rage that such a use was made of such a victory was no greater than that of scores of gentlemen with the army. Why must my name forsooth be given up to the Commander-in-Chief as that of the most guilty of the grumblers ? Personally, General Howe was perfectly brave, amiable, and good-humoured.

'So, Sir George,' says he, 'you find fault with me, as a military man, because there was a fog after the battle on Long Island, and your friends, the Continentals, gave me the slip ! Surely we took and killed enough of them ; but there is no satisfying you gentlemen amateurs !' and he turned his back on me, and shrugged his shoulders, and talked to some one else. Amateur I might be, and he the most amiable of men ; but if King George had said to him, ' Never more be officer of mine,' yonder agreeable and pleasant Cassio would most certainly have had his desert.

I soon found how our Chief had come in possession of his information regarding myself. My admirable cousin, Mr. William Esmond—who of course had forsaken New York and his post, when all the Royal authorities fled out of the place, and Washington occupied it,—returned along with our troops and fleets ; and, being a gentleman of good birth and name, and well acquainted with the city, made himself agreeable to the new-comers of the Royal army, the young bloods, merry fellows, and macaronis, by introducing them to play-tables, taverns, and yet worse places, with which the worthy gentleman continued to be familiar in the New World as in the Old. *Cœlum non animum.* However Will had changed his air, or whithersoever he transported his carcase, he carried a rascal in his skin.

I had heard a dozen stories of his sayings regarding my family, and was determined neither to avoid him nor seek him; but to call him to account whensoever we met; and, chancing one day to be at a coffee-house in a friend's company, my worthy kinsman swaggered in with a couple of young lads of the army, whom he found it was his pleasure and profit now to lead into every kind of dissipation. I happened to know one of Mr. Will's young companions, an aide-de-camp of General Clinton's, who had been in my close company both at Charleston, before Sullivan's Island, and in the action of Brooklyn, where our General gloriously led the right wing of the English army. They took a box without noticing us at first, though I heard my name three or four times mentioned by my brawling kinsman, who ended some drunken speech he was making by slapping his fist on the table, and swearing, 'By ——, I will do for him, and the bloody rebel, his brother!'

'Ah! Mr. Esmond,' says I, coming forward with my hat on. (He looked a little pale behind his punch-bowl.) 'I have long wanted to see you, to set some little matters right about which there has been a difference between us.'

'And what may those be, sir?' says he, with a volley of oaths.

'You have chosen to cast a doubt upon my courage, and say that I shirked a meeting with you when we were young men. Our relationship and our age ought to prevent us from having recourse to such murderous follies' (Mr. Will started up looking fierce and relieved); 'but I give you notice, that though I can afford to overlook lies against myself, if I hear from you a word in disparagement of my brother, Colonel Warrington, of the Continental Army, I will hold you accountable.'

'Indeed, gentlemen? Mighty fine, indeed! You take notice of Sir George Warrington's words!' cries Mr. Will over his punch-bowl.

'You have been pleased to say,' I continued, growing angry as I spoke, and being a fool therefore for my pains, 'that the very estates we hold in this country are not ours, but of right revert to your family!'

'So they are ours! By George they're ours! I've heard my brother Castlewood say so a score of times!' swears Mr. Will.

'In that case, sir,' says I hotly, 'your brother, my Lord Castlewood, tells no more truth than yourself. We have the titles at home in Virginia. They are registered in the courts there; and if ever I hear one word more of this impertinence, I shall call you to account where no constables will be at hand to interfere!'

'I wonder,' cries Will, in a choking voice, 'that I don't cut him into twenty thousand pieces as he stands there before me with his confounded yellow face. It was my brother Castlewood won his money —no, it was his brother: d—— you, which are you, the rebel or the other? I hate the ugly faces of both of you, and, hic!—if you are for the King, show you are for the King, and drink his health!' and he sank down into his box with a hiccup and a wild laugh, which he repeated a dozen times, with a hundred more oaths and vociferous outcries that I should drink the King's health.

To reason with a creature in this condition, or ask explanations or apologies from him, was absurd. I left Mr. Will to reel to his lodgings under the care of his young friends—who were surprised to find an old toper so suddenly affected and so utterly prostrated by liquor—and limped home to my wife, whom I found happy in possession of a brief letter from Hal, which a countryman had brought in; and who said not a word about the affairs of the Continentals with whom he was engaged, but wrote a couple of pages of rapturous eulogiums upon his brother's behaviour in the field, which my dear Hal was pleased to admire, as he admired everything I said and did.

I rather looked for a message from my amiable kinsman in consequence of the speeches which had passed between us the night before, and did not know but that I might be called by Will to make my words good; and when accordingly Mr. Lacy (our companion of the previous evening) made his appearance at an early hour of the forenoon, I was beckoning my Lady Warrington to leave us, when, with a laugh and a cry of ' Oh dear, no !' Mr. Lacy begged her Ladyship not to disturb herself.

'I have seen,' says he, 'a gentleman who begs to send you his apologies if he uttered a word last night which could offend you.'

'What apologies? what words?' asks the anxious wife.

I explained that roaring Will Esmond had met me in a coffee-house on the previous evening, and quarrelled with me, as he had done with hundreds before. ' It appears the fellow is constantly abusive, and invariably pleads drunkenness, and apologises the next morning, unless he is caned overnight,' remarked Captain Lacy. And my Lady, I daresay, makes a little sermon, and asks why we gentlemen will go to idle coffee-houses and run the risk of meeting roaring roystering Will Esmonds?

Our sojourn in New York was enlivened by a project for burning the city which some ardent patriots entertained and partially executed. Several such schemes were laid in the course of the war, and each one of the principal cities was doomed to fire; though, in the interests of peace and goodwill, I hope it will be remembered that these plans never originated with the cruel Government of a tyrant King, but were always proposed by the gentlemen on the Continental side, who vowed that, rather than remain under the ignominious despotism of the ruffian of Brunswick, the fairest towns of America should burn. I presume that the sages who were for burning down Boston were not actual proprietors in that place, and the New York burners might come from other parts of the country—from Philadelphia, or what not. Howbeit, the British spared you, gentlemen, and we pray you give us credit for this act of moderation.

I had not the fortune to be present in the action on the White Plains, being detained by a hurt which I had received at Long Island, and which broke out again and again, and took some time in the healing. The tenderest of nurses watched me through my tedious malady, and was eager for the day when I should doff my militia-coat, and return to the quiet English home where Hetty and our good General were tending our children. Indeed, I don't know that I have yet forgiven myself for the pains and terrors that I must have caused my poor wife, by keeping her separate from her young ones, and away from her home, because, forsooth, I wished to see a little more of the war then going on. Our grand tour in Europe had been all very well. We had beheld St. Peter's at Rome, and the Bishop thereof;

the Dauphiness of France (alas, to think that glorious
head should ever have been brought so low!) at Paris;
and the rightful King of England at Florence. I
had dipped my gout in a half-dozen baths and spas,
and played cards in a hundred courts, as my 'Travels
in Europe' (which I propose to publish after the
completion of my 'History of the American War')
will testify.* And, during our peregrinations, my
hypochondria diminished (which plagued me woefully at home); and my health and spirits visibly
improved. Perhaps it was because she saw the
evident benefit I had from excitement and change,
that my wife was reconciled to my continuing to
enjoy them: and though secretly suffering pangs at
being away from her nursery and her eldest boy (for
whom she ever has had an absurd infatuation), the
dear hypocrite scarce allowed a look of anxiety to
appear on her face; encouraged me with smiles;
professed herself eager to follow me; asked why it
should be a sin in me to covet honour? and, in a
word, was ready to stay, to go, to smile, to be sad;
to scale mountains, or to go down to the sea in ships;
to say that cold was pleasant, heat tolerable, hunger
good sport, dirty lodgings delightful; though she is
a wretched sailor, very delicate about the little she
eats, and an extreme sufferer both of cold and heat.
Hence, as I willed to stay on yet awhile on my native
continent, she was certain nothing was so good for
me; and when I was minded to return home—oh,
how she brightened, and kissed her infant, and told
him how he should see the beautiful gardens at home,
and Aunt Hetty, and grandpapa, and his sister, and
Miles. 'Miles!' cries the little parrot, mocking its
mother—and crowing; as if there was any mighty

* Neither of these two projected works of Sir George Warrington
were brought, as it appears, to a completion.

privilege in seeing Mr. Miles, forsooth, who was
under Doctor Sumner's care at Harrow-on-the-Hill,
where, to do the gentleman justice, he showed that
he could eat more tarts than any boy in the school,
and took most creditable prizes at football and hare-
and-hounds.

CHAPTER XCI

SATIS PUGNÆ

IT has always seemed to me (I speak under the
correction of military gentlemen) that the intrenchments of Breed's Hill served the Continental army
throughout the whole of our American war. The
slaughter inflicted upon us from behind those lines was
so severe, and the behaviour of the enemy so resolute,
that the British chiefs respected the barricades of the
Americans afterwards ; and were they firing from
behind a row of blankets, certain of our generals rather
hesitated to force them. In the affair of the White
Plains, when, for a second time, Mr. Washington's
army was quite at the mercy of the victors, we
subsequently heard that our conquering troops were
held back before a barricade actually composed of corn-
stalks and straw. Another opportunity was given us,
and lasted during a whole winter, during which the
dwindling and dismayed troops of Congress lay
starving and unarmed under our grasp, and the
magnanimous Mr. Howe left the famous camp of
Valley Forge untouched, whilst his great, brave, and
perfectly appointed army fiddled and gambled and
feasted in Philadelphia. And, by BYNG's countrymen,
triumphal arches were erected, tournaments were held
in pleasant mockery of the middle ages, and wreaths

and garlands offered by beautiful ladies to this clement
chief, with fantastical mottoes and posies announcing
that his laurels should be immortal ! Why have my
ungrateful countrymen in America never erected
statues to this general ? They had not in all their
army an officer who fought their battles better ; who
enabled them to retrieve their errors with such adroit-
ness ; who took care that their defeats should be so
little hurtful to themselves : and when, in the course
of events, the stronger force naturally got the uppermost, who showed such an untiring tenderness,
patience, and complacency in helping the poor disabled
opponent on to his legs again.   Ah ! think of
eighteen years before, and the fiery young warrior
whom England had sent out to fight her adversary on
the American continent.   Fancy him for ever pacing
round the defences behind which the foe lies sheltered ;
by night and by day alike sleepless and eager ;
consuming away in his fierce wrath and longing, and
never closing his eye, so intent is it in watching ;
winding the track with untiring scent that pants and
hungers for blood and battle ; prowling through midnight forests, or climbing silent over precipices before
dawn ; and watching till his great heart is almost
worn out, until the foe shows himself at last, when he
springs on him and grapples with him, and, dying,
slays him !   Think of Wolfe at Quebec, and hearken
to Howe's fiddles as he sits smiling amongst the
dancers at Philadelphia.

A favourite scheme with our Ministers at home and
some of our generals in America, was to establish a
communication between Canada and New York, by
which means it was hoped New England might be
cut off from the neighbouring colonies, overpowered
in detail, and forced into submission.   Burgoyne was
intrusted with the conduct of the plan, and he set

forth from Quebec, confidently promising to bring it
to a successful issue. His march began in military
state : the trumpets of his proclamations blew before
him ; he bade the colonists to remember the immense
power of England : and summoned the misguided
rebels to lay down their arms. He brought with him
a formidable English force, an army of German
veterans not less powerful, a dreadful band of Indian
warriors, and a brilliant train of artillery. It was
supposed that the people round his march would rally
to the royal cause and standards. The Continental
force in front of him was small at first, and
Washington's army was weakened by the withdrawal
of troops who were hurried forward to meet this
Canadian invasion. A British detachment from New
York was to force its way up the Hudson, sweeping
away the enemy on the route, and make a junction
with Burgoyne at Albany. Then was the time when
Washington's weakened army should have been struck
too ; but a greater Power willed otherwise : nor am
I, for one, even going to regret the termination of the
war. As we look over the game now, how clear
seem the blunders which were made by the losing side !
From the beginning to the end we were for ever
arriving too late. Our supplies and reinforcements
from home were too late. Our troops were in
difficulty, and our succours reached them too late.
Our fleet appeared off York Town just too late, after
Cornwallis had surrendered. A way of escape was
opened to Burgoyne, but he resolved upon retreat too
late. I have heard discomfited officers in after days
prove infallibly how a different wind would have saved
America to us ; how we must have destroyed the
French fleet but for a tempest or two ; how once,
twice, thrice, but for nightfall, Mr. Washington and
his army were in our power. Who has not speculated,

in the course of his reading of history, upon the 'Has been' and the 'Might have been' in the world! I take my tattered old map-book from the shelf, and see the board on which the great contest was played; I wonder at the curious chances which lost it: and, putting aside any idle talk about the respective bravery of the two nations, can't but see that we had the best cards, and that we lost the game.

I own the sport had a considerable fascination for me, and stirred up my languid blood. My brother Hal, when settled on his plantation in Virginia, was perfectly satisfied with the sports and occupations he found there. The company of the country neighbours sufficed him; he never tired of looking after his crops and people, taking his fish, shooting his ducks, hunting in his woods, or enjoying his rubber, and his supper. Happy Hal, in his great barn of a house, under his roomy porches, his dogs lying round his feet: his friends, the Virginian Will Wimbles, at free quarters in his mansion; his negroes fat, lazy, and ragged: his shrewd little wife ruling over them and her husband, who always obeyed her implicitly when living, and who was pretty speedily consoled when she died! I say happy, though his lot would have been intolerable to me: wife, and friends, and plantation, and town life at Richmond (Richmond succeeded to the honour of being the capital when our province became a state). How happy he whose foot fits the shoe which fortune gives him! My income was five times as great, my house in England as large, and built of bricks and faced with freestone; my wife—would I have changed her for any other wife in the world? My children—well, I am contented with my Lady Warrington's opinion about *them*. But with all these plums and peaches and rich fruits out of plenty's horn poured into my lap, I fear I have been

but an ingrate; and Hodge, my gatekeeper, who
shares his bread and scrap of bacon with a family as
large as his master's, seems to me to enjoy his meal as
much as I do, though Mrs. Molly prepares her best
dishes and sweetmeats, and Mr. Gumbo uncorks the
choicest bottles from the cellar.   Ah me! sweetmeats
have lost their savour for me, however they may
rejoice my young ones from the nursery, and the
perfume of claret palls upon old noses!   Our parson
has poured out his sermons many and many a time to
me, and perhaps I did not care for them much when
he first broached them.   Dost thou remember, honest
friend (sure he does, for he has repeated the story over
the bottle as many times as his sermons almost, and
my Lady Warrington pretends as if she had never
heard it)—I say, Joe Blake, thou rememberest full
well, and with advantages, that October evening when
we scrambled up an embrasure at Fort Clinton, and a
clubbed musket would have dashed these valuable
brains out, had not Joe's sword whipped my rebellious
countryman through the gizzard.   Joe wore a red
coat in those days (the uniform of the brave Sixty-
third, whose leader, the bold Sill, fell pierced with
many wounds beside him).   He exchanged his red for
black and my pulpit.   His doctrines are sound and his
sermons short.   We read the papers together over our
wine.   Not two months ago we read our old friend
Howe's glorious deed of the first of June.   We were
told how the noble Rawdon, who fought with us at
Fort Clinton, had joined the Duke of York: and
to-day His Royal Highness is in full retreat before
Pichegru: and he and my son Miles have taken
Valenciennes for nothing!   Ah, Parson! would you
not like to put on your old Sixty-third coat? (though
I doubt Mrs. Blake could never make the buttons and
button-holes meet again over your big body).   The

boys were acting a play with my militia sword. Oh, that I were young again, Mr. Blake ! that I had not the gout in my toe ; and I would saddle Rosinante and ride back into the world, and feel the pulses beat again, and play a little of life's glorious game !

The last '*hit*' which I saw played was gallantly won by our side ; though 'tis true that even in this *parti* the Americans won the rubber—our people gaining only the ground they stood on, and the guns, stores, and ships which they captured and destroyed, whilst our efforts at rescue were too late to prevent the catastrophe impending over Burgoyne's unfortunate army. After one of those delays which *always* were happening to retard our plans and weaken the blows which our chiefs intended to deliver, an expedition was got under way from New York at the close of the month of September, '77 ; that, could it but have advanced a fortnight earlier, might have saved the doomed force of Burgoyne. *Sed Dis aliter visum.* The delay here was not Sir Henry Clinton's fault, who could not leave his city unprotected ; but the winds and weather which delayed the arrival of reinforcements which we had long awaited from England. The fleet which brought them brought us long and fond letters from home, with the very last news of the children under the care of their good Aunt Hetty and their grandfather. The mother's heart yearned towards the absent young ones. She made me no reproaches : but I could read her importunities in her anxious eyes, her terrors for me, and her longing for her children. ' Why stay longer ?' she seemed to say. ' You have no calling to this war, or to draw the sword against your countrymen—why continue to imperil your life and my happiness ?' I understood her appeal. We were to enter upon no immediate service of danger ; I told her Sir Henry was only

going to accompany the expedition for a part of
the way. I would return with him, the reconnaissance over, and Christmas, please Heaven, should see
our family once more united in England.

A force of three thousand men, including a couple
of slender regiments of American Loyalists and New
York Militia (with which latter my distinguished
relative, Mr. Will Esmond, went as captain), was
embarked at New York, and our armament sailed up
the noble Hudson river, that presents finer aspects than
the Rhine in Europe to my mind : nor was any fire
opened upon us from those beetling cliffs and pre-
cipitous 'palisades,' as they are called, by which we
sailed ; the enemy, strange to say, being for once
unaware of the movement we contemplated. Our
first landing was on the eastern bank, at a place called
Verplancks Point, whence the Congress troops withdrew after a slight resistance, their leader, the tough
old Putnam (so famous during the war), supposing
that our march was to be directed towards the
Eastern Highlands, by which we intended to penetrate
to Burgoyne. Putnam fell back to occupy these
passes, a small detachment of ours being sent forward
as if in pursuit, which he imagined was to be followed
by the rest of our force. Meanwhile, before daylight,
two thousand men without artillery were carried over
to Stoney Point on the western shore, opposite
Verplancks, and under a great hill called the Dunderberg by the old Dutch lords of the stream, and which
hangs precipitously over it. A little stream at the
northern base of this mountain intersects it from the
opposite height on which Fort Clinton stood, named
not after our General, but after one of the two gentlemen of the same name, who were amongst the oldest
and most respected of the provincial gentry of New
York, and who were at this moment actually in

command against Sir Henry. On the next height to Clinton is Fort Montgomery ; and behind them rises a hill called Bear Hill; whilst at the opposite side of the magnificent stream stands ' Saint Anthony's Nose,' a prodigious peak indeed, which the Dutch had quaintly christened.

The attacks on the two forts were almost simultaneous. Half our men were detached for the assault on Fort Montgomery, under the brave Campbell, who fell before the rampart. Sir Henry, who would never be out of danger where he could find it, personally led the remainder, and hoped, he said, that we should have better luck than before the Sullivan Island. A path led up to the Dunderberg, so narrow as scarcely to admit three men abreast, and in utter silence our whole force scaled it, wondering at every rugged step to meet with no opposition. The enemy had not even kept a watch on it : nor were we descried until we were descending the height, at the base of which we easily dispersed a small force sent hurriedly to oppose us. The firing which here took place rendered all idea of a surprise impossible. The fort was before us. With such arms as the troops had in their hands, they had to assault ; and silently and swiftly in the face of the artillery playing upon them, the troops ascended the hill. The men had orders on no account to fire. Taking the colours of the Sixty-third, and bearing them aloft, Sir Henry mounted with the stormers. The place was so steep that the men pushed each other over the wall and through the embrasures ; and it was there that Lieutenant Joseph Blake, the father of a certain Joseph Clinton Blake, who looks with the eyes of affection on a certain young lady, presented himself to the living of Warrington by saving the life of the unworthy patron thereof.

About a fourth part of the garrison, as we were told,

escaped out of the fort, the rest being killed or
wounded, or remaining our prisoners within the works.
Fort Montgomery was, in like manner, stormed and
taken by our people ; and, at night, as we looked down
from the heights where the King's standard had been
just planted, we were treated to a splendid illumination
in the river below. Under Fort Montgomery, and
stretching over to that lofty prominence called St.
Anthony's Nose, a boom and chain had been laid with
a vast cost and labour, behind which several American
frigates and galleys were anchored. The fort being
taken, these ships attempted to get up the river in the
darkness, out of the reach of guns, which they knew
must destroy them in the morning. But the wind
was unfavourable, and escape was found to be impossible. The crews therefore took to the boats, and so
landed, having previously set the ships on fire, with
all their sails set ; and we beheld these magnificent
pyramids of flame burning up to the heavens and re-
flected in the waters below, until, in the midst of
prodigious explosions, they sank and disappeared.

On the next day a *parlementaire* came in from the
enemy, to inquire as to the state of his troops left
wounded or prisoners in our hands, and the Continental
officer brought me a note, which gave me a strange
shock, for it showed that in the struggle of the previous
evening my brother had been engaged. It was dated
October 7, from Major-General George Clinton's
divisional headquarters, and it stated briefly that
'Colonel H. Warrington, of the Virginia line, hopes
that Sir George Warrington escaped unhurt in the
assault of last evening, from which the Colonel himself was so fortunate as to retire without the least
injury.' Never did I say my prayers more heartily
and gratefully than on that night, devoutly thanking
Heaven that my dearest brother was spared, and

making a vow at the same time to withdraw out of the fratricidal contest, into which I only had entered because Honour and Duty seemed imperatively to call me.

I own I felt an inexpressible relief when I had come to the resolution to retire and betake myself to the peaceful shade of my own vines and fig-trees at home. I longed, however, to see my brother ere I returned, and asked, and easily obtained, an errand to the camp of the American General Clinton from our own chief. The headquarters of his division were now some miles up the river, and a boat and a flag of truce quickly brought me to the point where his out-pickets received me on the shore. My brother was very soon with me. He had only lately joined General Clinton's division with letters from headquarters at Philadelphia, and he chanced to hear, after the attack on Fort Clinton, that I had been present during the affair. We passed a brief delightful night together; Mr. Sady, who always followed Hal to the war, cooking a feast in honour of both his masters. There was but one bed of straw in the hut where we had quarters, and Hal and I slept on it, side by side, as we had done when we were boys. We had a hundred things to say regarding past times and present. His kind heart gladdened when I told him of my resolve to retire to my acres and to take off the red coat which I wore: he flung his arms round it. 'Praised be God!' said he. 'O heavens, George! think what might have happened had we met in the affair two nights ago!' And he turned quite pale at the thought. He eased my mind with respect to our mother. She was a bitter Tory, to be sure, but the Chief had given special injunctions regarding her safety. 'And Fanny' (Hal's wife) 'watches over her, and she is as good as a company!' cried the enthusiastic husband. 'Isn't

she clever? Isn't she handsome? Isn't she good?'
cries Hal, never, fortunately, waiting for a reply to
these ardent queries. 'And to think that I was nearly
marrying Maria once! O mercy! what an escape I
had!' he added. 'Hagan prays for the King, every
morning and night at Castlewood, but they bolt the
doors, and nobody hears. Gracious powers! his wife
is sixty if she is a day; and oh, George! the quantity
she drinks is——' But why tell the failings of our
good cousin? I am pleased to think she lived to drink
the health of King George long after his Old Dominion
had passed for ever from his sceptre.

The morning came when my brief mission to the
camp was ended, and the truest of friends and fondest
of brothers accompanied me to my boat, which lay
waiting at the river-side. We exchanged an embrace
at parting, and his hand held mine yet for a moment
ere I stepped into the barge which bore me rapidly
down the stream. 'Shall I see thee once more, dearest
and best companion of my youth?' I thought.
'Amongst our cold Englishmen, can I ever hope to
meet with a friend like thee? When hadst thou ever
a thought that was not kindly and generous? When
a wish, or a possession, but for me you would sacrifice
it? How brave are you, and how modest; how gentle,
and how strong; how simple, unselfish, and humble;
how eager to see others' merit; how diffident of your
own!' He stood on the shore till his figure grew
dim before me. There was that in my eyes which
prevented me from seeing him longer.

Brilliant as Sir Henry's success had been, it was
achieved, as usual, too late: and served but as a small
set-off against the disaster of Burgoyne which ensued
immediately, and which our advance was utterly
inadequate to relieve. More than one secret
messenger was despatched to him who never reached

him, and of whom we never learned the fate. Of one
wretch who offered to carry intelligence to him, and
whom Sir Henry despatched with a letter of his own,
we heard the miserable doom. Falling in with some
of the troops of General George Clinton, who
happened to be in red uniform (part of the prize of a
British ship's cargo, doubtless, which had been taken
by American privateers), the spy thought he was in the
English army, and advanced towards the sentries. He
found his mistake too late. His letter was discovered
upon him, and he had to die for bearing it. In ten
days after the success at the Forts occurred the great
disaster at Saratoga, of which we carried the dismal
particulars in the fleet which bore us home. I am
afraid my wife was unable to mourn for it. She had
her children, her father, her sister to revisit, and daily
and nightly thanks to pay to Heaven that had brought
her husband safe out of danger.

CHAPTER XCII

UNDER VINE AND FIG-TREE

NEED I describe, young folks, the delights of the
meeting at home, and the mother's happiness with all
her brood once more under her fond wings? It was
wrote in her face, and acknowledged on her knees.
Our house was large enough for all, but Aunt Hetty
would not stay in it. She said, fairly, that to resign
her *motherhood* over the elder children, who had been
hers for nearly three years, cost her too great a pang ;
and she could not bear for yet awhile to be with them,
and to submit to take only the second place. So she
and her father went away to a house at Bury St.
Edmunds, not far from us, where they lived, and

where she spoiled her eldest nephew and niece in private. It was the year after we came home that Mr. B—— the Jamaica planter died, who left her the half of his fortune; and then I heard, for the first time, how the worthy gentleman had been greatly enamoured of her in Jamaica, and, though she had refused him, had thus shown his constancy to her. Heaven knows how much property of Aunt Hetty's Monsieur Miles hath already devoured: the price of his commission and outfit; his gorgeous uniforms; his play debts and little transactions in the Minories;—do you think, sirrah, I do not know what human nature is; what is the cost of Pall Mall taverns, *petits soupers*, play—even in moderation—at the 'Cocoa-Tree;' and that a gentleman cannot purchase all these enjoyments with the five hundred a year which I allow him? Aunt Hetty declares she has made up her mind to be an old maid. 'I made a vow never to marry until I could find a man as good as my dear father,' she said; 'and I never did, Sir George. No, my dearest Theo, not half as good; and Sir George may put *that* in his pipe and smoke it.'

And yet when the good General died, calm and full of years, and glad to depart, I think it was my wife who shed the most tears. 'I weep because I think I did not love him enough,' said the tender creature: whereas Hetty scarce departed from her calm, at least outwardly and before any of us; talks of him constantly still, as though he were alive; recalls his merry sayings, his gentle kind ways with his children (when she brightens up and looks herself quite a girl again), and sits cheerfully looking up to the slab in church which records his name and some of his virtues, and for once tells no lies.

I had fancied, sometimes, that my brother Hal, for whom Hetty had a juvenile passion, always retained a

hold of her heart; and when he came to see us, ten
years ago, I told him of this childish romance of
Het's, with the hope, I own, that he would ask her
to replace Mrs. Fanny, who had been gathered to
her fathers, and regarding whom my wife (with her
usual propensity to consider herself a miserable sinner)
always reproached herself, because, forsooth, she did
not regret Fanny enough. Hal, when he came to
us, was plunged in grief about her loss ; and vowed
that the world did not contain such another woman.
Our dear old General, who was still in life then, took
him in and housed him, as he had done in the happy
early days. The women played him the very same
tunes which he had heard when a boy at Oakhurst.
Everybody's heart was very soft with old recollections,
and Harry never tired of pouring out his griefs and
his recitals of his wife's virtues to Het, and anon of
talking fondly about his dear Aunt Lambert, whom
he loved with all his heart, and whose praises, you
may be sure, were welcome to the faithful old
husband, out of whose thoughts his wife's memory
was never, I believe, absent for any three waking
minutes of the day.

General Hal went to Paris as an American General
Officer in his blue and yellow (which Mr. Fox and
other gentlemen had brought into fashion here likewise), and was made much of at Versailles, although
he was presented by Monsieur le Marquis de Lafayette
to the most Christian King and Queen, who did not
love Monsieur le Marquis. And I believe a Marquise
took a fancy to the Virginian General, and would
have married him out of hand, had he not resisted,
and fled back to England and Warrington and Bury
again, especially to the latter place, where the folks
would listen to him as he talked about his late wife,
with an endless patience and sympathy. As for us,

who had known the poor paragon, we were civil,
but not quite so enthusiastic regarding her, and
rather puzzled sometimes to answer our children's
questions about Uncle Hal's angel wife.

The two Generals and myself, and Captain Miles,
and Parson Blake (who was knocked over at
Monmouth, the year after I left America, and
came home to change his coat, and take my living),
used to fight the battles of the Revolution over our
bottle ; and the parson used to cry, ' By Jupiter,
General ' (he compounded for Jupiter, when he laid
down his military habit), ' you are the Tory, and Sir
George is the Whig ! He is always finding fault
with our leaders, and you are for ever standing up
for them ; and when I prayed for the King last
Sunday, I heard you following me quite loud.'

' And so I do, Blake, with all my heart ; I can't
forget I wore his coat,' says Hal.

' Ah, if Wolfe had been alive for twenty years
more ! ' says Lambert.

' Ah, sir,' cries Hal, ' you should hear the General
talk about *him !* '

' What General ? ' says I (to vex him).

' *My* General,' says Hal, standing up, and filling
a bumper. ' His Excellency General George
Washington ! '

' With all my heart,' cry I, but the parson looks as
if he did not like the toast or the claret.

Hal never tired in speaking of his General ; and it was
on some such evening of friendly converse, that he told us
how he had actually been in disgrace with this General
whom he loved so fondly. Their difference seems to
have been about Monsieur le Marquis de Lafayette
before mentioned, who played such a fine part in
history of late, and who hath so suddenly disappeared
out of it. His previous rank in our own service, and

his acknowledged gallantry during the war, ought to
have secured Colonel Warrington's promotion in the
Continental Army, where a whipper-snapper like M.
de Lafayette had but to arrive and straightway to be
complimented by Congress with the rank of Major-
General. Hal, with the freedom of an old soldier,
had expressed himself somewhat contemptuously
regarding some of the appointments made by
Congress, with whom all sorts of miserable intrigues
and cabals were set to work by unscrupulous officers
greedy of promotion. Mr. Warrington, imitating
perhaps in this the example of his now illustrious
friend of Mount Vernon, affected to make the war
en gentilhomme ; took his pay, to be sure, but spent
it upon comforts and clothing for his men, and as for
rank, declared it was a matter of no earthly concern
to him, and that he would as soon serve as colonel
as in any higher grade.   No doubt he added contemptuous remarks regarding certain General Officers
of Congress Army, their origin, and the causes of
their advancement : notably he was very angry about
the sudden promotion of the young French lad just
named—the Marquis, as they loved to call him—in
the Republican army, and who, by the way, was a
prodigious favourite of the Chief himself.   There
were not three officers in the whole Continental force
(after poor madcap Lee was taken prisoner and dis-
graced) who could speak the Marquis's language, so
that Hal could judge the young Major-General more
closely and familiarly than other gentlemen, including
the Commander-in-Chief himself.   Mr. Washington
good-naturedly rated friend Hal for being jealous of
the beardless commander of Auvergne ; was himself
not a little pleased by the filial regard and profound
veneration which the enthusiastic young nobleman
always showed for him ; and had, moreover, the very

best politic reasons for treating the Marquis with friendship and favour.

Meanwhile, as it afterwards turned out, the Commander-in-Chief was most urgently pressing Colonel Warrington's promotion upon Congress; and, as if his difficulties before the enemy were not enough, he being at this hard time of winter intrenched at Valley Forge, commanding five or six thousand men at the most, almost without fire, blankets, food, or ammunition, in the face of Sir William Howe's army, which was perfectly appointed, and three times as numerous as his own; as if, I say, this difficulty was not enough to try him, he had further to encounter the cowardly distrust of Congress, and insubordination and conspiracy amongst the officers in his own camp. During the awful winter of '77, when one blow struck by the sluggard at the head of the British forces might have ended the war, and all was doubt, confusion, despair in the opposite camp (save in one indomitable breast alone), my brother had an interview with the Chief, which he has subsequently described to me, and of which Hal could never speak without giving way to deep emotion. Mr. Washington had won no such triumph as that which the dare-devil courage of Arnold and the elegant imbecility of Burgoyne had procured for Gates and the Northern Army. Save in one or two minor encounters, which proved how daring his bravery was, and how unceasing his watchfulness, General Washington had met with defeat after defeat from an enemy in all points his superior. The Congress mistrusted him. Many an officer in his own camp hated him. Those who had been disappointed in ambition, those who had been detected in peculation, those whose selfishness or incapacity his honest eyes had spied out,—were all more or less in league against him. Gates was the chief towards whom the malcontents turned. Mr. Gates' was the only genius fit to conduct the war; and with a vain-gloriousness, which he afterwards generously owned, he did not refuse the homage which was paid him.

To show how dreadful were the troubles and anxieties with which General Washington had to contend, I may mention what at this time was called the 'Conway Cabal.' A certain Irishman—a Chevalier of St. Louis, and an officer in the French service—arrived in America early in the year '77 in quest of military employment. He was speedily appointed to the rank of brigadier, and could not be contented, forsooth, without an immediate promotion to be major-general.

Mr. C. had friends in Congress, who, as the General-in-Chief was informed, had promised him his speedy promotion. General Washington remonstrated, representing the injustice of promoting to the highest rank the youngest brigadier in the service; and whilst the matter was pending, was put in possession of a letter from Conway to General Gates, whom he complimented, saying, that 'Heaven had been determined to save America, or a weak general and bad counsellors would have ruined it.' The General enclosed the note to Mr. Conway, without a word of comment; and Conway offered his resignation, which was refused by Congress, who appointed him Inspector-General of the army, with the rank of Major-General.

'And it was at this time,' says Harry (with many passionate exclamations indicating his rage with himself and his admiration of his leader), 'when, by heavens, the glorious Chief was oppressed by troubles enough to drive ten thousand men mad—that I must interfere with my jealousies about the Frenchman!

I had not said much, only some nonsense to Greene and Cadwalader about getting some frogs against the Frenchman came to dine with us, and having a bagful of Marquises over from Paris, as we were not able to command ourselves ;—but I should have known the Chief's troubles, and that he had a better head than mine, and might have had the grace to hold my tongue.

'For a while the General said nothing, but I could remark, by the coldness of his demeanour, that something had occurred to create a schism between him and me. Mrs. Washington, who had come to camp, also saw that something was wrong. Women have artful ways of soothing men and finding their secrets out. I am not sure that I should have ever tried to learn the cause of the General's displeasure, for I am as proud as he is, and besides ' (says Hal) ' when the Chief is angry, it was not pleasant coming near him, I can promise you.' My brother was indeed subjugated by his old friend, and obeyed him and bowed before him as a boy before a schoolmaster.

'At last,' Hal resumed, 'Mrs. Washington found out the mystery. "Speak to me after dinner, Colonel Hal," says she. "Come out to the parade-ground before the dining-house, and I will tell you all." I left a half-score of general officers and brigadiers drinking round the General's table, and found Mrs. Washington waiting for me. She then told me it was the speech I had made about the box of Marquises, with which the General was offended. "I should not have heeded it in another," he had said, "but I never thought Harry Warrington would have joined against me."

'I had to wait on him for the word that night, and found him alone at his table. "Can your Excellency give me five minutes' time ?" I said, with my heart in my mouth. "Yes, surely, sir," says he, pointing to the other chair. "Will you please to be seated?"

'"It used not always to be Sir and Colonel Warrington, between me and your Excellency," I said.

'He said calmly, "The times are altered."

'"Et nos mutamur in illis," says I. "Times and people are both changed."

'"You had some business with me?" he asked.

'"Am I speaking to the Commander-in-Chief or to my old friend?" I asked.

'He looked at me gravely. "Well,—to both, sir," he said. "Pray sit, Harry."

'"If to General Washington, I tell his Excellency that I, and many officers of this army, are not well pleased to see a boy of twenty made a major-general over us, because he is a Marquis, and because he can't speak the English language. If I speak to my old friend, I have to say that he has shown me very little of trust or friendship for the last few weeks; and that I have no desire to sit at your table, and have impertinent remarks made by others there, of the way in which his Excellency turns his back on me."

'"Which charge shall I take first, Harry," he asked, turning his chair away from the table, and crossing his legs as if ready for a talk. "You are jealous, as I gather, about the Marquis?"

'"Jealous! sir," says I. "An aide-de-camp of Mr. Wolfe is not jealous of a Jack-a-dandy who, five years ago, was being whipped at school!"

'"You yourself declined higher rank than that which you hold," says the Chief, turning a little red.

'"But I never bargained to have a macaroni Marquis to command me!" I cried. "I will not, for one, carry the young gentleman's orders; and since Congress and your Excellency choose to take your generals out of the nursery, I shall humbly ask leave to resign, and retire to my plantation."

' "Do, Harry ; that is true friendship !" says the Chief, with a gentleness that surprised me. "Now that your old friend is in a difficulty, 'tis surely the best time to leave him."

' "Sir !" says I.

' "Do as so many of the rest are doing, Mr. Warrington. *Et tu, Brute,* as the play says. Well, well, Harry ! I did not think it of you ; but, at least, you are in the fashion."

' "You asked which charge you should take first ?" I said.

' "Oh, the promotion of the Marquis ? I recommended the appointment to Congress, no doubt ; and you and other gentlemen disapprove it."

' "I have spoken for myself, sir," says I.

' "If you take me in that tone, Colonel Warrington, I have nothing to answer !" says the Chief, rising up very fiercely ; "and presume that I can recommend officers for promotion without asking your previous sanction."

' "Being on that tone, sir," says I, "let me respectfully offer my resignation to your Excellency, founding my desire to resign upon the fact, that Congress, at your Excellency's recommendation, offers its highest commands to boys of twenty, who are scarcely even acquainted with our language." And I rise up, and make his Excellency a bow.

' "Great Heavens, Harry !" he cries—(about this Marquis's appointment he was beaten, that was the fact, and he could not reply to me)—"can't you believe that in this critical time of our affairs, there are reasons why special favours should be shown to the first Frenchman of distinction who comes amongst us ?"

'"No doubt, sir. If your Excellency acknowledges that Monsieur de Lafayette's merits have nothing to do with the question."

'"I acknowledge or deny nothing, sir!" says the General, with a stamp of his foot, and looking as though he could be terribly angry if he would. "Am I here to be catechised by you? Stay. Hark, Harry! I speak to you as a man of the world—nay, as an old friend. This appointment humiliates you and others, you say? Be it so! Must we not bear humiliation along with the other burthens and griefs for the sake of our country? It is no more just perhaps that the Marquis should be set over you gentlemen, than that your Prince Ferdinand or your Prince of Wales at home should have a command over veterans. But if in appointing this young nobleman we please a whole nation, and bring ourselves twenty millions of allies, will you and other gentlemen sulk because we do him honour? 'Tis easy to sneer at him (though, believe me, the Marquis has many more merits than you allow him); to my mind it were more generous as well as more polite of Harry Warrington to welcome this stranger for the sake of the prodigious benefit our country may draw from him —not to laugh at his peculiarities, but to aid him, and help his ignorance by your experience as an old soldier : that is what I would do—that is the part I expected of thee—for it is the generous and the manly one, Harry : but you choose to join my enemies, and when I am in trouble you say you will leave me. That is why I have been hurt : that is why I have been cold. I thought I might count on your friendship—and—and you can tell whether I was right or no. I relied on you as on a brother, and you come and tell me you will resign. Be it so! Being embarked in this contest, by God's will I will see it to

"We walked into Mrs Washington's
tea-room arm-in-arm"

an end. You are not the first, Mr. Warrington, has left me on the way."

'He spoke with so much tenderness, and as he spoke his face wore such a look of unhappiness, that an extreme remorse and pity seized me, and I called out I know not what incoherent expressions regarding old times, and vowed that if he would say the word, I never would leave him.' 'You never loved him, George,' says my brother, turning to me, 'but I did beyond all mortal men ; and, though I am not clever, like you, I think my instinct was in the right. He has a greatness not approached by other men——'

'I don't say no, brother,' said I, 'now.'

'Greatness, pooh !' says the parson, growling over his wine.

'We walked into Mrs. Washington's tea-room arm-in-arm,' Hal resumed ; 'she looked up quite kind, and saw we were friends. "Is it all over, Colonel Harry ?" she whispered. "I know he has applied ever so often about your promotion——"

'"I never will take it," says I.' 'And that is how I came *to do penance,*' says Harry, telling me the story, 'with Lafayette the next winter.' (Hal could imitate the Frenchman very well.) '"I will go *weez heem,*" says I. "I know the way to Quebec, and when we are not in action with Sir Guy, I can hear his Excellency the Major-General say his lesson." There was no fight, you know : we could get no army to act in Canada, and returned to headquarters ; and what do you think disturbed the Frenchman most ? The idea that people would laugh at him, because his command had come to nothing. And so they did laugh at him, and almost to his face too, and who could help it ? If our Chief had any weak point it was this Marquis.

'After our little difference we became as great friends as before—if a man may be said to be friends with a Sovereign Prince, for as such I somehow could not help regarding the General : and one night, when we had sat the company out, we talked of old times, and the jolly days of sport we had together both before and after Braddock's ; and that pretty duel you were near having when we were boys. He laughed about it, and said he never saw a man look more wicked and more bent on killing than you did. "And to do Sir George justice, I think he has hated me ever since," says the Chief. "Ah !" he added, "an open enemy I can face readily enough. 'Tis the secret foe who causes the doubt and anguish ! We have sat with more than one at my table to-day to whom I am obliged to show a face of civility, whose hands I must take when they are offered, though I know they are stabbing my reputation, and are eager to pull me down from my place. You spoke but lately of being humiliated because a junior was set over you in command. What humiliation is yours compared to mine, who have to play the farce of welcome to these traitors ; who have to bear the neglect of Congress, and see men who have insulted me promoted in my own army. If I consulted my own feelings as a man, would I continue in this command ? You know whether my temper is naturally warm or not, and whether as a private gentleman I should be likely to suffer such slights and outrages as are put upon me daily ; but in the advancement of the sacred cause in which we are engaged, we have to endure not only hardship and danger, but calumny and wrong, and may God give us strength to do our duty !" And then the General showed me the papers regarding the affair of that fellow Conway, whom Congress promoted in spite of the intrigue, and down whose

black throat John Cadwalader sent the best ball he
ever fired in his life.

'And it was here,' said Hal, concluding his story,
'as I looked at the Chief talking at night in the
silence of the camp, and remembered how lonely he
was, what an awful responsibility he carried; how
spies and traitors were eating out of his dish, and an
enemy lay in front of him who might at any time
overpower him, that I thought, "Sure, this is the
greatest man now in the world: and what a wretch
I am to think of my jealousies and annoyances,
whilst he is walking serenely under his immense
cares!"'

'We talked but now of Wolfe,' said I. 'Here,
indeed, is a greater than Wolfe. To endure is greater
than to dare; to tire out hostile fortune; to be daunted
by no difficulty; to keep heart when all have lost it;
to go through intrigue spotless; and to forego even
ambition when the end is gained—who can say this is
not greatness, or show the other Englishman who has
achieved so much?'

'I wonder, Sir George, you did not take Mr.
Washington's side, and wear the blue and buff yourself,' grumbles Parson Blake.

'You and I thought scarlet most becoming to our
complexion, Joe Blake!' says Sir George. 'And my
wife thinks there would not have been room for two
such great men on one side.'

'Well, at any rate, you were better than that
odious, swearing, crazy General Lee, who was second
in command!' cries Lady Warrington. 'And I am
certain Mr. Washington never could write poetry and
tragedies as you can! What did the General say
about George's tragedies, Harry?'

Harry burst into a roar of laughter (in which, of
course, Mr. Miles must join his uncle).

'Well!' says he, 'it's a fact, that Hagan read one at my house to the General and Mrs. Washington and several more, and they all fell sound asleep!'

'He never liked my husband, that is the truth!' says Theo, tossing up her head, 'and 'tis all the more magnanimous of Sir George to speak so well of him.

And then Hal told how, his battles over, his country freed, his great work of liberation completed, the General laid down his victorious sword, and met his comrades of the army in a last adieu. The last British soldier had quitted the shore of the Republics, and the Commander-in-Chief proposed to leave New York for Annapolis, where Congress was sitting, and there resign his commission. About noon on the 4th of December, a barge was in waiting at Whitehall Ferry to convey him across the Hudson. The chiefs of the army assembled at a tavern near the ferry, and there the General joined them. Seldom as he showed his emotion outwardly, on this day he could not disguise it. He filled a glass of wine, and said, 'I bid you farewell with a heart full of love and gratitude, and wish your latter days may be as prosperous and happy as those past have been glorious and honourable.' Then he drank to them.

'I cannot come to each of you to take my leave,' he said, 'but shall be obliged if you will each come and shake me by the hand.'

General Knox, who was nearest, came forward, and the Chief, with tears in his eyes, embraced him. The others came, one by one, to him, and took their leave without a word. A line of infantry was formed from the tavern to the ferry, and the General, with his officers following him, walked silently to the water. He stood up in the barge, taking off his hat, and waving a farewell. And his comrades remained

bareheaded on the shore till their leader's boat was out
of view.

As Harry speaks very low, in the grey of evening,
with sometimes a break in his voice, we all sit touched
and silent. Hetty goes up and kisses her father.

'You tell us of others, General Harry,' she says,
passing a handkerchief across her eyes, 'of Marion
and Sumpter, of Greene and Wayne, and Rawdon and
Cornwallis, too, but you never mention Colonel
Warrington!'

'My dear, he will tell you his story in private!'
whispers my wife, clinging to her sister, 'and you can
write it for him.'

But it was not to be. My Lady Theo, and her
husband too, I own, catching the infection from her,
never would let Harry rest, until we had coaxed,
wheedled, and ordered him to ask Hetty in marriage.
He obeyed, and it was she who now declined. 'She
had always,' she said, 'the truest regard for him from
the dear old times when they had met as almost
children together, but she would never leave her
father. When it pleased God to take him, she hoped
she would be too old to think of bearing any other
name but her own. Harry should have her love
always as the best of brothers; and as George and
Theo have such a nursery full of children,' adds
Hester, 'we must show our love to *them*, by saving
for the young ones.' She sent him her answer in
writing, leaving home on a visit to friends at a distance, as though she would have him to understand
that her decision was final. As such Hal received it.
He did not break his heart. Cupid's arrows, ladies,
don't bite very deep into the tough skins of gentlemen
of our age; though, to be sure, at the time of which
I write, my brother was still a young man, being little
more than fifty. Aunt Het is now a staid little lady

with a voice of which years have touched the sweet chords, and a head which Time has powdered over with silver. There are days when she looks surprisingly young and blooming. Ah me, my dear, it seems but a little while since the hair was golden brown, and the cheeks as fresh as roses! And then came the bitter blast of love unrequited which withered them ; and that long loneliness of heart which, they say, follows. Why should Theo and I have been so happy, and thou so lonely? Why should my meal be garnished with love, and spread with plenty, while yon solitary outcast shivers at my gate? I bow my head humbly before the Dispenser of pain and poverty, wealth and health ; I feel sometimes as if, for the prizes which have fallen to the lot of me unworthy, I did not *dare* to be grateful. But I hear the voices of my children in their garden, or look up at their mother from my book, or perhaps my sick bed, and my heart fills with instinctive gratitude towards the bountiful Heaven that has so blest me.

Since my accession to my uncle's title and estate my intercourse with my good cousin, Lord Castlewood, had been very rare. I had always supposed him to be a follower of the winning side in politics, and was not a little astonished to hear of his sudden appearance in opposition. A disappointment in respect to a place at Court, of which he pretended to have had some promise, was partly the occasion of his rupture with the Ministry. It is said that the most august person in the realm had flatly refused to receive into the R-y-l Household a nobleman whose character was so notoriously bad, and whose example (so the August Objector was pleased to say) would ruin and corrupt any respectable family. I heard of the Castlewoods during our travels in Europe, and that the mania for play had

again seized upon his Lordship. His impaired fortunes
having been retrieved by the prudence of his wife and
father-in-law, he had again begun to dissipate his
income at hombre and lansquenet. There were tales
of malpractices in which he had been discovered, and
even of chastisement inflicted upon him by the victims
of his unscrupulous arts. His wife's beauty and freshness faded early ; we met but once at Aix-la-Chapelle,
where Lady Castlewood besought my wife to go and
see her, and afflicted Lady Warrington's kind heart
by stories of the neglect and outrage of which her
unfortunate husband was guilty. We were willing to
receive these as some excuse and palliation for the
unhappy lady's own conduct. A notorious adventurer,
gambler, and *spadassin*, calling himself the Chevalier
de Barry, and said to be a relative of the mistress of
the French King, but afterwards turning out to be an
Irishman of low extraction, was in constant attendance
upon the Earl and Countess at this time, and con-
spicuous for the audacity of his lies, the extravagance
of his play, and somewhat mercenary gallantry towards
the other sex, and a ferocious bravo courage, which,
however, failed him on one or two awkward occasions,
if common report said true. He subsequently married,
and rendered miserable, a lady of title and fortune in
England. The poor little American lady's interested
union with Lord Castlewood was scarcely more
happy.

I remember our little Miles's infantile envy being
excited by learning that Lord Castlewood's second
son, a child a few months younger than himself, was
already an ensign on the Irish establishment, whose
pay the fond parents regularly drew. This piece of
preferment my Lord must have got for his *cadet* whilst
he was on good terms with the Minister, during which
period of favour Will Esmond was also shifted off to

New York. Whilst I was in America myself, we
read in an English journal that Captain Charles
Esmond had resigned his commission in His Majesty's
service, as not wishing to take up arms against the
countrymen of his mother, the Countess of Castlewood. 'It is the doing of the old fox, Van den Bosch,'
Madam Esmond said ; 'he wishes to keep his Virginian
property safe, whatever side should win!' I may
mention, with respect to this old worthy, that he
continued to reside in England for a while after the
Declaration of Independence, not at all denying his
sympathy with the American cause, but keeping a
pretty quiet tongue, and alleging that such a very
old man as himself was past the age of action
or mischief, in which opinion the Government
concurred, no doubt, as he was left quite un-
molested. But of a sudden a warrant was out
after him, when it was surprising with what agility
he stirred himself, and skipped off to France,
whence he presently embarked upon his return to
Virginia.

The old man bore the worst reputation amongst
the Loyalists of our colony ; and was nicknamed
'Jack the Painter' amongst them, much to his
indignation, after a certain miscreant who was hung in
England for burning naval stores in our ports there. He
professed to have lost prodigious sums at home by the
persecution of the Government, distinguished himself
by the loudest patriotism and the most violent religious
outcries in Virginia ; where, nevertheless, he was not
much more liked by the Whigs than by the party
who still remained faithful to the Crown. He
wondered that such an old Tory as Madam Esmond
of Castlewood was suffered to go at large, and was
for ever crying out against her amongst the gentlemen
of the new Assembly, the Governor and officers of the

State. He and Fanny had high words in Richmond one day, when she told him he was an old swindler and traitor, and that the mother of Colonel Henry Warrington, the bosom friend of his Excellency the Commander-in-Chief, was not to be insulted by such a little smuggling slave-driver as him! I think it was in the year 1780 an accident happened when the old Register Office at Williamsburg was burned down, in which was a copy of the formal assignment of the Virginia property from Francis Lord Castlewood to my grandfather Henry Esmond, Esq. 'Oh,' says Fanny, 'of course this is the work of Jack the Painter!' And Mr. Van den Bosch was for prosecuting her for libel, but that Fanny took to her bed at this juncture, and died.

Van den Bosch made contracts with the new government and sold them bargains, as the phrase is. He supplied horses, meat, forage, all of bad quality ; but when Arnold came into Virginia (in the King's service) and burned right and left, Van den Bosch's stores and tobacco-houses somehow were spared. Some secret Whigs now took their revenge on the old rascal. A couple of his ships in James River, his stores, and a quantity of his cattle in their stalls were roasted amidst a hideous bellowing ; and he got a note, as he was in Arnold's company, saying that friends had served him as he served others ; and containing 'Tom the Glazier's compliments to brother Jack the Painter.' Nobody pitied the old man, though he went well nigh mad at his loss. In Arnold's suite came the Honourable Captain William Esmond, of the New York Loyalists, as Aide-de-Camp to the General. When Howe occupied Philadelphia, Will was said to have made some money keeping a gambling-house with an officer of the dragoons of Anspach. I know not how he lost it. He could not have had much when he consented to become an aide-de-camp of Arnold.

Now the King's officers having reappeared in the province, Madam Esmond thought fit to open her house at Castlewood and invite them thither—and actually received Mr. Arnold and his suite. 'It is not for me,' she said, 'to refuse my welcome to a man whom my sovereign has admitted to grace.' And she threw her house open to him, treating him with great though frigid respect whilst he remained in the district. The General gone, and his precious aide-de-camp with him, some of the rascals who followed in their suite remained behind in the house where they had received so much hospitality, insulted the old lady in her hall, insulted her people, and finally set fire to the old mansion in a frolic of drunken fury. Our house at Richmond was not burned, luckily, though Mr. Arnold had fired the town ; and thither the undaunted old lady proceeded, surrounded by her people, and never swerving in her loyalty in spite of her ill-usage. 'The Esmonds,' she said, 'were accustomed to Royal ingratitude.'

And now Mr. Van den Bosch, in the name of his grandson and my Lord Castlewood, in England, set up a claim to our property in Virginia. He said it was not my Lord's intention to disturb Madam Esmond in her enjoyment of the estate during her life, but that his father, it had always been understood, had given his kinsman a life-interest in the place, and only continued it to his daughter out of generosity. Now my Lord proposed that his second son should inhabit Virginia, for which the young gentleman had always shown the warmest sympathy. The outcry against Van den Bosch was so great, that he would have been tarred and feathered, had he remained in Virginia. He betook himself to Congress, represented

himself as a martyr ruined in the cause of liberty, and
prayed for compensation for himself and justice for
his grandson.

My mother lived long in dreadful apprehension,
having in truth a secret, which she did not like to
disclose to any one. *Her titles were burned!* the deed
of assignment in her own house, the copy in the
Registry at Richmond, had alike been destroyed—by
chance? by villainy? who could say? She did not
like to confide this trouble in writing to me. She
opened herself to Hal, after the surrender of York
Town, and he acquainted me with the fact in a letter
by a British officer returning home on his parole.
Then I remembered the unlucky words I had let slip
before Will Esmond at the coffee-house at New York :
and a part of this iniquitous scheme broke upon
me.

As for Mr. Will : there is a tablet in Castlewood
Church, in Hampshire, inscribed, ' Dulce et decorum
est pro patriâ mori,' and announcing that ' This marble
is placed by a mourning brother, to the memory of the
Honourable William Esmond, Esq., who died in
North America, in the service of his King.' But
how ? When, towards the end of 1781, a revolt took
place in the Philadelphia Line of the Congress Army,
and Sir H. Clinton sent out agents to the mutineers,
what became of them ? The men took the spies
prisoners, and proceeded to judge them, and my
brother (whom they knew and loved, and had often
followed under fire), who had been sent from camp to
make terms with the troops, recognised one of the
spies, just as execution was about to be done upon him
—and the wretch, with horrid outcries, grovelling and
kneeling at Colonel Warrington's feet, besought him
for mercy, and promised to confess all to him. To
confess what? Harry turned away sick at heart.

Will's mother and sister never knew the truth.   They
always fancied it was in action he was killed.

As for my Lord Earl, whose noble son has been the
intendant of an illustrious Prince, and who has
enriched himself at play with his R—l master: I
went to see his Lordship when I heard of this astound-
ing design against our property, and remonstrated with
him on the matter.   For myself, as I showed him, I
was not concerned, as I had determined to cede my
right to my brother.   He received me with perfect
courtesy; smiled when I spoke of my disinterestedness;
said he was sure of my affectionate feelings towards
my brother, but what must be his towards his son?
He had always heard from his father: he would take
his Bible oath of that: that, at my mother's death, the
property would return to the head of the family.   At
the story of the title which Colonel Esmond had ceded,
he shrugged his shoulders, and treated it as a fable.
'On ne fait pas de ces folies là!' says he, offering me
snuff, 'and your grandfather was a man of *esprit!*
My little grandmother was *éprise* of him: and my
father, the most good-natured soul alive, lent them
the Virginian property to get them out of the way.
C'étoit un scandale, mon cher, un joli petit scandale!'
Oh, if my mother had but heard him!   I might have
been disposed to take a high tone: but he said, with
the utmost good-nature, 'My dear Knight, are you
going to fight about the character of our grandmother?
Allons donc!   Come, I will be fair with you!   We
will compromise, if you like, about this Virginian
property!' and his Lordship named a sum greater
than the actual value of the estate.

Amazed at the coolness of this worthy, I walked
away to my coffee-house, where, as it happened, an
old friend was to dine with me, for whom I have a
sincere regard.   I had felt a pang at not being able to

give this gentleman my living of Warrington-on-Waveney, but I *could* not, as he himself confessed honestly. His life had been too loose, and his example in my village could never have been edifying : besides, he would have died of *ennui* there, after being accustomed to a town life ; and he had a prospect finally, he told me, of settling himself most comfortably in London and the Church.* My guest, I need not say, was my old friend Sampson, who never failed to dine with me when I came to town, and I told him of my interview with his old patron.

I could not have lighted upon a better confidant. 'Gracious powers!' says Sampson, 'the man's roguery beats all belief! When I was secretary and factotum at Castlewood, I can take my oath I saw more than once a copy of the deed of assignment by the late lord to your grandfather : "*In consideration of the love I bear to my kinsman, Henry Esmond, Esq., husband of my dear mother Rachel, Lady Viscountess Dowager of Castlewood, I,*" &c.—so it ran. I know the place where 'tis kept—let us go thither as fast as horses will carry us to-morrow. There is somebody there—never mind whom, Sir George—who has an old regard for me. The papers may be there to this very day, and O Lord, O Lord, but I shall be thankful if I can in any way show my gratitude to you and your glorious brother!' His eyes filled with tears. He was an altered man. At a certain period of the port wine Sampson always alluded with compunction to his past life, and the change which had taken place in his conduct since the awful death of his friend Doctor Dodd.

Quick as we were, we did not arrive at Castlewood

---

* He was the second Incumbent of Lady Whittlesea's Chapel, Mayfair, and married Elizabeth, relict of Hermann Voelcker, Esq., the eminent brewer.

too soon. I was looking at the fountain in the court, and listening to that sweet sad music of its plashing, which my grandfather tells of in his Memoirs, and peopling the place with bygone figures, with Beatrix in her beauty; with my Lord Francis in scarlet, calling to his dogs and mounting his grey horse; with the young page of old who won the castle and the heiress—when Sampson comes running down to me with an old volume in rough calf-bound in his hand, containing drafts of letters, copies of agreements, and various writings, some by a secretary of my Lord Francis, some in the slim handwriting of his wife my grandmother, some bearing the signature of the last lord; and here was a copy of the assignment sure enough, as it had been sent to my grandfather in Virginia. 'Victoria, Victoria!' cries Sampson, shaking my hand, embracing everybody. 'Here is a guinea for thee, Betty. We'll have a bowl of punch at the "Three Castles" to-night!' As we were talking, the wheels of postchaises were heard, and a couple of carriages drove into the court containing my Lord and a friend, and their servants in the next vehicle. His Lordship looked only a little paler than usual at seeing me.

'What procures me the honour of Sir George Warrington's visit, and pray, Mr. Sampson, what do you do here?' says my Lord. I think he had forgotten the existence of this book, or had never seen it; and when he offered to take his Bible oath of what he had heard from his father, had simply volunteered a perjury.

I was shaking hands with his companion, a nobleman with whom I had had the honour to serve in America. 'I came,' I said, 'to convince myself of a fact, about which you were mistaken yesterday; and I find the proof in your Lordship's own house.

Your Lordship was pleased to take your Lordship's
Bible oath, that there was no agreement between
your father and his mother, relative to some property
which I hold. When Mr. Sampson was your Lordship's secretary, he perfectly remembered having seen
a copy of such an assignment, and here it is.'

'And do you mean, Sir George Warrington, that
unknown to me you have been visiting my papers?'
cries my Lord.

'I doubted the correctness of your statement, though
backed by your Lordship's Bible oath,' I said, with
a bow.

'This, sir, is robbery! Give the papers back!'
bawled my Lord.

'Robbery is a rough word, my Lord. Shall I tell
the whole story to Lord Rawdon?'

'What, is it about the Marquisate? *Connu, connu,*
my dear Sir George! We always called you the
Marquis in New York. I don't know who brought
the story from Virginia.'

I never had heard this absurd nickname before, and
did not care to notice it. 'My Lord Castlewood,'
I said, 'not only doubted, but yesterday laid a claim
to my property, taking his Bible oath that——'

Castlewood gave a kind of gasp, and then said,
'Great Heaven! Do you mean, Sir George, that
there actually is an agreement extant? Yes. Here
it is—my father's handwriting, sure enough! Then
the question is clear. Upon my o——, well, upon
my honour as a gentleman! I never knew of such
an agreement, and must have been mistaken in what
my father said. This paper clearly shows the property
is yours: and not being mine—why, I wish you joy
of it!' and he held out his hand with the blandest
smile.

'And how thankful you will be to me, my Lord,

for having enabled him to establish the right,' says
Sampson, with a leer on his face.

'Thankful? No, confound you. Not in the
least!' says my Lord. 'I am a plain man; I don't
disguise from my cousin that I would rather have had
the property than he. Sir George, you will stay and
dine with us. A large party is coming down here
shooting; we ought to have you one of us!'

'My Lord,' said I, buttoning the book under my
coat, 'I will go and get this document copied, and
then return it to your Lordship. As my mother in
Virginia has had her papers burned, she will be put
out of much anxiety by having this assignment safely
lodged.'

'What, have Madam Esmond's papers been burned?
When the deuce was that?' asks my Lord.

'My Lord, I wish you a very good afternoon.
Come, Sampson, you and I will go and dine at the
"Three Castles."' And I turned on my heel, making
a bow to Lord Rawdon, and from that day to this I
have never set my foot within the halls of my
ancestors.

Shall I ever see the old mother again, I wonder?
She lives in Richmond, never having rebuilt her house
in the country. When Hal was in England, we sent
her pictures of both her sons, painted by the admirable
Sir Joshua Reynolds. We sat to him, the last year
Mr. Johnson was alive, I remember. And the Doctor,
peering about the studio, and seeing the image of Hal
in his uniform (the appearance of it caused no little
excitement in those days), asked who was this? and
was informed that it was the famous American general
—General Warrington, Sir George's brother.
'General *Who?*' cries the Doctor, 'General *Where?*
Pooh! I don't know such a service!' and he turned

his back and walked out of the premises.   My worship
is painted in scarlet, and we have replicas of both performances at home.   But the picture which Captain
Miles and the girls declare to be most like is a family
sketch by my ingenious neighbour, Mr. Bunbury, who
has drawn me and my Lady with Monsieur Gumbo
following us, and written under the piece, 'SIR
GEORGE, MY LADY, AND THEIR MASTER.'

Here my master comes : he has poked out all the
house-fires, has looked to all the bolts, has ordered the
whole male and female crew to their chambers ; and
begins to blow my candles out, and says, 'Time, Sir
George, to go to bed !   Twelve o'clock !'

'Bless me !   So indeed it is.'   And I close my book,
and go to my rest, with a blessing on those now around
me asleep.

THE END